W9-AHE-683

The Sandburg Connection

Books by Mark de Castrique

The Buryin' Barry Series
Dangerous Undertaking
Grave Undertaking
Foolish Undertaking
Final Undertaking
Fatal Undertaking

The Sam Blackman Series
Blackman's Coffin
The Fitzgerald Ruse
The Sandburg Connection

The Sandburg Connection

A Sam Blackman Mystery

Mark de Castrique

Poisoned Pen Press

Poisoned Pen Press

Copyright © 2011 by Mark de Castrique

First Edition 2011

10 9 8 7 6 5 4 3 2 1

Library of Congress Catalog Card Number: 2011926963

ISBN: 9781590589410 Hardcover
       9781590589434 Trade Paperback

Poisoned Pen Press
6962 E. First Ave., Ste. 103
Scottsdale, AZ 85251
www.poisonedpenpress.com
info@poisonedpenpress.com

Printed in the United States of America

In Memory of Storyteller Louise Bailey
and Songcatcher Donald Lee Moore,
Two Treasures of the Blue Ridge Mountains

Chapter One

The beep caught me in mid-bite. I glanced down at the Black-Berry on the table next to my side order of hush puppies and read the text message, "She's leaving campus early."

Of course. I'd just stopped for a late lunch at Luella's Barbecue on the outskirts of the University of North Carolina at Asheville and should have known a sit-down meal was too good to be true. I rewrapped the barbecue sandwich, dumped it and the hush puppies back in the to-go bag, and headed for my car.

The BlackBerry beeped again. "Where r u?"

I waited till I was in my Honda CR-V before texting, "Luella's. Can u talk?" A few seconds later the cell number of my partner, Nakayla Robertson, flashed as an incoming call.

"How's the pig?" she whispered.

"Uneaten. What's up?"

"I'm not sure. She should be keeping office hours for students but she came out of the classroom and is headed toward the faculty parking lot. I'm walking about ten yards behind her."

"Where's your car?"

"The main visitor's deck. I don't think I can get to it in time to follow."

I started my engine. "I'm on the way. Stay with her to make sure she's not just getting something from her car."

"And if she leaves?"

"See which direction she turns. I should be in position to pick her up."

"Are we tag-teaming?"

I glanced at my watch. Three-thirty. "No. Go to the farm. Her daughter will be home from school soon. Janice is probably meeting her."

I crossed Merrimon Avenue and turned onto W.T. Weaver Boulevard. Traffic was light and I figured to reach the university in a few minutes. "How close is she to her car?"

"We still have a five minute walk."

"Good. I'll try for a side street close by so I can cover whatever direction she takes."

"Sam, keep your eyes on the road and your sandwich on the seat."

That was the problem with a partner. She knew me too well. But, Nakayla was the reason we had the case and I didn't want to screw up. We'd been tailing the professor all day, documenting her activities and searching for any indication that her claim of pain and suffering was a sham. Nakayla's former employer, The Investigative Alliance for Underwriters, a company devoted exclusively to insurance fraud, had subcontracted our detective agency. They hoped Sam Blackman and Nakayla Robertson would succeed where they failed. Janice Wainwright was suing an Asheville spinal surgeon, his clinic, and the hospital for an operation she said left her in more pain than the herniated disk it was intended to repair. She said standing to deliver a full lecture was now impossible and performing even the simplest chores at her small mountain farm left her in agony. Her life and livelihood had been irreparably altered.

Medical tests had been inconclusive, mediation efforts had failed, and the court date was scheduled for May 10th, less than three weeks away. Although North Carolina law only permit-ted plaintiffs to state their requested damages as "greater than ten thousand dollars," the mediation process revealed Janice Wainwright was seeking five million. The malpractice insur-ance company wanted to nail Janice with irrefutable proof that she was faking. In desperation, the Investigative Alliance hired us, not because we could do anything more than their own operatives, but because Nakayla and I had a certain star power. We'd solved two Asheville cases that caught the attention of the national media. We were the CYA factor for Investigative Alliance. "Cover Your Ass." If we failed, their excuse would be "but we bought the best."

Less than five minutes later, Nakayla called. "She's turning right on University Heights." Her voice rose with excitement. "That's not the direction to the farm."

I ran through my mental map of the campus. "If she stays on University Heights, she'll enter the rotary. I'll hang back and see which way she comes off the circle."

"You sure you don't want me to back you up?"

A two-car tail would be the normal way to go. Nakayla and I could alternate being ahead and avoid the target noticing the same vehicle in the rearview mirror for too long. But in this case, I felt the farm offered the best chance for catching Janice Wainwright in a lie.

"No. She's probably running some errands. She might pick up sacks of feed or fertilizer, and you need to be in position if she unloads them by herself. Go to the vista and be ready with the long lens."

The vista was a scenic pull-off on the county road overlooking the valley where the Wainwright property stretched along part of one slope. In the summer, tourists parked to photograph the panorama that featured the Appalachian Mountains encircling a mix of grazing land, Christmas tree fields, and apple orchards. White farmhouses dotted the landscape and a country church with an adjacent cemetery sat close to a bold stream bisecting the valley floor. The Wainwright farm was nearest to the overlook, and our surveillance camera could zoom in close enough that anyone by the house or barn could be identified.

"Okay. Keep me posted." Nakayla hung up.

When the rotary came in sight, I edged onto the shoulder about fifty yards away and clicked on my flashers. Within thirty seconds, Janice's green Ford Explorer entered the circle and took the first right. She was now on W.T. Weaver Boulevard and we were headed in the same direction. I immediately pulled onto the road and tried to narrow the distance. I was surprised at how fast she accelerated. Until now, the woman had been easy to tail. She kept her speed within the limit, gave ample warning with her turn signals, and rarely changed lanes.

A guy in a white Mercedes honked as I swung into the rotary without yielding. I pushed my Honda, trying to draw closer without looking like I was in a high-speed chase. Fortunately, the light caught Janice at the intersection with Broadway and let me catch up. She was turning right, away from downtown. I wondered if I'd made a mistake not using Nakayla. I thought about calling her back, but by now she'd be a couple miles away, traveling in the opposite direction.

We hit heavier traffic and Janice began switching lanes like an Olympic slalom skier as she passed everything on the road. I had trouble keeping up and nearly lost her when she suddenly swerved onto the exit for I-26 East. I braked hard, cut in front of a Fed-Ex truck, and barely made the edge of the ramp. As I merged onto the interstate, I saw the Ford Explorer already a half-mile ahead. My speedometer nudged eighty before the gap between us narrowed. She slowed through the construction by Biltmore Park Mall, but resumed her NASCAR pace as soon as the congestion cleared. I worried she was on some excursion to South Carolina. Hell, I-26 went all the way to Charleston.

As we crossed from Buncombe County into Henderson County, her right turn signal began flashing. We'd just passed an exit and the only signs were for a rest area ahead. We'd traveled less than fifteen miles from the university so I doubted she needed to use the facilities. Maybe she was a sensible driver and was stopping to text a message rather than steer with her knees while thumbing her phone's keypad.

She found a parking spot near the gray-sided, single-story building. I went beyond her at least fifteen spaces and pulled in where I had a clear view of the entrance. To my surprise she got out of her car and walked up the handicapped ramp. She carried a small backpack over one shoulder.

I called Nakayla.

"You almost here?" she asked.

"No. I'm at the I-26 rest stop near mile forty-one. She's gone inside."

"Why?"

"How should I know? Maybe she's got an overactive bladder."

"Doesn't sound like she's coming to the farm right away."

I checked the time. Ten minutes to four. "Has the daughter shown?"

"No. You think they're meeting somewhere?"

"Maybe. Janice is driving like she's late for a wedding." I knew Nakayla's next question would be whether she should abandon her stakeout. "Stay there until I get an idea what she's doing."

Nakayla sighed. "Obviously she's going farther down the interstate. No one drives to the next county to pee no matter how nice the décor."

"The hand dryers are top of the line."

"Nobody with any sense I should have said. The woman's not stupid. The verdict's still out on the guy tailing her."

A herd of Harley-Davidsons roared into the rest stop. At least ten spread across the spaces to my left. Most of the bikes carried two riders. This wasn't the weekend outing of doctors or lawyers; this was the real deal, tough scary dudes whose women looked like they could twist me into a pretzel.

"Are you at a chainsaw convention?" Nakayla asked.

"Bikers. Don't worry. Once I whip their leader's ass, the rest will run."

"I'll head over to the funeral home. Do you want a metal or wooden casket?"

I turned from the rumbling hogs and saw a woman with a backpack halfway down the ramp. I slapped the steering wheel. "Damn."

"What's wrong?" Nakayla asked.

"She changed clothes."

Janice Wainwright wore blue jeans, a brown flannel shirt, and hiking boots cut just above her ankles.

"She ditched her teaching wardrobe for L.L. Bean. Looks like she's going into the woods."

"That could be a good thing. You got your camera?"

I glanced at my Sony 700 reflex sitting on the seat beside my barbecue sandwich. "Yeah."

Nakayla figured out my problem. "You've got the Cadillac, right?"

She didn't mean a car. She meant my leg. Uncle Sam provided me with two prosthetic devices, my consolation prize for having my left leg blown off in Iraq. I called one the Cadillac because I wore it for normal activities like walking on level ground, standing in line, or sitting at a desk. It was made to absorb the minor shocks and protect the flesh below my knee that wasn't meant to bear the weight of my body. But running and jumping would bottom out that leg just like crossing open terrain would bottom out the suspension in a Cadillac. The car's cushy ride would become bone jarring as every ditch and gully overwhelmed shocks built for cruising the interstates. My second prosthesis had a stiffer design that could take the pounding of more strenuous action. It wouldn't be as comfortable crossing a Persian carpet, but it could get me up a mountainside without turning my stump to hamburger. That was my Land Rover and right now it lay on the floor of my bedroom closet.

"Yeah," I admitted. "I should have tossed the Land Rover in the backseat. What good's a detective with a leg up on the competition if he doesn't use it?"

Janice's Explorer passed behind me. I was confident she wouldn't notice a Honda amid a swarm of bikers. I backed up, careful to avoid the chrome chopper next to my front fender and the need for a decision between a metal or wooden casket.

"She's on the move again," I told Nakayla. "You come on. We want to photograph her on difficult terrain and I might not be able to keep up."

"Okay. I'm twenty minutes away. But, she could be going to look at livestock in some barnyard."

"Then stay where you are."

She laughed and hissed make-believe static in my ear. "Sorry. Bad connection. Call again when you leave I-26."

Janice held a steady seventy-five for the next twelve miles, and I began to fear she might be going to Charleston after all. I checked my fuel gauge. The needle had dipped below half a tank. When I looked up, the Explorer's turn signal was blinking. A green sign indicated the Upward Road exit. Two smaller brown signs bordered it top and bottom. The long one above read Carl Sandburg Home; the other, Flat Rock Playhouse. Janice barely slowed at the top of the ramp before turning right on a red light and heading in the direction of the two sites. She zipped through a second stoplight just as it changed from yellow to red and left me trapped on the wrong side of the intersection.

A rusty pickup on wobbly retreads turned in from the side road, shifted gears, and belched a cloud of blue smoke from a dangling tailpipe. Janice couldn't have hired a better roadblock to keep me from catching her.

I called Nakayla. "She exited on Upward Road south of Hendersonville, but I'm stuck behind a rattletrap truck that will fall apart if it tops thirty miles an hour."

"Where did you lose her?" Nakayla asked.

"Second light off the interstate."

"Which way did she go?"

"Straight ahead, but the road's a curvy two-lane and the oncoming traffic's so heavy I can't pass."

"You're headed to Flat Rock?"

"I guess so."

Nakayla was quiet for a minute. I looked down each side road I passed but no Explorer. The smell of the old pickup's burning oil seeped through the vents and I dropped back even farther. "You still there?"

"I'm thinking."

"What?"

"Goats."

"Goats?" It wasn't a word high on my list of her possible responses.

"They have at least one goat on the farm. We saw the girl taking care of it this morning. Almost like a pet."

"So? The relevance of a goat escapes my deductive powers."

"I think the goat's pregnant, but that probably escaped your deductive powers as well."

"Is this a woman thing? If so, I plead gender handicap."

"It's a knowledge thing which means you're really handi-capped. Carl Sandburg's wife raised goats."

I still didn't see the connection. "Don't a lot of people raise goats?"

"Mrs. Sandburg was a champion breeder. The national park service assigned a ranger who's a specialist with goats to manage the remnant of her herd."

Without the least hint of a signal, the pickup suddenly turned onto a dirt road. I stared ahead. Janice Wainwright had disappeared.

"Then I'll go to the Sandburg home because I deduce Janice is asking the ranger questions about delivering the baby."

Nakayla laughed in my ear. "They're called kids."

"I knew that. I'm not as dumb as I look."

"Sam, there's no way you could be."

I drove a few miles farther until the road dead-ended in a T intersection. Signs indicated both the Carl Sandburg Home and The Flat Rock Playhouse were to the left. I found myself driving beneath a canopy of giant pines spaced evenly on both sides of the narrow road. They'd either been specifically planted decades ago or the road graders had preserved them as a natural boundary.

A sign read, "Entering Historic Flat Rock, Established 1807." As far as I could see, there was no downtown. The houses seemed to be tucked away behind the trees, as hidden as the Past. I found the Flat Rock Playhouse on the right side of another three-way intersection. A large white house looked like a hybrid of Victorian and antebellum design. More buildings spread behind it. One was the playhouse proper and others might have been scene shops or housing for the cast. The theatrical complex sat on a giant flat rock, and I wondered if it was where the name of the village originated.

Another Sandburg marker at the intersection directed me to turn right onto Little River Road. In less than a tenth of a mile, an official National Park Service sign proclaimed I'd arrived at Carl's home. I cruised through the parking lot looking for Janice's Explorer. The cars were only a single row deep on either side and her vehicle wasn't one of them. So much for Nakayla's goat theory.

I exited, crossed the road, and entered the lot for the playhouse. The Explorer sat alone at the far end. Why would Janice change clothes to attend a play? I decided to keep my car a safe distance until I knew what she was doing. I returned to the Sandburg site and noticed it closed at five. I could check on Janice and still have plenty of time to move the Honda. I slipped the camera around my neck and strolled across the road to the playhouse.

The box office was at the rear of the white house. No one stood at the ticket windows. I walked to the single-story playhouse about thirty yards to the left and found the doors locked. I went around the building and saw a shirtless man in paint-splotched jeans rolling white paint on a flat leaned against a sawhorse. Several more flats lay drying in the afternoon sun. A second man stood just out of splatter range. He wore pressed khaki slacks, a pink shirt with the sleeves rolled above the wrists, sock-less loafers, and a straw Fedora. The dapper dresser appeared to be supervising.

"Excuse me."

Both men jumped. The painter turned quickly, holding the soggy roller like a broad sword. "Hey, man. You startled us." He looked to be in his early twenties and wore a blue bandana around his head to keep the sweat from his eyes and the paint out of his jet-black hair.

The other man was probably in his late thirties. "We're dark today."

"I know. But I'm supposed to meet a friend here. She's about five-six. In her early forties."

"Nobody's been by. That right, Rick?"

The younger man half-turned away, anxious to get back to work. "Nope. You sure she said the playhouse?"

"Her car's in the parking lot. A green Explorer."

The older man frowned. "That doesn't mean anything. She could be at the Sandburg farm. Their parking lot's too small and we have trouble with the overflow taking our spaces. Not a problem today but a real mess when we've got a matinee."

"Thanks. I bet that's where she is."

"No problem. Rick, I'm going to head on to the high school for the auditions. God, some of these kids think they're trying out for American Idol." He tipped his hat to me. "I'm Arthur Thrash. Visiting Artistic Director. You don't sing, do you?"

"No, not unless you can put my shower on stage."

He laughed. "Sounds like Rick. He paints flats and sings flat, but he's a hell of an actor. Someday you'll see the name Rick Torrence on a Broadway marquee." Thrash headed toward the parking lot, twirling his hat on his finger. "Come back tomorrow," he called over his shoulder. "You and your friend will love the show. *Steel Magnolias.*"

"He's chipper," I said.

Rick Torrence, future Broadway star, flat painter and flat singer, dipped the roller in the pan at his feet. "You would be too if you thought you were God's mentor."

"Sorry. I didn't realize I was in the presence of the divine."

"Oh, yeah." He waved his roller over the flat in the sign of the cross. "And Artie beheld the flat. And Artie saw that it was good."

"He said you were a hell of an actor."

"Because I laugh at his jokes. Believe me, that's an Academy-Award-winning performance."

I made no comment. Instead, I said, "I'd better see if I can find my friend at the Sandburg house."

Rick pushed the roller up and down the unpainted surface. "You should have set a more specific place to meet."

"Yeah, my mistake. Thanks for the advice."

"Artie's right about the show. It's a great production. The women are terrific."

"I'm all for terrific women."

He stopped painting, turned, and gave a conspiratorial smile. "I'm with you. Nothing like being a straight guy in the theatre."

I left Don Juan to his showbiz career. As soon as I was out of earshot, I phoned Nakayla. "You're a decent detective."

"So, she's at the Sandburg farm."

"Yep. Though I haven't found her yet. Where are you?"

"Coming off I-26. Ten minutes away."

"I'll look for the goats. When you get here, you'll find her car in the Flat Rock Playhouse parking lot. Better stay close to it in case I miss her."

"What about your leg? Maybe you should wait by the car and let me find her."

"No. She's already got a head start on us. How tough can it be to walk to a barn?"

Pretty damn tough. Adjacent to the parking lot were restrooms and a display of photographs of Sandburg. Quotations from his writings were interspersed among them. The white farmhouse stood across a pond and up a steep meadow. I followed the pathway over the dam of the pond and came to a trail marker warning the distance to the house was three-tenths of a mile and an elevated climb of 110 feet. Special transportation could be provided for those requiring assistance. I refused to use some old folks' minibus to chase down Janice Wainwright.

I started up the hill. The path was well maintained and cleared of roots and rocks, but the incline rivaled a staircase. Benches were scattered along the way, a precaution against visitors collapsing on the ground. I looked through the woods to the nearby service road. Maybe the minibus wasn't such a bad idea.

The temperature must have been in the high seventies, warm for late April, and I could feel perspiration starting to soak the sleeve of my prosthesis. That could create irritation, but sitting down and putting on a dry sleeve wasn't an option. About two-thirds of the way up the hill, the path split, the left ascending to the house and the right to the barn and hiking trails. I pursued the goats.

A man and woman sat on a bench where the path leveled and a rustic red barn and outbuildings were visible through the trees. The couple must have been in their sixties and looked exhausted. The woman gulped from a water bottle and the man leaned on a walking stick held between his knees.

I stopped to catch my breath. "I guess Mr. Sandburg didn't run down the hill to get his morning paper."

The man laughed. "You'd have to be half goat yourself to scamper up and down this mountain."

"Yeah. I'm trying to catch a friend. I got here late. She's in her forties. Jeans. Brown shirt. Might have had her backpack. Did you see her at the barn?"

"No," he replied. "But there was a woman with a backpack headed up Glassy Mountain."

"What's that?"

He pointed with his walking stick. "The mountain behind us. A rock dome's at the top. You can see almost thirty miles to Asheville."

"How long's the trail?"

"The marker says a mile and three-tens, but it sure seems longer."

"That's because we're out of shape, Fred." The woman wiped her forehead with the back of her hand. "We sat on a bench with her. We were coming down."

"And she was going to the top?"

The woman nodded. "That's kind of the point. But she seemed pretty tired. Maybe she's waiting for you."

"Thanks." I hurried on. The path forked and a sign indicated Glassy Mountain to the left. The incline rose sharply. I called Nakayla. "She's going up Glassy Mountain. If I can get a picture of her at the top, we may have a very happy client."

"Are you sure?"

"Yes. Some hikers described her down to the backpack."

"I'm pulling into the lot," Nakayla said. "Go on and keep your camera ready."

For over twenty minutes I struggled upward. A few people passed me on their way down. If one had been Janice, I would have greeted her with a smile because to ignore a fellow hiker would have drawn more attention.

The trail began to snake back and forth with greater frequency, an indication I was nearing the summit. I slowed my pace, mostly because I was tired but also to avoid suddenly overtaking Janice around a blind switchback. Mountain laurel and orange flaming wild azaleas obscured the trail above.

Footsteps sounded behind me and I glanced over my shoulder. Nakayla moved at twice my speed, climbing with short, quick strides that ate up the slope. She waved. I stopped and tried to catch my breath so I could talk without gasping. The stump of my leg burned like someone had put hot coals in the socket of my prosthesis.

"You left your car." I squeezed out the four words between gulps of air. Rivulets of sweat stung my eyes and tickled my neck. Nakayla's light cocoa skin glistened with a sheen of perspiration. It was amazing that the same activity could make her look beautiful and me want to dial for an ambulance.

She must have seen my pain. "I decided to follow because I remembered how steep the trail is. Why don't you let me go on? The rock outcrop's just around the next bend."

"No. I've come this far, I'm going to finish. We'll do it together."

Nakayla shook her head. "Not a good idea. We don't want her to notice us. It may be the 21st century but a black and white couple still draws attention here."

Unfortunately, she had a point. "Then you stay. The trail's steep and rocky. You can take photos of her going down after she passes you."

She jabbed me on the shoulder. "I think I know what to do. I didn't just fall off a truckload of turnips."

"No. It's been at least a year since that happened." I hurried away before she could hit me again.

In less than thirty yards, the trees thinned as bare rock broke through the soil. A sign reading "Glassy Mountain Overlook" pointed to a wider patch ahead. The gray granite began sloping downward and my artificial leg transferred every jarring step into a painful stab. I paused to switch on my camera. Janice had to be somewhere right ahead of me.

"No!" A woman's voice shouted. Then the word grew to a shrill scream. Abruptly the sound ceased, cutoff like a plug had been pulled on a radio.

"Nakayla, hurry!" I ran as fast as I could over the rock. It spread more than fifty yards, curving downward to the trees below and opening a spectacular view of the valley.

Rain and wind had carved ripples into the exposed stone making the footing uncertain. I turned sideways, putting my good leg lower so it bore most of my weight. On the granite, a splotch of smeared blood shone red in the sunlight. Then my chest tightened as I saw Janice's body twisted against a tree at the base of the rock. A sudden movement to my right caught my eye. A brown blur flashed beyond the rhododendron and disappeared.

"Sam. Be careful!" Nakayla stood above me.

"It's Janice. She fell." I sidestepped, as the descent grew steeper.

Nakayla scrambled past me, more agile on the slope. When I joined her, she was kneeling beside Janice with her fingers pressed against the carotid artery in the woman's neck. Blood flowed from a wound somewhere underneath her hair.

"She's still alive but she's taken a nasty crack to the head," Nakayla said. "I'm afraid to move her. Call 911."

I gave a brief account to the emergency operator, asked for an ambulance, and requested the rangers at the Sandburg home be notified. They might have some all-terrain vehicle that could come up the wide trail.

A moan slipped from Janice's lips and her eyes fluttered. She looked at us. Pain and confusion mingled in her gaze.

"We're going to get you out of here," Nakayla whispered.

"Wendy." The word was a wisp of breath.

"Don't talk. Help's on the way."

Janice reached up and brushed Nakayla's cheek with her fingers. "Wendy. It's the verses. Sandburg's verses." The "s" sounds hissed faintly and died on a gusty breeze. The injured woman's eyes closed and she spoke no more.

Chapter Two

We stayed with Janice Wainwright until three park rangers arrived in an all-terrain cart. An older woman introduced herself as Carol Hodges, Chief of Visitor Services, and said a second cart was bringing EMTs with a stretcher. She knelt beside Janice and saw the pool of blood congealing in her hair.

"My God, it's Mrs. Wainwright."

"You know her?" I asked.

"She bought one of our goats a few months ago." The ranger looked at me. "Did you see her fall?"

"No. I was just coming out on the rock. I heard a cry and found her. There are several smears of blood above us. I think she fell backwards and then rolled here."

Ranger Hodges turned to Nakayla. "How about you?"

"I was even farther away."

"She was hiking by herself?"

I shrugged. "I guess. Did you see anyone as you drove up?"

"No. We're near closing time and visitors are off the trail by now."

"Any other way down?"

"There's a back path that's not on park land. You think someone left her?"

The flash of motion I saw could have been a bird or squirrel or my imagination so I decided not to mention it. I also didn't mention we were following her. "No. Just ruling out possibilities."

She eyed me with curiosity and I realized I sounded like a cop. Nakayla jumped in. "Is there anything more we can do?"

The roar of a small gas engine announced the arrival of the EMTs.

"No," Hodges said. "Why don't you go back to the house. There's a room off the gift shop where you can wait."

"I know it," Nakayla said.

"Wait for what?" I asked.

Ranger Hodges motioned us aside as medics scurried down the rock with their equipment. "An investigating officer will have some questions."

"That's not you?"

Hodges shook her head. "Nope. And I'm not sure who will talk to you. That's a matter of jurisdiction above my pay grade."

"Between local and federal?" I asked.

"That's right. We're on National Park land but if a crime has been committed, then you've got the Henderson County Sheriff's Department and our L. E. rangers from the Blue Ridge Parkway who assist us in these matters."

"L. E.?" Nakayla asked.

"Law enforcement." Hodges looked at Janice who was now surrounded by the attending EMTs. "And if she doesn't make it, the FBI might get involved."

Nakayla and I exchanged glances. We must have been thinking the same thing. If Janice Wainwright died, a five million dollar lawsuit died with her. We were first on the scene and we were working for a client who had five million reasons for Janice to go away. Five million dollars. That would get the FBI's attention.

Nakayla and I descended Glassy Mountain. She kept her pace slow, knowing the steps down were tougher on me than climbing. As we neared the bottom, the all-terrain cart honked behind us and we stepped off the trail to let it pass. Janice lay on a portable stretcher with her head bandaged and an inflatable collar fastened around her neck. EMTs perched precariously on the cart railings, clutching the stretcher and trying to dampen the shocks from the uneven ground. The grim set of their faces told me things didn't look good.

The gift shop entrance was under the main steps at the front of the house. What looked to be the main floor of the farmhouse was actually the second level and the first floor had the feel of an aboveground basement, if there was such a thing.

The shop was unmanned. I suspected the rangers had been pulled from their posts to assist with the rescue. The shelves contained books by Sandburg and books about Sandburg. There were also picture postcards and flyers promoting upcoming events. Nakayla took me to a separate room on the left where about ten folding chairs faced a television.

"You know your way around," I said.

"My mother used to bring me. She liked the kitchen."

"The kitchen?"

"Yeah. They've kept it just like it was back in the sixties. It reminded Mom of her house when she was a little girl." Nakayla sat down. "When she got sick, we'd come over. The rangers would drive her up the hill and we'd walk around."

I sat beside her and took her hand. Nakayla's mother died of breast cancer over ten years ago and her father committed suicide six months later. Her older sister Tikima had been murdered almost two years ago. Nakayla and I met when I became involved in solving the crime. Now Nakayla was the last of her family.

"Did your mother like Sandburg's poetry?"

"She liked his philosophy." Nakayla gestured to the blank television screen. "There's a video they play of Sandburg being interviewed by Edward R. Murrow, the old TV newsman. One answer stood out for my mother. Sandburg said the word he hated most in the English language was 'exclusive.' He didn't buy into the marketing connotation used for ritzy neighborhoods or country clubs. He hated the word because it meant there were people who would be excluded, barred from participating in something. I guess if you're known as the poet of the people you care about all the people. As a black child growing up in the sixties, my mother understood exclusive all too well."

I said nothing. Although Nakayla and I shared a lot, there were some experiences that would always divide us. For me, exclusive never meant being denied my basic rights as an American citizen.

"Wendy's her daughter," Nakayla said.

"I know. Did Janice think you were Wendy?"

"Maybe. With a head injury like that, she could have hallucinated anything."

"Sandburg's verses. Was that a hallucination?"

"She was on his property. Maybe she went up there to read."

"A woman claiming chronic back pain hikes up a mountain to read a poem?"

"Sam, don't be sarcastic. I'm not a mind reader. We're making wild guesses."

I took a deep breath. I felt frustrated and anxious about what I knew was coming.

Nakayla gave a sympathetic smile. "Maybe they'll find a book of Sandburg's poetry in her backpack."

"Maybe." Then the significance of her words hit me. "Where was the backpack?"

Nakayla stared through me. Her eyes must have been reviewing the scene of the accident. "She wasn't lying on it. Maybe she left it in the car."

"No. The couple I met on the trail said she had it."

"I didn't see it on the rescue cart. It could have slid off the rock and into the woods. Should we mention it to the rangers?"

I thought for a moment. "No. We'll have enough other information to give them."

Nakayla nodded. "We need to tell them we were following her and why."

"Yeah. Better to come clean because they'll discover that when they run a check on us. "

"Why the concern with the backpack? It's probably where she stuck her change of clothes."

"She carried it to the top of the mountain. I doubt she planned to put on her dress again to enjoy the view."

Nakayla stood and paced in front of the TV. "The ranger knew her. The goat at her farm came from Mrs. Sandburg's stock so Janice has a connection to this place. Maybe she just wanted to get away for an hour or two and the backpack held water and a sandwich. My mother came here when she was in pain. Even though she never met the Sandburgs she said the place had a welcoming spirit."

"Did your mother climb Glassy Mountain in her pain?"

"No."

"No," I repeated. "That's what Janice shouted at the top. 'No.' I wonder if it was directed to someone."

"But you didn't see anyone."

"No."

Nakayla stopped pacing and stared at me. "That's why you want to find the backpack. Rule out the possibility an assailant took it."

I grinned. "Once a chief warrant officer, always a chief warrant officer." Before my injury in Iraq, I served with the Army's Criminal Investigation Command, also known as CID— Criminal Investigation Division. My first reaction to a suspicious event was to view it as a possible crime.

Nakayla shook her finger at me. "Then tell whoever interviews us what you suspect and let them investigate."

"I will. But not about the backpack. That could be something relevant to our case. If we don't find it, I can say I remembered it later and let them look for it."

Nakayla wasn't convinced. "If Janice was attacked, it's a police matter."

"You're saying a county deputy or parkway ranger is a better detective than me?"

"No. But I believe I heard Ranger Hodges say the initials FBI. They don't stand for Federal Bureau of Incompetence."

I raised my hands in mock surrender. "And if the FBI's on the scene, I'll back off. But we've got our client's interest to consider and like it or not that client is going to be dragged into this. I want to know if you and I are mixed up in more than a simple surveillance."

Her eyes widened. "You think the client might be involved?"

"Do you know anyone else who benefits if Janice Wainwright is out of the picture?"

She shook her head. "You're in no condition to climb back up Glassy Mountain."

"Aren't I lucky to have a partner who's not only beautiful but also in prime physical condition." I got up and walked into the gift shop.

In addition to the Sandburg literary collection, the park service sold books about the history of the house, the Flat Rock community, and the activities available. There were books on hiking, fishing, kayaking, even on nearby rock faces for serious climbers. I picked up a thin volume entitled, "Day Trails of Henderson County."

"What are you doing?" Nakayla leaned against the jamb of the doorway between the gift shop and TV room.

"Finding the safest way for you up the mountain. Hodges mentioned a second path."

Nakayla crossed the room to where pamphlets and brochures were displayed around the cash register. She lifted one, glanced inside, and then motioned me to put the book back on the shelf. "This will do. Let's look at it in the other room."

We sat in chairs out of sight of anyone entering the gift shop. Nakayla unfolded the pamphlet in her lap. It was a map of the Sandburg property highlighting the various buildings and trails. Nothing indicated a back way to Glassy Mountain.

The spring hinges of the screen door squealed as someone entered the shop. Nakayla folded the map.

"Mr. Blackman?"

I turned to see two uniformed men step into the room. One wore the bluish-gray shirt and dark green pants of the National Park Service; the other, a dark blue uniform. Both had service pistols holstered on their duty belts.

"Yes." I stood, and Nakayla rose beside me.

The ranger stepped forward. He was stocky and no more than five-six, at least three inches shorter than me. He looked to be in his forties. The other man couldn't have been much over thirty and was what my grandmother would have called a string-bean with a long horse face and close-set brown eyes that darted between Nakayla and me.

"I'm Bobby Ray Corn with the Parkway L.E. Rangers and this is Sidney Overcash. He's a county deputy."

We all shook hands.

"Let's sit." Corn grabbed a folding chair and spun it around. "We've got a few questions about the incident."

We sat in a makeshift circle and I knew we were undergoing an interview rather than an interrogation. Otherwise, Nakayla and I would have been split up and questioned separately.

"How's Mrs. Wainwright?" I asked.

Corn glanced at Overcash.

The deputy shrugged. "EMTs took her to Asheville. Something about specialists in cranial pressure."

That made sense. A severe head wound often caused swelling of the brain tissue. Treatment included inducing a coma to keep the patient as immobile as possible because the damage done by the swelling could be worse than the original injury.

"Were you hiking with her?" Corn asked.

I pulled my wallet out of my pants pocket. "Let's cut to the heart of the matter." I held up my license, angling it first to Corn and then Overcash. "Nakayla and I are private investigators. We were following Mrs. Wainwright for a client. Her hike caught us off guard and we have no idea why she was on the trail."

"Private eyes." Overcash muttered the words like they were synonymous with "dung beetles."

"Sam Blackman," Corn said to himself. He looked at us with new interest. "Blackman and Robertson. You broke the Peters' homicide."

"Detective Peters was a good man," I said.

"Some other P.I. got killed?" Overcash asked, the lack of concern rampant in his voice.

Corn's square jaw tensed. "Roy Peters was a detective with the Asheville police killed in the line of duty. More importantly, he was a friend of mine."

Lieutenant Peters had been working the investigation into the murder of Nakayla's sister. I provided him with a lead that got him killed. He left a wife and two children.

Overcash reddened. "Well, maybe they were pursuing the Wainwright woman a little too aggressively. She ran out on the rock and lost her balance."

"Deputy Overcash." Nakayla spoke his name like he might not have the sense to recognize it. "I don't know how you do it here in your county, but when we follow people, they don't realize they're being followed. That's the point."

The deputy leaned back in the chair and folded his arms across his chest. "And why were you following her?"

"A client hired us," Nakayla said curtly.

"Who?" Overcash asked her.

She said nothing.

I didn't want the conversation to turn into an us-versus-them standoff. "We'll inform our client what happened and recommend they cooperate with the authorities should such cooperation be required. But since they bear no responsibility for Mrs. Wainwright's unfortunate injury, there's no need to involve them."

"Says you," Overcash snapped. "We've only your word it was an accident."

"You have no such thing," I said.

Overcash and Corn looked at me with surprise.

"I can't tell you it was an accident. I heard her shout 'no' and then scream. The scream was cut off abruptly, and I assume that was when her head hit the rock. Whether someone pushed her or frightened her is an open question because I didn't see it happen."

"And you were the only ones up there," Overcash said.

"As far as I know. So, if we wanted to walk away, we could have. Or if we wanted to finish her off, we could have."

Overcash looked at Corn. "I still want to know who they're working for."

"We do confidential investigations," Nakayla said. "Do I need to get you a dictionary? You'll find confidential under the Cs."

"All right," Corn said. "Everybody calm down. Deputy Overcash, there's nothing to indicate anything occurred outside of National Park property. For now, this is my investigation. We'll deal with their client if the need arises."

Overcash sulked.

Corn took a flip pad out of his chest pocket. "Walk me through what happened."

I gave him the narrative from the time I saw Janice's car in the rotary until I found her at the bottom of the rock. Then Nakayla told how Janice spoke to her, apparently thinking she was her daughter.

"Sandburg's verses," Corn said. "Any ones in particular?"

"No," Nakayla said. "And she said nothing about being attacked."

"And she and her daughter have one of the Sandburg goats?"

Nakayla nodded. "That's what Ranger Hodges told us."

"I know Glassy Mountain," Corn said. "The rock's steep but not like a cliff. You can walk up and down it. Was it wet or did a mossy part break loose under her feet?"

"The section above where I found her was dry and bare," I said. I looked at Nakayla and thought I saw her approval to tell more. "One thing we will share is that she'd been prescribed some pretty heavy painkillers. Maybe she was on them."

"This is a medical insurance investigation, isn't it?"

Corn's leap to the correct conclusion surprised me. There was more to him than met the eye.

"We were given that information legitimately and haven't violated any patient-doctor relationship."

"Right," Corn said. "So, you're saying the woman could have been woozy."

"Yes." A second thought alarmed me. "If the Asheville doctors induce a coma, they need to know what's already in her system."

Corn turned to Overcash. "He's right. Their treatment could kill her. Get word to the hospital immediately."

The deputy jumped from the chair and ran from the room.

"What's his role?" I asked.

Corn understood what I meant. "He's all right. A little too eager to prove he's as good as the rest of us."

I caught the phrase "the rest of us." Corn was treating Nakayla and me as his professional equals, a rare compliment from someone on the law enforcement side.

"Sheriff Davis runs a good department in Henderson County," Corn said. "Overcash is positioning himself in case they wind up involved with the investigation."

"How would that happen?"

"Geography. If Wainwright had been attacked outside of National Park property and then dumped here, we'd have shared jurisdiction. Or if there were a conspiracy with roots in the county, especially if it's tied to an open case in their department, we'd mount a joint operation. But, most likely, it's an accident and the painkillers could have been what literally tipped her over the edge."

"Why were you brought in so soon?" Nakayla asked.

Corn smiled. "Ranger Hodges didn't like the looks of the wound. When most people fall, it's because they slip. They usually land on their side or hip and they don't topple headfirst into a slab of granite."

Nakayla arched her eyebrows. "So, you're considering us as more than hikers who were first on the scene?"

"I was."

"And now?" she asked.

"And now I'm considering you as the two people who made sure Roy Peters' widow and children received a financial gift that kept them in their home with the future Roy would have wanted for them. That's all the reference I need."

I felt my cheeks blush with embarrassment at his heartfelt words.

"Your client might be a different story," he said. "So, I can't give you a pass if worse comes to it."

I knew the "it" was if Janice Wainwright died.

The screen door of the gift shop slammed shut and Deputy Sidney Overcash stepped in the room. His ashen face told the story before he spoke.

"She died two minutes out from the hospital. In Buncombe County."

I figured he added the location to tell Corn the DOA would be beyond the jurisdiction of the Henderson County Sheriff's Department. The autopsy and M.E.'s report would be coming out of Asheville.

Corn sighed. "Jesus. Poor woman. How old's the kid?"

"Seventeen," Nakayla said. "She graduates from high school in June."

I made a decision. "Our client's Investigative Alliance. It's a sub-contract job. A five-million dollar malpractice lawsuit is at stake, and you'll need to get Investigative Alliance to give you the name of their client."

Overcash whistled under his breath. "Five million dollars."

Corn stood. "Thanks, Sam. Call and give them a heads up."

Nakayla and I rose. The interview was over.

"One more thing," I said. "Janice Wainwright had a backpack with her. I didn't see it on the rock or the rescue cart."

Corn turned to Overcash. "You got here before me."

The deputy shook his head. "There was no backpack when they loaded her in the ambulance."

Corn looked out the window at the waning light. "Then I guess I'd better get my butt up the mountain."

"I'd like to come with you," I said. "If one of those all-terrain vehicles is available."

"Okay. You know what the backpack looks like?"

"Yeah. Small and brown. More like a book bag."

"What about you?" Corn asked Nakayla.

"I'd better contact our client. I'll wait here if it's okay."

"That's fine. I'll let Hodges know." Corn turned to Overcash. "Can you hang with us? We could use the help."

The deputy relaxed, pleased to be included. "Sure. Should I get some crime tape from the car?"

"Yeah. Bring a roll. Let's meet out front in five minutes. I'll find Carol Hodges and let her know what's going on."

Corn and Overcash left.

"Oh, boy," Nakayla said as soon as we heard the screen door shut.

"Oh, boy, is right. After you talk to your contact at Investigative Alliance, see if you can reach Newly." Curt Newland had been Detective Roy Peters' partner in the Asheville Police Department and we'd formed a personal and professional relationship after Roy's death.

"Why?"

"I want a backdoor channel to the Medical Examiner. Tell Newly to get word to whoever does the autopsy that Janice Wainwright may have had a significant amount of painkillers in her system."

"Won't Ranger Corn cover that? He seems pretty sharp."

"Yes, but I also want Newly to suggest the M.E. look for damage in Janice's lower back."

"You still want to know if she was faking or not?"

"More than ever. If she wasn't faking, then why the hell did she endure a painful climb to the top of a mountain?"

"I don't know," Nakayla said.

"I don't either. But I'm going to find out."

"Sam, you're stepping over the line. You're letting this become personal."

"You're damn right I am. If Janice Wainwright was murdered, then you and I jump to the head of the line when it comes to suspects. No matter how much Ranger Corn appreciates what we did for Roy Peters' family, he can't help but take on the suspicions that Deputy Overcash expressed. I don't like being under a cloud and I sure don't like the possibility that someone set us up to take the fall."

"All right. How much do you want me to tell Newly?"

"Everything. If this winds back into Asheville, then we might need his help. Tell him to keep it quiet and that we're just making sure we're not caught up in something we didn't bargain for."

Nakayla laughed and kissed me on the cheek. "He knows we're always caught up in more than we bargained for."

Ranger Carol Hodges drove the all-terrain cart. Corn sat in the front beside her and Overcash and I were in the rear. The deputy checked the left side of the trail and I watched the right. We needed to rule out the possibility that Janice either dropped her backpack along the way, left it on one of the benches, or it had fallen off the rescue cart on the way to the ambulance. We reached the top without finding it.

Corn had me walk through my approach to the rock. I showed him where I was when I heard the shout and demonstrated how long it took me to reach Janice.

"What's wrong with your leg?" Overcash asked.

"I left it in Iraq," I said. "They'll buy anything over there."

His face flushed. "Sorry. Didn't mean nothing by it."

"I know. Not a big loss considering my buddies who came home in a body bag."

"You followed Mrs. Wainwright up here on foot?"

"Yep. And if I had two feet of my own, maybe I'd have seen what happened to her."

Corn pointed down the slope. "Let's look in the woods below where she landed. She might have flung the backpack loose while trying to keep her balance."

Overcash and Hodges followed Corn, fanning out as they entered the trees. I moved to the right where I thought my peripheral vision had caught the flash of movement. The rock surface narrowed into several fingers that probed into the foliage. I followed the top one till it ended, then came back and tried the next one. The third was level with where the first bloodstains appeared. A thicket of mountain laurel grew at the end. In the green-leafed branches lay the backpack.

"I found it," I cried. Although I was tempted to pull it free, I left it alone. The fabric of the bag and straps appeared to be slick nylon, not the best material for preserving fingerprints.

Overcash came first, his youth giving him the jump on the others. "Good eye. What made you look here?"

"The wind jiggled it. The brown looked out of place in a sea of green."

Hodges arrived, followed by Corn. The senior ranger took a handkerchief from his pocket and lifted the backpack clear of the branches.

"Let's set it on the flattest part of the rock where there's more light," he said.

We huddled over the backpack. The main pocket was unzipped. Inside were a light blue dress wadded in a ball and a pair of black, flat-heeled shoes.

"She wore those at the university today," I said.

"Is that all that's in there?" Overcash asked.

Corn ran his hand through the interior, and then opened two smaller side pockets. Both were empty.

"Why would she bother toting these clothes up here?" Hodges lifted one sleeve and the dress rolled out to its full length.

A slip of white paper fluttered from a fold in the cloth. I snagged it before the updraft carried it away.

"What's that?" Corn asked.

"A receipt." The thin paper was only about two inches wide and four inches high. "From Malaprop's."

"Malaprop's?" Overcash asked.

"A bookstore in Asheville." I looked at the smaller print. The receipt was a duplicate of a Master Card payment for one book. "It's for something that's been abbreviated as 'FGT NA TREES EAST.'"

"When was it purchased?" Corn asked.

"7:35PM. April 19th. She paid $19.95."

"Yesterday," Corn said.

"Yes." I turned to Hodges. "Does the dress have pockets?"

"No."

"And she wouldn't have stuck the receipt in one of her shoes. How did it wind up in the backpack?"

"Maybe she carried this like a purse," Overcash said.

"Then where's her wallet?"

"She locked it in her car."

"Which makes it even weirder that she brought this backpack up the mountain."

"We'll check the car," Corn said. "But let's keep looking while we've got daylight. Maybe we'll find a water bottle or sandwich wrapping that could have been in it."

Nothing else turned up. We stretched crime scene tape across the spot where the path opened onto the rock and then we returned to the Flat Rock Playhouse parking lot. Nakayla and I watched Overcash pop the lock to Janice Wainwright's Explorer. We found her wallet and cell phone in the glove box, but nothing else.

I followed Nakayla's taillights through the dark back to Asheville, eating my cold barbecue and wondering why the day had gone so wrong.

Chapter Three

At my apartment, I took off my prosthesis and sat at the small dining table, gently massaging the end of my leg. Nakayla opened a bottle of Biltmore Chardonnay, not to support the local economy but to support our spirits. The death of Janice Wainwright might have eliminated our client's problem but it wasn't how we wanted the case resolved.

"So, where do we go from here?"

Nakayla took a healthy sip of wine. "Into the bedroom. I'd like to stay over. I'm not nuts about being alone after watching a woman die."

"Okay."

"Don't worry. I'm not expecting anything more than a hug and good night kiss."

I topped off her wine. "Really? If my apartment's bugged, our listeners will think we're married."

Nakayla and I had developed a personal as well as professional relationship. I'd have gladly moved in with her, but she valued her independence. She also had the pragmatic view that sharing a home and sharing an office could be more than either of us could handle, especially in a business as unpredictable as running a detective agency.

She toasted me with her glass. "No, I treat you too nice to be your wife. That's why I'll fill out the paperwork tomorrow."

"What paperwork?"

"For Investigative Alliance. While you were up on the mountain, I briefed them. Their first response was 'we didn't tell you to do anything but tail her.'"

I shook my head. "They know the inquiry's going to focus on them and the doctor."

"That's why they want me to file a final report and submit an invoice immediately. They're insulating themselves by demonstrating we were hired and paid as independent operatives."

"That's the fate of a subcontractor. When we succeed, our client gets the credit. When we fail, we get the blame."

"At least we get the money." Nakayla reached across the table and stroked the inside of my wrist. "As a love toy, I'm very expensive."

"Yeah. If only you were tax deductible." I refilled my glass. "Tomorrow while you're collecting our money, I'll check in with Corn."

"You think he'll tell us anything?"

"I was straightforward with him. I'd like to get the scoop on the autopsy."

"Newly said he'd follow up if you need him to."

I ran my finger around the rim of my glass. The sound produced wasn't the ring of fine crystal but the squeak of a discount special. "That's a backup. I hope I've got enough rapport with Corn that he'll share what he can."

"And what will you do with the information?"

I shrugged. "Depends on what it is. But I know one thing. This case isn't over."

Nakayla stood and walked behind me. She bent down and gently nibbled my ear. "It's over for tonight."

She left at seven-thirty the next morning to run by her house in West Asheville for a shower and change of clothes. We planned to be in the office before nine, ready to field calls and investigate how Janice Wainwright died. Now we were working for our favorite client, ourselves.

On the way from the parking garage to our office, I stopped at City Bakery Café for a couple of blueberry muffins and two coffees to go. I also picked up a copy of the *Asheville Citizen-Times*. Beneath the fold on the front page was the headline, "UNC-Asheville Professor Dies In Fall."

The story was short, only four column inches. It identified the victim as Assistant Professor of History Janice Wainwright, and said she apparently slipped while walking on the steeper section of the Glassy Mountain dome. A quote from Ranger Bobby Ray Corn stated the trail would be closed today while they determined the exact cause of her fall. The paragraph that grabbed my attention came next: "Henderson County Deputy Sidney Overcash reported Mrs. Wainwright was discovered almost immediately. 'Two hikers heard her cry out and found her still conscious,' Overcash said. 'She was unable to say what happened. She died on the way to the hospital.' Overcash declined to identify the hikers, citing the ongoing investigation."

Great, I thought. He made us sound like prime suspects. If he'd simply given our names, most reporters would have ignored us. Now they saw uncovering our identity as worthy of a Pulitzer Prize.

Our office was in the Adler Court building on the southwest corner of Pack Square, the heart of downtown Asheville. Recent renovations beautified the multi-block combination of lawn, sidewalks, and amphitheater. The historic landmark once had the monument shop of Thomas Wolfe's father on its perimeter where the famed statue in *Look Homeward, Angel* first made an indelible impression on five-year-old Tom. A replica of the original marble angel was erected in front of the Asheville Arts Center on the square, reminding tourists of the city's literary pedigree. From our third-floor office windows, I can see them standing beside it, having their pictures taken like they were next to Thomas Wolfe himself. Tourists. You gotta love 'em, even though they double-park and head the wrong way down one-way streets. Without their money, the local economy would crash so hard the mountains themselves would tremble.

The glow through the frosted glass of our office door told me Nakayla had beat me to work. The words "Blackman &

Robertson" were centered in the half pane, our homage to "Spade & Archer" written on the door shown at the beginning of John Huston's version of *The Maltese Falcon*. Unlike Sam Spade, Nakayla and I vowed never to scrape off each other's name. We'd come close to being killed in two past investigations so we weren't playing out a fantasy. We'd have our business together or have no business at all.

I tucked the newspaper under my arm, juggled the coffees in one hand, pinched the bag of muffins between two fingers, and used my palm to turn the doorknob. I stepped in our waiting room. The leather sofa, matching chairs, oak end tables, and an oriental rug gave it the air of a British club where Watson, Sherlock, and his brother Mycroft might discuss a case. Nakayla's office was on the right; mine on the left. We had no receptionist because the state of the art phone equipment provided an easy way to leave a message or page us. And we didn't want anyone else involved in our business. Confidential means just that, and the fewer the ears and eyes the fewer the wagging tongues. Nakayla and I carried our own secrets, the most incriminating being a source of funds acquired through those two life-threatening investigations but not reported. Our agency kept us busy and also provided a way for funneling some of that money into our local bank accounts. We were topnotch investigators who feared being investigated.

"Is that the muffin man?" Nakayla called.

I started singing: "Do you know the muffin man, the muffin man, the muffin man? Do you know the muffin man who lives in Mulberry Lane?"

"No, but I know the guy from the Kenilworth Apartments who can't carry a tune and better be carrying something to eat."

"That's me, along with hot coffee." I set one coffee and the bag with the two muffins on the corner of her desk.

She looked up from her computer screen. "I thought the muffin man lived in Drury Lane."

"Not where I grew up. I guess Mom rewrote it because we had a Mulberry Lane near our house. When we rode down the street, my brother Stanley and I looked for a mailbox with Muffin Man on the side."

"You must have been a pair of geniuses. Now can you sing, 'Do you know the mystery hikers?'"

I tossed the newspaper on her desk. "You've read the story." I sat in her guest chair and removed the plastic lid from my cup.

"Online. After I heard Ranger Corn's voice mail." She touched a button on her phone.

"Mr. Blackman. Ms. Robertson. I need you to stay in town for the next few weeks. We could have an inquest and you'd be called to testify. Also I don't know why Deputy Overcash played cloak and dagger with your names. I went ahead and gave them to the media, not that I want you speculating beyond what you saw. I'll be back in touch."

"Inquest?" I asked. "Too soon for a medical report."

"He's anticipating more than a formality." Nakayla gestured toward the computer screen. "I got an email from Investigative Alliance requesting we send them an affidavit stating we never had direct contact with their client."

"Which one? The doc or the malpractice insurer?"

"Both, although the emphasis was on Montgomery."

Wyatt Montgomery was the surgeon named in the suit. He'd practiced for eight years and had something more valuable to lose than money: his reputation.

"They see the cops taking a good look at their guy," I said. "Does Corn know Montgomery's name?"

"Yes. He called the CEO of Investigative Alliance last night."

"He doesn't waste any time." I took a sip of hot coffee and mulled the developments. The fact that we'd never met the surgeon was as much to our benefit as his. "I wonder if Corn's contacted Montgomery?"

"Probably. He might have checked the hospital's surgical calendar, not only for this morning but also for yesterday afternoon."

"Then I'd like to do a preemptive call."

"To Corn?"

"Yes. I'll let him know we got his message and we learned he got Montgomery's name. I'll tell him we've never spoken to Montgomery, and if the doctor played a hand in what happened, we knew nothing about it. Given Janice Wainwright's medical history, Corn should understand why we were surprised she climbed Glassy Mountain."

"Ask him for more specifics about the inquest. Tell him you're planning a trip to Paris."

"Paris?"

"Why not? I've never been there." She pulled a muffin from the bag and broke it in half. "Tickets. Hotel reservations. All that's at risk if we're tied up with the inquest."

"What do I say when we don't go?"

She arched her eyebrows and glared at me.

"So I'm taking you to Paris."

Dimples appeared as her scowl transformed into an impish grin. "Why, Sam. What a surprise. How romantic."

I sipped my coffee. Nakayla had taken me from Glassy Mountain to the Eiffel Tower in less than fifteen seconds. Ambushed by my own partner.

"Here's his number." She handed me the business card Corn gave her the previous night.

I retreated to my office and placed the call. My name must have been circulating through the district office because as soon as I gave it, the ranger transferred me to Corn.

"What's up?" His voice sounded raspy and tired. He'd probably snagged a couple hours of sleep at the most.

I ran through my script. He responded with monosyllabic grunts until I posed Nakayla's fabricated trip.

"Paris? I thought you were in the middle of an investigation?"

His question stopped me. We should have anticipated that we already had a potential conflict.

I paused a second too long. "We were leaving when the case went to trial on May 10th."

"Wouldn't you have to testify?"

"If we uncovered anything. But Investigative Alliance knew they'd have to pay for lost deposits and re-booking fees. I assume that the National Park Service won't be cutting a similar check for reimbursements."

Corn laughed. "You got that right."

I said nothing, waiting for him to fill the silence.

"Look," he said. "We'll move this along as fast as we can. The body went overnight to the Chief Medical Examiner in Chapel Hill for the autopsy. It started at six this morning. I received an email that the verbal report might be delayed until tomorrow."

"Why?"

"Apparently the M.E. wants a more detailed look at a lower back injury."

"Mrs. Wainwright's lawsuit."

"Imagine that," Corn said sarcastically. "Amazing since I didn't have the chance to mention the injury to him. I didn't learn about it till eleven-thirty last night."

"He must be good."

Corn said nothing.

"What about the blood work?"

"He'll have a report later this morning."

"If it's clean and we learn her sense of balance wasn't impaired, will the FBI come in?"

"Are you kidding?"

"Don't you share jurisdiction on a federal land crime?"

"Do you know which federal officers have the highest risk of assault or death in the line of duty?"

I took a guess. "The FBI?"

"They'd like you to believe that. National Park Rangers are twelve times more likely to be in a life-threatening encounter. No bullshit. And I'm talking attacks from other people, not bears, snakes, or mountain lions. An official government study back in 2004 has the data to back it up. The wimps in the FBI don't want to come near us."

I doubted that was entirely true. A high profile case usually had agencies fighting for a piece of it. "So, you're solo on this?"

"That's the way I prefer, although I'm not adverse to a suggestion now and then, like checking out a lower back injury."

I got the message that Corn suspected I'd somehow tipped the M.E. I didn't confess and instead moved on to my most important question. "Does her doctor have an alibi?"

"No comment."

"Okay. How about the daughter?"

"I made the notification last night in person with a female ranger. The girl was understandably distraught. I went easy on the questioning. She's only seventeen so I avoided anything that smacked of an interrogation. I've informed social services because she has no next of kin in the area."

"She had to stay alone?"

"No. My colleague remained."

I figured I'd gotten all I could for the moment. "So, what about Paris?"

"Yeah, Paris." He sighed. "Give me a day or two. I'll have a better idea of where this is headed. Hopefully a more solid destination than your bogus trip." He hung up.

All and all the call hadn't gone badly. I knew the M.E. was checking the back injury, Corn would be the lead investigator, and something was still hanging out there with the doctor. My inquiry about him had generated the only "no comment."

I got up to share the information with Nakayla. As I stepped into the waiting room between our offices, the door from the hallway opened. A teenage girl stepped in and pushed the door closed behind her. She wore jeans and a green cotton-knit sweater. She held a black leather clutch purse that seemed too formal for the rest of her wardrobe.

"Mr. Blackman?" Her voice was tight with the hint of a sob beneath the words. Her brown hair hung in tangles to her shoulders. Her brown eyes were rimmed with red and tears glistened on her pale cheeks. She looked familiar.

"Yes. Can I help you?"

"Where's your partner?"

Nakayla came to the door of her office. Her eyes widened. "Wendy?"

The girl took a step backwards. I recognized her. Janice Wainwright's daughter. I'd only seen her through the long lens of our surveillance equipment. Where was the ranger that Corn left with her?

Wendy's right hand disappeared into her purse for a split-second, and then reappeared holding a small pistol. Her finger wrapped around the trigger, tightening till her knuckle smoothed. The barrel arced from Nakayla to me.

"So, you know me. You've been spying on us."

The gun shook with each word.

Nakayla took a step forward. "Put the pistol down and let's talk."

"No. You murdered my mother. There's nothing to talk about. You've taken her life and ruined mine."

The door behind her swung inward, hitting her square in the shoulder.

Wendy screamed as she pulled the trigger.

Chapter Four

A thirty-two caliber is a light weapon. There's not much stopping power but a well-placed shot to the head or chest can put you in a casket. A hit elsewhere on the body will ruin your day.

Although small in size, the exploding round in the revolver's chamber sounded like Wendy detonated a stick of dynamite in the room. I was grateful I heard it.

Whether because of the recoil or because of her alarm, Wendy flung the gun aside. I jumped forward, wrapping my arms around hers and pinning them to her sides. She screamed again and struggled against my grip.

I looked over her shoulder. Hewitt Donaldson, the attorney from down the hall, stood with his mouth open and his Hawaiian shirt steaming. He held a coffee mug pressed against his chest, its contents now turning his shirt's pattern of bright reds, greens, and oranges into a muddy brown. His face grimaced with pain but the shock of the gunshot smothered any cry.

"Come in and close the door," I shouted.

Hewitt shook himself like a burly bear, stepped aside, and pushed the door shut. "Jesus," he muttered.

Nakayla tugged at my arm. "Let me take her."

Instinctively, Hewitt wedged his hands against the doorjamb and became a human barricade blocking Wendy's escape.

I jumped away and Nakayla grabbed the girl's wrists.

"Look at me," she ordered.

The girl twisted her head away, trying to see who hit her from behind.

"Look at me," Nakayla repeated. "Let us help you. If not for yourself, then for your goat."

Hewitt's mouth opened even wider. The defense lawyer used his share of flamboyant dramatics in the courtroom, but I doubted they had ever involved a goat.

Wendy stopped struggling. "What can you do about Ida Mae?"

"Whatever you want us to do."

Wendy stared at Nakayla. I couldn't see my partner's face, but her expression must have offered reassurance. Wendy looked at me.

I nodded. "We'll make sure Ida Mae's taken care of." I assumed Ida Mae was the goat. "And her baby, uh, kid."

"She'll probably have two." Wendy's lower lip trembled. "And I won't see them." She flung herself around Nakayla's neck, her body convulsing with sobs.

"Help me get her to the sofa," Nakayla said.

I took Wendy's left arm and we guided her. The girl's knees were so weak we practically carried her. She plopped in a corner and tucked her feet under her legs.

Nakayla sat snug against her. "Give us a minute," she told me.

I pointed to the gun on the floor. "We need to know what happened to the ranger."

Nakayla took Wendy's hand. "Where's the woman who was staying with you?"

"In the tool shed," she murmured.

"Is she all right?"

Wendy shrugged. "I guess. She came with me to get a shovel to muck Ida Mae's stall. I ran out and threw the bolt."

"Could she radio for help?" I asked.

Wendy kept her gaze on Nakayla. "No. She only had a cell phone and it's charging in the house."

"Okay." I looked around the office.

Chipped plaster beside a wall sconce revealed the impact point of the bullet. When Hewitt opened the door and hit Wendy, the shove knocked the pistol to the left, away from

Nakayla, the window, and me. I stepped into my office and examined the other side of the wall. Its thickness stopped the slug from exiting. Other than the sound, no one outside the office would have been aware that a gun was fired.

I took an evidence bag from a cabinet by my desk, and then ran a ballpoint pen through the trigger guard of the revolver. I lifted the weapon off the floor and dropped it in the bag. "I'll hold onto this."

"It's my mom's," Wendy said.

"I'll take good care of it. For the time being don't tell anyone you fired the shot."

"It was an accident." Wendy started crying again.

I didn't say anything. It wasn't an accident that her mother's gun had been pointed at my chest.

Nakayla put an arm around Wendy. "You'd better call Corn," she told me.

"Okay." I turned to Hewitt. "Can I use your office?"

"Sure." He opened the door.

"Give us at least thirty minutes," Nakayla said.

As I closed the door behind us, Hewitt whispered, "Surely someone heard the shot."

"I know. But they might not know what it was."

"What do you want to do? The girl fired a gun in a public building. Hell, she practically fired it on the front steps of the police department."

The main site of the Asheville Police and Fire Departments was only a few hundred yards away on the south side of Pack Square. The county courthouse stood at the east side, opposite our office. Wendy Wainwright could be arrested, booked, arraigned, and jailed within a five-minute walk.

I pulled my BlackBerry from my belt. "I'll call it in but say I accidentally discharged my weapon. Are you good with that?"

As a trial lawyer, Hewitt Donaldson was a sworn officer of the court and technically I was asking him to ignore a crime.

He brushed his long gray hair out of his face and gave me a hard stare. "The girl nearly killed you. And she escaped from custody."

I pressed the speed dial button programmed for the police, a necessity of my trade. "She wasn't in custody. Her mother was the woman who fell off Glassy Mountain."

"The history professor?"

"Asheville Police Department." The woman's efficient voice rang in my ear.

I held up a finger signaling Hewitt to be quiet. "Good morning. This is Sam Blackman. I'm up at Adler Court."

"Hi, Sam. It's Louise. What do you need?"

I wasn't sure who she was but most of the officers knew my name. "Has anyone called about a gunshot in my building?"

"No." Her tone jumped to rapid-response mode. "I'll dispatch assistance. Anyone injured?"

"Just my pride. I accidentally discharged my handgun. I wanted you to know everything and everyone is all right. If you need to check out the scene for a report, then send someone to look at the hole."

She laughed. "Was the bullet contained?"

"Yes, it's buried in an interior wall."

"All right. I'll note your call in case someone else reports it."

"Is there a fine? I'll pay it."

She lowered her voice. "If no one mentions it by the end of my shift, it'll be our secret. I hope you learned your lesson."

"Believe me, I have. Nakayla's never going to let me forget it. Thanks, Louise." I returned the BlackBerry to my belt.

"What's going on?" Hewitt asked.

"I'll tell you in your conference room." I motioned him to lead the way.

His office was around the corner and farther from the elevator. The suite was larger than ours with a reception area, conference room, two private offices, and a storage room for case files. Hewitt's firm had one lawyer, one paralegal, and one business manager/receptionist. His specialty was criminal defense and he was often a hired gun for bigger firms. He enjoyed the perfect niche. A throwback to the 1960s, he was in his sixties and didn't care what he said or to whom he said it.

The police couldn't stand him because they considered him a smart-ass legal whore who defended anyone. Too often they saw suspects they thought they had dead-to-rights pronounced "not guilty" by a jury persuaded by Hewitt's legal skills and force of personality.

We met on a case and I uncovered information that helped him make peace with a family secret. Since then, people claimed Hewitt Donaldson was mellower. But not in a courtroom.

I followed him into his reception area. He glanced around to make sure no one was there except the woman at the desk. Her nose was buried in a file folder and only the top of her inky black hair appeared above her computer screen.

"Shirley," Hewitt shouted, "didn't you hear the gunshot?"

"Was that what that was?" She spoke casually and kept reading. "I thought it might be."

"Why didn't you call the police? I could have been out in the hall bleeding to death."

"You just answered your own question."

I laughed. Only then did Shirley look up.

"Hi, Sam."

As I expected, she wore chalk white makeup with her eerie blue eyes encircled in heavy black mascara. She looked like she grew up in the Addams Family and would melt in direct sunlight.

She stared at Hewitt's shirt. "I'll be damned. Someone did shoot you. I always knew you'd bleed coffee." She picked up the phone. "Should I call Mission Hospital or Starbucks?"

"Very funny." Hewitt stormed past her. "Is Cory in?"

"No. She's at the courthouse filing the motions in the Nicholson case."

Cory DeMille was Hewitt's paralegal. She looked like she grew up as one of the Brady Bunch.

Hewitt stopped. "What's my next must-do?"

"You're to see Judge Wood in his chamber at ten-thirty. It's now nine-twenty-five."

"Right." He looked at the front of his shirt. "I'll need to change."

"Ya think?" Shirley turned to me. "Isn't it awesome being in the presence of such a brain?"

Hewitt threw up his hands in defeat. Shirley always got the last word.

He walked on. "Sam, use the conference room for your call. Get me when you're done. Meanwhile I'll find another shirt."

"Not like that one," Shirley said. "Hawaii had to promise to stop making them if it wanted to become a state."

The conference room reflected Hewitt's personality: a round table where no one could sit at the head and walls filled, not with law books or law degrees, but with classic album covers from the 1960s. Plexiglas protected The Grateful Dead, Bob Dylan, The Rolling Stones, Iron Butterfly, and other bands whose names now survive as Trivial Pursuit questions.

I sat in a chair facing the door and used my BlackBerry to call Ranger Corn for the second time that morning.

"What's up now?" He sounded irritated. "Are you adding Italy and need to leave town even earlier?"

"Have you heard from your ranger with the Wainwright girl?"

"No. She's staying with her till someone arrives from social services."

"Wendy Wainwright's in my office. Your ranger is locked in Wendy's tool shed."

Corn sucked in a sharp breath. "What the hell!"

"The girl's very upset. She thinks we murdered her mother."

"She confronted you?"

"Yes. No one was hurt and she claims your ranger's unharmed. How did she get our names, Corn?"

He paused. "I may have mentioned them when I told her what happened."

"And may have mentioned we were detectives following her?"

"I asked the questions I had to ask. One of them was whether her mother said someone was following her."

"I think the phrase was 'spying on her.' What was the answer?"

"No. Her mother never said that. She did say the doctor and insurance company would do anything to get out of paying the money, but that she was working on another way."

"And what was that?"

"The girl claims she doesn't know."

"Does she know why her mother went to Sandburg's home yesterday?"

"She didn't know her mother was going. She assumes it was about the goat."

"Where was Wendy yesterday afternoon? My partner was watching the farm when she should have been there."

He paused longer. "I didn't ask. There was no reason to do anything but comfort the girl."

"You're right. Is she in trouble now?"

Corn cleared his throat to make an official pronouncement. "She locked up a law enforcement officer. That has consequences."

"Consequences? How about the consequences of telling her that two detectives working for the other side were at the scene of her mother's fatal injury. Maybe your tool shed prisoner speculated a little more after you left."

"I understand. But I can't let it slide."

"I'd think you'd want her as a cooperative witness for your investigation, not as an adversary." I looked at the closed door of the conference room and thought about the man changing his shirt. "If you're going to play it that way, then you'll be working through her lawyer."

"Who's that?"

"Hewitt Donaldson."

Corn muttered something I couldn't understand, but I doubted the Ranger Code of Conduct approved it.

"What do I tell the girl?" I asked.

"Let me spring my tool shed prisoner and hear what she has to say. Maybe the wind blew the door shut."

"It happens."

"Can you assure me you'll keep the girl where I can find her?"

"Yes."

"I'll call you back."

"Okay." I pulled the phone from my ear.

"Blackman." Corn shouted my name before I could disconnect.

"I'm still here."

"Sorry if something I said set her off. I had to check."

I said nothing.

"And it looks like the death was most likely an accident."

"Why?"

"This isn't for public consumption but the blood work came back about ten minutes ago. Janice Wainwright double-dosed her painkillers."

"How do you know?"

I heard him flipping through pages.

"She had a level of hydrocodone that was higher than it should have been. I'd already sent a ranger back to her car this morning and he radioed that he found a prescription bottle of Vicodin HP under the seat. It was filled yesterday morning and six tablets were missing. That's twice the normal dose. Hydrocodone and acetaminophen are the active ingredients. Dizziness and light-headedness are side effects. Janice Wainwright could have walked out on the slope, lost her balance, and cracked her head."

"But the backpack on the bush."

"She set it there so it wouldn't get dirty," Corn said. "You don't know for sure how far she was ahead of you on the trail."

Part of my mind was saying leave well enough alone. If an accidental fall was the conclusion, then Nakayla and I were in the clear. But the other part of my mind wanted to know why she hiked there at all. Why did she scream "no?" What were Sandburg's verses?

"But I'm not curtailing the investigation," Corn said. "I'm not settling for an accidental death until we've followed every lead and ruled out every other possibility."

We hung up with the understanding that Corn would call after he spoke with his ranger at the Wainwright farm.

Meanwhile, I planned to get as much information from Wendy as I could because once Corn took action, I might not have another opportunity.

I found Hewitt Donaldson sitting behind the desk in his office. He now wore a white linen shirt that seemed more appropriate for meeting a judge—if the judge was drinking a Mojito at a cabana in the Caribbean.

"How much do you charge an hour?" I asked.

He frowned. "What have you gotten yourself into?"

"Something that's none of my business."

His eyes lit up. "A man after my own heart."

"Good. Because I've already gotten you into it with me."

He laughed. "If you're Don Quixote, then I must be Sancho Panza."

"I see you more as Sir Galahad. We've a damsel in distress."

"That girl who tried to kill you?"

"No. I'll take care of Wendy. I'm counting on your legal genius to save Ida Mae."

"The goat? You want me to represent the goat? You're kidding?"

"The goat's kidding. She's pregnant. Hell, you should do it for Ida Mae pro bono."

Hewitt stared at me. There's nothing more pitiful than a defense lawyer who's run out of questions.

"Yes, I'm kidding," I said. "I want you to represent Wendy until she gets through this mess with the law enforcement rangers."

"Okay."

"And then we're going to find out who killed her mother."

Chapter Five

Hewitt looked at his watch. "I've got forty-five minutes till I see Judge Wood. How can we best use the time?"

I sat in his guest chair. "Let me share everything I know. Then we'll talk to Wendy."

I briefed him on the initial assignment from Investigative Alliance, the drive from the university to the Sandburg home, Janice's whispered words before losing consciousness, and the discovery of the backpack. I told him about the link between the goat and the Sandburg herd and the blood work that confirmed Janice had taken extra painkillers before attempting the hike. I concluded with Corn's commitment to a full investigation and his insistence that Wendy face some consequence for her actions.

Hewitt waved his hand dismissively. "Nah, he's just hot under the collar right now. The more he thinks about it, the less attractive it'll be to have his ranger publicly ridiculed for letting a seventeen-year-old girl get the jump on her."

"Can you be with Wendy when Corn speaks to her?"

"Yes. My meeting at the courthouse won't last over twenty minutes. I'm more interested in why you think Janice Wainwright was killed."

I shook my head. "I can't say exactly. Something about the way she yelled 'no.' Not in fear or as a reaction to losing her balance. It was defiant, almost a command to someone."

"Okay."

"And then there's the backpack. If it's what caught my eye, then it must have been in the air. I don't think I would have seen the bush from the first spot I stopped."

"Someone tossed it as he ran away?"

"Yes, but I didn't hear him."

Hewitt spread his hands like gesturing to a jury. "It could have been tossed to catch your eye and keep you from looking elsewhere. Then he hid until you and Nakayla were so absorbed with the Wainwright woman that he slipped away unnoticed."

"Why did he take her backpack? Did he hope it had something valuable or did he know?"

"Could have been either one. People are accosted on the trails from time to time. Sort of a mountain mugging gone bad."

"A five million dollar mugging. Maybe someone wanted it to look like a purse snatching. I'm going to check out that sales receipt from Malaprop's. It was in the backpack but there wasn't a book."

"She might have placed the book in there with the receipt when she bought it. Later, she took the book out and left the receipt. But it's worth a try." Hewitt looked out the window at Pack Square and thought a moment. "Who's the attorney representing Wainwright in the lawsuit?"

"I don't know. Won't that go away now?"

"No. The law states the estate can continue the suit on her behalf. The lawyers for the doctor and clinic will file a motion to dismiss, but that won't do any good. In addition to pain, suffering, and loss of income, there's also death as the ultimate damage."

He stood and walked around his desk closer to me. His eyes held mine and I felt what it must be like to have him cross-examine you in the witness box.

"There's an interesting twist that you'd better be aware of."

"A twist?"

"Yes. If I'm Janice Wainwright's lawyer, I immediately change the lawsuit to wrongful death and include the pharmaceutical company. If they didn't have 'hiking' on their warning label, then we bring them in as a proximate cause guilty of negligence.

North Carolina requires the new suit go to mediation where I'd tell the other side we're doubling our damages to ten million."

I saw the possibility. "So the botched surgery created the condition which required the pain medication. The prescription bottle didn't provide ample warning and the dosage caused her to fall. But wouldn't stating dizziness as a side effect cover them from liability?"

"She wasn't doing anything dangerous like rock climbing. She was simply walking in the woods. And if the autopsy shows conclusive proof of medical negligence and error, then I've got a hell of a case. At that point the defendants usually turn on each other, casting blame as to who was the most proximate cause. You were smart to have Detective Newland tell the M.E. to check her lower back. The defendants wouldn't want that examination going anywhere near her surgery."

"I wasn't that smart. I only wanted to know if she'd gone through pain and suffering to climb Glassy Mountain. The trek was hard enough on my leg. I can't imagine how it felt with a bad back, and I'm still left with the question of why she did it."

"That's the twist," Hewitt said. He waited, expecting me to finish his point.

"I don't get it."

"If Janice Wainwright met someone up there and that person caused her to fall, then the blame shifts. The defendants aren't responsible for her being knocked down. There's no negligence on their part."

"Even if she was dizzy?"

"How dizzy's dizzy when someone pushes you on a rock slope and rips your backpack away? The defense just has to paint that picture and my case is weakened. I'm back to seeking damages for pain and suffering only. The big settlement for death is off the table."

"So I'm working against you."

He grinned. "That's right. Your quest, Sir Galahad, to discover the truth about Janice Wainwright's death could cost her daughter a shit load of money."

"Ranger Corn might discover enough evidence to hand the defense that possibility."

"Yes. He might. But he won't. He's got the blood levels to explain the fall. Whatever the M.E. finds will be a bonus. Right now his only other suspects are you and Nakayla." Hewitt glanced at his watch. "Let's talk to the girl. Then we'll chart a course of action."

Nakayla and Wendy still sat on the sofa, but Nakayla had slid to the opposite end. Wendy held a can of Pepsi Cola in one hand and a handkerchief in the other. Her sobs had subsided to faint sniffles. I sat in the chair nearer to Wendy; Hewitt took the one by Nakayla.

"How'd you do?" Nakayla asked me.

"Okay." I looked at Wendy. "Ranger Corn is upset that you locked the woman in the tool shed."

"I know," she whispered. "And I'm sorry I came here with a gun."

"You and I are square, but you're going to have to deal with the ranger. Mr. Donaldson here is a lawyer friend and he's offered to help you."

She studied him for a second. "We already have a lawyer."

"Who's that?" Hewitt asked.

"Mr. Kirkland. I think his first name's Louis. He's working on Mom's case." Her mouth twisted as she thought about what she'd said. "I guess there is no case."

"There's a case, dear," Hewitt said gently. "Louis Kirkland's a good man and he should pursue it differently now. If your mom fell because of her medication, then the drug company may also bear responsibility. There's something called wrongful death and that's more serious. I'll talk to Mr. Kirkland about it. With your permission, of course."

"All right." She set the Pepsi on the floor and twisted the handkerchief with both hands. "What's going to happen to me?"

Hewitt leaned forward. "While Mr. Kirkland's working on the lawsuit, I'll be happy to help you with the rangers."

"I mean what's going to happen to me period." Tears welled in her eyes and she couldn't say anymore.

"Wendy doesn't have any kin in Asheville," Nakayla said. "Her mother's sister is flying in from Orlando this morning. Wendy says she's named as guardian in her mother's will. Wendy turns eighteen in October."

"I see," Hewitt said. "Wendy, what would you like to do?"

"What Mom wanted me to do. Go to college. Help on the farm."

"What college?" Hewitt asked.

"Warren Wilson. I'd stay on the campus but be close to home."

Warren Wilson was a progressive small liberal arts school between Asheville and Black Mountain and famous for its sustainable environmental policies, social consciousness, and land management practices including a working farm. I'd never been on campus, but for a girl of high intelligence and an interest in agrarian life, the college sounded like a perfect match.

"A good choice," Hewitt said. "Do you have any siblings?"

"No."

"How about your dad?"

"He and Mom are divorced. He's got a new wife and three-year-old twins. They live in Gainesville, Florida, and they don't need me."

"Your dad may feel differently."

"Maybe. But not his wife. She was his secretary at his law firm. You can guess the rest."

For a few seconds, an awkward silence hung in the air.

"Who's helping with funeral arrangements," I asked.

"Aunt Cynthia." Wendy wiped her nose with the handkerchief. "The family plot's in Florida. My aunt will want me to stay in Orlando. I want to stay here."

"That could happen," Hewitt said.

Wendy blinked back the tears. "Really?"

"Are you the sole heir?"

"Yes. Mom has some life insurance through the university. And my father sends child support."

"Is there a mortgage on the farm?"

Wendy nodded. "Mom hoped the lawsuit would pay it off and leave enough to hire some help."

Hewitt cleared his throat. "Then here's what I'll do. We'll find out about the insurance and other assets."

"I can't pay you much," Wendy said.

"I'm not worried about that. My fees will come when you win your lawsuit. I want to make sure you've got funds for funeral expenses and travel, and enough to live on and run the farm."

"What about my aunt? If she makes me stay with her, what'll happen to the farm this summer? Ida Mae's due in a week. Her udders are filling up already."

Now I understood why Wendy thought she wouldn't see Ida Mae give birth to her kids.

"People go away to college when they're seventeen," Hewitt said. "If we can show that you've got the financial resources and your aunt agrees, you should be able to stay. If your aunt says no, we can petition the court for an emancipation."

"Emancipation? You mean like a slave?"

"Sort of. It frees you from the limitations of being a minor. Emancipation of a Minor is the full legal term. You have to be at least sixteen and demonstrate the ability to accept adult responsibility."

Wendy took a deep breath. "Oh, God, I really shouldn't have locked that ranger in the tool shed."

Hewitt smiled. "No, you shouldn't have. And you shouldn't have brought the gun, but Mr. Blackman is covering for you on that. I'll work on the ranger problem."

Wendy dropped her eyes and gnawed on her lower lip.

Hewitt continued, "If the emancipation is granted, your aunt's duties as guardian will be ended. You'll still have other limitations like buying alcohol or representing yourself in the lawsuit, but running the farm and going to college will be your decisions."

She looked up, hope in her eyes. "That would be great."

"It also means your father's child support could end."

"He was supposed to pay for college. That was part of the settlement."

"I'll review the documents," Hewitt said. "Under the circumstances, he may understand why we're doing what we're doing. Do you know who your mother named as the executor of her estate?"

"I guess Aunt Cynthia."

"Is she married?"

"No. She and my uncle Tom divorced ten years ago. They didn't have any children. I'll be like a Martian in her house."

"That aside I'll need to talk to her about the lawsuit. We'll do that as soon as it's appropriate."

"Thank you." She looked at Nakayla and then me. "Thanks to all of you."

"You're welcome." Hewitt shifted uneasily in his chair. "There's another matter to bring up about your mother's death. What did the rangers tell you?"

"That my mother had fallen on Glassy Mountain and hit her head. They said she died in the ambulance." Wendy looked at me. "Then they asked me whether anyone had been following her and they mentioned your names."

"Did they imply that we had anything to do with your mother's fall?" I asked.

"No. But when I heard you were working for the other side, I, um..." She looked away.

"Right now no one knows what happened," Hewitt said. "Mr. Blackman suspects there could have been foul play."

Wendy's eyes widened. "Really?"

"Nakayla and I want to check it out," I said. "Mr. Donaldson wants us to proceed cautiously."

Wendy looked at the lawyer. "Why?"

"If someone else was involved, it will complicate the lawsuit. Our claim of wrongful death will be harder to prove."

Wendy shook her head so hard her long brown hair swished across her face. "But that's not right. Whoever killed my mother needs to be caught."

"I agree," Hewitt said. "By proceed cautiously, I mean Mr. Blackman and Ms. Robertson investigate discreetly so that the surgeon and his insurance company don't latch onto some theory that's not true."

"So, it's better if my mother's fall was an accident." Wendy grasped the heart of the matter.

"Yes," Hewitt said, "but not at the expense of the truth."

Wendy leaned forward, staring first at Nakayla and then me. The tears were gone and her eyes burned with determination. "Then find who killed my mother. I don't care if it costs the farm, Ida Mae and her kids, or the lawsuit. She deserves justice."

I nodded. "We'll do our best and we'll do it quietly."

"Promise me." Wendy reached out and clutched my wrist so hard that her fingernails dug into my skin.

"We promise," Nakayla and I said together.

At that moment, I knew we'd taken a vow to this seventeen-year-old girl. We weren't simply responsible for her case; we were responsible for her future.

"Good." Hewitt stood. "I've got to be in Judge Wood's chamber in ten minutes. I'll make him aware of our Emancipation of a Minor petition and ask him to fast-track it. Nakayla, can you stay with Wendy until her aunt arrives?"

"Certainly."

"Excellent. I'll see if the judge will notify social services that they're not required. Sam, call Ranger Corn and tell him Wendy and I will see him in his office at eleven-thirty."

"What if that's not convenient?"

Hewitt smiled. "Then tell him my client must not be all that important and he can speak to us after the funeral in Florida." He opened the door, and then paused. "I'll have Shirley start the emancipation paperwork. When you finish here, take Wendy to Cory. She'll help fill out the forms. I'll be back by eleven." He bowed and closed the door behind him.

Wendy looked bewildered. "He's not like any other lawyer I've met. Certainly not like my dad."

"You've seen the bumper sticker 'Keep Asheville Weird?'" I asked.

Wendy nodded.

"Hewitt Donaldson goes beyond the call of duty."

The girl thought for a moment. "Maybe I should have him do the lawsuit."

"No," I said. "I think you're better to keep things as they are. Your mother must have hired Kirkland on a contingency basis and you shouldn't cut him out."

"I wouldn't want to do that."

"And if Hewitt joins the team, it could alarm the other side. Force them to shift their strategy, which could mean they aggressively look for someone else who caused your mother's death. Nakayla and I are their best suspects, but if they try to pin it on us, they look bad because we were working for them."

She blushed. "That's why I came here with the gun."

"Well, we don't want them to look any further. Unlike us, they're not interested in the truth. They only need to create a plausible alternative for the cause of your mother's death that takes them off the hook."

"I see," Wendy said softly.

"We let Mr. Kirkland file the new lawsuit, Hewitt Donaldson navigates you through your personal situation, and Nakayla and I investigate what really happened."

"All right." Wendy brushed her hair off her face and picked up the empty Pepsi can. "I guess I should meet the person who's helping me fill out the papers."

"In a minute," I said. "There are a few questions we need to ask."

"Questions?" She wrinkled her nose. "About what?"

"You're the first source of information about your mother. Trying to understand why she was on Glassy Mountain might be our best approach."

"I told you I don't know why." The whine of a teenager sounded in her voice.

"Then we'll have to figure it out together."

She sighed. "Okay."

"Where were you yesterday afternoon?"

Wendy flicked her tongue across her lips. "Why do you need to know that?"

"Because we want to rule out that your mother thought she was meeting you." I glanced at Nakayla. She'd picked up that for some reason the question unnerved the girl.

"And eliminate the possibility the doctor's defense team can claim you met your mother and had an argument," Nakayla added.

"They'd do that?"

Nakayla nodded. "They'll play hardball. Too much is at stake."

I admired my partner's instinct for making Wendy feel vulnerable without accusing her. I guess it helps to have been a teenage girl.

"Now I know you didn't drive home straight from school," Nakayla said. "I was watching the house from the overlook."

Wendy reddened. "I still can't believe you were spying on us."

Nakayla and I said nothing. We weren't the issue.

"I went to Warren Wilson College."

"Why?" I asked.

"To hang out. Pretend I was one of the students. Classes are still in session."

"Anyone see you?" Nakayla asked.

"I was down at one of the barns. I talked to a couple people, but we didn't exchange names."

"What time was this?" Nakayla asked.

"Around three-thirty. Then I walked through some of the classroom buildings. I know it's silly but I feel more at home there than my high school."

Nakayla smiled. "You've got senioritus, the terrible itch to get out. Any professors see you?"

"No. Why should they?"

"No reason. It's just good to have some people confirm your alibi."

"Alibi. I don't need an alibi. I did nothing wrong!"

Nakayla ignored her outburst. "What time did you get to the farm?"

"Six-thirty. I started to get worried about eight when Mom hadn't come home. The rangers arrived about nine-thirty."

And so it began, I thought. "Did your mother go to the Sandburg home often?"

"Maybe once or twice a month. She's interested in its history. And then when I had a 4-H project with livestock we bought Ida Mae from them."

"How did that work?"

"We were lucky. Every August they auction off part of the herd. We missed that, but an extra doe got pregnant."

I looked to Nakayla. Pregnancy wasn't my thing.

"Is there a quota?" Nakayla asked.

"Yes, the ranger in charge of the barn allows two pregnancies each year because they can only manage a limited number of goats. Last winter one of the bucks got out of his pen, and, well, you know what happened. The ranger asked Mom if we wanted to buy Ida Mae."

"This was for a 4-H project?" I asked.

"Yes. The timing was perfect, although Ida Mae's due date is near the end of school."

"Does your mother study Sandburg?" I asked.

Wendy shrugged. "Some. She was more interested in the history of the farm and Flat Rock in general. American history's her specialty. Especially The Civil War and the South."

"How long have you been up here?"

"Four years. We moved after the divorce was finalized. She left a teaching position at the University of Florida for Asheville. She likes it okay."

"Does she have any close friends?" Nakayla asked.

"Not really. We're kinda by ourselves at the farm. She's made some friends on the faculty."

"Anyone she'd go hiking with?"

Wendy shook her head. "Mom didn't hike. Not since she hurt her back."

I stretched my bad leg. Sitting so long was starting to give me a cramp. "One last thing for now. There was a receipt for a book in your mother's backpack. She bought it the night before last. Do you know what it was?"

Wendy looked puzzled. "In a backpack?"

"Yes. Is that unusual?"

"We have a couple around the house. I use them for school, but Mom always carried a briefcase. The old kind that closed with buckled straps."

"So you don't know what book she bought? The receipt was from Malaprop's Bookstore."

"No. She said she had a faculty meeting that night."

I stood. "Thank you, Wendy. And we're very sorry about what happened to your mother."

Her eyes teared and she didn't say anything.

"Why don't you go with Nakayla to Mr. Donaldson's office. I'll phone Ranger Corn and set up the meeting."

Wendy got to her feet and steadied herself on the arm of the sofa. "Mr. Blackman, do you think my mother could have been killed because of her plan?"

"What plan?"

"The one she said could take care of us even if we didn't win the lawsuit."

"At this point anything's possible. What did she say about it?"

"Nothing. Just that maybe her degree would finally pay off."

"Did she often keep secrets from you?" I asked.

Again, Wendy hesitated as if the question made her uncomfortable. "Not really. She didn't talk much about work. I guess she thought I wasn't interested."

"We'll look for anything unusual in her schedule. Did she carry a calendar with her?"

"She has a computerized calendar at school that's synched to the university Internet. She keeps a paper calendar at home. Sometimes she forgets to coordinate the two."

"I'd like to see both of them. I know you've got a lot to do, but maybe before you leave for the funeral in Florida, I could come by the farm and we could also go by her office at the university."

Wendy took a deep, ragged breath. "That would be good. I'd like someone to be with me."

She and Nakayla left to start the emancipation paperwork. I wondered what she'd think of the Shirley cast straight out of *Night of the Living Dead* and Cory whose impeccable wardrobe made her the designated grownup of Hewitt Donaldson's law firm.

I went to my desk. It was only a quarter to eleven but it felt like two years had passed since Wendy pulled the trigger and nearly killed me. I picked up the phone and called Ranger Corn. As far as I was concerned, he'd never know how close Wendy came to being arrested for murder.

When I asked for him, the ranger said Corn was out. I told him who I was and said I needed to speak with Corn right away. The Blackman name must have the power to open doors because I was told to stay on the line and I'd be connected to his mobile.

"Blackman?" Corn's voice was curt and cold.

"Yeah. Hewitt Donaldson's bringing the girl to your office at eleven-thirty. She's very sorry for what she did."

"Is she? Well, she's not coming to my office. I'm on the way to her farmhouse and you get her ass there as soon as you can or I'll ask the Asheville police to bring her in handcuffs."

My stomach tightened. "What the hell's going on?"

"You tell me," Corn snapped. "My ranger wasn't in the tool shed. She's in the house and beaten to within an inch of her life."

Chapter Six

We traveled like a convoy. I drove my CR-V in the lead, Nakayla and Wendy followed in Wendy's Subaru Outback, and Hewitt Donaldson brought up the rear in his Jaguar. Shirley had reached Hewitt in the judge's chamber, and then she'd taken him his car. He caught up to us as we left the city limits. I hoped his vanity plate "NOT-GIL-T" accurately described his newest client.

Wendy's reaction had been total disbelief and denial. She swore she locked the ranger in the tool shed, got the revolver from her mother's dresser, and immediately left the farmhouse. On the way into Asheville, she called information on her cell phone to find our office location. If she wasn't telling the truth, then the kid deserved an Academy Award. She seemed so upset that Nakayla and I were afraid she might jump out of a moving vehicle. We belted her in the backseat of her own car and over-rode the door locks.

About halfway to the farm, an ambulance passed us heading the opposite direction. The wailing siren echoed off the hills, and I hoped the outcome for the ranger would be better than the one for Janice Wainwright.

Two cars from the Buncombe County Sheriff's Department and two SUVs with National Park Ranger insignias flanked the front porch of the farmhouse. Bent grass next to the steps showed where the ambulance must have backed in. Ranger Corn walked out through the screen door to the edge of the porch.

Protective crime scene boots covered his shoes. He bent over, yanked them off, and then stood with his hands on his hips and his lips drawn tight.

I braked to a stop, got out and hurried to meet him. I wanted to let Nakayla and Hewitt take their time bringing Wendy to the house.

"When was the girl in your office?" Corn asked the question without so much as a hello.

"Nine-fifteen."

"You sure."

"Positive. If anything, it was earlier. She caused a fuss. Hewitt Donaldson came into the office about that time and can vouch for it. She swears she only locked the ranger in the tool shed."

"Uh huh," Corn muttered as he looked at Wendy emerging from the Outback.

Hewitt and Nakayla stood on either side of her, helping her keep her balance.

"She's had quite a shock, Corn."

"I believe her."

"You do?" I couldn't keep the surprise out of my voice.

"My ranger regained consciousness before the ambulance arrived. We don't think she's hurt as badly as we first thought."

"That's good."

"Yeah. You always imagine the worst when you hear one of your guys has gone down." He paused and watched Nakayla and Hewitt escort Wendy across the lawn. "Wendy!" he called.

She looked up. Even from twenty yards away I saw tears sparkling on her cheeks.

"It's all right, dear," Corn said. "You're not in trouble. I just want you to help us learn if anything is missing. Okay?"

Nakayla and Hewitt looked at me. I shrugged. Something had happened that changed Corn's attitude.

He turned back to me. "Elsie Compton, my injured ranger, said she'd been in the tool shed about ten minutes when she heard a vehicle come up the driveway. She thought it was Wendy returning and she pounded on the door. When the girl still didn't let her out, she made a more thorough search of the shed. The light was better because the sun had cleared the ridge. She found a crowbar behind a wheelbarrow and went to work on the door. It took her another ten minutes to pry out the lock."

"What time was this?" I asked.

"A few minutes before nine. There's no way the girl could have been here and then at your office by nine-fifteen." He stepped back and let Hewitt and Nakayla help Wendy up the steps. "She can sit in the glider." He pointed to the rusty piece of green porch furniture to the right of the door. It looked like it came with the house.

"Can't I go inside?" Wendy asked.

"In a bit. But you'll need to put some booties on and not touch anything. The mobile crime lab won't be here for half an hour. We'll do a quick walk-through before then." Corn faced Hewitt. "Mr. Donaldson, I understand you're representing Miss Wainwright."

"That's correct."

"She's not being charged with anything. We are considering her actions to be the result of emotional distress."

"We appreciate that." Hewitt laid his hand on Wendy's shoulder and squeezed gently. "Don't we?"

The girl gave a barely perceptible nod.

"Good," Corn said. "Mr. Donaldson, if you'll wait here with Wendy, I need to go over a few details from yesterday with Sam and Nakayla."

We followed him into the yard and around the back of the farmhouse. The structure appeared in decent shape, although paint was peeling off underneath the second-story eaves where the gutters bent away from the roof. The house looked like it had been constructed back in the 1930s. Green pasture surrounded it except for an immediate circle of tall oaks, probably left to provide shade.

Corn led us to a shed halfway between the house and barn. Its wooden door was open and the jamb around the latch had been reduced to splinters. There were no windows, and I understood how the trapped ranger would have had difficulty seeing once the door was closed.

Corn turned around. "Look back at the house. See the problem?"

There was an enclosed porch across the right half of the rear of the building. I could see buckets and an upturned mop in the windows. Like in many farmhouses, the initial food preparation took place outside the main kitchen. There was probably a working sink on the porch. Game and fish could be cleaned, ears of corn shucked, butter beans shelled, and other vegetables scrubbed. While I was thinking about what I was seeing, Nakayla was thinking about what she wasn't seeing.

"None of the cars are visible," she said.

"Exactly." Corn smiled at me. "It's clear who's got the brains in your operation."

"No argument from me."

"Your ranger went in the back," Nakayla said. "She thought Wendy was in the house."

"Correct. Elsie and Wendy came out the backdoor to go to the shed. When Elsie got free, she returned that way, cutting through the kitchen and into the dining room. We figure someone ducked in the corner and she ran past him. He cracked her over the head before she reached the living room."

"She never saw her assailant?" Nakayla asked.

"No. And she never saw his vehicle. But she knows he must have heard her screaming when he arrived. If he knew Wendy, he had to know someone else was in the shed. Elsie's got a deeper voice and she was calling Wendy's name."

I gazed at the ridge line and saw where the ribbon of highway curved to the overlook. "Hell, he could have watched the whole thing from up there. That's where we staked out the house." I pointed to the spot. "If he had binoculars, he might have seen Wendy lock up your ranger and drive off. Once Wendy went past him, he came down. That would account for why he was here in only ten minutes."

Corn studied the overlook, squinting against the sun. "Or it could have been some scumbag who read about Wainwright's death and figured the family would be going to the funeral home this morning. It happens."

"You believe that?" I asked.

"It's possible. But, no, I don't believe it." He gestured to the house. "That's the theory the deputies are touting."

"What's their role?"

"The break-in and the assault happened in the county. The assault was on a federal officer so I'm claiming jurisdiction and if it ties to Wainwright's death I'll bundle everything."

"Was it a break-in?" Nakayla asked.

"You mean was there forcible entry?"

"Right," she said.

"No. Either the person had a key or the door wasn't locked. But the attack on my ranger proves he wasn't supposed to be there."

Nakayla looked at me and arched her eyebrows. I guessed what she was thinking.

"Why are you telling us this?" I asked.

He scratched the side of his face. "The way I see it, you've got no more reason to be in this case. Hewitt Donaldson doesn't go around representing minors who lock up a ranger and he isn't involved in the lawsuit which is where the money lies. Something else is going on."

"How about justice," I said.

"A nice concept. But when you're in the machine, that's all it is. You play your part, you do your job as much as you're allowed to do it, and you hope at the end of the day the system works."

"Is the system going to work for Janice Wainwright?"

He pivoted, faced the barn, and put his hands in his pockets. "I don't know. And that bothers me. She's been dead less than twenty-four hours and we've already involved three agencies: the Henderson County Sheriff's Department, the Buncombe County Sheriff's Department, and my department. All of us are understaffed and underfunded."

"All of you want to clear the case," I said.

"Yeah. Without expending any more manpower or money than necessary."

I realized Corn had led us away from the house, not to avoid being overheard by Hewitt, but by the deputies and his own rangers. "And you've got two ready-made solutions: Janice Wainwright's painkillers and a burglar who preys on funeral families."

"Without evidence to the contrary, those are the logical explanations."

Corn voiced the same opinion Hewitt Donaldson stated. The authorities would follow the trail that was widest and easiest, even though Corn appeared reluctant to settle for its conclusion.

"But," I said.

His lips twisted in a grimace. "But, my gut tells me there's more to it." The grimace eased into a grin and he patted his stomach. "Over the years, both my gut and my reliance on it have grown. We'll work the case as much as we can, but I'm afraid it won't be enough. Curt Newland says you two are a real pain in the ass when you get fixed on something. Like dogs with a bone who won't turn loose."

I glanced at Nakayla. "There's a testimonial for our brochure."

"I'm the same way," Corn said. "But I need more to go on than my gut. I have to stop where the evidence stops."

"We understand," Nakayla said.

We did. Corn was signaling that he wanted us to pursue those lines of inquiry he couldn't. Somewhere in the federal bureaucracy, a bean counter and a supervisor second-guessed his actions.

"We'll need access," I said.

"It can't look like I'm providing you leads, especially where our inquiries overlap."

"Like where would that be," I said. "Just so we don't get in the way."

He smiled and glanced over his shoulder to the house. "We'll interview Wendy about her mother's activities the past few days.

Then, I'll talk to the doctor involved in her lawsuit. His office said he took yesterday afternoon off and probably played golf."

"Are Tuesday afternoons his normal tee time?"

"Don't know. We've only had a few hours this morning to work the case. Montgomery's operating at the hospital now but he'll be in his clinic after lunch."

"Are you going to talk to Janice's doctor?" I asked.

"Yes. We need to determine if her medication could have other side effects."

"Like depression or suicidal tendencies?"

"They have to be considered."

"What about the ex?" Nakayla asked.

"Definitely. We'll get an address from Wendy."

"Gainesville, Florida," Nakayla said. "He's an attorney."

"Okay. Then we'll run through friends and colleagues." Corn didn't sound encouraged. "If nothing turns up and the autopsy report is consistent with an accidental fall, then I think we'll have exhausted the possibilities."

"What about her final words?" I asked. "'Sandburg's verses.'"

Corn sighed with exasperation. "Do you know how many verses Carl Sandburg wrote?"

"No, but one of the rangers might know what she meant. And we haven't asked Wendy."

"All right. Duly noted." He started for the house.

"Wait," I said. "We'd like to see the interior when you walk Wendy through."

"It's a crime scene."

"But we've been following Janice. Maybe we'll notice something."

"Like what?"

"Like if we knew we wouldn't have to see it."

Corn threw up his hands. "The Asheville police were right. You are a pain in the ass."

Wendy, Nakayla, Corn, and I donned the crime scene boots and gloves and left Hewitt on the porch. I could tell he wasn't happy, but he kept his mouth shut. He knew Ranger Corn was giving us an unusual opportunity.

The county deputies migrated to their patrol cars and Corn asked his rangers to wait outside and give us room to move around. Wendy grabbed Nakayla's hand and pulled her through the door.

Less than two yards inside, she froze. "Oh, my God."

I stepped behind her. Over her shoulder, I saw a room filled with contrasts. Pine paneling ran in horizontal boards along the walls. Oval braided rugs dotted the wide plank floor. The construction mirrored the style of the better built farmhouses and cabins across the valley. But other than the handmade rugs, the furnishings could have been in a beach house. An assortment of wicker chairs with aqua-pastel cushions, a bamboo-framed futon, chrome and glass bookshelves, and a coffee table with its glass top on a driftwood base looked more appropriate to southern Florida than southern Appalachia. I thought of Wendy's aunt and father being in Florida and realized her mother hadn't purchased new furniture since she moved.

That wasn't the contrast that caused Wendy's gasp. Books were strewn across the floor. At first I thought the attack on the ranger caused the disarray, but knickknacks and curios were neatly in place on the shelves. A television and an iPod hadn't been touched, the items most burglars would grab first. Someone had either been looking for a book or for something hidden within its pages.

Ranger Corn edged around us and walked closer to the mess. "After Ranger Compton was knocked unconscious, her attacker pressed on with his search."

"How do you know?" Nakayla asked.

"A few of the books were on top of her. She fell through the doorway from the dining room and landed in front of the hearth." He eyed Wendy. "There were books on the mantel, right?"

"Yes."

I noticed a bare spot amid the scattered volumes where the ranger must have lain.

Corn gestured toward the dining room. "Nothing in here is messed up, but see if something's missing. Don't touch anything."

The dining room furniture was traditional. A round oak table had a split along the diameter where a leaf could be inserted. Four matching chairs were spaced evenly around it, and two additional chairs stood on either side of a breakfront. The china and glassware inside seemed undisturbed.

"Anything missing?" Corn asked.

"I don't think so," Wendy said.

The kitchen and back porch showed no signs of an intruder. We followed Corn to the second floor where three bedrooms and a bathroom opened onto the landing. One of the bedrooms had been converted into an office. Corn went there first.

"This is the only other room that's obviously been searched." He swept his hand in an arc as if we needed help seeing the disaster.

Bookshelves covered three walls but their contents lay dumped on the floor. Some books were piled on a table that must have served as a desk. A printer stood on a stand next to it but the cables dangled uselessly.

"Was there a computer on the desk?" Corn asked Wendy.

The girl stared at the ravaged room in shocked silence.

Corn stepped in her line of sight, his face close to hers. "Wendy, did he steal your mother's computer?"

"No. She used a laptop and carried it back and forth to the university. It wasn't here last night. That's how I knew she hadn't been home."

"She didn't have it with her when she left work," Nakayla said.

Wendy stepped closer to the table. "The lamp's gone. "There's supposed to be a brass desk lamp."

"Did you find what he used to hit your ranger?" I asked.

Corn looked out the window. The shed and destroyed door were clearly visible. "That's it. He saw Compton break free and grabbed the lamp. He got to the dining room first."

"And he took the lamp with him." I said. "In case there were prints on it. Wendy, you said your mother kept a calendar at home. Was it here?"

She looked at the desk. "Yes. Right on the front corner."

"We have to assume he took that as well." Corn motioned us out of the room. "Wait on the landing while I ask a deputy to contact campus security and have them seal off her office." He disappeared down the stairs.

"What's happening?" Wendy asked. "Why is someone doing this?"

"We don't know," I said. "It would help if we knew what he was looking for." I gazed through the doorway at the chaos in Janice's office. "Were most of those history books?"

"Yes. Mom's specialty was the reaction of individual states to the Civil War. How politics and issues varied."

"Was she working on a particular project?"

"The turmoil in western North Carolina. Support for the Union and the Confederacy was split. That's part of why we moved here."

"Are goats why she got interested in Sandburg?"

Wendy shook her head. "Not at first. Sandburg's farmhouse was built before The Civil War by the man who became Secretary of the Treasury for the Confederacy. Mom wanted to see it. While she talked to the park people, I played with the goats. I wanted one for our farm."

"Did she have Sandburg's books?"

"She had his biography of Lincoln." Wendy glanced back in the office. "It should be in there somewhere."

"How about poetry books?"

"Yeah. Those are downstairs. And she bought the book with his songs."

"He wrote songs?"

"He collected them," Nakayla said. "*The American Songbag.*"

"That's the one," Wendy said. "It's on the coffee table. The Flat Rock Playhouse is doing a musical revue of Sandburg's favorite songs later this summer." She wiped her eyes with the back of her hand. "The director promised us complimentary tickets."

Nakayla paced the landing, thinking to herself. Then she stopped at the head of the stairs and looked down. She cocked her head, listening for Corn's return. I looked out a window and saw him talking to the county deputies on the front lawn.

"What is it?" I asked Nakayla.

She ignored my question and whispered to Wendy, "You got the gun from your mother's dresser?"

"Yes."

"Does she hide other things there?"

"Some jewelry."

"Was the pistol in a holster or case?" I asked. "If Corn finds evidence of a gun, he'll wonder what happened to it."

"No. It was loose."

"You're sure?"

"Yes. It was lying on a book under a nightgown. She showed me where she kept it. She taught me how to load and fire it."

Nakayla's eyes narrowed. "You want to double-check?"

Although her question was to Wendy, I understood the full meaning. In a house with shelves filled with books, why hide one with a gun?

"To make sure there's no empty holster?" Wendy asked. "So I won't get in trouble?"

"Yes," I said. "It couldn't hurt. You show me the drawer and I'll open it. We don't want to disturb any fingerprints."

We entered the front bedroom diagonal from the office. A waist-high bureau was under a wide mirror. There were eight drawers in two columns of four. Wendy pointed to the second drawer on the left. I checked the fingertips of my latex gloves to make sure they were clean. One of the nightgowns had been pushed aside. A black hardback book with frayed edges was tucked against the side of the drawer. Stamped in faded gold lettering on the front was the title, *Folk Songs of North America*. Beneath it was a silver line drawing of a banjo, fiddle, dulcimer, and a pair of clapping hands. I opened it to the flyleaf and saw the author was Alan Lomax. "Return to Cameron Reynolds" was printed in blue ink across the bottom of the page.

"Someone's coming up the drive," Nakayla said.

I closed the book and made a quick search through the rest of the drawer, finding only a few bracelets and a jade necklace. "You were right," I whispered to Wendy. "There's nothing here to indicate your mother owned a gun."

"Good."

"How long has the book been there?"

She shrugged. "I never noticed it before." She turned and looked out the bedroom window. A blue Jeep pulled to a stop beside Corn and the deputies. "Cammie!" She clapped her hands, bolted from the room, and flew down the stairs.

I joined Nakayla on the landing and we watched Wendy run across the lawn, her feet still covered in the booties. A dark-haired man about my own age got out of the car and seemed surprised by the scene. He turned to say something to Corn, but Wendy flung her arms around his neck. The motion of her shoulders showed she was sobbing.

"Who's that?" Nakayla asked.

"My guess is he's Cameron Reynolds."

"Who's that?"

"I have no idea."

Chapter Seven

Nakayla and I went downstairs and joined Hewitt on the porch.

"Who's that?" he asked.

"We don't know," I quickly replied. I didn't want to tell the lawyer about the book hidden in the drawer and put him in the position of withholding its existence from Corn. My years of experience as a military criminal investigator conditioned me to protect my access to evidence until I could determine its importance. I needed a chance to examine the book before it went into Corn's chain of custody.

"Well, let's find out," Hewitt said.

As we approached, the stranger stopped his conversation with Corn and eyed us curiously. Up close, he appeared older, probably in his late thirties. His black hair was short, not in a military cut but the style from a generation or two ago with the part down the middle. He wore brown corduroy pants and a charcoal pullover.

Corn made the introductions. "This is Hewitt Donaldson, an attorney who's helping Wendy with legal matters, and two of his colleagues, Nakayla Robertson and Sam Blackman. Cameron Reynolds is a friend of the family who read about Mrs. Wainwright's death. I told him about the break-in."

Reynolds glanced at Wendy. "You've got a team of lawyers?"

She stepped closer to him. "No, just Mr. Donaldson. He's going to fix it so I can stay in Asheville."

Hewitt jumped in before Wendy elaborated more on what she thought he could do. "Since Wendy's starting college in the fall, I'm helping her navigate a way to remain here this summer. We're hoping her aunt will give her blessing."

"Cynthia?" Reynolds asked.

Wendy nodded. "She's flying up this morning."

Reynolds looked at Nakayla and me. I knew what he was thinking. If we weren't lawyers, who were we?

I answered the unasked question. "Nakayla and I own a detective agency. We happened to be with Mr. Donaldson when the call came in about the break-in."

"Isn't this a police matter?" Reynolds asked Corn.

"Yes. But Nakayla and Sam are the ones who discovered Mrs. Wainwright yesterday and summoned medical aid."

"Did you work with Mrs. Wainwright?" I asked.

"No. I've known Janice since we taught at the University of Florida. I'm a professor at Warren Wilson College."

"Where you'll be going to school," Nakayla said to Wendy.

She said nothing and clutched Reynolds' arm.

"Is there anything I can do?" he asked. "This is such a shock."

Corn shook his head. "I still have some questions for Wendy and we need to go through all the rooms for an inventory of what's missing. Right now it's a crime scene and I can't allow you on the premises. I suggest you call later, after Wendy's aunt arrives."

Reynolds stared beyond us to the house. "Who would do such a thing at a time like this?"

"That's a good question, Mr. Reynolds." Corn handed him a card. "If you think of something, call me day or night."

Reynolds took it, and then studied Hewitt, Nakayla, and me one final time. The expression on his face revealed he wasn't comfortable with us being there.

"You're working for Wendy's interests, right? Not her aunt's."

Hewitt cleared his throat. "I assure you, Mr. Reynolds, we've already taken steps to make sure Wendy's rights are protected."

Reynolds looked like he wanted to say more, but decided against it. He turned to Wendy. "We'll talk later. Be strong and do what they say."

As he walked to his Jeep, Wendy stuck to him like a shadow. He slid into the driver's seat and she caught the door as he tried to close it. None of their whispered words were audible, but the man shook his head several times. Finally he peeled Wendy's gloved fingers off the window glass, slammed the door, and backed the Jeep down the driveway. Corn called to Wendy to come back to the house.

I wondered if Cameron Reynolds had arrived expecting to find Wendy alone or gone. The suspicious corner of my brain sent the signal that there was more going on than met the eye. Maybe Reynolds wanted to make an appearance so that no one would suspect he'd been there earlier.

Corn handed the three of us fresh booties from a box by the front door. "Shall we head upstairs?"

As we covered our shoes again, I said, "Wendy, the Sandburg books weren't on the coffee table or anywhere on the floor I could see."

"Maybe Mom took them to work."

"Were there others?"

"In her study."

Corn glanced up as if he could see through the ceiling. "The Sandburg verses," he muttered, and turned to me. "Do you think her words could be connected to the break-in?"

"I'd like to find the books and then think."

Not a single word of Sandburg's prose or poetry could be found. When the mobile crime lab arrived, Nakayla, Wendy, and I sat in the shade of one of the oaks while the team went through the house. Prints would be lifted and Corn would want Wendy to provide a list of persons who had been there. Her prints would be taken along with her mother's. The medical examiner had probably scanned them into a database already.

Wendy looked down the driveway. "My aunt should be here soon. Her flight landed at eleven."

"Is she renting a car?" Nakayla asked.

"Yeah. She said she didn't want me to worry about picking her up in case her plane was late." Wendy wrinkled her nose.

"She doesn't trust my driving. She has to be in control. My mom said that's why her marriage broke up."

"I'll need to talk to her," Hewitt said. "Is she staying here?"

Wendy's eyes swept across the police cars lining the lawn. "Aunt Cynthia's going to freak out. But I'll need to take care of the animals."

Nakayla turned to Corn. "Are you posting a ranger in case the guy returns?"

"No. As far as we know, he finished his search. There's no reason to think he'll be back."

Nakayla shook her head. "Unless he doesn't find what he's looking for in the calendar or those Sandburg books."

Corn sucked air between his teeth and tugged his earlobe. "I can't justify pulling a man out of the duty roster because some poetry books were stolen."

"Your officer was knocked unconscious," I said.

He flushed. "Damn it, I know that. If I thought there was a realistic chance we'd catch the guy here, I'd put in place whatever resources were needed."

The sound of a car came from the driveway. A white Toyota Camry swung wide around the police vehicles. Behind the steering wheel, a woman gaped in astonishment at the spectacle before her.

"Aunt Cynthia," Wendy whispered.

Corn took the lead, removing his hat as we walked toward the car. "What's your aunt's last name?"

"Howell."

Cynthia Howell emerged from the Camry like a swimmer surfacing after a lap underwater. She gulped for air and blinked in an attempt to clear away the sight before her. An attractive woman in her late forties, she appeared overdressed in high heels and a smartly tailored tan suit. Diamond earrings sparkled as she slowly shook her head in disbelief.

"Mrs. Howell, I'm Bobby Ray Corn. On behalf of the National Park Service let me offer our condolences."

She stared at him for a few seconds and then focused on Wendy. "What's going on?"

"Someone broke into our house, Aunt Cynthia."

"My God, are you all right?" She hurried to her niece and embraced her.

Wendy stood rigid, her hands by her side. Then, whatever was calcifying her emotions dissolved and she flung her arms around her aunt's neck.

The rest of us retreated to the front porch and left them to cry together while we speculated on our next steps.

"When do you think the body will be released?" Hewitt asked Corn.

"This afternoon. Tomorrow at the latest."

The lawyer glanced at me. "Wendy said she and her aunt were going to the funeral home but the burial's in Florida."

"I guess she wants to work out getting the body shipped."

"But if it's in Chapel Hill, why bring it back here?"

"That's true," Corn said. "I can give the Florida information directly to the medical examiner."

"Then that's what I'll recommend." Hewitt looked at the two women in the yard. "As soon as we're clear to re-enter the house, I'd like to sit down with her aunt. We might as well get all the options on the table."

Thirty minutes later, Ranger Corn released control of the farmhouse.

Cynthia Howell paled when she saw the disarray. "What did they steal?"

"We think some books by Carl Sandburg," Corn said. "Wendy hasn't had a chance to do an inventory."

"Sandburg?"

"Yes. Did your sister say anything about working on something involving Sandburg?"

Cynthia sat on the futon and Hewitt joined her. The rest of us stood.

She looked up at Corn. "No. Janice and I didn't talk that often. Not after she moved here." She turned to Wendy. "That's where you got that goat, isn't it? The Sandburg place?"

"Yes." Wendy's eyes met her aunt's in an unspoken challenge.

"Well, let's just hope they'll take it back."

Cynthia Howell may as well have slapped Wendy with a two-by-four. The girl's face turned beet red.

"No! Ida Mae is mine and you have no right to take her away. Tell her, Mr. Donaldson. I'm going to be emancipated. I'm going to be free to live my own life."

Cynthia stared at Hewitt like she suddenly realized Jack the Ripper sat beside her.

"There's no reason for anyone to get upset." Hewitt shifted on the futon, creating more space between Cynthia and him. "We have many options available." He looked at me. "Sam, take Wendy upstairs so she can go through her mother's study. Nakayla, why don't you stay with me and help fill in some of the background for Mrs. Howell."

Ranger Corn took the opportunity to excuse himself. "I think I've got everything I need for the moment." He leaned across the coffee table and offered Cynthia his card. "Please call when you know your travel schedule so I'll be able to reach you. Again, we're very sorry and we'll do everything we can to determine what happened."

Cynthia clutched the card without looking at it. "Thank you."

Corn turned to leave and then paused. "Oh, someone dropped by earlier. Cameron Reynolds. He said he'll call back later."

"Cameron?" Cynthia's eyes narrowed and she said the name with a tinge of contempt. She glanced at Wendy. "What did he want?"

Wendy said nothing.

Corn shrugged. "He was concerned about Wendy." Her response caught his interest. "You know him?"

Cynthia forced a smile. "Not really. I believe he and my sister taught together in Florida."

Nakayla looked at me only long enough to show that Cameron Reynolds had risen on her curiosity meter.

"Let's go," I told Wendy, and then nodded to Corn. "I'll let you know if anything else is missing."

My immediate interest lay in something that wasn't missing, Cameron Reynolds' book. However, I didn't want Wendy knowing that. Her first reaction might be to call Reynolds and give him a piece of evidence that he might have ransacked the house to find. Instead, I helped Wendy pick the books up from the study floor and place them on the shelves. Most were reference volumes regarding the Civil War. Some were compilations of first-hand accounts, bound copies of troop orders or minutes of governmental meetings of both the Union and the Confederacy, and photocopies of diaries and journals kept by individual soldiers. It was amazing how four years of conflict had unleashed an eternity of re-hashing, re-evaluating, and, in some ways, re-fighting our national catastrophe.

I was born a Southerner in the Piedmont section of North Carolina not far from the sites of the final battles of the war, but I never understood why four years out of the South's multi-century history should define "Southern Heritage." A friend in the army from Jackson, Mississippi argued that the South had the distinction of being the only region of the country to have been defeated and occupied. He said when the greatest growth industry in your state after the war was wooden crutches and prosthetics for Confederate vets, you aren't going to forgive and forget any time soon. Now that I'd lost a leg, I had a better understanding of his argument. But, ask the Cherokee about being defeated and occupied. You don't see them driving around with bumper stickers saying, "Forget, Hell!" over crossed tomahawks.

We worked for about five minutes in silence broken only by Wendy's sniffles. I wedged a three-ring binder titled "Major Disbursements of the Confederate Treasury" into the last slot on a top shelf. Several paperclips jutted out of the pages marking points of interest. I wondered if some scholar would ever bother to review what had once been significant to Janice Wainwright. I wasn't a scholar but I was definitely interested in what was significant about Carl Sandburg.

"Do you think Mr. Donaldson is selling me out?"

I turned from the bookshelf. Wendy sat on the corner of the desk and dangled her feet a few inches above the floor. She cocked her head, like a Bluejay examining a worm, and searched my face for any hint of duplicity.

I paused to choose my words carefully. "The last thing Mr. Donaldson would do is sell you out. He's—"

"Really?" she interjected. "Then what's the next to the last thing he'd do to me?"

"What?"

"I just want to know how far down his list is selling me out."

The girl was a challenge, quick-witted one second, weepy the next.

"As I was about to say, any selling he's doing is to your aunt. Nakayla's there to assure her that we have your best interest at heart. She's probably arguing that you're capable of staying on your own for the few months before you begin college."

"But Nakayla doesn't know me."

I shook my head. "That's not so important. Your aunt will judge Nakayla, not your relationship. I figure your aunt will want you to follow through with what you and your mom intended. But she's feeling very protective right now. Her sister dies, her niece is left alone, and she shows up to find more police than termites at the farmhouse."

I walked closer and Wendy looked away. "Cut her some slack. If you want to be treated as an adult, you'll have to act like one."

She snapped back to me, eyes blazing. "And who's cutting me slack? The first statement out of Aunt Cynthia's mouth is she's getting rid of Ida Mae."

"Nakayla and I will do what we can to help you." I softened my tone. "I promise. But, Wendy, you lose it again like you did downstairs and you'll undercut everything. Understand?"

She nodded.

"Good. Now let's finish here so we can be ready for Mr. Donaldson."

With renewed effort, Wendy and I returned the study to a presentable condition. Then she started arranging items on the desk and in the drawers as busy work while we waited. I wondered how long we were going to be trapped upstairs. Occasionally, muffled voices came from below but the fragments of conversation provided no clue as to what was being said. I pulled one of Janice's thin notebooks back off the shelf and flipped through photocopies of ledger pages.

The dates ranged from October 1863 to May 1864 and highlighted cotton production of the Confederacy. The months were what I considered outside the normal growing season, but the closest I came to unwoven cotton were the puffy balls in my bottles of Tylenol. Closer examination revealed records of shipments and allocations to war materials like uniforms and munitions. One section listed exports. Several cities had an X beside them—Charleston, Savannah, Wilmington—all ports along the South's Atlantic coast. I took the mark to mean the Union blockade had prevented trade ships from picking up cargo. New Orleans had the number 25 written beside it, but I didn't know whether the figure represented tons, bales, or shipments.

An asterisk had been penciled next to "Texas: Mexico." I turned through several months and found each "Texas: Mexico" entry had an asterisk beside it. The numbers were the highest of any exports; all were above fifty with the last being seventy-five. I speculated the Tex-Mex border would have been as porous as a sieve and immune to a blockade. Nations wanting southern cotton or other agricultural products would have used Mexico as the conduit with Mexican brokers or government officials profiteering on the exchange. In any war, some people die, some people make money.

"Wendy, your aunt and Mr. Donaldson want to talk to you." Nakayla stood in the doorway, relaxed and smiling. "Sam and I'll wait here."

Wendy closed the desk drawer harder than needed and eyed Nakayla suspiciously. "Why aren't you going with me?"

"Because your aunt prefers to talk to you without our being present. She may have some questions about us that could be awkward for you to answer if we were there."

Wendy paled. "Did you tell her about the gun?"

"No. But she wants to know how you'd feel about our supervision if you stay in Asheville."

"Really?" She jumped up from the desk and her eyes sparkled. "I don't have to go to Florida?"

"Talk to your aunt."

Wendy looked at me. Where her expression was one of relief, mine must have been slightly less than abject horror. What had Nakayla gotten us into?

"Don't worry, Mr. Blackman," Wendy said. "I won't lose it."

"Good." I replaced the notebook on the shelf. When the sound of Wendy's footsteps faded on the stairs, I said, "Are we now Blackman and Robertson Childcare Services?"

"What did you think was going to happen?" Nakayla crossed the room and sat on the edge of the desk. "I gave references, and the fact that we're licensed detectives made her comfortable, like our professional status satisfied her due diligence."

"Professional means you get paid."

"Professional means you finish the job. Our case is the death of Janice Wainwright and we're not getting paid for that, right?"

I paced in front of the bookshelf, agitated by the turn of events. "Caring for a goat and some chickens is one thing, being responsible for a high-strung teenager is another."

"I know. I'll be the one moving in with her when she returns from the funeral. You can focus on the case."

I stared at her. "You can't be serious."

"If we need access to the house and Janice's files, then what better way?"

"You'll be sleeping here?"

Nakayla laughed. "Ah, the real concern of the detective surfaces. Will the case interfere with his sex life?"

I felt my face flush and hoped words going down the stairs were as difficult to hear as those coming up.

"Don't worry. I'm sure we can arrange a date or two. Wendy will be tied up with the funeral for several days. She won't be back from Florida till next Monday at the earliest."

"When are they leaving?"

"Wendy's aunt had a flight set for tomorrow morning, but since there's no need to involve a local funeral home, she's going to try to book tickets on a plane late this afternoon."

"Seems kind of soon."

Nakayla glanced around the room. "When the house is in order, all Wendy needs to do is pack, show us the farm routine, and make the flight."

"What about Janice's computer at work? I hope we get a chance to examine it."

"Hewitt says the university will cooperate with law enforcement but deny access to private investigators without clear and legally authorized directives from either Corn or the court-appointed executor of her estate."

I knew Corn would go to the university immediately. If someone's desperate search hadn't already succeeded, Janice's office would be the next target.

"I figure we've got Corn as an ally for a few more days," I said.

"You mean until the Medical Examiner files his report."

Nakayla understood the reality of what we were facing. Without evidence that Janice had been attacked, Corn would be hard pressed to pursue his investigation beyond checking alibis of a few people, most notably the doctor and others involved in her lawsuit.

"We need to take a step back," I said. "I want to make sure I'm not creating a mystery where there isn't one."

Nakayla hopped off the desk. "Is that self-doubt or are you wanting to extricate yourself from the commitment I made to Wendy?"

"This has nothing to do with Wendy. I'm facing the fact that Janice was a dying woman who could have been delirious." I waved my hand across the study. "And there are scumbags who break into the homes of people who just died."

"And steal their Carl Sandburg books. Yes, the police files are jammed with those cases."

"Smart ass." I grabbed her wrist and pulled her close. "I hate you when you're right."

"That's bad news." She kissed me lightly on the lips. "Because then you'll never have a chance to love me."

"Sam? Nakayla?" Hewitt's voice boomed from the stairs.

"Yeah," I cried.

"Time for farm class 101."

"Coming." I returned Nakayla's kiss. "Meet me behind the barn?"

"Does farm class 101 include a roll in the hay?"

"I hope so. That's farming I could get into. With you as my project partner, of course."

She pushed me away. "I'd better be your partner, unless you want a first-hand demonstration of how to create a gelding."

We followed Wendy out the kitchen door to the tool shed. Her aunt and Hewitt remained in the house, Cynthia preferring to protect her shoes from the evils of the barnyard. That was just as well, since if Cynthia saw the demolished door, we'd have to explain the imprisoned ranger or create a lie on the spot.

"I've got to get Ida Mae's birth supplies together," Wendy said. "The ranger knocked them over."

Nakayla and I watched her pick up an assortment of boxes and bottles and load them in a wheelbarrow.

I nudged Nakayla. "What's all that stuff? I thought the babies just dropped out on the ground."

"Sshh. You pay attention and nod your head like you understand everything."

Wendy carefully rolled the wheelbarrow down the short ramp from the shed to the ground. "The goat ranger at the Sandburg farm recommended we have these on hand. Ida Mae's not due for another week, but that's just an approximation."

Nakayla picked up a clear plastic package protecting a milk-white cylinder attached to a blue squeeze bulb.

"Oh, that's to help if they're not breathing." Wendy took it. "You put the open end over the mouth and nostrils and pump air." With her other hand, she lifted a bottle. "Here's iodine for the umbilical cord."

I nodded like I severed umbilical cords before every meal. My stomach twitched and I hoped Nakayla's DNA was fused with an abundance of maternal instincts.

"And these tubes contain colostrum." She handed one to me. "Just squirt a dose in the kid's mouth and it will help it in case Ida Mae's natural colostrum is late."

I studied the label like it conveyed instructions for disarming a nuclear bomb. Beside the cute close-up of a newborn kid's face were the words, "Colostrum Oral Gel—A nutritional product for newborn goats which contains dried colostrum milk, a source of live (viable) naturally occurring microorganisms and vitamins."

"And this is a bottle of barn and stable cleaner for scrubbing the stalls." Wendy pulled a jug from the wheelbarrow.

"Let me see." I traded her the tube of viable microorganisms for the cleaner. Scrubbing sounded like something I could handle.

"I also have it in a powdered mix," Wendy said, "but we normally use that in the winter."

I nodded. "The liquid concentrate will be fine. Right, Nakayla?"

"Whatever you say." She turned to Wendy. "Sam is very thorough about cleaning."

I nodded a third time.

Wendy pushed the wheelbarrow toward the barn. "I'm going to leave the supplies next to Ida Mae's stall in case you need them. The thermometer and logbook are in a case just inside the door."

"Thermometer?" I asked.

"Yes. Now that we're getting close I take Ida Mae's temperature every morning. It's a rectal thermometer and her normal temperature is one-hundred-two degrees. When it drops to ninety-nine, the delivery should happen within twenty-four hours."

"Rectal thermometer?" I couldn't get the image out of my mind.

"Yeah," Wendy said in a matter-of-fact tone. "Don't worry. There's lubricant right beside it."

Nakayla laughed. "Yeah, Sam. Don't worry."

"The other sign of imminent delivery is vaginal mucous," Wendy said. "It's cream colored and you might see it on her or where it's fallen on the straw and dried."

I wondered if I looked as green as I felt.

Wendy spouted on, unaware she'd crossed into my male land of too much female information. "There's a good chance she'll deliver at night so keep a couple of flashlights and fresh batteries handy."

As we neared the door of the weather-beaten barn, she arced away toward the side.

"Isn't the goat in the barn?" I asked.

"Oh, when I say barn, I mean Ida Mae's. We had a smaller stall and feed storage building constructed in back."

Ida Mae's barn was more of a large shed. The new wood appeared very sturdy compared to the warped boards of the old barn. An electric fence formed a perimeter about thirty feet from each side, and a series of batteries were hooked to the bottom wire near the base of the gate.

"Let me disconnect the charge." Wendy opened a switch box on the fence post and broke the circuit. "The fence keeps her in, but also deters predators. Dogs are the worst. They can literally scare a goat to death."

Wendy slid back the latch and pushed the gate inward. "Ida Mae's been spending more time in her stall. She knows the birth is getting close."

My stomach twitched again.

"Ida Mae! You've got company." Wendy closed the gate behind her.

Nakayla and I held back, letting Wendy take the lead. I saw a shadowy movement behind stall slats deeper in the barn. Then a brown and white goat rounded the end and stepped into the sunlight. She came forward slowly, long ears hanging down on either side of her face like drapes framing a window. Large golden eyes with black horizontal pupils fixed on Wendy.

"These are your new friends who will take good care of you." Wendy dropped the wheelbarrow and scratched the goat behind the crown of her skull. "Y'all come and say hello," Wendy told us.

Ida Mae shifted her gaze to Nakayla. I noticed the width of the animal's stomach, like she would burst if you poked her too hard.

Nakayla scratched behind one of the droopy ears. "Nubia faces have the sweetest expression. Come closer, Sam."

As I stepped forward, Ida Mae lifted her head. The golden eyes looked me up and down. Then, with a quickness that belied her bloated figure, the goat jumped to the side and scampered behind Wendy. She peered over the wheelbarrow and bleated mournfully.

Ida Mae knew both she and I were in trouble.

Chapter Eight

Nakayla, Hewitt, and I watched from the front porch as Wendy and her aunt drove away in the Camry. I fingered the key to the farmhouse tucked in my front pocket. Goat Keeper Sam Blackman. That's a title I never expected to have.

Hewitt ran his fingers through his long gray hair. "Well, so it begins. Fortunately Cynthia said Janice had redrawn her will in North Carolina after she bought this property. I'll pull documents together and overnight them to Florida for Cynthia's review. When she and Wendy fly back Monday, I hope to complete the court appointment paperwork and also get Janice's attorney, Louis Kirkland, in agreement on filing the wrongful death suit. Surely we'll have the M.E.'s report by then."

"I'd better get to the office," Nakayla said. "I'll finalize our invoice for the surveillance of Janice. Since we're about to switch sides, the sooner we sever our relationship with Investigative Alliance the better."

"Can you fax it?" I asked.

"Yes, and they'll be all too happy to expedite a check and get us off their books."

"What's your next step?" Hewitt asked me. "Looks like there's precious little to go on."

"I guess I'll check out the book receipt we found in Janice's backpack, and I'd like to learn more about Cameron Reynolds."

Hewitt nodded and leaned against a porch post. "Yeah, his visit was a little strange. I'm also curious about Wendy's father."

"What about him?" Nakayla asked.

"He's invisible. The aunt's the guardian and as far as I know, the father hasn't been informed of his ex-wife's death."

"If he's a lawyer in Gainesville, maybe you should make a courtesy call," I suggested.

"Wendy and her aunt are my clients. I don't want them to think I've gone behind their backs."

I saw his point. "Corn said he was contacting him."

"Everybody needs an alibi. I'd like to know the gist of their conversation."

"So would I. Do you think Wendy's father could throw a wrench in the plan?"

Hewitt shrugged. "Depends on the will and the divorce settlement. If Cynthia's the legal guardian and the ex has no custody rights, then he has no control. But I can't believe an attorney, even a stupid one, would let himself be boxed in like that, especially if he's on the hook for college tuition."

"Maybe Janice Wainwright had great pictures," Nakayla said.

Hewitt didn't laugh. He gazed out at the ridge line. "Maybe," he muttered to himself. "I'll check for a safe-deposit box."

If Hewitt took the possibility seriously, then so did I. "Pictures could also fit in a book. Carl Sandburg's poems as you've never seen them illustrated before. I think I'll look around here a little more. Might be some goat information I could use."

Hewitt gave me a skeptical look, but knew better than to ask.

As soon as I was alone, I returned to Janice Wainwright's bedroom. I rolled on the pair of latex gloves I'd worn during the initial search of the house and pulled the folk song book from the drawer. I flipped through the pages, but there were no bookmarks, inserts, or dog-ears. I dropped the book on the bed a few times to see if it would consistently bounce open to the same page. No luck. So, I decided to sit at Janice's desk and read through it more thoroughly.

Folk Songs of North America had been published in 1960 and was a compilation collected by Alan Lomax. He credited Peggy Seeger for transcribing the melodies and guitar chords. I wasn't familiar with either person, but I wondered if Peggy was related to Pete Seeger, the famous folksinger.

The songs were divided into geographical regions and subdivided into types: work songs, love songs, frolic tunes, white spirituals, and a number of other categories. Black spirituals fell under a separate major heading, "The Negro South," that also included secular blues, ballads, and reels. All the tunes shared their origins in the English language and the sections were prefaced by general comments followed by specific notes about each song. I saw how an historian like Janice could use the book as a cultural reference source.

The book came out during Carl Sandburg's lifetime and was a volume that he, as a collector of songs, would have appreciated. I read the acknowledgments to see if Sandburg was credited. His name appeared twice: in a book list appendix referencing *The American Songbag*, and in an appendix of long-playing records for an album called *Ballads And Songs*. Neither of these entries were underlined or highlighted in any way that signified they held importance.

I read through the songs collected under the heading "Yankee Soldiers and Sailors," thinking of Janice's Civil War research, but nothing was marked. In the "Southern Mountains and Backwoods" category, I had better luck. There were numerous pencil notations in some of the margins with an occasional question mark or word variation written in. But, the handwriting was the same as the "Return to Cameron Reynolds" script on the flyleaf. I suspected I was reading his notes. If the book was an academic resource, then maybe he loaned it to Janice and she put it in the drawer for no reason other than to keep it from being misplaced among the others in the house.

I decided to cross-reference the songs in Sandburg's *The American Songbag* with those in the Lomax book. Either Malaprop's Bookstore or the library should have a copy. And

I'd ask Nakayla to do an Internet search for the songs on the Sandburg album. I had no idea what these activities could produce, but when you're clueless, you try anything.

I locked the house, checked the outbuildings, replenished Ida Mae's water, and admonished her not to even think about making me a midwife.

◇◇◇

"I have a question about a receipt." My statement drew a puzzled look on the face of the bookseller.

The young man with a neatly trimmed beard stepped to the side of the register and reached for the slip of paper in my hand. "Is the total wrong?"

I held onto it. "No. I want to know about the book."

Now he looked worried. "If it was a gift, we can exchange it, but Malaprop's policy is no returns." His gaze went past me and took in the whole bookstore as if to emphasize the issue was bigger than both of us.

I smoothed out the receipt and started improvising. "It was a tree book. You see, my friend had it in her backpack. She went into Woolworth Walk and I waited in the park across the street." Woolworth Walk was an old Woolworth's store a few blocks away that had been converted into a series of booths for artisans and craftsmen to sell their wares. Out of the corner of my eye, I saw a man edge beside me ready to make a purchase. "A woman can spend days in that place."

The customer chuckled. The clerk smiled sympathetically.

"I was supposed to watch her backpack, but I dozed off on the bench. Two beers at lunch were a big mistake. Anyhow, somebody snatched it."

"That's terrible," the man beside me muttered.

"I know. Certainly not the spirit of Asheville. I found the backpack by a trashcan at the other end of the park. The book was gone. Fortunately, my friend had her wallet with her. When I saw the receipt was from here, I thought I'd replace it. She only bought it the other night."

I let the clerk examine the receipt.

"The abbreviation stands for *The National Audubon Society Field Guide to Trees, Eastern Region*. It's in the nature section to the right as you head to the cafe."

"Thanks. Listen, is there someone here who might have been working when she bought it? Maybe there's another tree book she was also interested in and I'll get her both. I know you're helping other people." I glanced at the man beside me.

"That's all right," the customer said. "Sounds like you're making a peace offering."

"Yeah. She advised me not to have the second beer."

"Been there, done that. Good luck."

The clerk turned to a woman who was stocking shelves a few yards away. "Sarah, you worked Monday night, didn't you?"

"Turned out the lights and locked up." She stated the phrase like a mantra and continued placing the books.

"This gentleman has a question."

Sarah turned. Her brown hair hung in a long braided ponytail and she flipped it over her shoulder. "Okay. How can I help?"

The clerk handed her the receipt. "It's about this book. Would you show it to him?"

She flashed a bright smile. "My pleasure."

I followed her to a wall where the shelves held volumes on wildflowers, insects, reptiles, animals, fish, and trees. In other words, anything in the forest that could bite me, trip me, sting me, or scratch me.

"Here's the book." She extracted an eight-inch by four-inch, simulated brown leather book partially covered by a dust jacket that was more of a wrapper designed to come off so the long, narrow volume could be stuffed in a pocket or backpack. "I think I waited on the woman who bought it." She held the receipt close to her eyes. "Yes, it was near closing time and she couldn't make up her mind between this one and the Peterson Field Guide. You want the same book?"

I gave her the fabrication I told the clerk at the register. "So, I was thinking of buying her both."

Sarah shook her head. "That's a waste of money. Most of the information is duplicated. Besides, she seemed to be interested in only one tree and the Audubon Society had the description she liked."

"What tree was that?"

"The chestnut."

My arboreal knowledge ranked right up there with my proficiency in brain surgery, but I had a vague memory that the chestnut tree had disappeared. "Aren't they extinct?"

Sarah nodded. "That's what I thought." She flipped through the pages. "But the lady said they weren't extinct, they were stunted and sterilized."

"What's that mean?"

Sarah ran her finger down the index at the back of the book. "Page 377. The commentary and picture are what sold her." She read aloud, "'Fortunately, there is no threat of extinction; sprouts continue from the roots until killed back by the blight.'" Sarah closed the book. "So, this is the one she selected."

"Because of the section on chestnuts?"

"Yes. Frozen in time. That's what she said. Never able to move beyond their place in the 1930s when the blight appeared. Kind of sad. I wonder what they think."

"Excuse me?" The woman lost me.

"The trees. Constantly sending up new shoots only to have the blight slaughter them before they can make seeds." Sarah made it sound like "The Charge of the Light Brigade." "You've read *The Speaker for the Dead*."

"No."

"Oh, it's a wonderful book. Orson Scott Card lives in North Carolina. Greensboro, I think. He also wrote *Ender's Game. The Speaker for the Dead* has trees that can think." Her brown eyes widened at the idea. "Of course, they communicate by telepathy because they can't move."

"Of course." Again, the bumper sticker "Keep Asheville Weird" popped into my mind.

"We have his books in Science Fiction." Sarah started walking deeper into the store.

"That's okay. Maybe next time."

She stopped and handed me the tree book. "But you want this?"

"Definitely." I thought about the books I was collecting. The first, Cameron Reynolds' folk song book, was in my car. Books had played a major role in two cases that gained national recognition for Nakayla and me. An unknown journal by Asheville's Thomas Wolfe had brought us together and the hunt for a missing F. Scott Fitzgerald manuscript had been our first case as a detective agency. Now here I was with two more books holding secrets I couldn't fathom.

"Sir, will there be anything else?"

Sarah's question snapped me into the present. "Sorry. I was just thinking I'd like something by Carl Sandburg. Do you have *The American Songbag?*"

"No. But we could order it if it's still in print."

"Then maybe one of his more popular-selling works."

"Poetry or prose?"

Janice Wainwright's voice whispered in my head. "Wendy. It's the verses. Sandburg's verses."

"Poetry."

"Right over here."

We rounded a corner of a freestanding shelf and stopped at a wall of thin volumes and thick anthologies. I found contemporary poetry too obscure and so most of the authors were unfamiliar.

"We sell a lot of this one." Sarah handed me a paperback simply titled *Carl Sandburg—Selected Poems.* A black and white close-up photo of Sandburg formed the cover.

"Thank you. I'll take it."

Sarah rang up my purchases at the register and I paid with our company credit card.

"Need a bag?" she asked.

"No. Let's save the trees to think."

She laughed and offered her hand. "It's a deal."

We shook and I thanked her for her help.

"Remember, come back for *The Speaker for the Dead*."

"I will." The speaker for the dead. I looked at the two books in my hand. Who was speaking for Janice Wainwright and what was the message?

I walked to the Rankin parking garage around the corner where I left the CR-V. Finding an on-street metered space in Asheville, particularly on Haywood Road near Malaprop's, was like winning the lottery. I took the stairs to the third level, pressed the keyless remote, and heard my car chirp a few spaces away. I opened the driver's door, ready to toss the new books on the passenger's seat with the folk song book I took from the farmhouse.

Pieces of safety glass lay scattered on the tan leather like diamonds in the dust. A gaping hole in the far window showed where someone had smashed through.

Cameron Reynolds' book was gone.

Chapter Nine

"I can go online and see if the Pack Library has a copy." Nakayla made a few strokes on her keyboard.

I'd just briefed her on my adventures since she left the farm-house, ending with the car break-in.

"Why bother?" I leaned back in the chair across from her desk. "If a library copy of the Lomax book held the secret, why take Cameron Reynolds'? No, it has to be something written specifically in his."

"Maybe."

"Maybe?" I folded my arms across my chest to ward off what sounded like an assault on my unassailable logic. "What else could it be?"

She shrugged. "Let's say someone hears Janice talk about Sandburg verses that have some special meaning. Maybe a code or they have some good or bad significance for this person."

I made no objection. We'd solved cases with coded messages and symbols, so Nakayla's speculation was within the realm of our experience.

"Or whoever broke into your car and also stole the books and calendar from the farmhouse might be as clueless as we are. He just knows Janice discovered something important and he's grabbing up everything that could link to her dying words."

I thought about the implications. "Wendy said her mother had a plan B for financial security if the lawsuit failed and that her history degree would finally pay off."

"There's that," Nakayla agreed. "It could be some academic discovery."

"Nobody can be more jealous or pissier than those people whose world begins and ends in their ivory towers. Damn it, Nakayla. You're making our suspect pool larger when I hoped to narrow it down. So, Janice could have fallen by accident, word gets out through deputies, rangers, or even EMTs about what she said, and 'the Sandburg verses' means something to somebody."

Nakayla threw up her hands. "Who said being a detective was easy?"

"You haven't explained why Cameron Reynolds' book isn't important?"

She clicked a few more keys. "Ah, the library has it as well as *The American Songbag*." She rolled her desk chair closer to me. "I'm not saying it's unimportant. His copy might be. But I think someone spied on the farm from the vista just like we did. Did you hide the book when you left?"

"Hell, no. I carried it out under my arm."

She smiled. "And?"

I conceded. "And he or she doesn't know what it is but thinks it's important if I'm taking it. I'm followed to the Rankin garage and relieved of my Reynolds' copy."

"Yes. So it could have been a specific theft and the culprit now has everything he needs to get whatever it is he wants, or he could be staring at folk songs wondering what the hell this is all about." Nakayla turned off her computer. "I'm going to the library. Nothing wrong with your idea to cross-reference the contents of the two books."

"Thanks. I'm also good for sweeping up and emptying the trash."

"I think you should go to Corn's office and tell him you found the book and you were bringing it to him, but it was stolen while you were checking out Janice's receipt."

"Okay." I realized we hadn't discussed the one decent clue I'd uncovered. "Any ideas about this chestnut business?"

Nakayla shook her head. "Not really. Maybe she was look-ing for new growth or marking the sites of old trees. It could be completely unrelated."

A different idea sprang to my mind. "What if it was an old tree? Not roots or shoots but the real deal?"

"You mean a chestnut that survived the blight?"

"Why not? Mother Nature creates mutations in every species. Something's different about this one that makes it immune to the blight."

"You'd think it would have been noticed over the last eighty years."

I refused to concede this possibility. "But what if it hasn't been. There's a lot of acreage on Glassy Mountain. The tree could be smaller, off the beaten path, and the Sandburgs were interested in goats not timber."

"And the verses?"

"A poem or song that mentions it."

Nakayla stood. "Okay, Paul Bunyan. I've got nothing better to offer."

"Paul Bunyan cut down trees." I rubbed my thumb back and forth across my fingers. "I'm talking cloning, and I bet I'm talking big bucks."

"See Corn," she said. "And call Glass Doctor to come fix your window before it rains or you'll be drowning in water as well as theories."

"To be great is to be misunderstood."

"Right. Tell it to Ida Mae." She closed the office door and left me alone with my ideas that were so great even I didn't understand them.

◇◇◇

"A folk song book?" Ranger Bobby Ray Corn asked the question and laid his pen by the notepad on his desk. Evidently, the theft didn't warrant being written down.

"Yes. It caught my eye after you left. Sandburg's name wasn't on it, but since he collected folk songs, I thought maybe there was a connection."

We sat in his office at the Ranger Station adjacent to the Blue Ridge Parkway. I had a file folder on my lap containing only a few sheets: a copy of my statement regarding yesterday's events, contact information for the chief ranger at Connemara, the Sandburg farm, and the notes I'd taken on the plight of the chestnut. I'd come in person because I hoped Corn would make the file thicker.

"Well, what do you want me to do about it?" Obviously my folk song clue underwhelmed him.

"Maybe it was what the guy was searching for when he stole the Sandburg books."

Corn shook his head. "We found some Sandburg books in her office at the university including the one with folk songs. Without an exact inventory, we don't know for sure which if any books were taken from the house."

"But the theft from my car."

Corn spread his palms face up on his desk in a display of sympathy. "If it had happened in the parking lot at Connemara, I could investigate. But, the parking garage on Rankin isn't a scenic overlook on the parkway, and I've got nothing but coincidence to tie it to the Wainwright break-in."

"Coincidence?" My voice rose in exasperation. "You believe that?"

"I believe this." He reached in the in-box on the corner of his desk, grabbed several sheets of fax paper, and slid them to me.

I examined the first page. The seal of the Chief Medical Examiner for the state of North Carolina was prominently displayed. "What's the bottom line?"

"In medical terms, Janice Wainwright had 400 nano-grams of hydrocodone in her blood. That's consistent with the missing Vicodin pills and equates to a stumble-and-fall level. The M.E.'s words, not mine."

"Hmmm," was all I could say.

"Yeah. The report includes his examination of the lower back. He found evidence of a previous laminotomy and discectomy." Corn stumbled and fell through the unfamiliar pronunciations.

"Those are fancy words for her back surgery. But he also notes three abnormal conditions. There was scarring about the nerve root, minute disc fragments compressing the nerve, and a partial transection of the nerve root that probably occurred at the time of surgery."

"What's all that mean?"

"In short, any of the three could have caused pain. Janice had them all, and the nerve cut and disc fragments are directly tied to the surgery. Dr. Wyatt Montgomery screwed up."

"Why couldn't this be determined while she was alive?"

Corn pointed to the papers in my hand. "He covers that in a summation paragraph. An MRI can be helpful in revealing these complications but it isn't foolproof."

"Meaning it took an autopsy to disclose the extent of this surgeon's sloppiness."

"Yep." Corn sighed. "That's the size of it. The woman was definitely in pain. And the clearest cause of death is the M.E.'s phrase 'stumble and fall.'"

"Can I get a copy?" I returned the report without looking at it.

He nodded. "Unofficially. I've already had a request from Hewitt Donaldson. No question the findings bolster any lawsuit."

"So, you're closing your investigation?"

"No. I'm not. We're going to interview the surgeon, although it would be a hell of an irony if he killed her and thereby enabled an autopsy to prove his responsibility for the botched operation."

"We still have the fact that her calendar was stolen from her home."

"A copy was on her computer at work. We had the chair of the department review it. Most of the appointments were classes, faculty meetings, and student conferences."

"Most of them?"

Corn smiled. "There were some entered only by initials with no meeting location or purpose. I figure we'll ask Wendy when she returns."

"Did the history department chair say anything about what Janice might have been working on?"

"Not really. He knew she'd been researching economics of the Confederacy and she was also fascinated with Connemara's history. He said it's not unusual for someone to pursue two lines of interest. Maybe they intersect, maybe they don't."

"What about her colleagues? Was she working with someone?"

"As far as he knew, her research was independent. Although he said one of the other assistant professors claimed to be collaborating with her."

I paused to consider the implications. "Who owns the work done so far?"

"Good question. I assume Janice if independent really means independent in academic terms. Now her research and any written conclusions are part of her estate." Corn rubbed the side of his face thoughtfully. "I didn't pursue that angle."

I leaned forward. "Want to trade me her calendar and an introduction to the department chair?"

"On what grounds?"

"Janice's academic work is part of her estate. Hewitt Donaldson is handling the estate and I'm his investigator."

He nodded. "What have you got in return?"

I tried for my slyest expression. If he didn't buy my folk song, my chestnut was going to be an even harder sell. "I told you the receipt in her backpack was for a tree book."

"Well, she was hiking. Tree books, wildflower books, they should all come with a compass embedded in their covers. You know how many times we've had to mount search parties for people who wandered off the trail looking for a lady slipper?"

"How about a chestnut?"

He laughed. "An American chestnut? She was a history teacher, wasn't she?"

"Yes. And she'd know how valuable a blight-resistant tree would be."

"What's she going to do with it? Dig it up from park land, replant it at her farm, and then claim she found it there?"

"She doesn't need the tree. Just the cells or maybe a branch for some kind of grafting." I pulled the notes from my folder.

"The tree book says scientists are working on developing a blight-resistant hybrid by crossing American chestnuts with Chinese chestnuts, the ones who brought the blight in the first place."

Corn took a deep breath and looked at me like I was a misguided student. "Sam, there are trees that survived the blight. Only a few, but we're instructed to keep an eye out for any mature ones."

"Have you ever seen a mature chestnut?"

"No. But they exist and are used in cross-pollination procedures. And I'll grant you discovering a new one that widens the available gene pool will be cause for celebration. But a cause for murder?"

"You know that but maybe Janice and her killer didn't."

Corn looked doubtful. "She was a scholar. I think she would have done her homework. As for a killer?" He eyed the M.E.'s report.

"I know. 'Stumble and fall.' Well, I offer the chestnut theory anyway."

"For a trade."

"For her calendar and the introduction."

Corn drew his lips so tight they nearly disappeared. He got up from his desk, walked behind me, and closed the door. I had to swivel in the chair to see what he was doing. He went to a file cabinet and pulled a manila folder from the top drawer. He returned to the desk, laid the folder on the M.E.'s report, and rested his hands on top.

"I know we both want the same thing," he whispered. "And I know you and your partner are working this case gratis."

"I promised the girl I'd find her mother's killer."

"And if there is a killer, I want to bring him to justice." His eyes narrowed. "Justice is the key word here and I don't want to screw it up."

I knew I was going to get the calendar and maybe everything else that wouldn't break a chain of evidence custody. "You're helping Hewitt."

"I'm helping the girl receive the justice her mother should have gotten." He tapped his index finger on the stack of documents. "I know how the game's played. If I go around following leads about priceless chestnut trees, lost Sandburg poems, or anything else of value that interested Janice Wainwright, hell even some prize-winning goat, then I'm handing alternative theories to the defendants. I'll be called as a witness to discuss these theories for the sole purpose of creating doubt as to what happened."

I echoed Hewitt's words. "Proximate cause."

"You got it. The surgeon, the hospital, and the pharmaceutical company will latch onto anything or anyone they can put between Janice Wainwright and her bottle of pills."

"So your limited investigation wasn't about budget or manpower?"

"Oh, those were definite factors." He glanced again at the papers in front of him. "But I don't see evidence compelling enough to jeopardize Wendy Wainwright's future." He shoved the stack over to me. "And I don't think you do either. But neither one of us wants a killer to go free. Like I said before, you can work in ways I can't. Not only off the clock but also off the radar. My case file stays thin and of no help to the wrongful death defendants. Yours gets thicker and when you've got more than 'maybe this or maybe that,' you bring it to me and we nail the bastard."

"And the issue of proximate cause?"

"Well, it sucks, but I'm drawing the line at murder even if it costs Wendy a fortune."

I reached for the papers, and then hesitated. "Why shouldn't I walk away and let this thing play out?"

"Because you're in a tougher spot than I am. You made a promise to that girl."

I grabbed the papers and stood. "Let me know what the surgeon says."

"Will do. The chair of the history department is Bill Venable. I believe the assistant professor's name is Douglas McCaffrey, but I'll have to double-check my notes. I'll call Venable and tell him you'll be contacting him." Corn got to his feet. "And we're about to get a new player in the game."

"Who?"

"Paul Wainwright. Wendy's father."

"You spoke to him?"

"Yes. Talked to him about thirty minutes ago. He hadn't heard about his ex's death."

"How'd he take it?"

Corn gave a humorless smile. "He asked how she died and then he wanted to know the status of her lawsuit."

"What did you tell him?"

"That all I knew was Cynthia Howell and Wendy had hired Hewitt Donaldson and he was recommending they ratchet the case up to wrongful death."

"And?"

"And Wainwright said no hayseed mountaineer of an attorney was getting near the case and he was coming to Asheville to take charge."

"From Florida?"

"No. Pinehurst. He's in some amateur golf tournament representing his Gainesville country club." Corn glanced at his watch. "He'll be here by four."

"It's two now, and Pinehurst's a four-hour drive."

"Not when you have your own plane."

I returned Corn's smile. "He called Hewitt Donaldson a hayseed mountaineer?"

"Yep. His exact words. I'd love to be a fly on the wall when they meet."

"Well, I might just have to check in with my buddy Hewitt later this afternoon. Maybe bring him a Mason jar of moonshine to pay my legal fees, the standard charge of every hayseed attorney."

Corn laughed and stuck out his hand. "You give me that conversation and I'll tell you what the good doctor Montgomery has to say."

I clasped his meaty palm. "Ranger, we've got ourselves a deal."

Chapter Ten

As I drove down from the Blue Ridge Parkway to I-40, I formulated a to-do list. First, I wanted to review Janice Wainwright's calendar that lay with the M.E.'s report on the seat beside me. Corn had printed the past six months and the upcoming three months from her university computer and noted those appointments with unknown participants. Then I'd make an appointment with her department chair to see what light he could shed on why she might have been on Glassy Mountain. The assistant professor claiming a collaboration credit warranted an interview as well. He was probably more attuned to Janice's research.

I also planned to drop by Hewitt's office while Wendy's father was there, not that Hewitt needed any help dealing with him. I just wanted to size up the man for myself.

The stolen book of Cameron Reynolds held the most interest. Nakayla and Corn dismissed my surviving chestnut tree theory, and after hearing Corn's information that a few mature trees had escaped the blight, I had to admit the prospect that Janice was on the trail of a healthy chestnut seemed farfetched. But the Lomax *Folk Songs of North America* was a different matter. The wind whistling through my shattered side window signified someone thought the book was important. Unless the calendar offered another option, directly questioning Cameron Reynolds promised to be my best course of action.

I glanced at my watch. A quarter to four. I wouldn't see Reynolds today. Glass Doctor was meeting me at the parking deck near my office at five, and then I had my farm chores with Nakayla. I knew I'd better show up for our first encounter with Ida Mae or plan on sleeping in the barn till this case concluded.

Our office was empty and I figured Nakayla was still at the library. I photocopied the material from Corn, slipped the M.E.'s report into a manila envelope, and walked down the hall to give it to Hewitt. Shirley and Cory DeMille were huddled over Shirley's desk. Cory wore a crisp, white blouse and pleated navy skirt with a hem just below the knee. Short brown hair framed her rosy-cheeked face. Beside her, Shirley looked like Death coming to harvest Cory's soul.

"Hi, Sam," Shirley said. "Cory and I are going over Wendy's emancipation paperwork. Judge Wood was sympathetic to her predicament."

"Good. Is his highness in?"

"Yes," Cory said, "but he's with—"

"Paul Wainwright," I interjected.

Cory's eyes widened. "Wow, you really are a detective."

Not a single wrinkle of surprise appeared in Shirley's thick white makeup. "No, his partner's a detective. They just got two sets of business cards for the price of one."

I ignored Shirley and held the manila envelope up to Cory. "As the designated grownup in this alleged law firm, you should be aware I have urgent information that I need to give Hewitt immediately."

Shirley nodded gravely. "Must be his DNA analysis proving he's half horse. I don't need to read which end."

Cory held out her hand. "I'll give it to him."

"No. I promised to deliver it personally."

"Kind of small for a pizza," Shirley said. "When do you get your Domino's uniform?"

"I had my uniform, dearie."

The faintest tinge of color seeped into Shirley's cheeks. She knew my military record and what the war in Iraq cost me.

Making her blush made me feel like I'd crossed some line that actually embarrassed her. Shirley's rapier wit wasn't something I wanted to dull. "But if the hat's cute and the shoes match the insulated delivery bag, I might reconsider."

She smiled. "I recommend you stay with basic black."

"Yeah. Ninja Pizza Man." I circled around the desk. "He's in the conference room I trust?"

"Yes," Cory said. "Tell him you overpowered us."

"And don't stand too close to that Wainwright guy," Shirley whispered. "He's got a terminal tan that could be contagious."

I knocked on the door as I opened it. Hewitt sat at the table with his back to me. He swiveled around, annoyance stamped on his face. He rolled his eyes and mouthed the word "asshole." His expression matched that of the guest opposite him. The man's eyes glinted ice-blue, and he looked at me like I really was the pizza delivery boy. He wore a pink golf shirt with some country club emblem on the pocket. Under the table I saw sock-less Gucci loafers and the hem of chino slacks. Shirley pegged the tan. It looked part Florida and part salon. If the lights went out, he'd glow bronze.

"Here's the report," I said, and handed Hewitt the envelope. "Exactly what you expected."

"Thank you. I trust you covered your tracks." Hewitt infused a dramatic tone.

"Our source is protected." I backed out the door.

"Wait." Hewitt stood. "I want you to meet Paul Wainwright."

I forced a wide grin, and then pursed my lips as I faked sudden recognition. "Wainwright? You're that woman's?" I left the question hanging in the air.

He nodded solemnly. "Janice and I used to be married."

"I'm so sorry for your loss. I'm Sam Blackman." I stepped forward offering my hand.

Wainwright got to his feet, grave face intact, and reached out with his palm angled down to force me into a power handshake where he's on top. High-pressure salesmen and overbearing attorneys who live by that little psychological trick must have a hell of a time shaking hands with each other.

"Sam and his partner are the best private investigators in the state," Hewitt said. "They found Mrs. Wainwright on Glassy Mountain and are doing everything they can to learn exactly what happened."

The information cracked Wainwright's facade of solemnity. His blue eyes flickered with genuine concern. "What?"

Hewitt's introduction signaled he wanted to push Wainwright's buttons about the lawsuit. I grabbed Wainwright's hand and rotated it 180 degrees. Then I gave an extra squeeze for good measure. So much for his power play. "Yes, sir. Don't you worry. We'll pursue every angle we can. Every possibility for what or who caused her death will receive our full attention."

He yanked his hand away. "Jesus Christ, man. What the hell are you thinking?"

"That your former wife deserves justice. At least that's the belief of your daughter and her guardian."

Wainwright turned on Hewitt. "Do you realize what this clown is doing?"

I stepped closer. "I'm afraid he doesn't. You see, Hewitt's just a hayseed mountaineer of an attorney. As for being a clown, let me make you laugh with something funny. It's funny that Janice didn't name you the guardian for your daughter. Was that the price for her walking in on you and your secretary?"

Hewitt took in a sharp breath behind me. Wainwright didn't breathe at all. Even the multi-layered tan couldn't suppress the color bursting from his cheeks. He turned as pink as his shirt.

"What did she tell you?"

Not as much as you just did, I thought. His reaction mixed embarrassment with anger. Maybe Nakayla's comment about Janice having good pictures wasn't far from the truth. "Wendy didn't say anything."

"Then it was Cynthia. The bitch." He turned away. "She kept telling Janice that Wendy was traumatized. It was all posturing for the divorce and to turn Wendy against me."

I glanced at Hewitt. He mouthed, "Wendy," and I knew he understood that Janice Wainwright hadn't discovered her husband in flagrante delicto. Wendy had. She must have been eleven or twelve. In flagrante delicto. Latin for "cheating spouse taken to the cleaners."

Wainwright spun around and gripped the back of his chair till his knuckles went white. "Well, Cynthia's no saint, and neither was Janice, no matter what you were told."

"What I was told and who told it are confidential. But the source was neither your daughter nor her aunt."

He looked from me to Hewitt. "What's going on here?"

"Just what he said. Sam's going to find out what happened." Hewitt pointed a finger at Wainwright. "And I might be a hayseed attorney and Sam a clown, but we both understand proximate cause, and we both know how to tread lightly. Unless you want to blow this up with your arrogant grandstanding."

"I want what's best for my daughter."

"So do we," Hewitt said. "I'm working to see she gets the money, but I can't turn a blind eye to murder."

"Murder?" He laughed as if the idea was ludicrous. "Who'd want to kill Janice?"

I locked my eyes on his. "Anybody who benefits from her death. Someone who feels threatened by her. Someone who sees her as an obstacle to what he wants. Someone who has something to hide." I paused, and then added, "Someone who needs to settle an old score."

"I don't like your insinuation."

"I don't like it either. But in my business, insinuations are as common as lawyers trying to cover them up."

He glared at me but said nothing.

"Where were you yesterday afternoon?"

"This discussion is over." He tried to walk around me.

I slid sideways, blocking his path. "Then you'll have to tell Ranger Corn in a formal interrogation. It will go into the file and on the record. Any holes in your story and you can bet the legal teams for the surgeon and the pharmaceutical company will be all over it. Isn't that right, Hewitt?"

"Yep. But if you aren't a person of interest to the police, you might stay under their radar."

A flicker of doubt crossed Wainwright's face. "Why won't this ranger interrogate me anyway?"

I stepped away from him. "He's ninety percent sure Janice fell because of her painkillers and he doesn't want to raise the specter of some other proximate cause. He gets the game, but I have his silent approval to pursue his ten percent of doubt."

Wainwright looked down at the manila envelope on the table. "Our source is protected," he murmured, and put the pieces together.

"Where were you yesterday afternoon?" I repeated.

Wainwright gave a barely perceptible shake of his head as if clearing his mind for a new strategy. "Playing golf with my team mates. The tournament starts tomorrow."

I pulled a pen and notepad from my pocket. "Names. And I'll need cell numbers."

He froze.

"You don't have an alibi, do you?" I sensed Hewitt move behind me, taking a position directly in front of the door.

"I did not kill Janice," he said flatly.

"What's your alibi?" I demanded.

"Go to hell."

I dropped the pen and pad on the table, grabbed the phone from my belt, and punched in random numbers.

He threw up his hands. "All right, all right. I met a woman friend." He ran his palm over his face, wiping away the sweat that suddenly drenched his skin.

"Once a cheater, always a cheater." I picked up the pen and pad. "I need a name."

His arrogance withered. "Look, please, she's married. We met at a legal conference in Raleigh last month. Yesterday was just a stupid fling for both of us." With shaking hands, he pulled out his billfold. "I've got a receipt for fuel at the municipal airport near Goldsboro." He thrust a folded scrap of paper at me. "That should be enough proof without dragging her into this."

I stuck the paper in my pocket without looking at it. "Sit down. I have a few questions."

Wainwright sat at the table. "I told you I don't know who would kill Janice."

I took a seat, leaving an empty chair between us. Hewitt remained standing in front of the door.

"When's the last time you spoke to her?" I asked.

"A couple of weeks ago. Wendy called to tell me she'd been accepted at Warren Wilson. Janice got on the phone afterwards and gave me the cost and when payments were due."

"Was that going to be a hardship?"

His cheeks puffed out as he exhaled. "A hardship? Well, college ain't cheap. And I'm still paying child support till she's eighteen."

"Yeah, tough. You might have to sell your plane and fly coach with the rest of us."

"The plane's owned by the firm. Three of the partners have licenses so we often fly colleagues to meetings and depositions. Saves a lot of time and money."

"Any of your golfing buddies pilots?"

"No. And none of them are from the firm. We're playing because we're the top four golfers in the club."

I took a few notes just to appear interested. "What did you tell them when you skipped out of the practice round yesterday?"

He squirmed in the chair. "I said I had to see a client in Charlotte."

"So, you lie to your wife and you lie to your team mates. Why should I believe you're telling the truth to me, a total stranger?"

"If I were going to lie, would I tell you I was having an affair?"

I shrugged. "They don't have the death penalty for adultery in this state."

"I didn't kill her. I agreed to the tuition expense and I'll meet that obligation even if it takes my last nickel." He pounded the table. "And I hope Wendy gets every nickel those bastards owe for what they did to Janice."

I changed my line of questioning off his personal conduct. "Did Janice say she was working on anything special?"

"No. There was that pregnant goat." He shook his head. "I can't believe Wendy and Janice as farmers."

"Your daughter's dedicated to that animal. I understand it came from the Sandburg herd."

"Yeah, so they told me. Might as well have kept it there."

"What do you mean?"

"Seems like every time I called Janice the last few months she was there."

"Did she say why?"

He curled his lip dismissively. "Research. Some topic she'd probably publish a paper on that ten people would read. She didn't volunteer the exact subject and I wasn't interested enough to ask."

"Did she ever collaborate with Professor Cameron Reynolds?"

The smirk reappeared. "Collaborate? I guess that's one verb for it."

I said nothing, waiting for his explanation.

"I may have gotten caught with my pants down, but I'm pretty sure Cameron got into Janice's."

"Before you divorced?"

"Does it matter? I took the high road and never voiced my suspicions."

A regular boy scout, I thought.

Hewitt grunted. "In other words, you had no proof."

"What were your suspicions?" I asked.

"Well, she followed him up here as soon as she could land a job at the university. Warren Wilson was too small a college to hope for an immediate opening."

"Wendy said she moved after your divorce."

Wainwright nodded. "That's correct. But I think they'd been planning it ever since Cameron had the trouble in Florida."

"What trouble?"

His smirk turned into a full-blown grin. "You're the smart detective. Since you connected Janice and Cameron so quickly,

I'm surprised you didn't know about his dark past. Cameron Reynolds was accused of taking indecent liberties with a freshman at the University of Florida. She was only seventeen and he was over twenty-four. In Florida, that's not adultery, that's statutory rape."

Hewitt cut straight to the core issue. "Was he convicted?"

"No. But universities have a way of hushing things up."

"And he and Janice continued their friendship?" I asked.

"None of my business what they continued." He eyed me sharply. "I just hope Janice kept him away from Wendy."

Wainwright's words faded as my mind replayed the scene from the morning: Wendy clinging to Cameron Reynolds and then Cameron peeling her fingers off his car door.

Chapter Eleven

"You've got nerve, I'll give you that." Hewitt picked up the manila envelope and opened the metal clasp with his fingernail. "And maybe a few brains. How'd you figure out Wendy caught her father with his secretary?"

Hewitt and I sat at his conference table. Paul Wainwright had exited pronouncing half-hearted warnings that we'd better not screw up the lawsuit.

"I didn't. The guy pissed me off so I thought I'd toss in the hand grenade of him and his secretary. I was going for dramatic. I didn't know how Janice found out and was as surprised as you that it was Wendy."

"Lawyers." Hewitt spit the word off the tip of his tongue. "Your people."

"I can't stand them. That's why I'm a one-lawyer shop. Hell, I couldn't even work with my clone."

"What kind of lawyer is Wainwright?"

"Real estate development. The kind of guy who looks at a mountain ridge in autumn ablaze with brilliant hues from God's palette and only sees how many lots can be carved out of it."

"Not a good time to be in real estate development in Florida."

"No. I expect his practice took a hit and clients went belly-up owing him legal fees."

I mulled that prospect and wondered how long the flying time was from Goldsboro to the small airfield near Flat Rock and Sandburg's Connemara. "Wendy inherits her mother's estate with her aunt as guardian, right?"

"According to the will. They sent it by courier from the farmhouse earlier this afternoon."

"Now what happens if Wendy dies?"

His bushy eyebrows shot up. "You're saying Janice Wainwright's death might be the first stage of a two-part strategy?"

"I'm not saying anything. Just humor me."

"Janice Wainwright's estate flows to Wendy unless her daughter pre-deceased her. Then the estate goes to Cynthia Howell."

"Does Wendy have a will?"

"No. But minors rarely do."

"And Cynthia Howell will have fiduciary responsibility for her niece's financial affairs?"

"Correct."

"And if Wendy dies?"

Hewitt leaned back in the chair. "Ah, there's the rub. Janice gave no further instructions should Wendy die before reaching the age of majority. Janice's intention may have been to have the estate pass to Cynthia, but nothing is specified. North Carolina would view Wendy as having no spouse and no children. Without a will, the state would award the property to the next in line—the parents."

"In this case, Paul Wainwright."

"Yes. The estate's not worth much now, but when the lawsuit is settled in Wendy's favor, we're in a whole different league."

"You think Paul Wainwright has thought that through?"

Hewitt sat up straight and pulled the M.E.'s report clear of the envelope. "The guy may be a fellow attorney, but he's not stupid." He scanned the documents quickly and whistled under his breath. "Hot damn, and this report is made to order. Louis Kirkland will be dancing off the walls."

"You think a settlement's possible before the trial?"

Hewitt flipped through the pages. "They sure as hell won't want this to go to the jury. I've got an excellent orthopedic surgeon out of Charlotte, Dr. Tom Buter, and I'll encourage

Kirkland to put him on the expert witness list. Tom has the demeanor of a family doctor and can connect with the jurors. I can see him shaking his head sympathetically and saying 'stumble and fall.' His testimony will be hard to refute."

The intercom buzzed on the phone. "Hewitt?" Shirley asked.

"What?"

"Tell Sam that Nakayla called. She said Glass Doctor is here."

I looked at my watch. A quarter to five. "They're early."

"You want Nakayla to tell them to come back later?" Shirley asked.

"No. I'll be at the car in five minutes."

I gave Hewitt a quick update on the break-in.

He frowned. "Did you file a police report?"

"No. And I guess that means I shouldn't expect my insurance company to cover the repair."

"Just as well. I doubt if anyone on the outside would tie it to Janice's death but why take a chance. So, you and Nakayla will follow-up with Reynolds and the calendar?"

"Yes."

"Discreetly?"

"Definitely. We're so discreet even we don't know what we're doing."

◇◇◇

"Do you want the chickens or the goat?" I asked the question as Nakayla walked out on the front porch of the Wainwright farmhouse.

She'd left the office while I was watching the technician install my new safety glass and I followed forty-five minutes later. The interval allowed me to see if someone had parked at the overlook. No one seemed to be staking us out.

She clasped my hand and pulled me toward the barn. "I'll take the chickens. And the goat has a name. Ida Mae. Use it because you might soon be on intimate terms."

"Right. I'm sure the sound of my voice will give her great comfort. Especially when she sees the rectal thermometer in my hand."

We split and Nakayla went to the coop to count chickens, refill the water bottles and grain feeders, and lock the birds in for the night. Dusk was falling rapidly and the birds should already be roosting, or whatever it's called when they go to bed. Our instructions for tomorrow morning were to scoop poop from the coop, put down fresh wood chips, and collect eggs. I wasn't excited about either scooping or putting my hand under a chicken's butt so maybe taking care of Ida Mae wasn't such a bad deal. As for her temperature, lubricant be damned. I'd just write down one-hundred-two degrees even if the goat was on fire.

An early evening breeze blew steadily down the valley. Lightning flickered in the western sky, and I realized the growing darkness came more from gathering thunderclouds than the setting of the sun. I approached the gate to Ida Mae's pasture cautiously. In the gloom, I didn't want to walk into a strand of electrified fence. Kicking it with the metal part of my prosthesis would be my own little taste of lightning. I opened the gate, walked through, and securely latched it behind me.

The interior of Ida Mae's barn was cloaked in shadows. I went to the stall where she had been in the morning, but she wasn't there. "Ida Mae?" I whispered. A rumble of distant thunder rolled down the valley. I felt my way around the side of the stall to the wall bin containing the rectangular bale of hay. I thought maybe Ida Mae was standing by the lid, waiting for her supper.

No goat.

I should have paid attention to Wendy's instructions for getting the animal in the barn. What if she was outside dropping a kid in the face of the looming storm?

A board creaked in the wall and a soft bleat came from the other side. Ida Mae must have been standing against the outside rear of the barn where the structure blocked the wind. Wendy had told us around a three-inch sheaf of hay would be sufficient for the evening feeding; so I lifted the bin's lid and pulled a fistful from the bale.

With the bait in hand, I rounded the corner and saw a dark shape pressed next to the wall. "Ida Mae, here's your supper." I thrust the hay under her nose. Not so much as a nibble. "Come on. You can't spend the night outside."

Lightning flashed, closer now, and illuminated two golden eyes fixed on me.

"Wild dogs, coyotes, raccoons, they'll all be on the prowl so get your sorry goat hide inside." I sounded like my father scaring my brother Stanley and me with tales of ghosts in the attic who would snatch us if we weren't in bed. That didn't work either.

"How are you doing?" Nakayla called from the chicken coop.

I parroted the line from the old film *Cool Hand Luke*. "What we have here is a failure to communicate."

"Lure her with the hay."

"Tried that. She's not falling for it."

"Well, she can't stay outside. I'll come help as soon as I finish with the chickens."

The idea that Nakayla would have to bail me out of a showdown with a stupid goat rankled. I'd been a Chief Warrant Officer with the Criminal Investigation Command. Our motto was "Do What Has To Be Done." Even generals had to answer my questions and they could be as ornery as any goat.

"Ida Mae, it's your damn hay. You're supposed to like it." I pushed the stalks against her mouth but her lips stayed shut. Then a large splatter hit me on the forehead. Rain. The skies opened and the storm engulfed us.

Ida Mae moved forward, pushing her head into my stomach. She wasn't trying to butt me or knock me over. She wanted to shield her face.

"Don't like water?" I scratched behind one of her drooping ears. "Well, that makes two of us." I backed up and she followed, keeping her head against me. When we crossed into the barn, she broke away and walked to her stall. She turned around and took the hay from my hand.

"Okay, Ida Mae, we're going to get along just fine."

"Finally found a friend?" Nakayla closed the barn door to keep the rain from blowing in. She clicked on a small flashlight and caught Ida Mae and me in the beam.

"We're doing all right. I'm used to working with hard-headed women."

"Takes a goat to know a goat more accurately describes your kinship."

I listened to the wind howling against the barn and the rain pounding on the tin roof. The fury of the storm increased with every second. "Do you want to make a run for it?" I shouted.

She stepped closer. "We'd be soaked before we got ten yards. I think hail's mixed in. Feel how the temperature's dropped."

I'd been so intent on getting Ida Mae inside I hadn't noticed what must have been a fifteen degree plunge. I shivered.

Nakayla switched off the flashlight and wrapped her arms around me. "This won't last long. I've got a bottle of wine and sandwiches from Lenny's Sub Shop waiting inside. There's dry wood stacked on the back porch. Maybe you can build a fire."

"This farm life isn't so bad after all." I pulled her down and we sat with our backs against the stall, snuggling together for warmth. "We'll probably have to hang our wet clothes from the mantel to dry."

Nakayla squeezed me. "The sacrifices we make for our clients."

Thirty minutes later the storm had diminished to a fine drizzle. We ran hand in hand to the porch, wiped our shoes on the welcome mat, and stepped into the front room. On the glass-top coffee table sat a bottle of Chardonnay and two glasses. A pair of sleeping bags were rolled out in front of the fireplace.

"Did you stop by my apartment?" I asked.

"I brought you a change of clothes and some sleeves. Ida Mae needs to be fed and let out at seven so I thought we might as well stay over. If the floor's too hard, we can put the sleeping bags on the futon. I didn't want to fool with washing sheets."

"Great." The sleeve buffering my stump from the socket of my prosthesis was soaked from the downpour and rubbing my skin raw. "Where'd you put them?"

Nakayla headed for the kitchen. "I stowed your bag behind the whicker chair by the door. Get changed into dry clothes while I reheat the sandwiches."

When the wine bottle stood empty and the sandwich wrappers burned in the fireplace, I caught Nakayla up on the encounter with Wendy's father.

"Funny that he would be in North Carolina," she said.

"Pinehurst is a mecca for golfers. And his little tryst sounds believable given his past history." I reached in my wallet where I'd tucked Wainwright's receipt. "He paid for fuel at an airfield at the other end of the state."

Nakayla looked at the slip of paper. "There's no date."

"There's not?" I grabbed the receipt. The company name, Halport Aviation Services, was printed across the top. A fuel quantity and total price had been handwritten in the lined columns, but there wasn't a date. "Damn. He could have flown there the day before."

"Yes, but I doubt it. In some ways this confirms his alibi."

I was too busy mentally kicking myself to follow her logic.

"He paid cash. He didn't want an account statement coming to his home or office. A credit card would generate a printout that he'd have to sign. The date and time would be part of the recorded transaction."

"You don't think he was trying to pull something?"

Nakayla shrugged. "Maybe. Call Halport Aviation Services tomorrow. A guy who pays cash to fuel a plane would be memorable."

Her theory made sense. A philandering husband using a company plane to hook up with his paramour de jour had twice the reason to cover his trail. "No. I'm handing Paul Wainwright to Ranger Corn."

"You sure that's a good idea?"

Nakayla's question let me know she didn't think so.

"Like you said, odds are he was at that airport. Let Corn put it on the record. It shuts down ex-husband-as-murderer theory and shows Corn pursuing likely suspects."

"And if Wainwright's alibi doesn't wash?"

"Then he screwed up and the rangers should be all over his ass." I spread the computer printout of Janice Wainwright's calendar across the coffee table. "Janice used initials rather than the complete spelling for some of her appointments. Corn had the university identify those that signified student conferences and faculty meetings."

"Any pattern to which were written out?" Nakayla asked.

"Mostly doctor visits and construction appointments."

She bent over the papers. "Construction appointments?"

"Must have been the new barn for Ida Mae. Janice probably got a few estimates. The appointments started about five months ago when the initials CS began to appear."

"Carl Sandburg."

"That's what I figure. Has to be her trips to Connemara unless she was contacting Carl through a seance."

"That's about the time they got Ida Mae."

I pointed to a date back in March. "This one's interesting. It has both CS and a new set, ES."

"Maybe ES works at Connemara."

She slid March aside. "What are some of the other initials?"

"LB occurs a few times. RT. CR."

"Cameron Reynolds."

I nodded. "Most likely. We should see him tomorrow. I've got a meeting with Janice's department head at nine in the morning. I'll cover that while you track down Reynolds and try for a later appointment."

"I pulled his profile off the Warren Wilson web page. He teaches courses in music and American culture. Warren Wilson has a special program for the preservation and promotion of Appalachian music. Every year they sponsor The Swannanoa Gathering. Folk arts and folk music. There's celtic week, fiddle week, dulcimer week—"

"That could connect to Sandburg," I interjected. I got up from the futon and threw another log on the fire. "And it explains why Cameron would have the Lomax book."

"The question is who has it now."

I stabbed the fire with a poker, popping sparks into the room.

"Careful," Nakayla said. "We don't want Wendy coming home to a smoldering ruin."

"I'm frustrated that I can't get a clear picture. According to Paul Wainwright, Janice and Cameron might have been romantically involved. And there's the relationship with the underage college girl."

"An accusation coming from a peach of a guy."

I paced in front of the hearth. "Yeah, I know. It could be unfounded character assassination. But both Janice and Cameron shared an interest in history, he in music and she in the Civil War. That could have fueled a more intimate relationship."

"What were her most recent unknown appointments?"

I picked up the April sheet. "Last Saturday at noon. DLM at Hawg Wild, spelled H A W G. Is that a word?"

"A barbecue restaurant in Brevard. Right up your alley. Maybe if we show her picture, someone will remember the person she met."

Brevard was a small town about thirty minutes from Asheville, equidistant from Flat Rock and close to the Pisgah National Forest.

"Better do that tomorrow around lunch." I sat beside her on the futon. "Work Reynolds around it."

She laughed. "Solely in an effort to get the same wait staff."

"Of course. That's what makes me a good detective."

She elbowed me. "I knew there had to be some reason. What else stands out on her calendar?"

"Then RT is marked for Sunday afternoon. Nothing was scheduled for Monday or yesterday."

"No CS?" Nakayla asked.

"Nothing to indicate she planned to go to Connemara. There was nothing for this week other than university appointments. Next week she'd blocked out time for LK, which must stand for Louis Kirkland, her lawsuit attorney."

Nakayla pulled out the three bottom pages. "And the months ahead?"

"Corn printed May, June, and July. Her trial starts a few days after the end of Spring term. There's an educational conference in Chicago in mid-June and a trip to Florida in July."

"To see her sister?" Nakayla asked.

"Possibly. June also has an evening blocked out for the Flat Rock Playhouse. Wendy told me they were getting some complimentary tickets."

"Wendy might be able to decipher some of the initials," Nakayla suggested.

I collected all the months into a pile. "Right. But I don't want to wait till she returns Monday to follow-up on the barbecue lead."

"Or Connemara," Nakayla said. "I think we need to talk to the rangers on-site. More was going on between Janice and Sandburg than a pregnant goat."

"What did you find at the library?"

Nakayla pulled two books from her overnight bag. One was a copy of Lomax's *Folk Songs of North America* and the other was Sandburg's *The American Songbag*. "I cross-referenced song titles from each. Sandburg's book came out in 1927 and has 267 songs. Lomax's in 1960 with over 300. Combined there are around 570 songs. What's amazing is only twenty-eight are duplicates. Songs like 'Turkey in the Straw,' 'Down in the Valley,' and 'Careless Love.'"

I looked at the two table of contents lying open side by side. "Are the verses the same?"

"Minor variations but they're all versions I've heard. Nothing stands out." Nakayla tapped one book and then the other. "If Sandburg's contains something important, then how does the Lomax book fit in unless as a comparison?"

I didn't have an answer. "Maybe there's so little overlap because Lomax didn't want to duplicate Sandburg's work."

"Possibly." She flipped through *Folk Songs of North America* to the appendix. "Sandburg is credited as the source for several of the songs in common. I examined Lomax's commentary and the verses and have no idea what could be significant."

I understood why Nakayla sounded discouraged. "And if it's a Lomax song that's not also in Sandburg's collection, then we're looking at nearly 275 songs and God knows how many individual verses for a clue."

"And why would Janice have said 'Sandburg's verses' but hidden Lomax's collection?"

I closed the books, knowing that finding the answer in either was impossible without more information. "That's why we'll see Cameron Reynolds and ask him point blank why Janice had his book."

"And if he doesn't know?"

I put my arm around her shoulder. "Then we console ourselves at Hawg Wild. My philosophy is when life hands you lemons, cover them in barbecue sauce and eat them."

Chapter Twelve

New Hall. The last name I expected to see on a building housing a history department. But, that's where the University of North Carolina at Asheville chose to keep its explorers of the past. The chairman, Dr. William Venable, ushered me into a small conference room. He must have been in his early sixties, portly with a circular fringe of white hair reminiscent of the popular style of medieval monks in the fourteen-hundreds.

"Would you like some coffee?" He pointed me to the nearest chair.

"No, thank you." I sat and put my notepad on the table. "I appreciate your seeing me on short notice and don't want to take up your time."

He waved my concern away and took the seat across from me. "We'll do anything we can to help. I speak for the whole department. We're like a family and we're grieving." Tears formed at the corners of his eyes and he turned his face away.

"I understand. And you have my sympathies." I waited, letting the man compose himself.

"Janice was very special. An excellent lecturer and an imaginative researcher." He turned toward me. "That's a rare combination."

"She must have been strong willed. To have persisted through what I understand was excruciating back pain."

"The last nine months were a living hell. You know a few weeks ago she collapsed in the classroom?"

"No."

"Her back just went into a spasm and she fell from the pain."

"Even after taking her Vicodin?"

Venable sighed. "She used painkillers as little as possible. Said they fogged her brain."

"And still she went up on that mountain."

"I don't know what the hell for. Janice was tenacious. You had to give her that."

I opened my notepad. "Can we assume it was part of her research?"

Venable touched the tips of his fingers together, forming a hollow triangle with his hands. "A logical guess, but still a guess. When a faculty member like Janice does independent research, I don't get involved with the details."

"What do you mean by independent?" I wrote the word on my pad and underlined it.

Venable smiled. "Money. There's no departmental funds or university grant involved. She's either raised the money herself or spending her own funds. Or sometimes a researcher might be collaborating with a colleague from another institution and that person has the funding."

"Was she?"

"No. She was flying solo. I assume from my conversation with Ranger Corn, you're interested in papers and materials that belong to the estate?"

"Yes. I think there are two issues. First, we want to identify and collect what's legally Janice's intellectual property, and second, recommend to her daughter Wendy what course of action to take. Would you be willing to help with guidance in that area?"

"Certainly," he said without hesitation. "It will depend upon how far along Janice had gotten toward a publishable manuscript."

"I understand." I flipped back a page and reviewed the notes from my meeting with Corn. "And you're sure there aren't any complications of authorship? Corn mentioned Douglas McCaffrey and that you said he and Janice were collaborating."

"Collaborating was too strong a word. I know she'd asked him for some data on agricultural production. As far as I know, he wasn't contributing any ideas or conclusions. I'm sure she would have acknowledged him in whatever she published."

"Okay." I ventured into the more delicate aspect of my visit. "Has Janice's office been locked since her death?"

"She locked it when she left Tuesday afternoon. The police were over here mid-morning the next day. Since then not even the cleaning crew has been allowed inside."

"Good."

Venable fidgeted in his chair. "How long do you think it will need to stay that way?"

I shrugged. "The police have a say, and then Wendy will need some time to collect her mother's things. Is there a problem?"

"Well, someone's going to have to pick up Janice's classes. We're too close to the end of term to have students, especially the seniors, left hanging with incompletes."

"Are there course outlines another professor can follow?"

"Each class has a syllabus. I'm talking about her grade books, tests that might be outstanding, and the final exams she's probably already drawn up."

"Some of that must be on her computer."

He nodded. "Yeah, but the police have it off-limits as well."

"I'll check with them and see what I can do." I closed my notepad. "You know my role is strictly to watch out for Wendy's interest. I don't mean to be an obstacle to what you have to do for your department."

Venable wiped his palms on his thighs. The thought of his pending administrative problem seemed to agitate him. "I understand. I've met Wendy many times. I hoped she'd attend here, but Warren Wilson is a fine school and a good match for her interests. I assume those plans will still go ahead."

"That's what we're working toward." I gave him my best look of concern. "But, Wendy says her mother hoped to earn some extra income out of whatever she was researching. Maybe a book deal, maybe something else."

"Really?" He sat up straighter. "I didn't know that."

"Well, this was Wendy's impression. Maybe she was making more of it than her mother meant."

"Janice wasn't one to exaggerate. If anything, she understated her work." He shook his head. "What a tragedy. If there was book potential, then we'll do what we can to bring it to publication. A fitting legacy for Janice and, I'll admit, a nice reflection on our department and the university."

I stood. "Thank you. I'll be in touch. Next week either I or my colleague will come back with Wendy to start sorting through the office."

He got to his feet. "Just call Trudy, my administrative assistant, and let her know when. We'll stop by her desk on the way out so I can introduce you."

He started for the door, but I stayed put.

"Dr. Venable, would it be possible for me to speak to Professor McCaffrey?"

He stopped. "Is there something else you need to know?"

"I thought maybe he'd have the most accurate assessment of where Janice stood in the completion of her work."

"That's possible, but like I said she kept her progress to herself."

"Any bit of information is useful at this point."

He started to say something else, and then changed his mind. "Okay. He should be in his office. You might have to wait if he's with a student."

"That will be fine. I shouldn't need more than five minutes."

I followed Venable down the hall and around a corner. Some doors were open, some closed. He halted before one at the end that was cracked a few inches. No voices came from inside, only the rhythmic squeak of a spring.

"Douglas?" Venable called, and rapped on the door.

The squeaking stopped.

"Bill. Come in."

Venable pushed open the door but stayed in the hall. A young man with curly brown hair sat behind a small desk. He looked to be in his early thirties, no more than a year younger or older than me. He wore a white shirt with frayed collar and a wide purple necktie that looked like a wardrobe prop from the 1970s.

His desktop was bare except for a single file folder open before him. His swivel chair faced the door and a computer stood on a credenza behind him. A word document filled the screen. In his left hand, he held a black hand-grip exerciser with a pitted chrome spring.

"Multitasking, I see," Venable said. "Can we interrupt you a few minutes?"

"Certainly. My nine o'clock student didn't show for her conference. Surprise, surprise." He looked at me curiously.

"This is Sam Blackman," Venable said. "He's assisting Janice's daughter Wendy in dealing with estate matters involving Janice's research."

McCaffrey stared at me.

"He'd like to talk with you a few minutes," Venable continued. "I told him all of us in the department are glad to help."

McCaffrey continued to stare as if his chairman had said nothing.

"Douglas?" Venable called his name with a sharper edge.

Whatever spell I'd cast on the assistant professor broke. He dropped the hand-grip and stood, pushing back his chair till it bumped into the credenza. "I'm sorry. I can't get used to Janice being gone."

He offered his hand. "I'm Douglas McCaffrey."

I stepped past Venable and through the doorway. As I expected from a man who exercised his hands, his grip was firm but not painful. Unlike Paul Wainwright, he wasn't trying to make a statement.

"Janice and I worked closely together." A slight tic tugged at the corner of McCaffrey's right eye and he looked away.

"Douglas is our resident jock," Venable said. "A competitive kayaker."

I smiled and pointed to the hand-grip. "I see you'll never lose your paddle. I should get one of those."

"Do you kayak?" he asked.

"I enjoy drifting downstream. My girlfriend and I are strictly recreational splashers. We avoid whitewater like the plague."

"I'll leave you to swap river stories," Venable said. "Sam, good to meet you. I'll tell Trudy, my assistant, you'll be in touch."

We shook hands and he closed the door, leaving me confined in a room no bigger than a prison cell. Two of the walls were floor-to-ceiling bookshelves. The volumes seemed to be neatly arranged. The other walls held various diplomas and certificates mixed in with framed photographs of kayakers shooting through rapids or running slalom gates. I assumed some of the pictures must be of McCaffrey, but in the heavy spray, the helmeted kayakers were unidentifiable.

"Please, sit down," he said. "We could go some place else except I'm supposed to be keeping office hours for students now."

"This is fine." I took the only other chair, a straight-backed one that must have escaped from someone's dining room. Anything larger wouldn't have fit in the cramped office.

He sat and leaned across the desk. "So, Janice's family has hired you to finish her research?"

"No. I'll just be identifying and collecting her papers."

"You're not an historian?"

"I'm afraid not."

The tension visibly lifted from McCaffrey's body. His shoulders eased down a few inches and the tic disappeared from his eye. I realized he thought I was some outside academic competitor hired to complete Janice's work, work that he obviously sought to appropriate. I decided to keep him on the defensive.

"I'm a private detective. I'm securing everything that rightfully belongs in Janice's estate including all intellectual property."

The tic returned. "Janice and I were collaborating. I'll need our papers to finish."

"And where does the project stand now?"

"Ready to have the conclusions drafted into narrative form."

"What are those conclusions?"

"I'm sorry. They're not ready to be made public."

"Then what is the project, or is that not ready to be made public?"

He reddened. "It has to do with the economy of the South and its effects in this region, particularly its influence on the policies of the treasury of the Confederacy."

"So, you actively researched the topic?"

"My area of specialization is the American economy of the 19th century. Janice was a Civil War historian. Our complementary expertise made a perfect combination."

"And Connemara?"

"It was the home of Memminger, the Secretary of the Treasury for the Confederacy."

"If you were collaborating, how many visits did you make there? How many interviews did you conduct with park rangers and archivists?"

His brown eyes darkened. "That wasn't my area of responsibility."

"So, a woman whose back was so bad that she collapsed during a lecture took on the physical aspects of your shared research including climbing to the top of Glassy Mountain while you sat in your office exercising your wrists."

He said nothing.

"I want to be fair with you, Dr. McCaffrey. But from what Dr. Venable has said and what seems obvious to me is that Janice Wainwright was very protective of her work. I will be also. You did provide her data." I thought back to my brief scan through the books in her study. "Cotton production, agricultural sales, minutes of meetings on economic matters."

McCaffrey's jaw dropped. "You've seen all that?"

"Yes. It's material she could have gotten elsewhere, but you were of assistance and we'll bear that in mind as we move forward."

He sat perfectly still for a few seconds, weighing his options. Then he sighed. "Okay. For the record, Janice was guarded about her work. Overly so. But she did come to me with questions and I tried to help as best I could. I would really like the opportunity to evaluate her research. Believe me, there's no one any closer."

"Not even Cameron Reynolds?"

"Who?"

"A professor at Warren Wilson College. He and Janice worked together at the University of Florida."

His brow furrowed. "Her friend the music guy? What's he have to do with this?"

"He also provided research assistance." I stood quickly and reached for the doorknob. "As to what he has to do with it, if you knew what Janice was working on, you wouldn't have to ask."

As I closed the door, I heard the hand-grip begin squeaking in double-time. I stopped by Venable's assistant, and reiterated that no one under any circumstances was to go in Janice Wainwright's office.

Then I called Nakayla and learned I should pick her up for round two of Sam Blackman's college tour.

Chapter Thirteen

The white letters WWC stood out crisp and bright on the side of the weathered barn. At first I thought a local radio station must have paid for the space. Throughout the mountains, "See Rock City" and "Chew REDMAN Tobacco" signs could still be seen as faded reminders of when companies compensated farmers for using their roadside outbuildings as billboards.

"WWC," I said. "Warren Wilson College?"

"Yes. We're entering the school's farmland." Nakayla drove along the two-lane blacktop and played the dual roles of my chauffeur and tour guide through an area of Buncombe County unknown to me. "This little valley is one of my favorites."

The road swung in a wide arc and woods gave way to cultivated fields. After another mile, Nakayla turned into a campus entrance, a narrow lane running along the side of a hill with buildings scattered above and below. Some housed classrooms; others administrative offices.

"Do you know which one's Kittredge?" I asked.

"At the end of the loop. I'll try to park close and then call his cell."

Nakayla had used the college directory to track down Cameron Reynolds' office phone number. She'd called a few minutes after nine and caught him before his morning class. She told him we were helping Wendy and her aunt continue Janice Wainwright's lawsuit and we had a few questions. That sparked his curiosity and his concern. Nakayla refused to divulge any specifics, only that Wendy said we could count on his cooperation and we needed to see him as soon as possible. Reynolds suggested eleven at Kittredge Music Center where we could either meet outside or in one of the rehearsal rooms.

Nakayla wedged her small Hyundai into a grassy spot between the road and a legitimate parking space. "I'm not blocking anyone and you'll probably piss off Reynolds so quickly we'll be leaving in five minutes."

I grabbed the library copies of the Lomax and Sandburg songbooks from the backseat. "Me? Mr. Charm? You should have seen the way I wowed Douglas McCaffrey." I got out of the car while she phoned Reynolds. The air was chilly but invigorating, the sky a cloudless blue, and the mountains surrounding the campus vibrant green with spring growth. I took a deep breath and thought had I known about a college with this setting, I probably wouldn't have defied my father by joining the Army right out of high school.

Nakayla got out and closed the driver's door. "He asked if it was okay to meet in the garden."

"What's that mean? We're going to pick vegetables while we talk?"

Nakayla started walking back the direction we'd driven. "The formal garden on the other side of the street across from the music building."

"Is he afraid we'll corner him in his office? It can't be any smaller than McCaffrey's."

"I bet he wants the privacy of the great outdoors. Everybody can see us but nobody can hear us."

We crossed the road and followed a path that looked like it had been created by a thousand footsteps. This garden would never be confused for one of the Biltmore Estate's pristine terraces. There was a centralized area with wooden slat benches and chairs spaced among a series of plant beds, and the overall impression was Mother Earth contributed the flora and humans occasionally tidied her handiwork.

"I guess the students are in class," I said.

"Or working." Nakayla took a bench that faced the direction of Kittredge Music Center. "Add a working farm to scholastic pursuits and these kids have a full plate."

I checked my watch. Ten minutes to eleven. "I hope Reynolds is on time."

Nakayla laughed. "You're so obvious."

"What?"

"I said full plate and you immediately thought about lunch at Hawg Wild."

I sat beside her. "Janice's appointment calendar said she met DLM at lunch. Maybe DLM is an employee working the lunch shift. And we're an hour away."

"Don't worry. They won't run out."

"Hey. It's not about the food."

She laughed louder. "Right. I bet when I'm not around you put barbecue sauce on ice cream."

"Only if it's heated first."

"That would be funny if I thought you were kidding." She looked across the garden. "Here he comes."

The man we'd met in Janice Wainwright's front yard hurried toward us, a battered guitar case in his left hand. He wore a green windbreaker and blue jeans. At first I thought the guitar case was held together with tape, but as he drew closer, I saw the colored strips were bumper stickers. We stood to greet him.

"Thanks for meeting me here." He offered his hand first to Nakayla and then to me. "Otherwise there's someone always waiting to catch me in the hall when I'm running late."

He set the guitar case on an opposite bench. The most prominent sticker read "This Machine Kills Fascists." Others sported slogans, "Sing What You Believe" and "A Song Will Set You Free."

"How many fascists have you killed?" I asked.

"As of today?" He shrugged. "None. That was the phrase Woody Guthrie pasted on his guitar. I like to think my guitar kills fascist attitudes."

"Sounds like a more reasonable expectation than storming a Nazi machine gun while singing *This Land Is Your Land.*"

Reynolds laughed good-naturedly. "Maybe not. You've never heard me sing." He looked at Nakayla and then back at me. "I'm afraid I'm on a tight schedule and you didn't come here to talk about my music."

"Oh, but we did, Mr. Reynolds." Nakayla sat on the bench and indicated for him to join his fascist-killing guitar on the one opposite us. "That's precisely why we're here."

Reynolds couldn't have looked more surprised than if we told him he was nominated for a Grammy. "But I thought we were discussing Janice's lawsuit?"

"We are," I said. "More importantly it's now Wendy's lawsuit and we're making sure the defendants' lawyers don't fabricate some other explanation for Janice's death."

"Like what? I thought she fell off Glassy Mountain."

"Like murder."

He recoiled at the word. "Murder?"

I held up the Lomax book. "Why did Janice have this?"

"That's mine. I loaned it to her last weekend." His face contorted in confusion, not alarm. "What's my book have to do with anything?"

"This isn't yours. Nakayla got it from the Pack Library along with *The American Songbag.*" I held Sandburg's book in my other hand. "I found your copy in Janice Wainwright's house. Then someone broke into my car and stole it."

He shook his head with disbelief. "That's crazy. There's nothing special about that book."

"Why did she have it?"

"She asked me if I had a copy of a song. A song that Sandburg was interested in, but she couldn't find in his collection."

"What was it?"

"'I'm Troubled.'"

"That's the song?"

"Yes. Lomax includes it in his section on the southern mountains and backwoods." He reached out his hand and I gave him the book. He opened it about a third of the way through and flipped a few pages. "Here it is."

Nakayla slid closer and we shared a look. On the page lay the musical score for piano, chord notations specified for guitar or banjo, and four verses:

> I'm troubled, I'm troubled,
> I'm troubled in my mind,
> If trouble don't kill me,
> I'll live a long time.
>
> My cheeks was as red,
> As the red, red rose,
> But now they're as pale as
> The lily that blows.
>
> I'll build me a cabin
> On the mountain so high,
> Where the wild birds can't see me
> Or hear my sad cry.
>
> I'm sad and I'm lonely,
> My heart it will break,
> My true love loves another,
> Lord, I wisht I was dead.

"Not much to it," I said.

"There's not much known about its origins. A typical plaintive ballad of unrequited love. If you heard similar words down in the low country, it would be among the field hands. A pre-Blues lament."

"Does Lomax make any comments about the song?"

Reynolds shook his head. "That's rather odd. I hadn't paid attention to the song until Janice asked about it. I remembered Lomax had it in this collection. His only comment is a quote from Davy Crockett about what it felt like to be a rejected suitor."

"Davy Crockett? The Davy Crockett?"

Reynolds laughed. "Coonskin hat and all. Maybe Lomax was namedropping."

"Does the song date back that far?" Nakayla asked.

"Probably. The Crockett reference is from 1803 when he'd just turned seventeen. I can only assume Lomax used the story because it linked to the time of the song's popularity. Lomax died in 2002 or else I'd ask him."

Nakayla picked up *The American Songbag*. "Sandburg didn't include it."

"Sandburg didn't include a lot of folk songs. There are thousands, and when you consider all the variations, you're talking about a building full of books." Reynolds pointed to the volume in my hand. "But I'd say 'I'm Troubled' is just what Lomax indicated. A lonesome love song brought over by English settlers in the 1700s. The similes of flowers run rampant through those ballads. The verse about a cabin on the mountain supports its evolution in this locale. I'd say Lomax categorized it correctly."

"Are you a musician or a historian?" I asked.

"A little of both. Some might say not much of either."

"Was Janice Wainwright a musician?"

"No. She was first and foremost a historian. We met at the University of Florida when she was working on a paper about songs of the Civil War."

"Were you close?"

"We were good friends. I felt like Janice had gotten a raw deal from her husband. And Wendy's a sweet kid."

I looked to Nakayla. It was time we got down to the more personal aspects of this interview, and we agreed she would broach the subject. Something about me being a bull in a china shop when it comes to sensitive issues.

She cleared her throat. "We spoke to her husband yesterday. He said she followed you up here."

"Paul's a first-class asshole. What else did he say?"

Nakayla looked him squarely in the eye. "That you left Florida because of your involvement with an underage freshman and that the university covered up the charges."

Instead of getting angry, Reynolds laughed. "Paul spouts that fantasy to ease his own conscience. So he can claim his wife ran off with a pervert."

"We know about the secretary," Nakayla said. "And about Wendy discovering them."

Reynolds leaned forward. "Wendy told you?"

"No. We figured it out from the terms of the divorce and meeting Paul Wainwright in person."

Reynolds stared at us for a few seconds without speaking. Then he relaxed against the back of the bench and rested his arm on the guitar case. "You're good. And I'm sure you'll learn a good bit about me if you put your minds to it. But let me save you the trouble because we're on the same team here. I want to see Wendy get what her mother would have wanted her to have."

"Okay," I said. "We're listening."

Reynolds gave a quick glance around the garden to insure no one was within earshot. "I had nothing to do with Janice's death. She and I were good friends. She didn't follow me here. I told her about the opening at UNC-Asheville because I thought the job would be a good fit for her research. I came to Warren Wilson College because they appreciate our heritage of folk music and the impact it's had on our culture." Again he pointed at the Lomax book. "I don't know why Janice found that particular song important. She only told me it had been important to Sandburg and might be key to what she was researching."

"And you don't know what that research was?"

He shrugged. "Something to do with the Civil War. Sandburg had certainly seen it through the eyes of Lincoln. And he would have grown up surrounded by veterans. An historian is always looking for primary sources and maybe Janice wanted to retrace Sandburg's footsteps as he researched Lincoln's life."

His explanation sounded plausible but not a motive for murder. Something more primal had to be involved.

"And you don't think she had feelings for you that went beyond good friends?" I asked. "The song is about love that's not returned and the final line is, 'Lord, I wisht I was dead.'"

"Janice Wainwright wasn't wishing she was dead. She was very much alive despite the pain she suffered. As for feelings, Janice and I loved each other, but she wasn't my gender of choice. Is that clear enough for you?"

"Perfectly," I said. "Then it's also clear the incident with the freshman girl was hogwash."

"'I'm Troubled' would have been an apt description of her. She earned a bad grade in one of my classes and fabricated the allegation out of spite."

"But if you're gay, why'd anybody believe her?"

"Because I've always felt my sexual orientation was nobody's business. My personal life is just that, personal. When the university officials investigated her claim, they discovered she'd made the same accusations against one of her high school teachers. He'd also given her a bad grade. I was cleared, but Paul Wainwright forgets that fact when smearing my name."

Reynolds seemed sincere and after meeting both men he came across as the more decent guy. But I'd investigated enough military cases to know many a man appears decent right up to the second he commits the crime.

"Do you have any reason to believe Wainwright would harm his ex-wife?"

His mouth dropped open. "You think Paul killed Janice?"

"No, I don't. But the other side is looking for any wedge they can put between their clients' liabilities and Janice's death."

He shook his head. "Paul's a lot of things. Arrogant, demanding, narcissistic. But I can't see him pushing Janice off a mountain. I can't even see him on a mountain unless there was a golf course atop it."

"Good." I glanced at Nakayla, cuing her to pick up the interview baton.

"Did Janice ever talk to you about chestnut trees?" she asked.

Reynolds threw up his hands. "You guys ask the weirdest questions. No. Does this connect to Sandburg somehow? I know he didn't write the line, 'Under the spreading chestnut tree, the village smithy stands.'"

Nakayla ignored his sarcasm. "Mr. Reynolds, the night before Janice died she bought a book about trees specifically for its section on American chestnuts. The book has disappeared. Can you think of any way that could be related to her work?"

"I can't. Honestly, I'd help you if I could."

"We've been given access to her calendar. She entered her appointments using only initials."

"I do the same thing. Students are very adept at reading things on your desk upside down. Neither of us wanted them to know what other students might be coming in for conferences."

"Makes sense." Nakayla took a notepad and pencil out of her purse. "Let me run some initials by you from her recent appointments. LB."

He thought a few seconds. "Could be Leonard Branagh. But he's still at the University of Florida. If he was coming into town, I would have known it. Maybe it was a scheduled phone call."

I hadn't thought about that. We'd have to check the initials against friends and colleagues everywhere. When Wendy returned, she'd have to guide us through all those possibilities.

"What about ES?" Nakayla asked.

"No. But I'm sure I'm missing people. It's difficult matching initials without at least part of a name to go by." He pulled his own notepad and pen from the pocket of his windbreaker. "I'd like to write these down. Maybe something will come to me later."

"There are more. RT."

"Still initials?"

"Yes."

"Rebecca Taylor is her physical therapist. Janice saw her frequently."

"Okay." Nakayla wrote down the name under Leonard Branagh. "How about DLM?"

"DLM," he repeated. "Nothing comes to mind. That's a tough one because you don't know how to consider the first two letters."

"What do you mean?" Nakayla asked.

Reynolds smiled. "Because we're in the South. Could be two first names like Billy Ray, Bobby Earl, or in this case Donna Lynn." He laughed. "You know the old joke about the difference between a southern wife and a northern wife?"

"No," Nakayla said.

"A southern wife has two first names, a northern wife has two last names. That was popular when Hillary Clinton suddenly became Hillary Rodham Clinton. So we don't know if the middle initial goes with the first or the last name. Any more?"

Nakayla closed her notepad. "No. These were the appointments that couldn't be identified."

"I'll give it some thought." He stuck the pen and pad back in his pocket and grabbed the handle of his guitar case. "Well, I've got to be in Flat Rock for a rehearsal. Have you got a card so I can contact you?"

While Nakayla fished one out of her handbag, I had another thought.

"We noticed when you dropped by the farmhouse this morning that Wendy didn't want to let you go. I assume you and she are also close."

Reynolds stiffened. "I've known Wendy since she was a baby. Yes, we're close, and it's only natural she'd be clinging to me under the circumstances."

His defensive tone surprised me. "How does she see you?"

"What do you mean?"

"I mean her father abandoned her after she discovered him in bed with another woman. Would you describe yourself as a father figure or more like a big brother? Or does she have a crush on you?"

His eyes narrowed. "Mr. Blackman, Wendy is a complicated girl. To be honest, she might have all three feelings jumbled together. She knows my preference, but if anything that makes her more flirtatious."

"I don't understand."

"You're safe," Nakayla told Reynolds.

He nodded. "Exactly. Wendy is dealing with her sexuality. She's seen the power of sex destroy her home. It's made her guarded in establishing basic friendships with girls and boys. She's a loner at school and not into trite, superficial relationships. In some ways, she's more mature than her peers, in others, she's less. But she's growing into womanhood and confronting her own impulses. She's role-playing with me, knowing I won't respond. I've discouraged that, but I also don't want her choosing promiscuity as a response to her father's infidelities. I think she's vulnerable to making poor choices, and I want her to be able to talk to me about anything."

"How was her relationship with her mother?"

"No question they loved each other. But she's a teenage girl." Reynolds looked at Nakayla.

"Oh, yeah. At that age, I was always butting heads with my mother and I'd do things just because she told me not to."

"So Wendy didn't have a boyfriend?" I asked. "Someone Janice didn't like?"

"Wendy's fixated on that goat. I don't know when or where she'd have time for a boyfriend. But, like I said, when the time comes, I don't want her falling for the wrong guy."

"Wendy said her mother didn't tell her about what she was working on. Why she climbed Glassy Mountain when the hike was such a painful ordeal. Does that ring true?"

"That's a little odd. I don't think they kept secrets from each other."

"Was Janice seeing anyone?" I asked.

"No. Janice was about three things. Her daughter, her work, and her lawsuit."

"Regarding her work, I spoke with Douglas McCaffrey this morning."

"Poor Dougie," Reynolds said.

"You know him?" I asked.

"No. That's what Janice called McCaffrey."

"He was very eager to take over Janice's research."

"I bet he was."

Nakayla and I looked at each other, and then waited for Reynolds to explain.

"Janice liked McCaffrey, but she said he was more interested in a river of whitewater than the river of time."

"He was lazy?" I asked.

"No. He does his work and the students like him. She considered him a colleague, but he didn't share her enthusiasm for scholarship. Teaching was more of a means for keeping him in his kayak."

"So why the poor Dougie?"

"He's up for tenure at the end of the fall term. She didn't think he was going to get it and the university might look for someone more motivated."

"They'd cut him loose?"

"P O P. Publish or perish, my friends. The cardinal rule of academia."

"He wanted to latch onto Janice," I said.

"Like a lifeline thrown from the riverbank. Practically begged her. Janice took some of the statistical data he provided but then regretted it when he came on so desperate to be a co-author."

"Would he be a good candidate to complete her work?"

"I don't know. I'd have to know more about the nature of her conclusions. I'd be glad to review her research."

"I'm surprised she didn't tell you more."

"What can I say? Scholars are good at keeping secrets." Reynolds stood. "I really must be going. Arthur Thrash at the playhouse will be in a snit if I'm late."

"That's your rehearsal?"

"Yes. I'm helping with the revue he's producing of Sandburg's favorite songs. It's a collaboration with Connemara. I'm organizing the musical material and consulting on the authenticity of the performances. Arthur's a stickler for starting promptly."

Nakayla and I got to our feet. She handed him a business card. "Call us any time."

"Are you going to the funeral?" I asked.

"Yes," Reynolds said. "I'm flying down Saturday morning on the first flight out."

"Tell Wendy that Ida Mae is doing fine."

"You two are caring for her?"

"We're regular farmhands."

"Thank you for helping. I know Wendy's worried about that goat."

As we shook hands, I said, "I'd prefer you not mention our conversation to anyone. No reason to give the defense material to concoct some story that enables them to wiggle out of their responsibility for Janice's death."

"I understand. Count on me for anything I can do. Janice stood by me during that ordeal in Florida." His eyes filled with tears and his voice choked. "I'll be there for her and Wendy now."

Then I asked my last question, the one that had been circling in the back of my mind the whole time. "Tuesday afternoon, when Janice fell, Wendy said she was here at the college. Do you know if that's true?"

"Yes. She and I were practicing her song."

"What song?"

"She was trying out for the Sandburg revue later that afternoon."

"She told us she didn't see any professors."

Reynolds smiled. "That's because Wendy kept our meetings a secret. Nothing devious or inappropriate. I was helping her work up a number for her audition. I've taught her guitar for several years. I hoped she get in a band just for the camaraderie. But like I said, Wendy's a loner. This audition was a big step for coming out of her shell. The audition was supposed to be a surprise. She didn't want her mother to know unless she got a part. She was probably performing at East Henderson High School the same time Janice had her accident." He sighed. "The irony is Arthur Thrash emailed me his cast list Tuesday night. Wendy made the cut."

"Her number wasn't 'I'm Troubled,' was it?"

"No." Pain flashed in his face. "She sang 'Motherless Child.'"

Chapter Fourteen

"Happy now?" Nakayla eyed the large plate filled with minced pork, barbecued beans, and hush puppies the waitress set in front of me.

"Yes. And for your information, I'm not simply eating, I'm establishing rapport."

"Oh, is that the new word for stuffing your face?" Nakayla took a small bite of her Greek chicken salad, an entree I considered heretical in a barbecue restaurant.

I popped a hot hush puppy in my mouth. The sweet corn meal tasted wonderful.

We sat in a booth at Hawg Wild Bar-B-Que. The table surface and seats were constructed of smooth knotty pine. There were no cushions, no brass rails, and no ferns. Just plenty of good food. Business was brisk and we'd waited ten minutes to be seated.

"Now we're customers," I said. "Not just people showing up and bothering them with questions during their busiest time."

I waved to our waitress as she refilled the glasses of tea at the next table. She hurried over.

"What'cha need, darlin'?" Her face showed concern that I might be suffering from insufficient doses of either vinegar-based or tangy tomato-added sauce. Hawg Wild served both eastern North Carolina and western North Carolina barbecue, a raging battle of sauce styles that made the Union-Confederacy clash look like a civil debate rather than a civil war.

"Did you work lunch last Saturday?" I asked.

"Sure did." She eyed us closely. "Were you here? Did you leave something?"

She must have been in her late forties and worked as a waitress for half that time. The way she moved among the tables, showing up right when needed, told me not much got past her.

From my pocket, I pulled the university's personnel photo of Janice Wainwright that Ranger Corn had given me. "No. But this woman was here last Saturday for lunch. Do you remember her?"

The waitress studied the picture. "Did she leave something?"

"I'm afraid it's a sad story. She died a few days ago."

She shuttered. "Oh, honey, that's terrible." Then her voice fell to a whisper. "Something she ate here?"

I hadn't thought about her reaction jumping immediately to bad pork. "She fell. It was an accident."

"I'm so sorry." She examined the photo again. "She doesn't look familiar. Not one of our regulars."

"She met someone here. That person may have been a regular or even an employee. The family found the appointment on her business calendar with a follow-up scheduled for this coming Saturday. Same time, same place. There were only the initials DLM and we were hoping to get word to the person about her death." The story sounded lame but I was hoping the impact the waitress felt holding a dead woman's photograph who only days ago sat in the restaurant masked the lack of credibility.

The waitress frowned. "DLM. A man or a woman?"

"We don't know," Nakayla said. "This woman lived on the other side of Asheville and the Brevard paper might not have carried her obituary. We'd hate to have someone sitting here thinking she just didn't show up."

"Do you mind if I pass this around to the other girls?"

"We'd appreciate it," Nakayla said. "Take your time. We know you've got other customers to deal with."

The waitress left with a sweet tea pitcher in one hand and the photograph in the other. Between bites, I watched her intercept the staff whenever a quick conversation was possible.

"That was a hokey story," Nakayla said.

"I agree. Good thing I established rapport."

Five minutes later, the waitress returned with a woman at least twenty years her junior. "This here's Darlene. She waited on your friend."

The younger woman had short brown hair and wore a pink tee shirt with Hawg Wild inscribed across the front. The diamond stud in her nose showed she and our waitress were a generation apart.

"They sat right where you're sitting," Darlene whispered, as if Nakayla and I now occupied a haunted booth.

"You're sure?" Nakayla asked.

"Positive. After I'd taken their order, they asked to move to a table with chairs. The woman said the bench seat didn't give her back enough support." Darlene laid her hand on the table behind her. "So I put them here. It was still in my zone."

Any doubt that Darlene could be mistaken about Janice's identity vanished with the reference to the bad back.

"Did you know the person with her?" I asked.

"No. But I think I've seen him before. He was older and had gray hair. He carried a CD in his hand, but I couldn't see who recorded it. It must have been old too."

"Why do you say that?"

She looked amazed at the question. "Nobody buys CDs anymore, except for old people who don't have iPods."

"Did he give the woman the CD or had she given it to him?"

Darlene shook her head. "I'm pretty sure he had it when they sat down and he took it when they left."

"And the CD was store-bought?"

"What do you mean?"

"Did it have a professionally made label? He hadn't just burned stuff on a blank disk?"

"No, just a CD in a clear case with handwriting on top." She thought a moment. "Now why would he bring it in the restaurant if there wasn't anything to show her?"

Her question was the one I asked myself. I gave her an answer I hoped satisfied her curiosity. "Maybe she gave it to him at the door."

"That's so sad," Darlene said. She looked at her colleague. "I bet he's probably coming back Saturday to return it."

"What do you want us to do?" the older waitress asked.

Nakayla opened her purse and gave each woman a card. "If either of you see him, please ask him to call us. Don't tell him his friend died. We'd prefer to break the news."

"Blackman and Robertson," they said, reading in unison.

"Yes, I'm Nakayla Robertson and this is Sam Blackman."

"I'm Darlene," our waitress said. She smiled. "We have the same name. You can't never have too many Darlenes."

They left us to our lunch. As I bit into my last hush puppy, Nakayla said, "You think they have a phone book?"

"Yes. But it probably lists people by first name so they can keep the Darlenes straight."

"Don't make fun of my people."

I looked around the restaurant. There wasn't another African-American in the place. "Your people?"

"I grew up in the mountains too, and my best friend in kindergarten was Darlene Middleton."

"I sit corrected. How many Nakaylas have these mountains produced?"

"I'm one of a kind. So you'd better hold on to me."

I held out the half-eaten hush puppy. "What's mine is yours. And great idea about the phone book."

She pushed my hand away, got up, and headed for the cashier. When she returned, I'd eaten everything but the paint on the plate. She passed me a check slip. A ten-digit number and street address were written across the front.

"The price is kinda steep," I said. "I guess I should have ordered the small plate."

"That's the phone number for a Donald L. Moore, Jr. His was the only listing that matched the initials DLM. In fact, it was the only name that could be abbreviated with a DM. So, we can't be missing someone who doesn't use his middle name."

"And if Darlene number two thought she'd seen him before, maybe he's local. Good work. Let's call from the car."

Nakayla sat in the passenger seat, a notepad and pen in her lap. She started to punch the number in her cell phone, but hesitated. "What if I get voice mail, do you want to leave a contact number?"

"No. This might not be the guy. Janice and DLM could have met here for convenience, a half-way point between Asheville and Rosman or Lake Toxaway. I'd prefer not to leave cryptic messages until we know who we're dealing with."

She held the phone to her ear for a few seconds, and then flipped it closed. "Voice mail. He didn't give a name. Just repeated the number reached and said leave a message."

"What was his voice like?"

"Mature, but not the whispery, garbled sound of someone really old. I could put his street address in the GPS and we could check out the house."

I glanced at my watch. Twenty minutes after one and we had a half-hour drive to Connemara. "No, let's leave him for now. We'll call later this afternoon. Phone Ranger Hodges and see if we can meet. Can we make it by two?"

"If you follow my directions for the back-roads."

"Always, dear. Always."

◇◇◇

Ranger Carol Hodges welcomed us to her office in the park headquarters. The building was off a service road completely separate from the visitors' entrance. We'd been instructed to ignore the Authorized Vehicles Only sign, park directly in front, and ask for her upon our arrival.

"Any more information on what happened to Mrs. Wainwright?" Carol Hodges asked the question as we took seats around a small conference table.

"I don't want to pre-empt Ranger Corn's report," I said, "but the M.E. found high levels of hydrocodone in her blood. That was her prescribed painkiller."

Hodges shook her head. "Poor woman. I know she suffered. Sometimes when we were talking, she had to get up from her chair and walk around. She could never get comfortable, standing or sitting."

"The evidence points to a dizzy spell and she simply took a fatal tumble."

"Then the case is closed?" Her question begged her unspoken one. If the case is closed, why are you here?

"Probably. But Nakayla and I are working for Wendy's interests. She's pursuing her mother's lawsuit and expanding it to wrongful death. The defendants will look for any excuse or alternative theory that gets them off the hook."

"And you want to stay ahead of them."

"Exactly. Our greatest concern comes back to why Janice Wainwright hiked up Glassy Mountain."

Hodges crossed her arms over her chest. "I have no idea. As far as I know it was the first time she'd been to the top. Usually, she'd come to the barn with Wendy or talk to the volunteers at the farmhouse. We met a few times here in my office."

"Do you know what she was working on?"

"Her questions focused on the history of Connemara."

"So she wasn't so much interested in Sandburg or the research he might have conducted?"

"She was interested in Sandburg but she never asked about his research. She did ask if we found a copy of a song among his papers."

"A song?"

"Yes." Hodges leaned forward and rested her arms on the table. She seemed encouraged to have mentioned something that caught our interest. "I believe it was called, 'I'm Troubled.'"

The hair on my neck lifted. Finally, a connection appeared between the stolen songbook and Sandburg.

"Did you find it?"

"No. But that doesn't mean it doesn't exist somewhere. Have you toured the house?"

"I have," Nakayla said. "But Sam hasn't."

Hodges smiled. "Take him through this afternoon. Then he'll understand."

"How did she learn about the song?" I asked.

"From Eli Smyth."

"ES," Nakayla whispered, connecting the name to the initials in Janice's calendar.

"Who's that?" I asked.

"A great-grandson of Captain Ellison Smyth. Captain Smyth and his brother bought the farm in 1900 and named it Connemara for the beautiful region in Ireland with the same name. Captain Smyth was a confederate veteran from Charleston who became a major textile industrialist after the war."

"Was the song the reason she contacted Mr. Smyth?" I asked.

"No," Hodges said. "Mrs. Wainwright was interested in any survivors of former owners who could share facts or stories about Connemara. The Smyth family used the home for a summer place from 1900 to 1925 and then moved in permanently. They sold to the Sandburgs in 1945, so that's forty-five years of history with the same family."

"So they held it for multiple generations?"

"Actually, Captain Smyth didn't die until 1941. He worked until he was 93."

"Did Eli Smyth know the Captain?" I asked.

"He was a youngster when the Captain died. Eli is short for Ellison, so he's a namesake. Eli's been here from Charlotte for several house events, and he knows a lot of stories from the Smyth era."

I could see why Janice Wainwright would want to talk to him. "So Eli Smyth told Janice about this song?"

"Yes. Evidently Sandburg found it in the house somewhere and wanted to know its history. Mrs. Wainwright didn't say much more than that. She just wanted to know if we had it catalogued among his papers."

"And you don't?"

"No."

"Do you have a contact number for Mr. Smyth?" I asked.

"Yes," Hodges said. "I'll be glad to give it to you."

I looked at Nakayla. I'd run out of questions.

She studied her notepad a few seconds and then said, "The Smyths weren't the original owners. Did Janice Wainwright speak with any descendants of the Memmingers or Greggs?"

"Not that I know of. And they'd be much more removed from memories of the house even if she could have tracked them down."

Douglas McCaffrey had mentioned Memminger but Gregg was a new name. "Sorry. Were they both former residents?"

Ranger Hodges nodded for Nakayla to answer my question.

"You know more about the history than I do," Nakayla said.

Hodges angled her chair toward me and I wondered if I was in for a long lecture.

"C.G. Memminger built the house in 1838 and used it as a summer home until his death in 1888. He named it Rock Hill. The family would come up from Charleston to escape the summer heat and mosquitoes. Memminger was Treasurer of the Confederacy, and at one point in the war he tried to convince Jefferson Davis to make Flat Rock the capital of the Confederacy."

"Really?" I found it hard to image the small, one-stop-light village of today being the South's seat of power in the 1860s.

"Yes," Hodges said. "Memminger thought it would be difficult for the Union forces to get to. The problem was it was difficult for anybody to get to."

"Was Memminger away during the war?"

"Yes, but he still spent time here. He removed the front entrance steps, fortified the ground floor, and put in gun ports. You can still see one of them on the side of the house. Memminger was here when Lee surrendered."

"Did Union soldiers ever attack him?"

"No. And the biggest danger was from marauding deserters of both armies. For a time, the Memmingers locked their valuables in a secret room at the Woodfield Inn down the road."

"And the Greggs?"

"William Gregg, Jr. was heir to his father's cotton manufacturing mills. He and his wife used it as a summer home and made some improvements. They rebuilt the steps, added a bay window, and made some minor interior changes. Gregg died in 1895 and his wife sold Rock Hill to Captain Smyth five years later. That's when the Captain renamed it Connemara."

"And Janice Wainwright's conversation with the Captain's descendant sparked her interest in the song, 'I'm Troubled?'"

"Yes. Sandburg had been interested in folk songs since riding the rails as a hobo. In fact, we're collaborating with the Flat Rock Playhouse on a musical revue of Sandburg's favorites."

I decided not to reveal we'd already spoken with Cameron Reynolds about the project. Instead I asked, "Was Janice Wainwright involved with the production?"

"Not to any great extent that I know. She might have spoken to Arthur Thrash about what he was planning to include and the historical contexts of the selections."

"Could she have been promoting 'I'm Troubled' as one of the songs?"

Hodges looked away, considering the possibility. "I hadn't thought of that. Yes, if the song was tied to an interesting story she could have shared that with Thrash." Then her eyes narrowed. "Excuse me for asking, but what does this have to do with the lawsuit?"

"I don't know. You brought it up." Fortunately, she had.

She laughed. "I guess I did. When you asked about Mrs. Wainwright's research. How else can I help?"

"I'd like another look at the site where she fell. But in case you didn't know, I walk on a prosthesis. Would it be possible to use one of the all-terrain carts on the trail?"

"Sure. I'll drive you myself."

Ten minutes later, the three of us stood on the rock bald of Glassy Mountain. A dark spot on the gray stone marked where Janice bled from her fatal head wound. I couldn't believe that had been only two days ago. I made a slow, 360-degree pivot, trying to see the scene as Janice would have viewed it. Nothing matched the lyrics of the song. I identified no spreading chestnut towering at the edge of the bluff, not even fog creeping on little cat feet. Instead, a steady breeze flowed directly down the valley, propelling fluffy white clouds across a sky so blue the intensity hurt my eyes.

"What are you looking for?" Ranger Hodges asked.

"I don't know. Anything that could cast doubt that Janice fell because of her back problem or medication. This slope seems fine for anyone with normal balance and decent shoes."

"Yes," Hodges agreed. "Otherwise we'd fence it off."

"For the sake of argument, if someone else had been up here with Janice, is there another way they could have arrived or left without using the main path?"

"Kenmure."

"What's that?" I asked.

"An exclusive development and golf course that borders the Sandburg property. Years ago, people hiked up Glassy Mountain using a trail that didn't cross Connemara. Part of the path still exists."

I glanced at Nakayla.

"That was before my mom and I came up here." She turned to Hodges. "Can we see it?"

"Sure."

Hodges led us back along the main trail. As the path began its descent, she veered right onto a narrower one that I hadn't noticed before. About ten feet into the woods, I saw the back of a wooden sign. On the other side was written, "Entering National Park Land." Ten yards farther, the path ran beside a high wrought-iron fence with stone pillars spaced approximately fifteen feet apart. The fence formed a perimeter around a matching stone building about the size of a one-room cabin.

"What's that?" I asked.

"You mean who's that?" Hodges said. "Roger Richardson Hill. The sole occupant of his mausoleum."

I looked around the woods. The structure was the only building in sight. "Who picks up his mail?"

"I think it's safe to say any correspondence goes to the dead letter box at the post office. The story is Mr. Hill came to the mountains because of his tuberculosis. He bought land on Glassy Mountain in 1926. He didn't build a house. His brother found him living in a tent, a recluse in terrible health, waiting for the end. His brother got him to a sanatorium and finally to Texas. Mr. Hill died in 1927 and his brother carried out his wishes to be buried in a mausoleum constructed on this spot. A bank trust pays for upkeep." Ranger Hodges shook the locked gate. It clanked against the latch but stayed shut. "I guess you could say he had the first gated community on Glassy Mountain. Now he's surrounded by National Park land on one side and million dollar homes on the other."

"Must be spooky after dark," I said.

"Yeah, but at least he's a quiet neighbor." Hodges kept walking.

"So, in 1926 the Smyths would have been his full time neighbors?"

"That's right. Although I doubt there would have been any social calls between the Captain and a tubercular patient living in a tent. But, the Smyths certainly would have been aware of the mausoleum's construction. I've spoken with locals who remember their parents talking about the four horses pulling the wagon with Hill's casket up the narrow dirt road to this spot. Eli Smyth would know."

I wondered what else Eli Smyth knew. Glassy Mountain and Connemara were turning out to have a very interesting past.

"Here we are." Ranger Hodges stopped beside a knee-high sign reading, "Private Property." "This is where Kenmure begins."

I turned around. Through the trees I could see a corner of the mausoleum's fence. "We're not more than forty yards off the trail. How close is the road?"

"Not far." She stepped by the sign and Nakayla and I followed.

In less than twenty yards we saw the back of a gray house with a driveway running out to the street.

"We can't have come more than a hundred yards," I said. "The distance to Sandburg's farmhouse is nearly a mile and a half." In my mind, I saw defense attorneys claiming most of western North Carolina had easy access to the top of Glassy Mountain. Hewitt Donaldson wouldn't like this development. "Why wouldn't Janice Wainwright have driven up here?"

"Because Roger Richardson Hill doesn't have the only gated residence on Glassy Mountain. Those roads are all private, and the Kenmure guardhouse is the one way in or out. You have to be a homeowner or country club member to come through the electronic gate. Everyone else has to sign in and state the reason for the visit."

"How far is the walk in?" I asked.

"About two and a half miles."

"That makes me feel better," Nakayla said. "It reduces the chance someone would use Kenmure to head Janice off."

"I'd still like to get a look at the guard's logbook for Tuesday afternoon," I said.

"And a list of the homeowners and club members," Nakayla added. "Sounds like a job for your new best friend Ranger Corn."

Hodges laughed. "Bobby Ray would go for that. He's the kind of guy who thinks gates are meant to be opened, not closed." She turned back toward the mausoleum. "He'd subpoena the bones of Roger Richardson Hill if he thought they were with-holding information."

"I bet he would," I said. But I wasn't laughing. Right now the mausoleum's secrets might be as meaningful as anything else Nakayla and I had to go on.

Chapter Fifteen

"Did the two-thirty tour start on time?" Ranger Hodges asked the question of her colleague manning the gift shop register.

The young woman behind the counter wore a jacket identifying her as a volunteer, not a park ranger. "Yes." She looked at the wall clock. It was nearly three. "They should be on the top floor."

"I'll take these two guests through now," Hodges explained. "No need to ring them up."

We followed her into an adjoining room filled with glass-shielded floor-to-ceiling bookshelves.

"I'm surprised you have these stored in the basement," I said.

"Actually this isn't the basement since everything is above ground. What we call the main floor is actually the second. That was the primary living space." She waved her hand across the shelves. "As you'll see, these are just some of Sandburg's volumes. There are over ten thousand books and thousands of papers still here."

And Janice was looking for one song, I thought. A needle in a haystack.

Ranger Hodges led us up a flight of stairs to the main floor. We emerged in a hallway. Piles of magazines from the 1960s were stacked against the wall. A young Elizabeth Taylor graced the yellowing cover of *LIFE Magazine*.

"We've kept the house just like it was when Sandburg lived here," Hodges said. "People over sixty find they're stepping back in time to the era of their childhood."

I understood the attraction the house would have for Nakayla's mother. If my own parents were still alive, I know they would have felt the same way.

"Please stay on the tan carpet," Hodges instructed. "We're trying to preserve the original rugs. You'll notice the furniture looks like it came from a yard sale."

She led us to a front room with a baby grand piano tucked in one corner and more floor-to-ceiling bookshelves in another. A fireplace with a white wooden mantel was centered in the interior wall. I walked to the edge of the carpet runner and saw a stringless guitar lying on top of the piano.

"Was this the music room?" I asked.

"The living room, but, yes, Sandburg often played his guitar and sang for guests after dinner. His daughter Margaret played the piano. Sometimes Sandburg was joined by others who knew folk songs or the mountain tunes. They'd swap verses and compare versions."

"Did he know Alan Lomax?"

"Was he a local?"

"No. He collected folk songs and published an anthology."

Hodges shrugged. "I don't know for sure, but I bet Sandburg was aware of his work. His book's probably here somewhere."

We retraced our steps to the adjoining room. There was a desk and a table piled with papers, more floor-to-ceiling bookshelves including a ladder for reaching the upper volumes, and an old Remington typewriter on a wooden stand.

"This is the downstairs study," Hodges said. "Sandburg and his part-time secretary worked on correspondence and proofing manuscripts."

"He didn't write in this room?" Nakayla asked.

"No, he did that in his upstairs study. He often worked late into the night and early morning. His bedroom was next door so that he wouldn't disturb anyone. Mrs. Sandburg slept on this floor."

I stepped closer to one of the bookshelves and noticed slips of paper sticking out from the tops of book pages. "Why are there so many bookmarks?"

Hodges smiled. "Our curator placed those. Sandburg would mark pages with whatever was handy—paperclips, cigar wrappers, envelopes, even bits of cardboard. We were afraid they'd deteriorate over time. Why he marked the pages isn't always clear. It could be passages for research or an idea he wanted to return to. Most books have multiple marks so you can see how much he utilized his library."

If a reference to "I'm Troubled" occurred on one of the pages, then we weren't looking for a needle in a haystack. We were looking for a needle in a hayfield.

"Here's something you might find interesting." Ranger Hodges pointed to a silver plaque lying on the corner of the desk. "In 1965, Sandburg was given this award by the NAACP for his staunch advocacy of civil rights."

Nakayla and I leaned over to read the inscription which included the phrases "a major prophet of civil rights in our time," and "he has strengthened our vision as we struggle to extend the frontiers of social justice." The plaque was signed by NAACP Executive Director Roy Wilkins.

"Sandburg's wife said he looked at it every day," Hodges said. "Here was a man who won two Pulitzer Prizes, one in history and one in poetry, and kept them out of sight. This was the award that gave him the greatest satisfaction."

As I read the inscription again, I understood why Nakayla's mother found the house and farm so welcoming.

Hodges chuckled softly. "Ironic, isn't it?"

Her comment eluded me. "What?"

"C.G. Memminger must be spinning in his grave. The beloved home of a slave-owner who rose to become the Treasurer of the Confederacy now houses the plaque honoring a literary champion of equality and brotherhood with a lifetime membership in the NAACP. If there ever was a symbol of the Old South replaced by the New South, we're standing in it."

We moved through the rest of the house quickly. The only rooms in which I didn't see bookshelves were the bathrooms and the kitchen. We returned to the ground floor by a back staircase that brought us to a concrete-floored area with several large work sinks and washing machines.

"This is the kids' room," Hodges said. "You know why they call it that?"

Nakayla looked at me to guess, not because she didn't know but because she did.

"The children couldn't get in trouble? There's nothing to break?"

Both women laughed. "Kids, as in baby goats," Hodges said. "They would be brought here after birth, kept warm in the adjacent furnace room, and then bottle fed every three or four hours. The mothers kept producing milk that could be sold."

Panic rose in my chest. "Are we going to have to do that for Ida Mae?"

"No," Nakayla said. "Wendy's not going into production of goat milk. We just have to make sure the kids are okay at birth."

"Are you helping Wendy?" Hodges asked.

"While she's in Florida for her mother's funeral. Sam's getting experience as a midwife."

I said nothing. This wasn't a laughing matter.

"Don't worry," Hodges said. "Mother Nature is the best midwife. If you get in trouble, call Sarah Parker. She's the ranger in charge of the herd. She'll be happy to help." Hodges gave a final look around the room. "That's the end of the tour. We can leave by the side entrance."

She opened the door and we stepped onto the gravel driveway. "Notice the side of the house where the high foundation wall changes building materials. That's where the Sandburgs expanded the rear in 1945. They needed more room, particularly on this ground floor for the kids' room." She pointed to a vertical indentation above my head. "That's the last vestige of Memminger's gun ports he installed toward the end of the war."

The covered slot appeared just wide enough to accommodate a rifle. With the front steps removed and the gun slots manned, the house would be like a fort at the top of a hill. Tough to capture.

Hodges walked toward the all-terrain vehicle that had transported us from headquarters. "Anything else you'd like to know?"

"We'd like to get the number for Eli Smyth," Nakayla said.

"And that goat ranger," I quickly added. "Mother Nature might be a great midwife, but I want back up in case Mother Nature forgets to show."

While I drove to Asheville, Nakayla worked the phone. She first tried the number for Donald L. Moore, Jr.

"Voice mail again," she said. "If this is his home number, he might not be there till later this evening."

"Then we'll keep trying. If we haven't reached him by tomorrow morning, check the phone directories for any DLM listings in adjacent towns where Hawg Wild would have been a convenient meeting spot."

"Okay." She unfolded the slip of paper Hodges gave us with Eli Smyth's and Ranger Parker's phone numbers. "How much do you think I should tell Mr. Smyth?"

"See if you can get by with saying we're doing some research on the house when his family owned it. If he gets too inquisitive, mention Janice Wainwright's name and she suggested he could help us."

"What if he knows she's dead?"

"Then say we're following up on her research for the university. I'd prefer to do most of our questioning face to face where we can read body language."

"I agree," Nakayla said. "I've heard people speak with absolute calm while their knees literally knocked together in nervous anxiety."

"Tell him we'll meet him in Charlotte any time tomorrow."

Nakayla punched in the number, held the phone to her ear, and waited. I hoped he wasn't someone who used voice mail to screen his calls and only answered a number he recognized. Maybe that was the case with Donald L. Moore, Jr. If so, we'd either have to leave a message or drive by the house to see if someone was there.

"Hello, Mr. Smyth? My name's Nakayla Robertson. Ranger Carol Hodges suggested I call you."

Referencing the ranger was a nice touch. Hodges was the one who pointed Janice to Eli Smyth so Nakayla's story was perfectly plausible.

"I'd like to talk to you about your memories of Connemara." She listened. "No, at your convenience."

"We can do it any time," I reminded her.

She waved me to shut up. I guessed she thought she was doing all right without my help.

"No, not on the phone," she said. "It would be great if we could meet in person. I've got some old photographs of Connemara and maybe you could help us identify some of the people. Would you have any time tomorrow? My friend and I would be glad to treat you to lunch."

Nakayla's smooth handling of the call got us a meeting at 11:45 the next morning at a restaurant near South Park Mall in Charlotte.

When she hung up, I said, "I know. We'll have to allow time before or after for you to shop."

"No. Before and after."

"And where are we getting these pictures we need Eli Smyth to identify?"

"I have a book about Connemara. I remembered some of the photographs have captions saying unidentified Smyth grandchildren. That's all we need to show him. It doesn't matter whether he can identify them or not. We'll work the conversation around to the song he mentioned to Janice."

"You're pretty slick. Do you think some year you could talk us into the Super Bowl?"

We made it back to the farmhouse a little after five. Nakayla volunteered to take care of Ida Mae and the chickens while I checked in with Ranger Corn. I agreed to handle the morning chores while Nakayla used the time to go to her house and dress for her big-city shopping spree. We'd need to be on the road by eight the next day.

I sat in the old green glider on the front porch and called Corn. He was still in his office.

"What have you got?" he asked.

"Not much. I spoke with Venable and McCaffrey at the university. Venable's keeping Janice's office locked until Wendy can go through her mother's files."

"And McCaffrey?"

"He's anxious to add his name to Janice's research by angling for more credit than he deserves. He's the real reason I urged Venable to keep Janice's office secure."

"Does McCaffrey have an alibi for Tuesday afternoon?"

"I didn't ask. Maybe you should check him out. Cameron Reynolds told me Janice confided that McCaffrey was bugging her to be cited as a co-author of any paper. He needs to publish or risks being denied tenure."

"You interviewed Cameron Reynolds?" Corn asked.

"Yes. Nakayla and I went to Warren Wilson. Reynolds said Janice Wainwright had asked him about a song called, 'I'm Troubled.' A song that interested Sandburg."

"Is that why she had the book?"

"Yes, but Cameron claims he didn't know what was special about it."

"You believe him?"

"At this point I don't have any reason not to. Then Ranger Hodges at Connemara confirmed Janice asked her about the song after she spoke to Eli Smyth, a descendant of the family that owned Connemara before Sandburg. We're seeing Smyth tomorrow."

"So, where's this going regarding her death?"

"I have no idea. Right now I'm just trying to keep Hewitt Donaldson ahead of any theories the defense might concoct."

I heard Corn's chair squeak as he leaned back.

"I spoke with our esteemed surgeon," he said. "The one the M.E.'s report depicts as being unqualified to cut meat at Ingles supermarket."

"What did you think?"

"That I was talking to a sweaty, nervous weasel. Dr. Wyatt Montgomery spent most of the time lamenting how hard he works. I think he's heard from his attorneys that the autopsy turned him into toast."

"Where was he Tuesday afternoon when Janice fell?"

"Playing golf at Reems Creek near Weaverville."

"Corroboration?"

"He reserved a tee time as a single for four o'clock, but he got paired up with another member so his alibi checks out. He said he has his scorecard."

Weaverville was a small town about ten miles north of Asheville.

"Does he live up there?" I asked.

"No, he lives in Kenmure. It's a ritzy development in Flat Rock."

Six hours ago I'd never heard of Kenmure. Now the name popped up twice in connection to Janice Wainwright.

I hopped off the glider and paced across the porch's wide floorboards. "Kenmure has the nearest access point to where Janice Wainwright fell. It's much closer than climbing up from Sandburg's farmhouse."

"That's right."

Now I understood why Corn said "No comment" when I asked whether he was investigating the surgeon. "If Montgomery lives on a golf course, why'd he drive to Weaverville? That gives him an hour commute home."

"That's what I asked him. He said Kenmure has reciprocal club privileges with Reems Creek. His Tuesday afternoon opened up and he went there on a lark."

"On a lark," I repeated.

"Yeah. He said he wanted to play a different course."

"What about this other person in his twosome? Could he be involved?"

"He is a she," Corn said. "Mary Collier. She lives in the Reems Creek golf community. It's like Kenmure, although not quite as expensive. I reached her by phone and she said they played fifteen holes before it got too dark."

"Wait a minute. Montgomery drove to Weaverville knowing he wouldn't have time to complete a round?"

"Maybe. Or maybe the woman slowed him down."

"Well, if they teed off as a twosome the course couldn't have been that crowded. They could have easily played as singles."

I heard Corn take a deep breath. Then he said, "You're suggesting he used Mary Collier as an alibi?"

"I don't know. I just don't like the coincidence of Kenmure being in the picture. Wyatt Montgomery could have gotten to Glassy Mountain through their gate without any problem or record."

"And how did he know Janice Wainwright would be on Glassy Mountain?" Corn asked. "I don't like coincidences either, but Montgomery does live in Kenmure and so do many other doctors and lawyers in the area."

Corn had me there. As far as we knew, no one was aware of Janice's plans to climb the mountain. I'd only been there because I'd been following her. What if I wasn't the only one?

"So Montgomery reserves a tee time and is paired with Mary Collier. Didn't anyone see them together?"

Corn understood where I was headed. "You think our doctor followed Janice Wainwright, but covered himself in advance?"

"Or on the fly. Maybe he does more with Mary Collier than play golf."

Corn said nothing for a few seconds. Then he grunted as he reached a decision. "I'll check with the Kenmure guards to see if anyone remembers seeing Montgomery return Tuesday afternoon. And I'll get a copy of their visitor logbook."

"Good. Maybe we'll get lucky."

"Lucky," Corn repeated. "This is the damnedest case. Remember lucky means we don't find anything. The inquest rules accidental death and Montgomery and the insurance companies pay Wendy a fortune."

"I know. But it goes against my nature not to discover evidence of a crime."

Corn laughed. "I hear you. Here's hoping I get back to you with no news. I should also have the list from her cell phone carrier of incoming and outgoing calls. Let me know what you learn from Eli Smyth."

I promised to check back with him tomorrow. After I hung up, I realized I wouldn't be seeing Eli Smyth tomorrow. Nakayla could handle him on her own. I wanted a closer look at Dr. Wyatt Montgomery and his alleged golfing partner. And I needed to warn Hewitt Donaldson that I could be destroying Wendy's case in the process.

Chapter Sixteen

When Ida Mae saw me enter the barn, she backed away from the gate of her stall. I have that effect on women. The pregnant goat moved slowly, her extra weight rocking her from side to side as she retreated into the shadows.

"Please, Ida Mae. Just hold on a few more days and we'll both be happier." I scooped out her daily dose of medicated food pellets from the metal bin and poured them into her feeder.

Breakfast proved stronger than her dislike for me. As she began munching, I gently rubbed her neck. She didn't balk at my touch. Even Ida Mae knew not to bite the hand that fed her.

Nakayla had left the Wainwright farm before dawn for her day in Charlotte. I hoped she wouldn't be sleepy during the morning drive because we'd stayed up past midnight working on the case. Through an Internet search, she got the address for Dr. Wyatt Montgomery's clinic, his vehicle make and registration, and the parking lot he used at the hospital. She found his home in Kenmure and used Google Earth to download a satellite view of the distance and terrain between his house and the clearly visible rock face of Glassy Mountain. The two were less than a quarter mile apart.

As soon as I took care of Ida Mae, I planned to head for the hospital where I expected Montgomery would be either performing surgery, making rounds, or both. I envisioned catching him off guard, maybe in the parking lot, and challenging his convenient golf game the afternoon Janice died.

"But first I'll check with Hewitt," I told Ida Mae. "Never blindside your lawyer."

The goat looked up from her feed and bobbed her head.

"You're a rare breed. A woman who agrees with me." I placed my palm between her eyes. "Just as I thought. One-hundred-two degrees."

She followed me out into the surrounding pasture and watched me fill her water trough from the hose. Then she stayed beside me as I walked to the gate. I checked that the transformer was properly electrifying the fence so that Ida Mae would be protected from predators while I was gone.

"All right. You're in charge. Just stay pregnant."

She bleated a goodbye.

◇◇◇

Wyatt Montgomery drove a red Porsche 911 Carrera. I easily spotted it in the restricted lot at Mission Hospital and was surprised that the car wasn't a convertible. Either Montgomery didn't want his patients to think he was making an obscene amount of money slicing them up, or he had the convertible model hidden at home.

Mission was a mammoth complex of buildings on a hill just south of downtown Asheville. The campus and surrounding streets seemed to be in a perpetual state of construction. I pulled over next to a barricade set up to keep vehicles from driving onto a road that was being demolished, probably to make room for either a new building or parking deck. I had a clear view of the physicians' lot about a hundred feet below.

I turned on my flashers, lifted the hood of the CR-V, and became just another poor guy whose car had died on him. The workers on the other side of the barricade ignored me. Leaning against the fender, I kept my ear against my cell phone like I was calling for help and my eyes on the hospital exit nearest the surgeon's red toy.

It was seven-thirty. I suspected Montgomery might not be operating on a Friday morning, preferring to avoid Saturdays and Sundays as the first days of recovery for his patients. If he were simply making rounds, then he could soon be heading to the clinic. I phoned Hewitt.

"Something better be up," he said groggily, "because I'm not."

"I'm calling for advice."

Silence.

"Hewitt?"

"I keep pinching myself but I'm still dreaming."

"I'm about to question Wyatt Montgomery."

Bedsprings groaned. Hewitt must have sat up. "Why the hell do you want to do that?"

I gave him a condensed version of the key events from the previous day: Cammie Reynolds' mention of the song "I'm Troubled;" Ranger Hodges' confirmation that Janice had learned about the song from a descendant of Captain Ellison Smyth, the owner of Connemara prior to Sandburg; the shortcut to Glassy Mountain through the exclusive Kenmure community; and Dr. Montgomery's Kenmure address and the seemingly spontaneous round of golf an hour away from his home course.

"What do you hope to accomplish?"

"Rattle him a little. See how he reacts. You told me something that might fuel his fear."

"This is a double shock. You want my advice and I've already said something useful. What did I say and why didn't I bill you for it?"

"You told me when a case is going badly for the defendants, they often turn on each other. If I understand things correctly, the pharmaceutical company you've named in the lawsuit is not just a co-defendant but the deepest pockets."

"That's true," Hewitt said.

"And if a proximate cause can be determined that makes their product less likely to have played a role—"

"They'd happily provide the drugs for Wyatt Montgomery's lethal injection," Hewitt interrupted. "I see where you're going. If a case can be made that Montgomery confronted Janice Wainwright in such a way that she fell, regardless of whether he may have actually pushed her or simply startled her, then the other defendants will be home free. We couldn't include them if we dropped wrongful death and returned to pain and suffering because the hydrocodone was relieving her pain and suffering."

A jackhammer started breaking concrete behind me. I stuck my finger in my open ear and shouted. "I thought I'd say I'd been hired to investigate the cause of Janice Wainwright's death for another party to the lawsuit. I'll only confirm it's not his defense team. I'll say I've seen he lives a quarter mile from the scene of the alleged accident and I'm very interested in talking to anyone who's providing him an alibi."

"What do you think he'll do?"

"I don't know. That's the point."

I got back in the car and closed the door, only slightly muffling the staccato booms of the road demolition.

Hewitt cleared his throat. "I think he'll evade your questions, go straight to his defense team, and they'll check it out with their counterparts. When the other legal teams deny it, Montgomery will know you're playing games."

"Can I give you some advice?" I said.

"Sure."

"Don't ever trust another lawyer."

Hewitt laughed so loudly he drowned out the jackhammer. "Yeah. I forgot. His lawyers won't trust the insurer's or pharmaceutical company's lawyers, and after they deny it, those lawyers will think maybe they should hire an investigator to go after Montgomery, especially given his botched surgery."

"Exactly."

"Which is exactly why it's a bad idea, Sam. You don't think deviously enough to be an attorney. I'm hoping the report from the M.E. and Dr. Tom Buter on the expert witness list will push an out-of-court settlement. I've alerted Louis Kirkland to expect an offer and that Wendy and her aunt should consider it."

"I thought you wanted to nail them for everything you could get?"

"I do. But you're doing too good a job. This song thing, the stolen books, Janice's unbelievable hike up the mountain, those are all unexplainable elements that could blow the case up in our faces. Right now, we've kept some of those factors quiet, but putting Montgomery on notice he's your chief suspect runs the risk of making him everyone's chief suspect."

"I should just drop it? That goes against my instincts."

"Your instincts are spot on. His alibi is fishy. So use your investigation ploy on the woman. See how she reacts. If she seems completely innocent, then I'm confident your charm will set her mind at ease. If she conspired with him, then I doubt she'll want Montgomery telling anyone about your visit because she'll have something to hide."

Hewitt raised good points. I could see why he earned the big bucks. A blur of red went by my window.

"Okay," I conceded. "But not because you told me so."

"Yeah, I know, you came to that conclusion before you called. You just wanted to wake me up."

"No. While I was so engrossed by your wisdom, Wyatt Montgomery got in his Porsche and drove away."

Rather than chase Montgomery, I decided to head directly to Reems Creek and scout Mary Collier's home. If I was lucky, I might catch her before she left for work. If I missed her, I'd drop by the golf club and see if anyone could give me information in addition to what Ranger Corn had learned. Sometimes people will tell the police more than they tell me, but often they'll confide their suspicions and gossip if they believe I'm not using it in some official report and if I promise to keep them an anonymous source.

Morning traffic was light and I zipped through Asheville and onto the northbound expressway without any delay. I exited near Weaverville and stopped in the parking lot of a CVS drugstore to program Mary Collier's address into my GPS.

A few miles farther, the road became a two-lane blacktop cutting through a valley of small farms, not unlike the landscape of Warren Wilson College. Then larger, newer homes began to appear along the upper ridges. The emotionless female voice of my electronic navigator warned me a left turn was approaching. I followed her explicit instructions until I was driving parallel to a narrow fairway curving against the base of the mountain. Homes were sprinkled in the forest above it.

"Your destination is approaching on the left," said my computerized comrade. I saw a sign for Highland Pointe, A Reems Creek Golf Community. Unlike Kenmure, there was no gate. Nicely designed condominiums lined either side of the street. The good news was the addresses were well marked at the curb. The better news was that Mary Collier's address was blocked. By a red Porsche.

I parked along the street a few driveways down and grabbed my camera from the back seat. The drapes were drawn on Mary Collier's windows which meant if I couldn't see in, they couldn't see out. I took several photos of Montgomery's Porsche with the condo in the background. He couldn't have arrived more than a few minutes ahead of me because metal clicks still sounded as the rear engine cooled off.

With the camera around my neck, I rang the front door bell. After a few minutes without a response, I rang again. I knew they hadn't left in her car because the Porsche blocked any exit from the garage. Finally I pounded on the door so hard the adjacent windows rattled.

"I'm coming," a woman yelled sharply from the other side.

She flung open the door and I snapped her picture.

"Hi, Mary. Did Wyatt come to finish playing your holes?" I took another picture.

She wore a red bathrobe a shade darker than the blood rushing to her cheeks. A pretty woman in her late twenties with curly, black ringlets, she stood paralyzed by conflicting emotions of anger and fear. I admit I was uncouth, but I suspected she collaborated with the man who had either directly or indirectly caused Janice Wainwright's death. Hewitt Donaldson's advice to avoid Montgomery was swallowed by my own anger.

"I need to speak to him now or I'll speak to Ranger Bobby Ray Corn instead. He'll be really pissed that you misrepresented your relationship with Dr. Montgomery. So pissed that his obstruction of justice charge will be pushing for jail time. You've crossed the feds, baby, not some local boy you can bat your eyelashes at and say you didn't understand."

She took an unsteady step backwards. I took that as an invitation to come in.

"Wyatt," she screamed. "Get out here."

Her histrionics took me by surprise. I didn't realize I played the tough guy so well. Her meltdown made me wonder what sort of woman I was dealing with. She had the emotional reaction of a ten-year-old. I never liked men who categorized women, but I couldn't get the word "bimbo" out of my head.

"Wyatt!"

The doctor came running into the living room, his shirt tail streaming like a flag behind him. I'd not seen him before, as we'd been hired to follow Janice and had nothing to do with the man whose ass we'd been trying to save. That ass was very low to the ground because Wyatt Montgomery couldn't have been more than two or three inches over five feet in height. And he had to be pushing fifty.

"Who the hell are you?" he demanded.

I flipped open my wallet. "Sam Blackman. Private investigator. I'm working for a party attached to the Wainwright lawsuit."

"Which party."

"Not your defense team. Someone else's team." I indulged myself in my most obnoxious smirk. "You understand proximate cause, don't you?"

He did. Where Mary's face had erupted red his turned chalk white.

Mary Collier stepped closer to him. "What's he talking about?"

"I'm telling an old joke," I said. "Before your time. Say, you and he were being chased across the fairway by a bear. Wyatt doesn't have to outrun it, he just has to outrun you. Now the bear is a big bad lawsuit that's going to turn your boyfriend into a pauper. And rightfully so since it appears his picture is now in the dictionary beside incompetent. Other people are making sure they can outrun him. Even his Porsche won't be fast enough to help him."

She turned on him. "What's going to happen to me? What's going to happen to this place?"

"Shut up," he snapped.

"Nice set up," I said. "Not a gated community. You come and go as you please. Tell people you're taking advantage of the reciprocal golf arrangement and keep your little mistress and your Viagra tucked away for whenever you need them."

"This has nothing to do with the lawsuit," he protested.

"Maybe not. But you two gave Ranger Corn a phony alibi for when Janice Wainwright fell to her death a quarter mile from your house, and you had the gate pass to get you in Kenmure unnoticed. Sounds like it has a lot to do with the lawsuit."

"I was here," Montgomery insisted. "We played golf."

"Fifteen holes?"

"Yes. It got dark and we quit."

"Why the charade of being paired up by chance?" I asked.

Montgomery ran his hands through his thinning brown hair. "Mary has a membership here, I have the reciprocal privileges. We don't draw attention to ourselves as a couple, but occasionally we like to play a round."

"As opposed to playing around."

"Look, smart ass. Do you want answers or do you just want to entertain yourself?"

"I think your playing around has affected your surgery. I'm calling it as I see it. Did you hurry through Janice Wainwright's operation to get to your little love nest?"

Montgomery puffed out his chest. "Her operation was complicated. The same outcome could have happened to any top-ranked surgeon."

I raised the camera to my eye and shot a photograph of the two of them together. "So Mary wasn't in the picture last fall when Janice Wainwright went under your knife?"

He said nothing.

"And the club records won't show you having a morning tee time that day, or that Mary lived here?"

He said nothing.

"Well, I think I've got enough to take to Ranger Corn, and my client will be very happy."

He swallowed hard. "You've got to believe me. I had nothing to do with that woman's death. I was here playing golf, but I wasn't going to tell some cop more than I needed. I have a wife and two kids."

Mary Collier's jaw muscles tensed at the mention of Montgomery's family. I wondered what she'd been told. "My wife doesn't understand me? As soon as I get through this lawsuit, I'll divorce her?"

I turned to his trophy-bride-in-training. "So, when Ranger Corn comes back are you going to claim you and Prince Charming just happened to be paired together last Tuesday? Are you continuing this deception at the risk of going to prison?"

"No." She looked to Montgomery. "It's time she knew, Wyatt. I'm not lying any more."

He stiffened. I let my camera dangle from the strap around my neck so that both my hands were free. If Montgomery was a cold-blooded killer, now would be the time he made his move.

His shoulders slumped and he sighed. "Okay. Tell them whatever."

Mary Collier pulled her robe tighter around her. "Wyatt helped me buy this place last summer. We met at a conference earlier in the spring. I work freelance in hospitality. You know, registering convention guests, preparing packets. I have contacts at all the hotels."

I glanced around the room for the first time. The furnishings were pricey, more than what a part-time convention hostess could afford. Dr. Montgomery had made quite an investment in his sex life.

"Wyatt's wife doesn't understand him," she said. "He's under a lot of pressure. Life and death cases every day."

He's under a lot of pressure all right. A family to support and two expensive hobbies—fast cars and fast women. "And last Tuesday?" I prompted.

"We played golf," Mary said. "The only lie was saying we hadn't known each other." She smiled broadly. "But now it doesn't matter. The whole world can know we're in love." She clutched his arm, towering a head taller above her sugar daddy.

Wyatt Montgomery looked close to throwing up.

"Is that your story?" I asked him. "You admit to being here in this condo with her?"

"Yes," he whispered. "It's the truth. I wasn't near Glassy Mountain. Lots of people live in Kenmure and go through those automatic gates every day. Homeowners, renters, country club members. They all bypass the guardhouse."

"And the reciprocal privileges?"

He shrugged. "There are restrictions on how often you can play the other courses. But if you show your home club membership card, you're waved through the gate without signing in."

My gut told me Montgomery was what he appeared, an egotistical, self-absorbed little man compensating for his insecurities with an eighty-thousand-dollar car and a woman half his age.

I thought about Paul Wainwright, another golfer cheating on his wife and wondered if his country club in Florida was part of the reciprocal network.

"All right." I turned to leave.

"All right what?" Montgomery called after me. "What are you going to do?"

I stopped at the door. "Nothing. I don't think any of your co-defendants should be let off the hook. Wendy Wainwright deserves every nickel she can get."

"But what about your client? Determining proximate cause?"

I looked at Mary Collier. "I have no idea what he's talking about."

Chapter Seventeen

I wasn't sure what Wyatt Montgomery would do next, but I had a pretty good idea it would be nothing. I believed his story about the Tuesday golf game because committing a murder and using your secret mistress as an alibi seemed like a really dumb plan. Now I had photos of them together and a suspicion that, on the day of Janice's surgery, Montgomery sped away to Mary Collier for his post-op recovery, leaving his patient damaged in the process. If Mary Collier and his love nest came to light, Montgomery knew his insurer and the pharmaceutical company would throw him under the bus and then repeatedly back over him.

Mary Collier had lied to Ranger Corn about the relationship and panicked at the prospect of jail time. Once her initial fear wore off, she'd realize her lie was leverage to hold over Montgomery's head. She'd be pushing him to ditch his wife and kids or she'd tell the truth. I smiled. Whatever happened, Montgomery was in for a rough ride.

I was the wild card. Neither of them could be certain what I'd do, but Montgomery would hope my parting comment indicated I was working for Wendy and would say nothing. He probably suspected I wanted the big money to stay on the hook and making him sole proximate cause created an escape route for his co-defendants as wide as the interstate. Montgomery might be a sloppy surgeon, but he wasn't stupid.

I ran all this by Hewitt Donaldson as I drove back to Asheville.

"Well, since you ignored my advice about confronting Montgomery, why should I bother with an opinion?"

"It helps me determine what not to do?

He laughed. "Given the circumstances you encountered, I admit you played it well. The girlfriend shifts the whole dynamic."

"So you agree they'll keep my visit to themselves?"

"Absolutely. But I'll provide a little encouragement."

"What do you mean?"

"I'll draft a letter to Montgomery stating that as legal counsel to Blackman and Robertson I'm notifying him that you have made discoveries in the normal course of an investigation that might prove embarrassing to him if they were made public. Since at present there appears to be no reason to make these discoveries known, you are planning to keep them from any public disclosure. You are doing this at your own discretion and neither expect nor will accept consideration or remuneration of any kind."

"You're making sure no one can interpret that I'm blackmailing Montgomery."

"Correct. But, I'll say, and I'll word this more carefully, should circumstances of the investigation or pending trial change, such as the attempted character assassination of Janice Wainwright or Wendy Wainwright, then we will have no recourse but to refute such allegations with evidence as to the character of any and all parties involved in such allegations."

"Like what allegations?"

"Like whatever," Hewitt said. "I'll leave that vague, but it could be claiming Janice had addictions to alcohol or other drugs. The lawyers may want Montgomery to say he warned her against excessive doses of hydrocodone and that she used bad judgment in not following his instructions. Our goal is to get him to think twice about opening his mouth to anyone—his attorneys, the court, the press. Your presence in the courtroom, should it come to that, will also be an unpleasant reminder of what you know."

"Okay," I agreed. "So I can check him off the suspect list."

"Unless he hired someone."

"That still means he had to know Janice was going to be on Glassy Mountain."

Hewitt stayed silent for a few seconds, considering my point. "And there's nothing," he finally asked, "nothing to indicate, either on her calendar or in her cell phone calls, that she called anyone who could have met her there?"

"Not that we've found so far. Corn told me he should have her phone records today."

"Will he share them with you?"

"Maybe." I took the exit for I-240 East, making the snap decision to see Corn in person. "I'm going to give him a tip, if he hasn't thought of it already?"

"What's that?"

"Check out reciprocal golf privileges between Kenmure and Paul Wainwright's Gainesville club."

"That's a real long shot."

"Tell me something about this case that isn't."

◇◇◇

"Here's another example of the eighty-twenty rule," Ranger Corn said.

We sat in his office where he had spread two sheets of computer printouts on his desk.

"What's that?" I asked.

"Eighty-twenty? It's a ratio. If you're a church, eighty percent of your donations come from twenty percent of your members. If you're a salesman, then eighty percent of your sales come from twenty percent of your customers. With Janice Wainwright, eighty percent of her calls involved twenty percent of the numbers listed."

"Going back how far?"

Corn flipped the pages around so I could see them. "The last thirty days. Most are to Wendy's cell. Then university colleagues, her sister, a few to her ex-husband, and an assortment of other people, but no one leaps out as unusual."

"What about those made or received within the last week?"

"There weren't that many. She and her daughter spoke at least four times a day. Two calls went to Paul Wainwright."

"When?"

"Last Friday."

"Exactly a week ago. He told Hewitt Donaldson and me he hadn't talked to her in the past two weeks."

"One was only a minute so she might not have reached him. The other lasted ten. None since he's been in North Carolina."

"And that golf tournament has been scheduled for months." I decided to mention the reciprocal playing possibility without admitting I'd seen Montgomery. "He might have access to Kenmure through the privileges of his Florida club."

Corn mulled that prospect for a moment. "I'll check their procedures. Maybe all Wainwright had to do was show his club ID card. But he's still got his Goldsboro airport alibi."

"You checked on the cash receipt for the fuel?"

Corn nodded. "Yeah. They remember him peeling his payment from a wad of fifties."

"You get a time?"

"The guy said it was in the morning. Between nine and ten."

I eased back in the chair. "Early. He must have filled up right after landing. Say his side dish picks him up at ten. They hit a motel or maybe her house. Take a break for lunch. He's in the air by two and here by four. He has a confrontation with Janice. Maybe she'd wanted to show him something on the mountain. Then if he's instrument rated, he flies back to Pinehurst after dark and uses a credit card to refuel or pays cash if the extra gas use would draw attention."

Corn wrote a few words on a legal pad. "We'll make inquiries at those airports. Not all of them keep the kind of records they should."

"What about McCaffrey? Where was he when Janice died?"

"We checked his class schedule. He doesn't teach Tuesdays. I spoke to him under the guise of asking if he saw Janice Tuesday.

I said I was trying to learn how she was feeling when she left the office. He claimed to be kayaking on the French Broad alone."

"He's a kayaker. No reason to doubt him." I picked up the printouts and scanned the previous week's calls. One number looked familiar. Someone had written the name Moore beside it. "This call to Moore lasted fifteen minutes."

"That's the Brevard call?"

"Yes. We found the same number while tracking the initials DLM Janice had scheduled on her calendar for last Saturday."

"Damn. I didn't make the connection. I was told the number was for Don Moore and he'd been a long time Brevard resident. When was the call?"

"Friday. He and Janice met the next day at Hawg Wild Bar-B-Que. Nakayla and I checked it out and the waitress said he had a CD at the table. One that someone had burned. We don't know whether it was pictures, music, or just document files."

"We tried his phone number and no one answered."

"Same here. Can you have someone do a quiet background check? We'll keep trying to reach him."

"Okay. Have you got any other leads?"

"Not really. I believe we're headed to the conclusion that Janice stumbled and fell."

"That's what we want, isn't it?"

"Yes. And if Eli Smyth turns out to be nothing more than a research source and Donald L Moore is only a friend, then barring some unlikely revelation about Paul Wainwright or Wyatt Montgomery, we should have exhausted the alternative possibilities and given Wendy's lawyers a slam-dunk legal case."

Corn smiled. "You're too experienced to use slam-dunk and legal case in the same sentence."

I stood and handed him the phone records. "Yeah. What was I thinking?"

"Keep digging," Corn advised. "There are still too many unexplained oddities to suit me."

"This song 'I'm Troubled' has got me troubled. I'm going to talk to the director of the Sandburg revue at The Flat Rock

Playhouse. Maybe he can shed some light on Janice's obsession with the song."

"Well, keep me posted. And if something more solid develops, I'll be all over it and to hell with the budget."

◇◇◇

A placard at the entrance to the parking lot read "No Matinee Today." A few cars were clustered close to the main house, but at ten on a Friday morning, The Flat Rock Playhouse looked as deserted as it had the previous Tuesday afternoon when I found Janice Wainwright's Explorer in a space at the far end.

I parked and retraced my steps around the side of the theatre. Rick Torrence, future Broadway star, stood shirtless with the paint roller in his hand. His weapon was coated in black this time and he covered with broad swaths the white surface of what appeared to be the first of multiple flats stacked against the sawhorse.

"Creating a new set?" I asked.

He turned to face me and his eyes widened with recognition and maybe a trace of fear. "That woman you were looking for. She was Mrs. Wainwright? The woman who died up on Glassy?"

"She was. And I found her. But she didn't die on the mountain."

"Any idea what happened?"

"The police think she fell."

He nodded, and then hesitated a second before asking, "What do you think?"

I shrugged. "I think what I think doesn't matter."

"I guess not. Dead is dead. That's tough. She seemed like a nice woman." He bit his lower lip and looked away.

Was this Rick Torrence, actor, displaying contrived sorrow for someone he thought might have been my friend, or Rick Torrence, distraught young man, who had his own connection to Janice Wainwright? The unidentified initials RT on her calendar jumped into my mind.

"Did you know her?" I asked.

"Hey, man, I just saw her around here once in a while."

"Did you know she was here Tuesday?"

"No. Like I told you then, I hadn't seen anybody. I was paint-ing these flats, just like I'm repainting them now." He looked at the roller in his hand. "And I've gotta get back to work."

I stepped between him and the sawhorse. "When she came here, was it to buy tickets or to see someone?"

Rick Torrence looked beyond me to the office. "I guess she got tickets. And she would talk to Artie if she talked to anyone."

"Arthur Thrash, the man who was with you on Tuesday?"

"Yes. He's directing the Sandburg music program and evi-dently she was a Sandburg nut."

"So, she was talking to Thrash about songs?"

"I guess."

"Are you involved in that show?"

He raised the roller. "This is my involvement. Like Artie said, I can't sing. So, I paint the flats. First, white, and now he wants black swaths cut across them for dramatic effect. I wish he'd make up his mind."

Something didn't ring true about Torrence's quick disclaimer that he hardly knew Janice or her interest in the playhouse. Then I remembered the Wainwright connection involved both Janice and Wendy. Wendy was cute, closer to his age, and, as Cameron Reynolds said, discovering her sexuality.

"How well did you know Wendy Wainwright? I hope enough to understand she's only seventeen."

Rick Torrence reddened, a physical reaction that stretched even an Academy-Award-winning actor's ability to fake. "All we did was talk. She was interested in being in the Sandburg revue, and I gave her some pointers for her audition."

"What did Mrs. Wainwright think about the attention you were paying her daughter?"

"She didn't think anything about it because nothing happened."

"She never met with you about Wendy or anything else?"

"No. For one thing, Wendy didn't want her mother to know she was auditioning. That was going to be a surprise."

His answer matched what Cameron Reynolds had said.

"Your advice must have done the trick."

"What do you mean?"

"I understand she made the cast."

"Really?" He grinned, and then the grin turned to a grimace. "Man, the audition was the same time her mother fell on the rock. Can you believe it?"

I stepped away to let him return to his painting. "Yeah, a real tragedy. Especially since she was so close to finishing some important work."

Torrence dipped the roller in the paint pan. If Janice's work meant anything to him, he didn't show it. "What's Wendy going to do?" he asked.

"She hopes to go to school at Warren Wilson like she'd planned."

He squeezed the excess paint off the roller and then began a looping stroke over the center of the white flat.

"But that might be up in the air," I added. "I think her mother was counting on her current project to provide a financial boost to her college fund."

There was a barely perceptible halt in the smooth motion of the roller. "What about her dad?" Torrence asked.

"You know. He'll probably try to weasel out of any obligation."

"Yeah," he grunted and kept painting.

Wendy and he must have talked enough that Torrence was aware of her family situation. At least more than a casual conversation. I decided pressing him for more information at this time would only make him suspicious.

"Well, I'll let you work in peace. You say Mrs. Wainwright usually spoke with Thrash when she came here?"

He straightened and wiped his brow with his forearm. "Yes. Artie should be here shortly. He only lives down the road."

"Does he have an office? I thought I'd let him know we're uncertain about whether Wendy will be able to be in the show."

He pointed with the roller to the main house. "He's working out of a room off the ticket windows. That's the way he'll come in, unless he's got an appointment elsewhere. He works his own hours and God knows they're more erratic than ever."

"What's he been doing?"

"Brooding. Ever since Mrs. Wainwright died he's been in a black funk."

"Were they close?"

"I could tell he liked her, but everybody felt bad about it. He doesn't have to take it out on me. He'll probably make me paint these flats again. Claim the black's not the right shade." Torrence thrust the roller across the top of the flat.

"My grandfather's favorite saying was, 'Don't worry that the mule's blind, just load the wagon.'"

Torrence had to laugh. "Except in this case, Artie's the blind mule who can't see what a pain in the ass he's turning into. I'll give him a message if you like."

"Thanks. I can hang here for a while." I walked away. "If I don't see him, I'll let you know."

I waited on the sidewalk to the right of the box office behind a white board fence that shielded the first-floor windows of the house from the parking lot. After ten minutes, I'd read the season schedule so many times I could recite by heart the performance dates and the promotional blurbs for each upcoming play. I was on the verge of heading back to my office to work the phone and Internet when I heard someone humming. The sound grew louder and I recognized the mournful tune as "Black is the Color of my True Love's Hair."

I stepped around the fence squarely in the path of Arthur Thrash. He stared down at the ground, his straw fedora clutched at his side. His brown hair lay close to his head in tight, damp curls like he'd just come from the shower. He wore a white linen shirt hanging over designer jeans, and just in case someone might think he was a plumber rather than an artistic director, he had a powder-blue silk scarf knotted around his neck.

"Mr. Thrash."

He froze, the tune abruptly severed.

"I'm Sam Blackman. We spoke the other afternoon when I was looking for Janice Wainwright."

"I didn't realize she was here." He slapped the hat against his thigh. "You never said her name."

"That's right. I didn't."

He shook his head with dismay. "If I'd known I would have helped you find her. Maybe we could have prevented her from making that climb. She had no business going up Glassy in her condition."

"I agree. That's why I want to talk with you."

He looked at me warily. "Were you going to help her up the mountain?"

"No. We were just going to meet. We had some things to discuss regarding her lawsuit."

He relaxed. "Well, I don't know how I can help, but I have a little time now." He stepped around me and walked away from the ticket office. "There's a picnic table over on the rock that gets the morning sun. We can talk there."

I slid onto the cool metal bench across from him.

Thrash set his fedora upside down on the white table. "You were helping her with her lawsuit?"

"That's how our paths originally crossed. Then I got interested in her last project." I decided not to lie to Thrash but to let him draw his own conclusions from my incomplete statements.

"Are you a historian?"

"Actually I'm a detective. But I guess there are a lot of similarities between the two."

His eyebrows arced in surprise. "So, she was bringing in outside help."

"You know how time consuming the lawsuit became, and then her physical condition limited her energy. At least I thought it did."

He leaned closer across the table. "Any idea why she went up there?"

I threw up my hands. "Oh, a few theories, but nothing that I claim to be the truth."

"Like what?"

I leaned back and pressed my palms face down like I was getting ready to rise. "Nothing I've worked out enough to share. Don't get me wrong, I'm not trying to be mysterious, but Janice was secretive and I don't want to violate any confidence."

"I know. The same with me."

I settled down again. "Well, maybe we could reinforce each other's information. How did you meet her?"

"Cameron Reynolds. He's a professor at Warren Wilson College. He's advising me on the Sandburg musical revue I'm directing. He and Janice Wainwright had worked together on Civil War songs and he suggested I have her assist with program notes."

"I know Cammie. They'd both be a good resource."

Thrash nodded. "That's what I thought. And it never hurts to have those Ph.D. credentials attached to the production. The grant foundations and park service eat that stuff up." He unconsciously straightened the knot in his scarf. "I have an M.F.A. from Yale but that and five bucks will get me a latte at Starbucks."

"Is that how Wendy got interested in performing?"

Thrash cocked his head and studied me. "You're on top of things. That was supposed to be a secret. Did Wendy tell you about her audition?"

"Cammie did. He said you selected her."

"I did." He crossed his arms across his chest. "I probably shouldn't have because there were others who were more polished in their technique. And her audition wasn't that strong so you shouldn't bring it up with her. But folk songs weren't sung by trained vocalists and she has good pitch and a good ear. She also doesn't have the nasal twang so many of the locals infuse in their performance, as if we were at the Grand Ol' Opry instead of the state theatre of North Carolina."

"You were kind to give her the part."

He shrugged. "Thanks. I did it as much for Janice. I was going to invite her to the first rehearsal and surprise her when Wendy came on stage."

I glanced beyond Thrash to where I could see Torrence painting the flats. "Leonardo Da Vinci over there says he gave Wendy some pointers."

Thrash rolled his eyes. "That's not all he'd like to give her. I told him in no uncertain terms she's underage and off limits."

"What did Janice think?"

"I'm not sure she knew. At first the girl came to see the goats at the Sandburg barn. I guess she met Rick when Janice and I started talking about the musical and Wendy waited around for her."

"And Janice and Rick never had a confrontation?"

"Oh, Lord, no. Rick would have told me right away. He'd be afraid Janice would mention it. Do you have reason to think otherwise?"

"Not really. Rick mentioned Wendy's name and I thought he was a little fast for the kind of guy Janice would want her daughter dating." I decided not to mention the letters RT on Janice's calendar until I had a chance to talk to Wendy.

Thrash looked down at his gold wristwatch. "Anything else?"

"Why was Janice interested in the song, 'I'm Troubled?'"

Thrash snapped his head up, clearly surprised. "She told you about that?"

"It's why I got involved."

"Then I wish I could help you. I wish I could have helped her. She just told me Sandburg had been very interested in it. I'd never heard of the song. It wasn't on the list we were considering for the show."

"You ever hear of Alan Lomax?"

"Yes. He collected songs like Sandburg. I've got his book as a reference."

"'I'm Troubled' is in it."

"Damn." Thrash shook his head. "Now I feel bad that I didn't take Janice's inquiries more seriously. I could have at least lent her my copy."

"I doubt it would have made a difference."

"That makes me feel better." Again, he leaned across the table. "So, between us, what's your theory? Why was she up on Glassy Mountain?"

"Because she had to be." I got up from the bench. "Carl Sandburg and that song gave her no other choice."

Chapter Eighteen

I fed Ida Mae and got her in her stall, counted the chickens, and checked that the transformer was electrifying the fence. Just another glamorous Friday night in the life of a detective. As I headed toward the backdoor of the Wainwright farmhouse, I heard a car pull into the front yard.

Nakayla met me in the kitchen. She held a large takeout box from Barley's Taproom and Pizzeria. "Date night," she said. "There's a jug of Green Man porter in the car."

Local pizza and local beer. The perfect start to the weekend.

Nakayla had called from the road to say she had a good meeting with Eli Smyth and would fill me in when she got here. I had my encounter with Wyatt Montgomery to share, plus the conversations with Ranger Corn, Rick Torrence, and Arthur Thrash. Then I hoped to set the case aside until Wendy returned from her mother's funeral on Monday. A few hours of kayaking on the French Broad tomorrow would be a welcomed break.

We sat at the Formica-top table in the kitchen. I poured two glasses of beer while Nakayla slid pizza slices onto our plates.

"All vegetables," she said. "You've had enough barbecued meat to choke a lion."

I tipped my glass to her. "Okay by me. Beer makes anything taste good. Now, skip the shopping report and tell me about Eli Smyth."

"You first. You'll talk with your mouth full anyway."

I ran through the course of events, highlighting that Montgomery's affair probably dated back to Janice's initial operation and that Hewitt suggested intimidating him into keeping my visit from his lawyers. I went over my conversation with Ranger Corn and that the number for DLM appeared on Janice's phone records from last Friday.

"I tried the number several times today," she said. "I only got voice mail."

"Corn's doing a background check. Maybe he'll find a work number for Moore."

"Too bad Investigative Alliance didn't bring us in earlier. Then we would have tailed her to Hawg Wild and seen him."

"Better yet, I could have sat at the next booth, had lunch, and overheard their conversation."

Nakayla put another slice of pizza on my plate. "Here. Eat your vegetables."

I poured a second glass of beer and summarized my conversations with Rick Torrence and Arthur Thrash. When I finished, I asked, "What do you think?" and then waited for Nakayla's reply. I knew her well enough not to push for a response because, unlike me, she would think thoroughly before expressing her opinion.

After a few minutes of silence, Nakayla said, "RT appeared a few times on her calendar during the past few months, right?"

"Correct. And if RT is Rick Torrence, why the multiple meetings?"

"Why indeed?" she agreed. "And the last one was Sunday afternoon. Wendy said her mother kept two calendars. The one from home has disappeared. We can't assume they were exact duplicates."

"You mean there might have been more on the home calendar?"

"I mean there might have been less. That's the one Wendy would have seen."

"Why would Janice have left off RT?" Then the light bulb went off. "Oh, maybe she was tracking when Wendy met Rick Torrence."

"Unlikely. Why keep that a secret? She would have confronted Wendy."

The voltage in my light bulb increased. "Oh, you think Janice was meeting Rick Torrence? Our historian was a cougar?"

"She had the same opportunity to meet Rick that Wendy did. She's an attractive woman. Her closest male friend is gay. Is Rick the kind of guy who would get an extra kick from nailing a mother and a daughter?"

"Geez, Nakayla. I never figured you for one to think the worst of people."

"It comes from hanging around you. What if Wendy found out her mother was involved with the guy she had a crush on? Wendy may have confronted Janice and not the other way around."

"On top of Glassy Mountain?"

"I'm just saying we should check her alibi from the time she left Cameron Reynolds at Warren Wilson College to her audition with Arthur Thrash."

"But we're doing all this investigative work for her benefit," I protested. "Now she's a suspect?"

"I admit it's improbable but I'm simply looking at one explanation for the unknown RT appointments. If Janice wasn't alone when she fell, it's more likely the person with her was tied to the song, especially now that it's the strongest link. But at least let's do due diligence and rule Wendy out."

Nakayla was right. I was letting my compassion for the girl cloud my judgment. Too many things were at play to disregard any of them.

"Okay. We'll verify Wendy's whereabouts for Tuesday afternoon." I calmed down and the full impact of Nakayla's statement hit me. "You said 'now that it's the strongest link.' You learned something about the song from Eli Smyth, didn't you?"

She smiled. "I did. He's the source. Janice Wainwright became obsessed with 'I'm Troubled' because of the story Eli Smyth told her."

I poured her another glass of beer. "And now you're going to tell me."

She took a sip and then slowly spun the glass between her palms. "Eli was a real nice guy. I guess he must be in his early seventies."

"Doesn't sound like he was old enough to know his great grandfather."

"Eli said he quite vividly remembered 'Grand Pay,' he pronounced it with a long 'a.' Eli was born in Hendersonville and visited Connemara every Sunday. More frequently in the summer. He said he has a picture of him and Captain Smyth when the old man was in his sick bed. Anyway, I played the role of amateur historian and told him how my mother loved to come to Connemara and I was interested in talking to anyone who actually lived in the house. We spent a few minutes looking at the pictures in the book I brought. He identified some family members. Then I told him I'd known Janice Wainwright and I was impressed with what she knew about the history of the house. That she had been a real historian."

"Did he react to her name?"

"Yeah, with a wide grin and a comment on how much he enjoyed meeting her. She'd also driven to Charlotte and they ate at the same restaurant where we were. Then he realized I'd spoken about her in the past tense."

"You brought up her death."

Before Nakayla could continue, my BlackBerry beeped an incoming call. I glanced at the display. A local number I didn't recognize.

"You want to get that?" Nakayla asked.

"I'll check it later. If it's important they'll leave a message."

She took another sip of beer, and sighed. "I played it like I assumed he knew she'd died. He was upset, of course, and surprised the accident happened on Glassy Mountain."

"That didn't seem significant to him?"

"No. Just ironic. Then I said I was disappointed not to have gotten to know Janice better. We'd planned to meet and she said she had a great story about Carl Sandburg and a song."

"Smooth," I acknowledged.

"And Eli Smyth said, 'I'm Troubled. I told her that story.'"

My phone beeped again, signaling a new voice mail. I ignored it and scooted forward on my chair. "Jackpot."

"Yes. Evidently Janice was curious if Eli had any personal memories of Sandburg. You know, maybe they'd gone back to visit the homestead at Sandburg's invitation. He said the only contact came in 1945, that first year the Sandburgs owned the house. The Captain had died in 1942 and so the sale had been handled by his direct heirs. Eli said his mother told him a few months afterwards Sandburg wrote with a question about something the workmen uncovered in the foundation of the house."

"This was during the renovations?" I asked. "Where Ranger Hodges showed us the old gun portal?"

"Yes. The expansion in the rear. When they were digging out the back foundation wall, the crew foreman found a metal box, like a small payroll chest, and brought it to Sandburg. It was rusty but intact, and when the dust had been brushed away, he saw the clasp was closed by a seal imprinted with the letters CSA."

"Confederate States of America."

Nakayla nodded. "Sandburg opened it and found a single document tightly wrapped in oilskin. It was the song 'I'm Troubled.' He knew Captain Smyth had fought for the Confederacy when he was only sixteen and thought maybe it held special significance for the family."

"Does Eli Smyth have the song?"

"No. He said his family never heard of it, and enough of the old timers had been around the Captain long enough to feel certain he would have mentioned it."

"Something about it piqued Janice Wainwright's interest," I said. "Did Eli have Sandburg's letter?"

"No. No one knows exactly what happened to it."

"The story's got too much detail to be a fabrication. And why would you even make something like that up?"

"Eli swore it was true," Nakayla said. "And he claimed Janice got very excited at the possibility that Memminger himself had buried the box in the foundation."

"The Treasurer of the Confederacy. The man who wanted to move the capital to Flat Rock."

"Right."

. I leaned back in the kitchen chair. "No wonder Janice Wainwright became obsessed with the song. If it had been hidden by a high-ranking Confederate official, there had to be some importance attached to it." I thought about the chain of events. "Then Janice came back to Connemara and asked Ranger Hodges about the song. She claimed she knew nothing about it. If Hodges told the truth, that would seem to be a dead-end."

"Not necessarily," Nakayla said. "Eli Smyth gave Janice another source to check. Louise Bailey. She's got to be our unknown LB initials on the calendar."

"Who's she?"

"A resident of Flat Rock. Her family's been there for genera-tions and she was once Carl Sandburg's secretary."

"Excellent." I split the remainder of the porter between our two glasses. "She might link the story of the song to the actual words of the song, or at least the verses Janice referenced with her dying breath."

Nakayla got up and carried the plates from the table. "I asked Eli Smyth how widely known was the discovery of the box in the house's foundation. He said it wasn't of particular interest outside his family. Other than Janice and me, the subject hadn't been discussed for years."

"Good. We might have information that the person who broke into my car doesn't know."

Nakayla ran hot water in the sink and added a squirt of dish detergent. "I think we should see Louise Bailey this weekend as soon as we can. I'll track down her phone number and address."

I crumpled the empty pizza box and crossed to the back porch to throw it in the large trash can. "Okay. Let's take the copy of the song in the Lomax book. That might prompt her memory." I paused for a moment, looking out at the old barn and chicken coop. The scene was peaceful. A faint glow of red haloed the ridges as the sun fell below the distant horizon. I called back through the doorway, "I'm going to walk out and double-check Ida Mae."

Over the running water, Nakayla said, "Do I detect a nervous father?"

"No. I'm simply looking for the best place to faint when the time comes."

An owl hooted from the woods beyond the pasture. His night of hunting was just beginning. I circled the barn, stepping carefully in the dark shadows. Ida Mae snorted. Maybe she sensed my presence. I stopped and heard the trickle of water. It wasn't coming from the farmhouse kitchen. The source was either the spigot on the side of Ida Mae's shed or the hose nozzle by one of the troughs. I entered the gate and went first to the spigot. It was on the darkest side and I pulled my BlackBerry to use it for a flashlight. As I suspected, I'd forgotten to turn the water off and the pressure created a steady trickle from a weak spot in the connector's washer.

After I shut the stream off, I noticed the "Voice mail" and "Missed Call" icons on the BlackBerry's touch screen. I leaned against the shed and punched in my retrieval code.

"Sam Blackman. This is Cammie Reynolds." He paused, and then stuttered like he wasn't sure what to say. "I've been doing some investigating on my own and I thought you ought to be aware of something that's a little odd. I'll have the chance to check it out tonight. You're good at asking questions so I thought you might have a way to bring it up without sounding accusatory. Give me a call as soon as you can. I'll be here in the office." His breath sounded like a rush of wind as he sighed. "I'm afraid I knew a little more about Janice's research than I told you. Like I said, scholars are good at keeping secrets." On that enigmatic note, the message ended.

Something that's a little odd. Cameron was supposed to be flying to Florida early tomorrow morning for Janice Wainwright's funeral. Whatever it was, it was clear he wanted to talk tonight and he'd withheld information. I called him back and got his voice mail. He'd phoned me about thirty minutes earlier and it was only seven o'clock now. I left him a message and expected to hear from him within a few minutes.

A half hour later he still hadn't phoned. Nakayla had found a number for Louise Bailey, but there was no answer, not even a machine. She may have figured if people wanted to talk to her, they'd call again.

I tried Reynolds' number and got voice mail again.

"Maybe something's wrong with his phone," Nakayla said.

"Maybe. You know I could be there in forty minutes."

She closed her laptop. "Let's go. It's a beautiful night for a moonlit drive."

We took my Honda CR-V and opened the sunroof. The air was brisk, but invigorating and dispelled the buzz of the half-jug of porter. Nakayla assumed the role of navigator and got us to Warren Wilson College by the back-roads.

"Drive to the farther entrance closer to the music center," she said. "I don't want you running over a student on that narrow campus lane."

"They should all be in bed so they can get up and milk the cows in the morning."

"Right, Mr. Farmer. Two days tending chickens and a goat and you're an expert?"

"I prefer fast learner."

We parked in the lot beside the Kittredge Theatre and Music Center and met three students coming out carrying guitar cases.

"Professor Reynolds is expecting us," Nakayla said. "Do you know if he's in his office?"

The boy in the middle said, "We didn't see him, but we were rehearsing on stage." He turned and pointed behind him. "That door's unlocked. Follow the hall to the right and you'll see his office on the left. It's about the third or fourth one down."

We found Reynolds' office without difficulty. The door was closed, but a light shone through the crack underneath.

I knocked. "Cameron? It's Sam and Nakayla."

No answer.

I knocked louder. "Cameron?"

No answer.

"Try the knob," Nakayla said.

The door was unlocked. I opened it just far enough to slide my head in.

The single desk stood against the far wall. Bookshelves lined the sides of the small office. A guitar sat in a chair in the corner. Cameron Reynolds occupied the only other chair. I assumed it was Cameron. He was face down on the desk, his head enshrouded in a white plastic bag with a thick string tied securely against his neck.

Chapter Nineteen

I reached back and grabbed Nakayla by the arm. "Come in quickly and close the door." Then I hurried to the desk. Preserving a possible crime scene ran a distant second to saving a life.

Nakayla gasped behind me. "Is he dead?"

Without answering, I grabbed the plastic bag with both hands, simultaneously lifting and driving my fingers through it. If he had a chance of survival, he had to get air. The rip exposed the side of Cameron Reynolds' face. His skin had a blue cast. I touched his cheek and its temperature matched the room's.

"Yes. And he's been dead a while. Probably soon after he phoned me."

"Should I get help?"

"Not from here. Call 911 and say we found a possible suicide victim. Do you have a number for Corn?"

"Only the ranger office. Not his direct or his cell."

"Someone will be on duty. Tell them to find him."

Nakayla pulled her phone from her purse.

I rethought the situation. "Wait. A deputy might be only a few minutes away or they'll alert campus security. I need a little time."

"What if somebody comes by?"

"Then immediately dial 911 and put the phone to your ear. All I need is five minutes. I want to know what we're dealing with. This has the potential to blow our quiet investigation right out of the water. Like it or not, Cameron Reynolds' call ties us to him. It's the reason we came and they'll find it on his phone record."

Nakayla licked her lips nervously. "Okay. This is your specialty."

"Yep. Although now I've got to investigate the scene without leaving any traces."

"Where do you want me?"

"Stand with your back against the door. That way you'll block someone's sudden entrance."

She leaned against the jamb with her phone ready in her hand. "Five minutes and counting."

I pulled a handkerchief from my pocket and wrapped it around the fingers of my right hand. Then I gently probed under the cord encircling Reynolds' neck. Tight enough to seal air out but not tight enough to choke him. He would have exhausted the oxygen in the bag in a matter of minutes.

I rolled the edge of the plastic bag higher. A thin dark bruise ran like a tattoo, not matching the exact indentation of the cord. It appeared to be a separate wound. Would Reynolds have pulled his noose so tightly it bit into the flesh and then loosened it? Maybe it slackened when he lost consciousness. I looked for the ends and found them knotted under his chin. Either he or someone else had tied the cord to make the bag airtight after applying what must have been strangulation pressure. Had Reynolds played some auto-erotic asphyxiation game that went horribly wrong?

I checked his clothing. The only disarray was the shirt. The collar was rolled under itself and the second button from the top was missing. Frayed white threads showed where it had popped free. To see any more I would have had to rearrange the body.

Both arms sprawled across the desk. The fingers of Reynolds' left hand curled upwards. I bent to within a few inches of the tips and saw traces of skin under the nails. Maybe his own; maybe an attacker. If there had been a struggle, it had been brief. The office was messy, but nothing appeared to be knocked askew.

The biggest surprise, aside from the dead body, lay under Reynolds' head. Alan Lomax's *Folk Songs of North America* was open to the page with "I'm Troubled." I wanted a peek at the inside cover but hesitated to jostle the body further.

Reynolds' left hand lay closest to his computer. The monitor and keyboard were on a side wing of the desk. A screen saver of flashing musical notes floated in a kaleidoscopic sea of colors. I nudged the spacebar with my knuckle and the psychedelic display was replaced by an open Word document. One sentence had been typed: Janice, I'm sorry.

I examined the plastic bag. It looked like a standard trash liner. I turned and saw the wastebasket by the second chair. There was no liner and no trash in the wire-mesh container. Three guitar strings and three square, white envelopes lay on the floor alongside it. The wire strings were each coiled in imperfect loops. I saw a purple box about three-inches square and half-an-inch thick in the seat of the chair next to the guitar. I walked closer. The label on the box read Elixir Acoustic Guitar Strings. Three white envelopes were visible inside containing new strings.

I examined the guitar. The two thicker strings appeared to be made of shiny wound bronze. They looked new. Next to them, a string was missing, and the remaining three were thinner and duller in appearance. I stooped to check the three on the floor. Two were the same size as the new ones, but all were dull and worn. Either Cameron Reynolds or a visitor had been re-stringing the guitar. I didn't know much about the instrument, but the name Martin was a brand I heard was a favorite of professional musicians.

I looked under the chair and carefully lifted the wastebasket. Nothing more. I had a total of six white envelopes, three still in the box, three empty on the floor, three old strings on the guitar and three by the wastebasket, two new strings on the guitar, and one new string unaccounted for.

Each of the strings had a brass eyelet at one end. It locked the string in place below the guitar's bridge as the other end was wound around the tuning peg at the top of the neck.

I understood why I was looking at a murder scene.

"Have you got your pad in your purse?" I asked Nakayla.

"Yes."

"I'm going to check Reynolds' phone. Jot down the numbers as I read them."

Using the handkerchief, I pulled his cell out of his belt holster. I quickly followed the menu prompts to recent calls. My number was first on the sent list. The second had a 321 area code I didn't recognize. There were eight others for the day: three incoming, two more outgoing, and three missed. The number with the 321 code was repeated in both the sent and received categories. The three missed calls were from me, my attempts to reach him from the farmhouse. In addition to the phone numbers, Nakayla wrote down the time and whether they'd been sent or received. I saw no point in going back further than a day because I believed the oddity Reynolds said he discovered must have occurred shortly before he called me.

I replaced his phone and took a deep breath. "Would you make the calls from out front and then bring the responding officers back?"

"Okay. How about campus security?"

"If you see a call box or a guard, that's fine, but call 911 and Corn first."

"Are you sure you don't want to talk to Corn yourself?"

I shook my head. "No. That will come soon enough. I'll stay here. I know it sounds funny, but I don't want to leave him alone. I liked him."

Nakayla gave me a sweet smile of sympathy. "I understand."

She left, closing the door behind her.

In the quiet, I became aware of the dull pain in the stump of my leg. It was a common occurrence at the end of a long day, an annoyance and nothing more. I sat down on the floor in a bare corner of the room and stretched both legs out in front of me.

I looked up at Reynolds. Scholars are good at keeping secrets. "My God, Cammie. What was it you wanted to tell me?"

◇◇◇

"All right. What do you really know?" Ranger Corn asked the question as he slid into the backseat of my Honda.

Nakayla and I sat in front and twisted around to see him. We were still parked outside Kittredge Theatre and Music Center. Crime scene tape was now strung across the entrances, students huddled together and some were visibly crying, the college president and other staff were consoling them, and Buncombe county deputies cleared the way for an ambulance to back close to a far door. Cameron Reynolds' body was finally being moved. It was ten minutes after midnight.

"Did the deputies give you our story?" I asked. Nakayla and I had been separated and interviewed soon after they arrived.

"Yes," Corn said. "And they seem fine with it. I confirmed Cameron Reynolds was a friend of Janice Wainwright and I was looking into her death. That was why you called me. You were working for the daughter and her lawsuit and you had recently spoken to Reynolds about Janice's frame of mind."

"Did you see the crime scene?"

"They were protecting their turf till they saw a note to Janice written on the computer. Then they became more interested in what I could offer and they let me examine his office."

"They tell you I let them listen to my voice mail from him?"

"Yeah, I don't think you two are under suspicion. Clearly Reynolds contacted you. The deputies found the students who gave you directions to his office. The time sequence works in your favor."

"Good, because that's the way it happened."

Corn leaned closer. "But I want to hear what you know and what you think. With your training, you can't tell me you didn't make at least a cursory examination of the body and surroundings. And you saw the computer screen because you haven't asked me what the note said."

Corn had played square with us and I wasn't going to jerk him around now. But that didn't mean I would give him everything.

"I know Reynolds was murdered."

"How?"

"It makes no sense he would call me and then kill himself. He wasn't that distressed. And why commit suicide in the middle of stringing your guitar?"

"I meant how was he killed?" Corn said impatiently. "I know it wasn't suicide."

"Garroted. The killer used a guitar string. That's why there are six old strings but only five new ones."

"Hmmm. I didn't think to count strings. I was expecting the M.E. to find he'd been knocked unconscious and then suffocated with the bag."

"No. The M.E. will find the neck wound inconsistent with the cord. The steel string cut deeper, probably cutting off the carotid arteries and rendering Reynolds unconscious in a matter of seconds. That's why there are no signs of a struggle. Reynolds was probably looking at the book and the killer pushed his chair into the desk as he pulled the noose taut. Reynolds couldn't move."

Corn grunted approval. "And it happened so quickly he couldn't utter a sound."

"The steel strings have an eyelet at one end. He simply threaded the string through it, made a loop, and he had the perfect killing device, silent and efficient."

"Premeditated?"

"I've been thinking about that. I'm inclined to say yes, but maybe he came prepared to kill only if necessary."

"What do you mean?"

"He brought the song book. Why do that? Either he was pumping Reynolds for information about the song or he planned to leave it as evidence that would be tied to my car break-in."

"Or both," Nakayla interjected.

"Or both," I agreed. "And maybe Reynolds confirmed some fear. Something he knew. He confronted someone with what he was going to tell me. The killer may have brought a hidden weapon like a gun or knife, but he saw the guitar strings and improvised. Staging a suicide by gunshot carried a lot more risk. The noise would bring students or staff. No time to dress the scene. A knife is a highly unlikely choice for suicide. The better option was silent strangulation, then an attempt to make it look like suicide by using what was handy in the office."

"They found the twine and scissors in a drawer in his desk," Corn said.

"Anybody see Reynolds with anyone, or notice someone hanging around?"

"No. There was a rehearsal in another part of the building, but Reynolds' corridor was deserted."

"What's your role in the case?" I asked.

"Courtesy sharing of information. I have no jurisdiction here. I told them it might be linked to Janice Wainwright's death, but I had neither evidence nor suspects to give them. They're treating it as a homicide, although a suicide makes it a whole lot easier. They wanted to know how distraught Reynolds had been over Janice's death."

"Will they be thorough?"

Corn paused, choosing his words carefully. "Yes, they'll be thorough. But they won't be imaginative. I hope they uncover the killer and we find indisputable evidence he either did or didn't confront Janice Wainwright on Glassy Mountain. I suggested they leave the computer note out of any public report."

"Why?" I asked.

"To keep something back to weed out false confessions. That's the reason I gave them. I also thought there was no need to alert the defendants in your lawsuit. They'd use it to develop so many wild theories the girl would never get a just settlement."

"You're a good man, Corn."

"Yeah? Well, right now I'm just tired."

"Are you going to make sure they notice the missing guitar string? That's the killer's slip up. He should have tried to wipe it clean rather than take it."

"You spotted it. You tell them."

"Take the credit. I don't want any links to this."

Corn leaned back. "All right. What do you think's the motive?"

"Money. A cover-up of Janice's death." I thought about McCaffrey. "Theft of her research. Maybe a combination of those and more."

"My money's on money. Have you got a favorite?"

"I wish I could say. Did you get a look at the book under his head?"

"Yes," Corn said. "The inside cover had 'Return to Cameron Reynolds' written on it. It's the same copy that was stolen from your car. I told the lead deputy about it."

"What did he think?"

"He said it looked like someone returned it. From his perspective, it wasn't an item out of place."

"Did you find anything about Janice's call to Moore in Brevard?"

"Don Moore. Upstanding citizen whose family's been there since the early 1900s. His construction business is in Savannah so he splits his time between the two. I don't have a Savannah number for you yet."

"That's okay. We can take it from here."

"What's your next move?" Corn asked.

"I'm going to get Hewitt Donaldson's ass out of bed and tell him we're meeting first thing in the morning. The connection between Janice and Reynolds won't stay hidden forever."

"Why'd you wait so late?"

"And have those deputies see the first call on my phone was to a lawyer?"

Corn laughed. "You think like a cop."

"I was a cop."

Corn got out, waved good night, and headed for a cluster of deputies.

"Are you really calling Hewitt?" Nakayla asked.

"Yes. But not right away. Let's drive till we hit a gas station or somewhere we can park without drawing attention to ourselves. I want to find out who's at the 321 area code number. I think that's Florida."

"Paul Wainwright?"

"Your guess is as good as mine."

We drove to Highway 70 and pulled into an Exxon station. I dialed and concentrated on the first words I would hear in an effort to recognize the voice.

An answering machine picked up. "This is the Howell residence. We can't come to the phone right now. Please leave a message."

"Cynthia Howell. This is Sam Blackman. Please call me immediately, no matter the time. It's urgent that I speak with you."

I disconnected.

"Why would Cynthia Howell call Cameron Reynolds?" Nakayla asked. "It was clear she didn't like him."

"I don't think it was Cynthia. My money's on Wendy. And something about that phone call cost Cameron Reynolds his life."

Chapter Twenty

Nakayla and I traded places so that I would be free to talk without worrying about driving along the mountain roads.

It was a smart move because Cynthia Howell called back in less than two minutes. "Mr. Blackman, what's wrong?" Her voice was strained and breathy.

"Is Wendy asleep?"

"She's in the guest bedroom but I don't know if she's sleeping. None of us are sleeping very well the night before her mother's funeral."

"I'm sorry to bother you so late. It's about Cameron Reynolds."

"What about him?" she asked curtly.

"He was found dead in his office this evening."

Silence. Then a gasp and a choked, "Oh, my God."

"We're not sure what happened, but I know he called this number earlier."

"Oh, God," she whispered. "What am I going to tell Wendy?"

I needed to learn who spoke with Reynolds and what was said. I was sympathetic to the shock the news created but I couldn't let Cynthia Howell get emotionally overwhelmed. "I'll talk to Wendy."

"No," she said emphatically. "Not before her mother's funeral. That would destroy the poor girl."

"I understand, Mrs. Howell, but someone from this number called Cameron Reynolds tonight. He returned the call and then phoned me. He left a message that he wanted to talk, but I don't know why. Would Wendy have called him?"

"Yes. I gave her permission and she used my phone. Her cell battery died and she forgot to pack her charger. She wanted to invite Cameron to come back to my house after the memorial service. I may have had my differences with him and his lifestyle, but at times like this all of Janice's friends are welcome." She hesitated, and then asked the question I'd been expecting. "Did he take his own life?"

"We don't know. But the police will find your number in his cell log and they'll want to know what he and Wendy discussed. I need to know that first. Not only to determine Reynolds' state of mind but to assess the impact on your sister's lawsuit."

"What's the lawsuit have to do with it?"

"A note was found in Reynolds' office. 'Janice, I'm sorry.' If the lawyers for the other side connect Reynolds' death to Wendy and the note to Janice, they'll try to build something out of it."

"Like what?"

"Like maybe Reynolds and Janice had a rendezvous on Glassy Mountain the day she died, or Reynolds had wronged her in some way that caused her to become unbalanced, mentally and physically. They'll grasp at anything to distance themselves from responsibility for her fall. I don't want to be blindsided, and I think there was something about the call between Wendy and Reynolds that triggered his contacting me."

Cynthia Howell sighed in resignation. "It's nearly one in the morning. Do you think the police will call tonight?"

"No. It will take them a while to start their investigation. Probably late tomorrow morning or tomorrow afternoon. Maybe even not until Monday."

"Then I'm not hitting Wendy with this news tonight. In the morning, I'll tell her Cameron won't be able to fly down for the service. Then we'll call you afterwards."

"What time?"

"Around three."

"And if the Buncombe County Sheriff's Department contacts you in the meantime?"

"Then I'll tell them I'm burying my sister, Mr. Blackman. If that's not a good enough excuse to postpone their questions, they can just arrest me."

Wendy had labeled her aunt a control freak, but in this case her domineering personality and protective instincts would probably keep the police at bay until after the funeral.

"Okay," I said. "I'm going to talk to Hewitt Donaldson. If you feel undue pressure from the authorities, call him. He'll be up to speed on the situation."

"Thank you. Then we'll talk tomorrow."

"Mrs. Howell," I added quickly. "I have one more question."

"Yes."

"After Wendy spoke to Reynolds, did she seem upset?"

"Just the opposite. He cheered her up. Although she got a little teary."

"About what?"

"Reynolds told her she'd been cast in some play. Wendy was pleased because she thought her audition had been a disaster." Cynthia Howell's voice broke. "Wendy had wanted to surprise her mother. She got the part but now Janice will never see her performance."

◇◇◇

At nine the next morning, Nakayla and I met Hewitt Donaldson in his office. He'd been so surprised by Cameron Reynolds' death that he didn't even grumble about me waking him. We sat around his conference table with a large carafe of coffee in the middle.

Hewitt wore a Grateful Dead tee shirt and his long gray hair looked like it had dried on the way to his office. Each strand pointed in a different compass direction. He had a file open beside his steaming mug and a legal pad under his right hand.

"So, they're calling you at three," he said.

"Yeah," I replied, "though I expect it to be later. The service is at eleven with a light lunch back at Cynthia Howell's home."

"Eleven? Reynolds was cutting it close."

"I checked flight schedules," Nakayla said. "He had a six AM commuter to Atlanta and then a quick connection to Orlando. He'd have arrived shortly after nine."

Hewitt took a sip of coffee, and then asked, "Do you think the trip precipitated the murder?"

"It could have," I said. "If someone wanted to keep him from going, last night was the time to stop him. But why? How would being there in person be any different than talking on the phone?"

The silence let me know the others didn't have a theory either.

"And the book?" Hewitt asked.

"We know the song's key to whatever Janice was working on. Nakayla learned that from Eli Smyth. I can't buy that Reynolds' copy of the song happened to show up in his office the night he died."

"Maybe that was the oddity," Hewitt said.

I shook my head. "Then he would have said so. He sounded puzzled, like he wanted to talk through something with me. Whoever left the book may simply have wanted us to think Reynolds had stolen it from my car. And that's why the message to Janice was typed on the computer. Make it look like a suicide note. Reynolds is dead and can't say otherwise."

Hewitt stared at his legal pad for a moment but didn't write anything down. "Well, if we're baffled, then Wyatt Montgomery, his clinic, and the pharmaceutical company will also be hard pressed to make any connection between Janice and Reynolds that indicates he caused her fall. Louis Kirkland called late yesterday afternoon. Montgomery's attorneys had received a copy of Janice's autopsy and they'd like to have an informal discussion about an out-of-court settlement."

"I bet they would."

"Kirkland was gung-ho to tell them to put any preliminary proposal where they'd need a proctologist to retrieve it, but I cautioned him we might be facing some unknown elements that could weaken the case. I suggested he be tough on no-informal preliminaries and demand a firm offer."

"How does the law work if he negotiates a settlement and then something bad comes to light?" I asked.

"That depends on the terms. They might be angling for a payment with no admission of wrongdoing and eliminating any further redress. Kirkland could protest but push for a little more money. If there is no admission of wrongdoing and no redress, then it could cut both ways. They can't come wanting their money back."

"I understand. We've got a potential window to wrap this up before we uncover a proximate cause that lets everyone, including Wyatt Montgomery, escape the wrongful death suit." I weighed the options. "Maybe we should back off for a few days and see what Kirkland works out."

"That might be safer," Hewitt agreed. "You're under no obligation to continue and you're not impeding or obstructing justice in any way. The Sheriff's Department and the Park Rangers are both working their respective investigations and all you're dealing with are speculations."

Nakayla looked from Hewitt to me. Her brown eyes bore into me.

"What?" I asked.

"You two are missing an important consideration."

"What?" Hewitt echoed.

"We don't know what happened to Janice but we're positive someone murdered Reynolds. How they tie together might be important to the lawsuit, but it's not the compelling reason for continuing the investigation."

"Then what's the reason?" I asked.

"The fact that our killer thinks he's on the trail of whatever Janice was seeking. We don't know what that is, but who's to say it's not extremely valuable. And we might be ahead in the race because no one spoke to Eli Smyth other than me and Janice. We have new leads with Louise Bailey and Don Moore and we'd be crazy not to take advantage of them."

"Nice argument, Counselor," Hewitt said. He pointed his finger at me. "The best investment you can make is send this woman to law school."

"No way. I don't win enough arguments as it is."

Nakayla stood. "So, I think I should try to reach Louise Bailey this morning and look for a Savannah number for Don Moore."

Hewitt closed his file folder. "All right. But let me give you a piece of free advice."

"What's the catch?" I asked.

"No catch. I like you. That's why the second fact to consider is whatever Janice was seeking now involves murder. The closer you get, the more likely you'll cross the path of someone who won't hesitate to kill you."

Chapter Twenty-one

Once again, Nakayla and I were on I-26 headed to Flat Rock. She'd reached Louise Bailey after our meeting with Hewitt and we'd been invited to the woman's home at eleven. From the directions, her house appeared to be just down the road from Connemara.

"How do you want to handle this interview?" I asked.

"Why don't you wait in the car?"

"No, seriously."

"I am serious. Why don't you wait in the car?" Then Nakayla laughed. "I don't care. It's not like she's a suspect."

"Take the lead. Obviously you didn't come across as threatening on the phone and you're more familiar with Connemara than I am."

"Okay." Nakayla sat in the passenger's seat and flipped through papers in her lap. "She's a fascinating lady. While you were allegedly thinking in your office, I did some online research."

"She's got to be up there if she was Sandburg's secretary."

"Ninety-four this year."

I gave a low whistle. "How'd she sound on the phone?"

"Very sharp. She writes a weekly column for the Hendersonville newspaper. It's called 'Along The Ridges' and she's been writing it for forty-two years."

"Human interest?"

"Yes, along with a mixture of history and mountain lore."

I stole a quick glance at Nakayla and smiled. "Then I think we're talking to the right person."

"I agree. Louise Bailey may be the one who can connect the song to both Sandburg and Janice Wainwright." Nakayla straightened the papers before slipping them in her purse. "And what were you pondering while I was tracking her down?"

"Wendy. I was trying to put myself in the mind of a seventeen-year-old girl."

"There's a stretch," Nakayla said. "Especially since you have the maturity of a fourteen-year-old boy."

"Fourteen was a good age for me."

"Right. And how did you find the mind of a seventeen-year-old girl?"

"Complex and contrasting. On the one hand she shows responsibility in caring for the goat, prepping for college, and working toward her audition. On the other hand, her emotions are so volatile, she comes after us with a revolver."

"She thought we'd killed her mother," Nakayla argued.

"Yes, that might be all of it or only part of it." I turned onto Little River Road between the Flat Rock Playhouse and Connemara.

"We go about a mile," Nakayla said. "Her driveway will be on the right." She shifted in her seat to face me. "What do you mean only part of it?"

"You asked what I was thinking. Janice Wainwright whispered, 'It's the verses. Sandburg's verses.'"

"I know. I heard her too."

"And she thought she was talking to her daughter Wendy."

"Unless there's some other Wendy we don't know about."

"My point is Janice said 'Sandburg's verses' as if Wendy knew what she was talking about. She didn't try to give an explanation."

"But Wendy said she didn't know what her mother was working on."

I slowed as I saw the driveway for Louise Bailey's house. "Yet she and her mother were close. I think Wendy knows more than she's telling us."

"But has she told someone else?" Nakayla asked.

"That, my dear, is the key question we need answered."

The gravel road gradually curved up the hill. Mountain laurel thrived on either side, a natural fence creating a green border that in a few months would burst into bloom. As the grade leveled, we entered a clearing where the house stood on the crest, moderate in size with a wide, covered porch.

The driveway split. The left fork looped back in front of the house and the right continued, probably leading to outbuildings and a garage. I parked near the steps, facing the way out. No other vehicles were visible.

An elderly woman walked onto the porch through the front door. She must have been watching at a window. She leaned on a wooden cane and raised her right hand in greeting.

Nakayla was first out of the car. "Mrs. Bailey, I'm Nakayla Robertson. Thank you for seeing us." Without waiting, she bounded up the steps.

I came slower, allowing Nakayla a moment to introduce herself. As I stepped on the plank floor, both women turned to me.

"This is my partner, Sam Blackman."

Mrs. Bailey extended her hand.

"I'm pleased to meet you," I said.

"The pleasure is mine," she replied in a quiet voice.

Her hand was thin and delicate with age.

Mrs. Bailey shook her head. "I'm sorry it has to be about the tragedy of Mrs. Wainwright's death. I have a special fondness for historians and would loved to have talked with her again."

She wore a light-blue checkered dress that matched the eyes sparkling behind wire-framed glasses. The collar of the dress was neatly spread over a darker blue sweater that came to her waist. A double string of pearls graced her neck. Whether she was dressed for company or not, I got the feeling Mrs. Bailey wasn't one to lounge around in a housecoat and fuzzy slippers. This woman led an active life.

"Well, come on in before ants crawl up your legs."

She laughed at what must have been looks of simultaneous confusion on our faces and pointed with her cane to the floor. "It's spring and the ground's warming up. I noticed ants are marching single file across the length of the porch. They're not coming inside, mind you, but unwavering in their route. Stand in their path and you could soon be doing a quick step."

I realized the first leg of mine they'd reach was my prosthesis and I wouldn't feel the invasion until they were nearing tender territory. "Yes, let's go in," I urged.

The home had high ceilings and comfortable furnishings, a place where people lived and not a showcase for designer fabrics and colors. Photographs on walls, tabletops, and end tables connected the past to the present with memories that must have burned with bright immediacy in Mrs. Bailey's keen mind.

She stopped at a cushioned chair facing the front window. "If you don't mind, I'll take this one. Since my stroke last fall, my balance hasn't been all that it should and it's easier for me to get up from here." She laughed. "My oldest son is always fussing at me to use my walker. I'm lucky if I remember my cane."

We sat in chairs on either side of her.

Mrs. Bailey turned to Nakayla. "What is it you'd like to know?"

"As I said on the phone, we're helping Mrs. Wainwright's daughter sort through some of the things her mother was working on. We got your name from Eli Smyth."

"Old Captain Smyth's great grandson. I knew the Captain. I thought he was ancient at the time, and here I sit, matching his longevity. A very nice family. Eli's father was in charge of the sale of Connemara to Mr. Sandburg, being the oldest living grandson at the time. Their overriding desire was to keep Connemara in one piece and not fall victim to a developer. I'm grateful for their stewardship of the property."

"Eli Smyth told us Carl Sandburg found a small chest in the foundation wall. He said Sandburg asked his family if they knew anything about it."

"That's what Mrs. Wainwright told me. I might have seen the box, but Mr. Sandburg was always sticking stuff everywhere. He never asked me about the song."

I was disappointed. I'd hoped Mrs. Bailey would burst out singing "I'm Troubled."

"How did you meet Sandburg?" Nakayla asked.

"Through his daughter Helga. If not for my audacity, I wouldn't have met the Sandburgs so soon after their arrival in the neighborhood. My husband Joe was a doctor and I was at home waiting for him to return from military duty in Japan. This was right after the war. A friend in town asked me to keep his horse for a while and give it the exercise he couldn't provide. I was delighted. I loved horses. One day I rode along the back drive to Connemara. As I passed the barn, the herdsman suggested I ask Helga to ride with me. I said I hadn't met her. He said, 'Oh, that doesn't matter. Just go to the window there and call her.'

"So that's what I did. I yelled under the window that I didn't realize opened into Mr. Sandburg's study. Helga finally appeared and said she would like to go with me and that I should wait in the kitchen while she changed clothes. Mrs. Sandburg welcomed me and we were having a lively conversation when Mr. Sandburg came in. Satisfying himself that it was I hollering under his window, he then asked, 'Can you type with as many as two fingers, and, if so, would you be free to come here in the afternoons to help me get *Remembrance Rock* ready for my publisher's deadline?' *Remembrance Rock* was his one and only novel. And, believe me, it was a long one.

"Well, two fingers grossly exaggerated my expertise on the typewriter, but I was on the job next day. And what an experience it was to be in the presence of that great mind at work—and to find I could sit perfectly still and keep quiet for three hours on a stretch lest I disturb Mr. Sandburg's concentration.

"Once in snow too deep for me to drive, I put on my brother's boots and walked the mile from my house to Connemara. When I needed to leave in order to get home before dark, Mr. Sandburg asked if I might spend the night so we could work after supper. That was fine with me, but we never got around to the work. He brought out his guitar and we had an evening of music. Then Mrs. Sandburg, maybe five feet tall, lent me a pair of her pajamas. Lillian was her name, but he called her Paula.

"I walked home next morning. That evening was the most we ever talked about music, and I don't remember him singing the song that interested Mrs. Wainwright."

Mrs. Bailey moved her cane to the side of her chair and hooked it on the armrest. She took a deep breath, and then looked at me to see if I'd been paying attention.

"How long did you work for him?" I asked.

"I guess a little over a year. There are few places I have been made to feel more at home or where I've experienced a warmer atmosphere than the Sandburg household. But when Joe returned from the service to start his practice of medicine, I told Mr. Sandburg I would have to leave my job. He said simply, 'Would you bring me someone I would like?' I took a friend, a real typist who'd just returned from overseas duty. She stayed with him for twenty years."

"Did you keep in touch after that?" Nakayla asked.

"Yes. We'd see each other occasionally. I guess the next time I saw Mr. Sandburg was when he walked over to my house to look at some of our books. Suppertime came and he accepted our invitation to join us for a plain country-style meal. He seemed to enjoy it—especially the green beans cooked with a chunk of salt pork—southern fashion. He kept helping himself to beans until the serving bowl was empty, then, saying 'Don't you ever tell anybody I did this,' he turned up the bowl and drank the pot liquid."

I laughed, and looked back in the kitchen, envisioning the scene.

Mrs. Bailey turned in her chair, following my gaze. "Sometimes my husband would see Mr. Sandburg walking along the back-roads late at night. Joe would be returning from an emergency house call, and I guess Mr. Sandburg was out thinking beneath the stars. You know he wrote nearly a third of his works after he moved to Connemara."

"Have other people recently come to ask you about Sandburg?" Nakayla asked.

She chuckled softly. "No. I'm not a Sandburg expert. Until they came to Flat Rock I knew nothing about them. Of course I read his poem 'Fog' in a high school literature book because I had to." She laughed louder. "I can't say it inspired me to read his other works and I was relieved to hear him say in later years that he had written that particular poem to amuse one of his children and he had no idea why it was singled out for study. I came to know Mr. Sandburg not as a celebrity but as a neighbor. I saw the Sandburgs as a family with little time for social activities, but with satisfaction in their extremely productive lives, and with a closeness seldom seen in families today."

She made the statement with undisguised admiration, and I figured Sandburg had lost a kindred spirit when Mrs. Bailey left him to raise her own family.

Nakayla looked at me and I nodded for her to continue. "Did you and Janice Wainwright talk about anything else, say the history of the house?"

"Oh, yes, and not just the house. She was curious about the legends of the area."

"Like what?"

Mrs. Bailey fingered one of the strands of her necklace while she thought a moment. "Some of the oldest go back to when De Soto passed through here in the late fifteen-hundreds, supposedly looking for gold but also carrying gold coins. A few were claimed to have been unearthed on Glassy Mountain."

"Do you believe that?"

She smiled. "I believe it's a good story. Personally, I'm drawn to tales with more evidence. Most of those are during the time of the War Between The States. That was Mrs. Wainwright's specialty, you know."

In the phrase the War Between The States, I heard Mrs. Bailey's upbringing in a South that never called it the Civil War.

"Yes," Nakayla agreed. "What did you tell her?"

"I said there were a few isolated families living at the top of the mountain during the war, and a handful remain today. Back then, some of them, fearing being robbed, dug into the clay to bury valuable items. Not many years ago I was shown where a short trench had been dug several feet into a clay bank bordering a seldom traveled road. Silver and gold pieces had been put into the trench, then the opening was filled back up with the clay, keeping the items safe until the war was history."

"You think some of those items are still buried?"

She shrugged. "Who knows? Very likely if the owners died before retrieving their valuables."

"Could C.G. Memminger, the original builder of Connemara, have done that?" Nakayla asked.

"Sure. But he lived well after the war and would have dug up all his personal possessions."

I caught her emphasis on the word personal. "He was Secretary Treasurer of the Confederacy, right?"

"That he was. He resigned in 1864 but kept close ties with the leadership." She gave me an approving nod. "You put your finger on the point that interested Mrs. Wainwright. She wondered if any government assets were held at Rock Hill. That's what Memminger called his estate."

"Were they?" I asked.

"There were rumors. My family passed down such tales."

Mrs. Bailey had our full attention.

Nakayla scooted forward on the edge of her chair. "How long has your family been here?"

"Well, the earth had cooled." Her eyes twinkled as she looked first at Nakayla and then me. "My great-great grandfather built one of the first cottages. We were here along with the Memmingers. Flat Rock became an enclave and escape from the Charleston heat in the summer. As time passed, some of us found we had more in common with the mountaineers than the city's socialites."

"What sort of Confederate assets?" I prompted.

"For more than twenty years after the war, my family heard the Great Seal of the Confederacy had been evacuated out of Richmond and hidden here. But in the 1880s, the Seal surfaced elsewhere and is now in a South Carolina museum. Other government valuables were scattered for safekeeping during those days before Richmond fell. Especially the assets of the Treasury."

Mrs. Bailey lowered her voice as if someone outside might be eavesdropping. "When C.G. Memminger recommended moving the capital of the Confederacy to Flat Rock, I wondered if he didn't have two meanings in mind, the seat of government and the funds, that is the monetary capital of the Treasury."

"I thought the South was broke at the end of the war," I said.

"For the most part. But it had some hard currency and reserves. My personal theory is that Memminger received the Mexican silver that was smuggled out of Richmond."

A tingle ran down my back. Now Mrs. Bailey was talking about a clearer motive for murder. "How much silver?"

"I read reports of thirty-nine kegs of Mexican silver dollars. The money was payment for the sale of cotton to Mexico."

My mind flashed to the books in Janice Wainwright's study. She had the ledgers, the minutes of Confederate cabinet meetings, and the accounting records I hadn't understood at the time. Was this the explanation for Douglas McCaffrey's cotton production numbers and the circled entries for Texas-Mexico?

Mrs. Bailey continued. "When Jefferson Davis fled Richmond, the Mexican coins went with him to Danville, Virginia. Then when his party was forced to move further south, the weight of the silver slowed them down. Most people believe the treasure was buried in Danville and has never been recovered. But I wonder if they didn't split up, Jefferson Davis heading south with the Yankees on his trail and the treasure heading west. C.G. Memminger was a trusted confidant and the fact that Flat Rock was too remote to be the government's capital would make it desirable to keep the silver out of Union hands. There were just too many rumors floating around here after the war for there not to be some germ of truth."

She sat back in her chair, finished with her story.

"And you told this to Mrs. Wainwright?"

"Yes. She was actually much more knowledgeable about the finances of the Confederacy and immediately grasped the possibility."

"How much money are we talking about?"

Mrs. Bailey laughed. "Good Lord, I don't know. The kegs were supposed to weigh almost nine-thousand pounds. Mrs. Wainwright said today it would run into the millions of dollars."

Janice Wainwright's Plan B. As much if not more than her lawsuit.

"Mrs. Bailey," I said, "did Mrs. Wainwright tell you she thought the song uncovered in the foundation of the Sandburg home was connected to hidden Confederate assets?"

"No. But I could see the interest glowing in her face." She paused and stared at me a second. "Just like I can see it glowing in yours."

I nodded. "There's certainly nothing wrong with either your eyesight or your insight."

"But you couldn't help her with the song?" Nakayla asked.

"No. I did suggest one person Mr. Sandburg might have discussed it with. There was a funeral director over in Brevard. He was a composer and songwriter and he collected mountain tunes. He and his brothers would come to Connemara to play music with Mr. Sandburg. I did a column on him maybe twelve or fifteen years ago."

"What's his name?" Nakayla asked.

"Donald Lee Moore. But he since passed away."

DLM, I thought. The initials for Janice Wainwright's Saturday meeting. It had to be with his son, the man we were trying to track in Savannah.

"I can give you a copy of the column," Mrs. Bailey offered.

"We'd appreciate it," Nakayla said.

A trace of sadness crept over the older woman's face. "Mr. Moore used to sit out in a storage room behind his funeral home and compose sacred music surrounded by caskets. What an image. The temporal and the eternal merged into the creation of beautiful hymns." She sighed. "Sometimes our best stories aren't said, they're sung. Mr. Sandburg understood that and Mr. Moore understood that. It's ironic if neither understood the full meaning of Memminger's song."

"And maybe Janice Wainwright did," I said.

"Maybe," Mrs. Bailey agreed. "And like so many unwritten stories, maybe we lost it when she died."

Chapter Twenty-two

"No! He's not dead. I don't believe he's dead!" Wendy managed to shout the words through the phone before her speech disintegrated into garbled sobs.

I sat at my desk, BlackBerry to my ear, and waited. After a few minutes, the torrent of grief subsided enough for her to whimper, "Mr. Blackman, what happened?"

"We don't know," I said calmly. "I think someone attacked him in his office while he was studying a song called 'I'm Troubled'." Her crying stopped.

"Wendy, do you know the song?"

No response.

"Cameron Reynolds called you shortly before he died. You're not in trouble but I need to know what he talked about. He left me a message a few minutes later saying he was puzzled by something he found odd. I never got a chance to ask him what he meant."

"I don't know about the song." Wendy's voice sounded low and strained, barely more than a whisper. "We just talked about my mom's service and that Aunt Cynthia invited him back to her house."

"Nothing else?" I pressed.

"He told me Mr. Thrash cast me in the Sandburg musical." Her voice broke. "Cammie said he was proud of me. I told him I was surprised to be selected because I got so nervous waiting for my audition."

"And you didn't talk about your mother's work? Anything about Mexican silver or how your mom discovered a Sandburg connection to Glassy Mountain?"

"Who told you that?"

"Not Cameron Reynolds," I said. "Now do you want to tell me about it?"

She took a sharp breath. "You're talking crazy."

"Am I? Then tell me something sane."

"I don't know anything. I don't know why anyone would hurt Cammie."

I wasn't getting anywhere, and Wendy verged on hysterics. I looked at my watch. Three-thirty. The poor girl had buried her mother only four hours earlier. "Okay. So there was nothing discussed last night other than your mother's funeral and your audition?"

"That's right."

"Was anyone either coming or not coming to the service who was a surprise?"

"No. Cammie asked if my father would be there. I told him my father sent a gaudy display of flowers and that was the most we expected to see of him. He was at some golf tournament. Sure enough, he didn't show and Aunt Cynthia told the funeral home to put his flowers somewhere inconspicuous."

"Any reason Cameron Reynolds was interested in your father?"

"He couldn't stand him." Wendy gave a humorless laugh. "That was one point of agreement between Cammie and Aunt Cynthia and probably why she invited him back to her house."

I thought through my conversation with Paul Wainwright. "Your father told me he hadn't talked to your mother for a couple weeks, yet his phone number showed up in her records from last Friday. Do you know why he called?"

"Probably to complain about the overdue tuition bill he was supposed to be paying. He kept pushing me to attend a state school."

"Was he behind in his other payments to your mother?"

"I don't know," Wendy said. "Mom shielded me from those things. But she did say she thought times had gotten harder for my father and he was looking for the cheapest way out of his obligations."

"Did Cameron know all this?" I asked.

"Probably. He and Mom talked about what Cammie called my father's self-exonerating rationalizations."

I remembered Reynolds' claim that Paul Wainwright propagated the story of Reynolds' involvement with the underage freshman to make his own infidelity seem as innocuous as ordering the wrong wine with dinner. But Wainwright's actions involving Janice's funeral or his phone call complaining about Wendy's tuition didn't seem out of character. Certainly not the oddity that Reynolds referenced in his voice mail to me.

"Okay, Wendy. That's all I need right now. If you think of anything else, call me. Will you do that?"

"Yes, sir," she said. A tone of contrition underscored her sincerity.

"Then I'll see you Monday. Have a safe trip home."

"Mr. Blackman?"

"Yes."

"How's Ida Mae?"

"Fine. We're getting along great."

"I won't forget what you and Miss Robertson are doing for me."

"We're glad to help."

"I'll repay you. I promise." She hung up.

I clipped my BlackBerry to my belt, left my desk, and walked to the window. Looking out over Pack Square, I saw the sunlight reflecting off the courthouse at the far end. Tourists filled the sidewalks below, enjoying the warm Saturday afternoon and fresh mountain air. Asheville wasn't the kind of town where you expected to find a harmless college professor murdered in his office. "This machine kills fascists." Cameron Reynolds should have carried a weapon with more firepower than a guitar.

"How was the call?" Nakayla asked the question as she stepped through my doorway.

"Of no help." I turned to face her. "Wendy claims there was nothing in her conversation with Reynolds that was unusual. His only question was whether her father was coming to the funeral."

"What's the significance of that?"

I shrugged. "I guess he didn't want to run into him."

"You look troubled," she said.

"'I'm troubled.' That's the motto for this case, isn't it? I still think Wendy's holding out on us. When she returns Monday, we need to put her under surveillance."

"For what?" Nakayla asked.

"Damn it! If I knew, I wouldn't need to follow her." I snapped the words in frustration.

"Don't bark at me," Nakayla shot back.

"I'm sorry." I crossed the room and took her hand. "I think she's hiding something and I pushed her as hard as I could to confide in me. We're going to have to uncover the truth another way."

Nakayla raised my hand to her lips and kissed my fingers. "Dinner and a movie tonight would be a good start."

"To uncovering the truth?"

"To thanking me for tracking down Donald Lee Moore, Jr."

"You found him?"

"I spoke to him. I discovered he has an apartment in Savannah and he's been working there this week."

"Did his father know the song?"

Nakayla smiled. "Better than that. Don Moore has a CD of Carl Sandburg singing it. That's what he played for Janice Wainwright."

"Can we get a copy?"

"No. He made it from tapes his father and Sandburg recorded for fun. Sort of a song swap. His father told him they weren't to be made public. Sandburg said some of the songs and stories weren't suitable for the PTA."

"Doesn't he have the words?"

"He let Janice listen to the CD. They sat in his car at Hawg Wild."

"Then that's the CD the waitress saw."

"You're brilliant, Sam. Why do you need me?"

"I've got to have someone to take to dinner."

"And a movie. We're meeting Don Moore at Hawg Wild tomorrow for lunch. He's bringing the CD."

I took her in my arms and kissed her. "I love it when you talk barbecue."

◇◇◇

A phone rang somewhere in the room. Nakayla nudged me through her sleeping bag. "Answer your cell."

I opened my eyes and saw the screen of my BlackBerry flashing like a lighthouse in the dark. It lay on the coffee table and its glass top amplified the annoying chirp.

Last night Nakayla and I had unrolled our sleeping bags in front of the fireplace. I slid out of mine like a snake shedding its skin and crawled across the floor. My prosthesis was under the futon on the other side of the room.

The caller ID showed Cynthia Howell's number and the time was two-fourteen in the morning. "Hello," I croaked.

"Mr. Blackman, Wendy's gone." She sounded both distraught and angry.

"Gone where?"

"I don't know. I was asleep but woke when I heard a car start. I looked out my window to see Wendy drive off in my Volvo."

"What time was this?"

My head began to clear. Had the girl just wanted to drive around for awhile? Maybe have time alone? Nakayla turned on a light and I mouthed, "Cynthia Howell."

"Shortly after midnight."

"How did she seem earlier in the evening?" I asked.

"She was quiet, but I could tell she was agitated. I thought it was normal grief. This isn't a happy time. First her mother and now Cameron."

"Maybe she was restless. She'll return when she's calmed down."

"That's what I thought. But I got a text from her a few minutes ago. It read, 'Sorry, Aunt Cynthia. I'll bring the car back. See you in Asheville."

"She's driving here?"

"I guess."

"Did she say anything after I spoke to her?"

"She hung up and muttered, 'He betrayed me.' I thought maybe she was talking about you."

"I don't think so." I flashed back to our conversation. "She thanked us for helping her. The only person we talked about was her father."

Cynthia Howell gave a derisive snort. "What a waste of space. He betrays everybody."

"Is it possible Wendy made some effort at reconciliation you're unaware of?"

"Extremely unlikely. If Paul Wainwright cared for her, he would have come to Janice's funeral for Wendy's sake."

Maybe, I thought. Or maybe he didn't want to put himself through the hostility so clearly radiating from his sister-in-law. Then there was Wendy's promise to repay us. With what? Kindness? Proceeds from the lawsuit? Or did she have something more definite in mind?

"Paul Wainwright is in a golf tournament in North Carolina this weekend," I said. "Do you think Wendy could be heading to see him?"

"I don't know why. Unless it's to punch him. The son of a bitch sure deserves it."

If Wendy felt her father betrayed her, she could do more than punch him. I'd looked down the barrel of the pistol she'd pointed at me. 'He betrayed me.' Was that her father, or some other man? Maybe someone Wendy had trusted. Maybe someone Janice had trusted. Someone who understood what "The Sandburg verses" really meant.

"Did you text Wendy back?" I asked.

"No. I tried to call but she wouldn't answer."

"What's the drive time between Orlando and Asheville?"

"Around ten hours."

That was probably close to the same length as driving to Pinehurst. Wendy would arrive around ten o'clock in the morning. But where?

"Text her at seven," I said. "She'll read that because she won't have to speak to you. Tell her Nakayla called." Nakayla sat erect on the futon wondering what I was scheming. "She said Ida Mae is giving birth. That should get Wendy's attention. Maybe she'll call Nakayla and we can find out what she's up to."

"Okay," Cynthia Howell agreed. "But why wait till seven?"

"Because we wouldn't call in the middle of the night, and seven is the time we feed Ida Mae." I also figured that was a little before Wendy would split off I-95 for either Asheville or Pinehurst. I hoped to lure her here in case she was planning something foolish.

"Mrs. Howell, do you have a gun in the house?"

"A gun?" Her words trembled in the receiver.

"Yes. I know your sister had a small revolver."

"Our father gave us each one and taught us how to shoot it."

"Would you check that it's still in your house?"

A clunk in my ear signaled she'd dropped the receiver. I waited a moment, hearing only a few muffled sounds; then a panicked whisper.

"It's gone. I hide it in a dresser drawer, but it's not there."

Just like your sister, I thought, and the first place Wendy would look. "All right. She probably took it for protection if she's planning on driving all night alone."

"What should we do?"

"Nothing. Send the text at seven like we planned. I'll let you know when I hear from her."

I hung up and briefed Nakayla on the developments.

"Do you think we should warn Paul Wainwright?" Nakayla asked. "If Wendy comes at him like she came at you, there could be real trouble."

"Maybe. Let's see what happens after Cynthia sends her text message. Wendy won't get to Pinehurst before nine unless she's really speeding. I doubt she'd risk getting pulled by a state trooper. And she'd have to find her father on the golf course. Hell, we don't even know whether Wendy's headed there. She might just be coming home because she can't stand being away till Monday."

"Coming home with a gun."

"I love the way you always look on the bright side."

Nakayla got up and paced in front of the fireplace. She wore a pair of light-weight pajamas cinched loosely at the waist. Her bare feet trod noiselessly on the plank floor. "The reason you think she's coming for her father is because you and she talked about him on the phone, and then Cynthia Howell overheard Wendy say 'he betrayed me' when she hung up."

"Correct."

Nakayla stopped and thought a moment. "That's not good logic. She's felt like he betrayed her for years now."

"I know. But that's what I want Cynthia Howell to think. If Wendy shared information about her mother's research, it's with someone else. That's the person Wendy believes killed Cameron Reynolds, and just like she did with us, she's going after him."

"Should we notify Ranger Corn?"

"Not yet. I want to see how strong a pull Ida Mae has on her. If we hear nothing from Wendy after seven, then we'll call Corn and tell him to alert Paul Wainwright. You and I'll go over to Connemara. That holds the key to everything. It's where Wendy will go and where we'll find Cameron Reynolds' murderer."

"Who?"

"I don't know. My best guess is one of the rangers Wendy befriended, probably the supervisor of the goat herd. Or RT from Janice's calendar. I think that's Richard Torrence from the playhouse. He's a good-looking young man with whom Wendy could have become enamored. I believe Cameron Reynolds suspected as much."

"Okay. I agree with you. What do we do now?"

I scooted back to my sleeping bag. "We go to bed and take care of Ida Mae and the chickens at seven."

She turned out the light and lay down beside me.

But I stayed awake, my mind racing as each passing moment brought Wendy and the gun closer.

Chapter Twenty-three

At five minutes after seven, Nakayla's cell phone began beeping. We were working side by side in Ida Mae's shed. I mucked out her stall and Nakayla spread fresh straw on the ground. When Ida Mae dropped the kids, we figured they'd appreciate a soft spot to land.

"It's from Wendy," Nakayla said, glancing at the number before answering. She stepped out into the barnyard. "Oh, hi, Wendy." Her feigned surprise sounded genuine.

I followed, still holding the shovel.

"No, nothing yet. Ida Mae just seems a little different this morning. She's refusing her food and staying in her stall. Sam and I are with her. I'll call the vet if there's any sign of trouble." Nakayla paused, listening to Wendy's response. "Really? We thought you weren't returning till tomorrow." A longer pause. Nakayla's brow furrowed and her brown eyes locked on mine. She didn't like what she heard. "Can you tell us a little more?" This time Nakayla stood motionless for a good minute. Then she said, "All right. I'll tell him, but if things get out of hand, we'll intercede. I'll call back if there's any change with Ida Mae." She flipped her phone shut.

"What?" I asked.

"Apparently Wendy's devised a scheme to discover what happened to Cameron Reynolds."

"What?" I repeated the question with undisguised concern.

"Yes. We have an unwanted investigative partner. She's coming straight here. She wants us to be hiding."

My stomach tightened. "Hiding from what?"

"The person she thinks killed Reynolds. She wouldn't tell me because she thinks we'll call the police. She plans to lure him here and make him confess while we're listening."

I banged the shovel blade on the dirt in frustration. "My God, Nakayla, that's a terrible plan. A distraught, grieving seventeen-year-old with a pistol facing a killer?"

"I know. But what would you have said? Our goal was to get her here. That's accomplished. We can jump her as soon as she arrives, or we can play it out and see who shows."

"How did Wendy sound?"

"Surprisingly confident."

"Damn. I don't like it." What I didn't like was Wendy as the linchpin. As for the plan, luring a suspect out in the open was something I wouldn't hesitate to do. "Where are we supposed to hide?"

"In the old barn. And we need to park the cars out of sight. Wendy's going to be with Ida Mae."

I looked around. The barn wasn't large enough to house the vehicles.

"She suggested taking them over the brow of the pasture," Nakayla said. "There's a farm road that runs along the woods. We'd have a short hike back."

"What time is this going down?"

"Ten o'clock. Wendy was just coming off I-95 onto I-26."

"Well, I guess we're along for the ride then. You might have to push back the noon appointment with Don Moore."

"I'll call him at eleven," Nakayla said. "We'll know something by then."

"If we're all not in police custody."

◇◇◇

We used the time between Wendy's call and her expected arrival as productively as we could. Rather than try to hide two cars,

I followed Nakayla to her home in West Asheville where she dropped her Hyundai and then rode with me to my apartment in the Kenilworth Inn. I armed and legged myself, picking up my Kimber forty-five semi-automatic and changing my prosthesis to the Land Rover for more strenuous activity. If I needed to move quickly over open terrain, I wanted to be prepared.

We returned to the farmhouse around nine-thirty. Nakayla offered to drive the CR-V across the wide field and save me the hike back, but I needed the exercise to adapt to the feel of the stiffer prosthesis. I parked behind a clump of cedars that had advanced into the pasture and started walking. A light breeze from the woods carried the scent of pine. The tan windbreaker I wore to cover my shoulder holster blocked the morning chill, but the cool air felt pleasant on my neck and the soft earth made my steps easy. When I was about fifty yards from Ida Mae's shed, my BlackBerry beeped.

"Someone's coming down the drive," Nakayla said.

"Wendy?"

"It's not a Volvo. It's a pickup. I can't see who's behind the wheel."

"Damn it. Wendy should have allowed more time to get here."

"Whoever it is came nearly thirty minutes early."

"Lock the house. Try to do it without being seen."

"What are you going to do?"

I started running. "I'll be in the old barn. You stay where you are. If our visitor tries to break in, I'll apprehend him. Otherwise watch him and let me know what's happening. If he heads toward the barn, tell me and then go silent. He might hear the phone."

"Okay. I've got the front door locked and I'm moving to the kitchen."

"Do you have your gun?"

"Yes."

Nakayla carried a twenty-five caliber semi-automatic and was an excellent shot. I didn't worry about her firing wildly. She'd stay calm no matter what happened.

"Okay. Both doors are dead-bolted. I'm going to position myself in the dining room where I can see the front and back windows. I hear footsteps on the porch."

"Stay out of sight."

"You keep yourself hidden and don't worry about me."

I crouched in a corner of the barn behind a rusted plow. Through a crack between the warped slats of the wall, I could see the rear of the house.

"A young man's looking through the window of the front door and rattling the knob," Nakayla whispered. "He's about six feet with straight black hair. He's got a blue bandana tied around his forehead."

"Rick Torrence," I said.

"Wendy?" The name came as a distant cry.

"He's calling for Wendy," Nakayla said.

"I know. I can hear him."

"Now he's walking off the porch."

After a few seconds, I saw the tall figure walk into the backyard. He wore ragged black jeans, a yellow tee shirt, and a lightweight denim jacket. The blue bandana headband looked to be the same one I saw when he was painting flats at the playhouse. "It's Rick," I confirmed. "I'm going silent."

The actor/stagehand entered the unlocked back porch and knocked on the kitchen door. "Wendy?" he called again. He tried the knob and peered through the window. Then gave up and headed for the barn.

I pulled back from the wall and slipped the Kimber from my shoulder holster. Torrence hadn't appeared armed, but I wasn't taking any chances. The sound of his footsteps grew louder.

The crunch of gravel came from the front of the house. The footsteps halted. My BlackBerry vibrated and I saw Nakayla's text, "Wendy's here." I put my eye to the crack and saw Torrence pivot and quickly walk to the farmhouse.

Whatever happened, we were set. Nakayla could watch the front while I covered the rear and barnyard.

"Hi, Babe. Where'd you get the wheels?" Torrence shouted the question as he disappeared around the corner of the house.

If Wendy answered, I couldn't hear it. Obviously, she hadn't told Torrence she'd been driving from Orlando. I wondered what she'd said to get him here.

I had a pretty good idea when I saw the two of them walking together. Wendy snuggled into his side. He wrapped his arm around her waist, his fingers spreading across her abdomen, the maestro preparing for his performance.

Wendy adjusted the strap on her shoulder bag and glanced at the barn. She trusted I was inside just as I trusted the gun was in her bag. I hoped it would stay there.

"Where are you taking me?" Torrence asked. "Out behind the barn?" He laughed and pulled her closer.

She wiggled free. "I told you I've got to give Ida Mae her medicine."

Torrence lunged at her playfully, but she scampered out of his reach.

"Don't be so anxious," she said.

"When you said you wanted to go all the way, I didn't know you meant all the way to the barn."

I crept along the inside wall to the rear. The crack between the closed double doors gave me a wider angle and I watched Wendy step into the shadowy interior of Ida Mae's shed. She took the bag from her shoulder. Torrence stopped to the left about halfway between us, allowing me a clear view of both of them.

"Oh, I'll be going all the way." Wendy pivoted and held the pistol level and pointed squarely at Rick Torrence's chest. Unlike in my office, her composure was rock-solid. "I'll go as far as I have to. Make a move and I'll shoot. My mother taught me well."

Torrence froze. I couldn't see his face, but his voice quavered.

"Wendy. What are you doing?"

"You think I'd sleep with you the day after I bury my mother?" Suddenly she sounded close to tears.

I put my palm on the right-hand door, ready to push it open. Her gaze shifted briefly in my direction and then returned to Torrence.

She shook her head. "You're a jerk, Rick. Cammie Reynolds warned me about you."

"Who?"

"The man you killed. It had to be you. You were the only one I told about my mother's plan."

"You're crazy. I didn't kill anyone."

"You went to his office, you tried to make him reveal what he knew about the song, and then you killed him. I know because you left evidence behind that a detective found. Evidence of my mom's theory of the silver and a song clue."

Wendy had constructed her own theory. She thought I must have learned those things from something in Reynolds' office because yesterday I told her I hadn't learned them from Reynolds.

"I didn't even believe that shit," Torrence screamed. "I knew you were just saying it to try to impress me with how smart your mother was."

Wendy's jaw muscles twitched. Torrence was pushing her too far. She pulled back the hammer and the cylinder rotated.

"Liar. You killed my mother. I see it now. That's why you weren't painting the flats."

Torrence dropped to his knees in the dirt. He was sobbing. "Wendy, I swear. I killed no one. I don't know what you're talking about. Painting flats? I painted the damn flats, I re-painted the flats."

"Mr. Thrash was late for the auditions because his assistant had skipped out leaving him to finish the work. I didn't think about it at the time. I was too nervous. But I understand now. You were stalking my mother and you pushed her off that mountain." She stepped closer and aimed the revolver at his head.

Torrence raised his hands in front of his face as if they could stop a bullet. "No. That's not true."

He was right. It wasn't true. I pushed open the barn door and walked into the light. I knew the truth. The oddity that drew

Cameron Reynolds' attention. The reason he was murdered. Who had confronted Janice Wainwright on Glassy Mountain.

"Wendy," I said. "Lower the gun and ease down the hammer."

Torrence whipped his head around. Tears streaked his face. "Man, she's crazy. She tried to kill me."

"No, she didn't. Or else you'd be dead."

Wendy shook her head. "He didn't confess."

"That's because he didn't kill anyone. But he's about to tell me who did. Otherwise he'll be charged with conspiracy in the death of Cameron Reynolds."

Torrence looked at me with surprise. "But I don't know anything?"

"Yes, you do. Answer one question. Where does the Flat Rock Playhouse put up its visiting directors?"

"A condo," he said quickly, anxious to please. "One of the patrons lets them rent it."

"Where?"

"Down the road. In Kenmure."

"Right answer." I looked to Wendy. "Your plan worked. Now lower the gun."

Torrence followed my gaze. A cold smile formed on Wendy's lips. She pulled the trigger.

Torrence screamed.

The hammer clicked on an empty chamber.

"It's not loaded," Wendy said. "I remembered what happened last time."

Chapter Twenty-four

Do What Has To Be Done. The motto of Criminal Investigation Command. The directive I followed as a Chief Warrant Officer in the U.S. Army's CID. CID. The initials go back to the founding of the Criminal Investigation Division before it was elevated in the 1970s to Command status, and CID is still used as an acknowledgment of the proud heritage that empowered me to "seek diligently to discover the truth, deterred neither by fear nor prejudice." At least that's the way the CID's mission is phrased on the web site. And actually that was the way we operated, no matter the consequences, no matter the rank of the suspect.

But now, out of the army and out of the Command, I felt the dilemma the truth imposed. Seeking the truth is not the same as acting upon the truth. I had a clearer picture of what happened but a murkier picture of what lay ahead. Do What Has To Be Done. But done for whom? And for what purpose? I faced the paradox that justice for Janice Wainwright's death created injustice for her daughter by undermining the wrongful death suit and costing her millions of dollars. And, on the other hand, Cameron Reynolds deserved to have his killer pay the price for his crime.

These thoughts tumbled through my mind as we walked from the barn to the farmhouse. Torrence took slow, measured steps and his complexion was as white as porcelain, not only from his point-blank confrontation with Wendy's pistol, but also from my threat to turn him over to the police for complicity in the murder of Cameron Reynolds.

Nakayla met us at the back porch and instinctively hugged Wendy without asking any questions.

"We didn't take Ida Mae's temperature this morning," I told Wendy. "I think you and Nakayla should do that now."

"But I want to hear what he has to say," Wendy protested.

Nakayla caught my eye and nodded. She grabbed Wendy gently by the arm. "Sam knows what he's doing. You need to trust him."

The girl glared at Torrence. "All right. Ida Mae's worth two of you. I hope you rot in jail." She spun around and headed for the barn.

As Nakayla followed her, I said, "Call our noon appointment and see if you can slide it to one."

"You got it."

I nodded to Torrence. "Let's go inside."

"No, man." He backed away and balled his hands into fists. "You can't hold me against my will."

I reached under my jacket and pulled out the Kimber. "Suit yourself, asshole. This gun's loaded, I'm licensed to carry, and I've shot so many people I've lost count."

His brief flare of bravado dissipated like a snowflake in a campfire.

"Now up the steps and into the house." I waved the revolver toward the backdoor. "You say you're an actor? Well, I'm going to give you the role of a lifetime."

The damnedest thing happened. Torrence looked at me, dropped his hands, squared his shoulders, and said, "A role? For me?" He bounded up on the porch.

I holstered the Kimber and led him to the living room. He perched on the edge of the futon and I sat in the chair opposite him.

"There's a way for you to come out of this clean," I said. "Assuming you are clean."

He nodded his head vigorously. "I am clean. I haven't touched Wendy. She lured me here."

I felt reassured that Torrence believed his only crime had been trying to seduce a seventeen-year-old girl. I decided to push that button. "Fine. If you don't cooperate, Nakayla and I will claim we discovered you forcing yourself on her. It'll be your word against ours, and you can guess which side Wendy will back."

He threw up his hands. "What the hell do you want? Just tell me."

"I want to make sure we don't have a failure to communicate. Is that clear?"

"Yes." He leaned back, folding his arms across his chest. "Now what's this role?"

"Arthur Thrash wanted you to find out what Wendy's mother was working on, didn't he?"

Torrence looked skeptical. "You don't believe what she's saying about me stalking Mrs. Wainwright?"

"No, I don't. But we need to prove it to Wendy. You can see she's disturbed and making wild accusations. But who can blame her? She just buried her mother."

He considered the point. "Well, she shouldn't have pulled a gun on me."

"No, she shouldn't have. But you did betray her confidence, didn't you?"

He sighed. "Look, Artie told me to ask Wendy if her mother was making progress on her project. He said Janice Wainwright was holding back some of her findings that he'd like to use in the narrative of the Sandburg revue."

"I thought they'd been collaborating?"

"They had been. That's how I met Wendy. She was hanging around the theater while her mother was talking to Artie. I guess Artie thought there was more to the story. He can be a demanding bastard when he wants something."

"What story?"

"Some song Sandburg found. Janice Wainwright thought it had historical importance. The guy who wrote it had been a hotshot in the Confederacy and built the Sandburg farmhouse. I don't know much about what else he did."

"Did Wendy tell you her mother thought it might be the key to some missing Confederate silver?"

"She said her mom believed the song described where the guy buried something he wanted hidden from the Yankees. Maybe silver, maybe secret papers, but Wendy said her mom would be famous."

"Famous?"

"Yes."

"Not rich?"

"No. Famous. These college types get off on discoveries. Normal people like you and me would just sell or pawn whatever we found. You know what I mean?"

"Yes," I agreed. "And Arthur Thrash probably wanted to know the whole story because it would add dramatic significance to his show."

"You got it. Artie says it's all about the story."

"When did you talk to Wendy last about her mother's project?"

He thought a moment. "I guess it was a week from today. Sunday night."

I remembered Janice Wainwright's calendar with RT marked for last Sunday afternoon. "But didn't you talk to Janice Wainwright that day?"

"Me?"

"Yes. She had RT on her calendar."

Torrence look baffled. "What's a meeting with Artie have to do with me?"

RT. They weren't initials for Rick Torrence. Janice used RT for Artie instead of AT for Arthur Thrash. A little word play? I recalled Cameron Reynolds' comment when I mentioned RT on Janice's calendar and he asked if they were initials. His first thought was Artie, but I'd already given him initials for the other appointments so he went with the pattern.

"Nothing directly to do with you," I said, covering my mistake. "I wondered if you'd spoken to Wendy after Janice met with Artie."

"I did. Artie asked me to. Janice didn't show last Sunday. He was pissed and wanted me to find out from Wendy what was going on. That's when Wendy told me her mother got a copy of the song."

The back of my neck tingled. "The song Sandburg found?"

Torrence started to answer and then paused a second. "No, that's wrong. Wendy didn't say her mother had the song, she'd heard the song. Wendy didn't know the verses."

The CD Don Moore brought to Hawg Wild. Janice would have listened to it the day before and blown off the meeting with Thrash. Maybe she sensed his interest was more than academic. "And you told this to Artie?"

"Yes. But I think it wasn't until the next morning."

Monday. That evening Janice Wainwright bought a tree book at Malaprop's because of a sudden interest in chestnuts. The next afternoon she fell on the rock outcropping after I told Arthur Thrash I was looking for a woman matching her description. He immediately left, claiming he was going to the auditions, and probably saw Janice's Explorer in the parking lot. Driving through Kenmure, he could be on the rock face ahead of her, watching her undetected. When he thought they were alone, he confronted her.

"Has Artie asked you to talk to Wendy since her mother's death?"

"Yes. He wanted me to give his condolences. And he asked if I could find out if Janice had the song sheet. This was the day after the woman died. I thought that was a little pushy, even for Artie."

I nodded my agreement. I was also relieved. Arthur Thrash didn't know that Janice Wainwright had learned the original song sheet no longer existed. Maybe that's why he cast Wendy in the play, to keep her close and ingratiate himself. "Okay. Here's what you need to do. In a few days, I'm going to get you more information about that song. You'll tell Artie you heard from Wendy that she found the verses in her mother's dresser drawer and she's not sure what to do with them. She's thinking of sharing them with her mother's colleagues at the university. That way any academic discovery will be credited to her mother's research. It's what her mother would have wanted."

"But Wendy wouldn't have told me that. She said I wasn't worth a goat."

"Artie doesn't know that. We're going to keep what happened this morning a secret."

Torrence wasn't the brightest bulb in the chandelier. Comprehension slowly dawned on his face. "Oh, right. We're making this stuff up."

"I'll have you wear a wire so we can hear what Artie says. Will you do that?"

"Like in the cop shows?"

"Yes."

"Cool."

"Artie will ask what you told her. You'll say you thought that was a good idea, but to wait because maybe Artie could help her. He could verify what her mother was working on and give Janice credit in the show. Tell Artie you suggested Wendy could even sing the song."

"Yeah. That's a good idea I had. Artie will like that."

"And when Wendy hears you taking her side with Artie, she'll know you meant her and her mother no harm. Everything will be fine."

Torrence sat quietly for a few minutes, mulling over the proposition. "Then can I tell Artie I was acting? I want him to be impressed."

"No. Not immediately," I said firmly. "That will ruin it. After Artie talks to Wendy and everything is ironed out, then you can tell him. Artie doesn't strike me as the kind of guy who likes being tricked. After the show's a big success will be the best time. Then he'll be too happy to care."

"Right." Torrence smiled. "This is great. Can I keep a copy of the recording of me and Artie? Maybe use it for an audition some time?"

"Sure," I lied. "Meanwhile, play it normal with Artie. Don't tell him you've seen Wendy. As far as you know, she's still in Florida. I'll contact you when we're ready."

"Okay. Let me give you my cell number. In a couple days, right?"

"Yes. Certainly by the end of the week."

We stood. He shook my hand. Any memory that I'd pulled a gun on him or threatened him with a false accusation of attempted rape had vanished from his mind. He had a role to play. Actors. What a bunch of lunatics.

I waved as he drove off in his pickup. Now what the hell was I going to do? I'd launched the first stage of an operation without a plan for its culmination, designed a deception on the spot without knowing when or how to pull the trigger. Oh, well, I couldn't be expected to think of everything. That's why I had a partner.

I found Nakayla in the fenced pasture with Wendy. Ida Mae was drinking water from her trough.

"Where's Rick?" Wendy eyed me suspiciously.

"He's gone. I'm satisfied he had nothing to do with your mother's death or Cameron Reynolds' murder."

"But Rick must have told someone. You knew about the song and the silver. I figured you found something in Cammie's office. Something Rick left behind."

"No. Nakayla spoke to the same man your mother did."

"Eli Smyth," Nakayla said. "His family owned Connemara before the Sandburgs."

"I know about him. Mother told me."

"And we pieced together what the song possibly means," I said.

Wendy's face fell. "So, I was wrong about Rick?"

"No. Not really. He didn't kill anyone, but he was pumping you for information." I decided it was best to crush any resurrecting romance. "Cameron Reynolds was right about him. Rick's a jerk interested only in himself." I looked at Nakayla. "Did you manage to move our appointment?"

"Yes. We're on for one."

"You need to stay with Wendy."

Wendy frowned. "I can stay by myself. She doesn't need to babysit me."

"I know. But someone broke into your house and someone killed Cameron. Until we find him, I don't want you left alone. Have you talked to your aunt?"

"We called while you were talking to Torrence," Nakayla said. "Cynthia's coming up tomorrow on the originally scheduled flight."

"Okay. So we'll stay here tonight." I grabbed Wendy by the shoulders and looked her square in the eye. "Are you good with that?"

"Yes."

"And you'll do exactly as we say?"

"Yes."

I released her, but she kept staring at me, her expression a mixture of anger and determination.

"What was your mother going to do with the song?" I asked.

"She was going to decode what it meant and see what was buried."

"If it was silver, was she going to try and sneak it out? Was that her backup plan if she lost the lawsuit?"

Wendy looked horrified. "Steal it?"

"That's what Rick Torrence was going to do."

"Rick's a jerk. You said so yourself. Mother was going to find what she thought was the spot and then notify the rangers and the university so they could set up a proper archaeological dig. If they found what she hoped they'd find, it would make her career. She would have academic papers to write and maybe a book deal."

"And is that what you want to happen now?"

Wendy's eyes filled with tears. "More than anything, Mr. Blackman."

Do What Has To Be Done. Wendy Wainwright had just narrowed my options for what had to be done to a delicate balance of deceit and provocation. At last, the vague outline of a plan began to take wispy shape in my mind. Like the fog comes on little cat feet.

Chapter Twenty-five

I arrived at Hawg Wild fifteen minutes before one. The lot was crowded but I found a parking space in a far corner and backed the CR-V into the spot. By facing out, I could see patrons arriving and leaving. I didn't know what Don Moore looked like, but Darlene number two had described him as carrying a CD when he met Janice Wainwright. I figured there was a good chance he'd do the same this time.

I wanted him to enter the restaurant first so that I could see if he had a tail. I was fairly confident Moore's relationship to the case wasn't known beyond Nakayla and me, but I'd seen over-confidence become a quick ticket to a casket too many times to take any chances.

About ten minutes later, a Lexus SUV stopped close to the front entrance and waited while another vehicle vacated a choice parking place. I couldn't see the features of the Lexus' driver, but reflecting sunlight highlighted silver-gray hair. As soon as the space was clear, the driver smoothly arced into it. He emerged from the car a moment later and glanced around. His height above the Lexus pegged him at over six-feet and he looked to be in his mid-to-late sixties. As he walked toward the restaurant, he carried a single CD case in his right hand.

I sat patiently for another five minutes, studying the arriving cars. Arthur Thrash wasn't in any of them, and there was no indication he had an accomplice cruising the lot. My rendezvous with Don Moore appeared to be secure.

I stepped inside and the hostess at the door asked if I was alone. Before I could answer, Darlene number one saw me and came running over.

"He's here," she whispered, her eyes wide with excitement. "He just sat down in Darlene's zone. She said he's got the same CD and he's waiting on someone."

"Me." I nodded to the hostess. "Thanks. Darlene can show me to the table." Darlene number one led me the length of the restaurant.

Halfway there, the younger Darlene caught up with us. "Does he know about his friend?"

"Yes," I said. "We've spoken on the phone."

Both Darlenes visibly relaxed. No person of kind heart likes to see someone receive bad news, and the waitress duo from different generations shared that admirable quality of compassion.

"He's fine," I added. "I'm sure your good food will make him feel even better." I left the women and walked to the corner table where the man with the CD idly glanced over the menu. He sensed my approach and looked up, then beyond me, obviously expecting Nakayla.

"Mr. Moore?" I stopped in front of him.

"Yes."

"I'm Sam Blackman. You spoke with my partner, Nakayla Robertson."

He stood and extended his hand. "Call me Don. Isn't she coming?" A hint of worry flickered in his blue eyes, as if somehow he'd been set up.

"No, she's not. She's staying with Mrs. Wainwright's daughter. We hated to leave her alone at a time like this."

He nodded sympathetically. "Yes, of course. A terrible thing. I didn't learn about it till I got your partner's call." His voice was soft and southern, but with cultured diction. A blend of the mountain and low-country dialects. He wore a green V-neck sweater over a tan, collared shirt. He appeared fit and trim. A man who took care of himself.

"Thanks for seeing me." I motioned to his chair. "Please sit."

We both tucked up close to the table across from each other.

Moore gave me the menu. "I don't know why I bother to look at it. I always order the same thing."

Young Darlene stood beside me in an instant, pencil at her pad. "You gentlemen know what you want?"

"My treat." I indicated for Moore to order first.

"I'll take the western barbecue dinner."

"Sounds good for me too." I handed her the menu.

"Tea?" she asked.

"Make mine a mixed drink," Moore said.

"I'll have the same."

"They'll be out shortly." Darlene scampered away.

Moore chuckled. "That's the nice thing about a barbecue joint. Not too many choices."

"And only one mixed drink." A mixed drink in reference to iced tea meant half sweetened and half unsweetened.

"So, what happened to Mrs. Wainwright?" Moore asked.

I told him the story of how she'd been taking medication for severe back pain and evidently stumbled and fell on the bald rock of Glassy Mountain. I shared that her last words for her daughter had been "The Sandburg verses" and we knew she had come to him for the song. Since it had been a pivotal point in her research on Connemara's history, we didn't want her work to be incomplete.

When I finished, Moore looked unconvinced. "How did you know Mrs. Wainwright?"

"She was suing the surgeon, hospital, and pharmaceutical company for the consequences of her back operation. My partner and I became involved in the case. Now we're helping her daughter Wendy follow through. This is sort of a side issue, but it goes to evaluating Mrs. Wainwright's value to society and academic research."

Moore nodded. "For determining a settlement."

I shrugged, letting him draw his own conclusion. The best lie is the unspoken one.

He picked up the CD. "I can't let you have this."

"I assumed so. Otherwise you'd have given a copy to Mrs. Wainwright."

"My father was the funeral director here in Brevard. He also composed music and collected mountain songs. He and his two brothers would get together and sing. Today, we'd call it a jam session. Somehow they got connected to Sandburg and they'd gather at Connemara. My dad had a Wollensak reel-to-reel and one night they recorded the session for their own amusement. Sandburg was in lively form, singing and telling stories, although everyone contributed. One of my uncles must have brought some moonshine just to enrich the spirit of the evening."

"Do you know when this happened?"

"My Dad said it was in January of 1956. He told me they all agreed never to make the recording public. It was strictly fun. Record a number, play it back, and pass the jug."

"But they're all gone now," I said.

Don Moore gave me a hard stare. "Not to me. Not my father and not my uncles. And the promise is very much alive."

It was the answer I wanted to hear. I knew Don Moore wouldn't want to draw attention to either the song or his conversation with Janice Wainwright.

"I understand completely. That's very commendable. But if you've got Sandburg's version of 'I'm Troubled,' I'd like to hear it, or have you write down the lyrics for me."

Moore smiled. "I don't see any reason for you not to listen to the song. It's not like someone's making money off it."

Darlene arrived with our food, sparing me the awkwardness of a reply.

After I paid the bill, we walked together into the parking lot.

"I've got a CD player in my car," I said. "All right if we listen there?"

Moore pointed to the Lexus two cars away. "I'm right here, and I know how to work the controls on mine. We need to fast-forward through about three-fourths of the disk. I digitized the original tape as one long clip."

I sat in the passenger's seat and watched as he slid the CD into the dashboard player. Suddenly Carl Sandburg's baritone voice surrounded us. From more than five decades in the past, he introduced a song about a country bumpkin going to London. Don Moore let it play about thirty seconds till Sandburg started singing. The quality of the recording was marginal with hiss and pops occurring throughout, but the words came through clearly enough.

"Did they record this in Sandburg's living room?" I asked.

"Yes. My father plays the piano for one of the songs."

Sandburg's guitar accompaniment to his voice was more punctuation than rhythmic strumming. He plucked the strings rapidly, particularly at the end of phrases, and infused the words with musical energy. I was surprised how taken I was with the sound, and I conjured up the image of that long ago evening in the room I'd visited only a few days ago.

Don Moore pushed the fast-forward button and watched as the digital counter displayed the running time. "The song you want is about thirty minutes in."

"How long's the recording?"

"A little over forty." He laughed. "They were just getting warmed up when they ran out of tape."

He paused the CD and hit play. A different voice, higher and more plaintive, sang a slow ballad.

> "I'm sad and I'm lonely,
> My heart it will break,
> My true love loves another,
> Lord, I wisht I was dead."

"That's it," I said. "That's the last verse of the song."

Moore let it play on.

Off-mike, Sandburg asked, "Do you know the origin?" "It's been circulating in these hills for years," the singer said.

"I believe that's my uncle Alvin," Moore said. "Now Sandburg tells his story."

Sandburg gave a brief account of how a handwritten version of the song was found in the wall during the renovations. He'd been familiar with it, but not the two verses added before the last one. Then Sandburg began singing in a sorrowful tone while lightly plucking the treble strings.

> "I'll dig me a grave hole
> On the rocky north side,
> To seal neath the chestnut
> A lost lover's pride.
>
> I'll cover it over
> With stones blue and gray,
> And leave it forgotten
> Till the pain dies away."

Then Sandburg said he thought someone in the Memminger household must have put the chest with the song in the foundation wall, but he never figured out why. None of the Moore brothers could offer an explanation. One of them asked to see it. "It's gone," Sandburg said, and strummed his guitar dramatically. "Disappeared." He laughed. "The box was so rusty I think someone threw it out. Paula won't admit it, but I don't think she liked any ghost of the Confederacy underfoot." That got a big laugh all around.

I asked Moore to replay Sandburg's verses two more times so I could make sure I copied the words correctly. Then he played his uncle's version. Those four verses didn't seem to be altered from the text in the Lomax collection. He ejected the CD.

"Thanks," I said. "I really appreciate the help."

"What are you going to do now?" Moore asked.

"Give these lyrics to Janice's colleagues at the university. They'll add them to her work."

Moore nodded his approval. "Makes for an interesting story. It's times like this I wish I'd sat down with my father and recorded him. He was a treasure trove of mountain stories."

I opened the door and shook his hand before slipping out. "I know. I'm afraid too often we overlook the treasures right before our eyes."

I sat in the front seat of my CR-V and watched him leave. Then I opened the Lomax book and read the song lyrics again, inserting Sandburg's verses where he said they appeared.

> "I'm troubled, I'm troubled,
> I'm troubled in my mind,
> If trouble don't kill me,
> I'll live a long time.
>
> My cheeks was as red,
> As the red, red rose,
> But now they're as pale as
> The lily that blows.
>
> I'll build me a cabin
> On the mountain so high,
> Where the wild birds can't see me
> Or hear my sad cry.
>
> "I'll dig me a grave hole
> On the rocky north side,
> To seal neath the chestnut
> A lost lover's pride.
>
> I'll cover it over
> With stones blue and gray,
> And leave it forgotten
> Till the pain dies away.
>
> I'm sad and I'm lonely,
> My heart it will break,
> My true love loves another,
> Lord, I wisht I was dead."

The new verses fit seamlessly into the song. A lover burying his pride under the pain of his loss. No one would see anything unusual in the lyrics or tone. But now I looked at them through the eyes of Janice Wainwright, Civil War historian who immersed herself in the world of C.G. Memminger, Secretary of the Treasury for the Confederacy.

Several words jumped out at me. Lost, pride, blue, gray, pain. But the song didn't have a final ending. The singer wasn't buried in the grave. He was biding his time "Till the pain dies away." Then what? His pride would be restored? The covering stones of blue and gray would be stripped away so something could emerge from a hole beneath a chestnut on the rocky north side?

I imagined Janice Wainwright standing on the rocky face of Glassy Mountain, directly above C.G. Memminger's home, facing north, and looking for the vestiges of new growth constantly shooting forth from the roots of a chestnut tree that died in the 1930s. A struggling sentinel marking the hopes of a fallen rebellion and the resurrection place of the last remnants of its treasure.

Chapter Twenty-six

"You're creating a difficult situation," Nakayla said.

She and I stood on the front porch of the farmhouse and waved as Wendy and her aunt Cynthia drove away. It was a few minutes after three on Monday afternoon. Wendy had met her aunt at the airport while Nakayla and I debated our next move. When they returned, we'd convinced them to check into a hotel for a few days and promised to notify Wendy if there was any change in Ida Mae's condition.

"No," I argued. "We're facing a difficult situation. I didn't create it." I pulled my wallet from my back pocket and extracted the slip of paper with Rick Torrence's cell number.

"And you think Torrence can pull it off?"

I followed Nakayla into the living room. "All he has to do is make a simple statement. Wendy's back from Florida and she found song lyrics in her mother's dresser. We know Thrash didn't search it or he would have taken the Lomax book. Then Torrence goes into his spiel about Wendy wanting to give the verses to her mother's colleagues and his recommending she also give Thrash a copy of the song for the show."

"And when Thrash tells Torrence to bring him the lyrics?"

"I don't think that's going to happen. Thrash doesn't want anyone else to see them. Not Torrence, not the history department at the university, and not the Connemara rangers. He'll try to get his hands on them as fast as possible."

"All right. That makes sense. But what if he doesn't? Torrence isn't exactly Sherlock Holmes. Thrash might believe the actor doesn't have a clue as to what the verses mean."

I had to give my partner credit. She pushed me to consider all possibilities. Maybe that was because a few of my plans in the past had gone awry with nearly fatal consequences. "If he tells Torrence to get a copy of the lyrics, we'll give him one. I think changing the words from the rocky north side to the rocky south side should protect the actual location. Then we'll have to wait for him on the mountain."

"Yeah, sitting in the dark on federal land." She stared at me with disbelief. "You're not exactly the world's best camper."

"If Thrash is coming to the south side, then we won't be on federal land. We don't have to camp. We can stay with Roger Richardson Hill in his mausoleum. At least Roger doesn't snore."

"He's got that over you." Nakayla sat on the futon. "The smart thing to do is call Ranger Corn, give him what you've got, and let him set the trap."

I paced the floor in front of her. "But we know Corn's case will tie directly to Janice Wainwright. If we bring Thrash down for Reynolds, then Ranger Corn won't be involved. It's the Buncombe County Sheriff Department's investigation. Thrash isn't going to admit he attacked Janice and anyway it's the weaker case to prove as a homicide. All we'll do is create a proximate cause that blows the wrongful death suit."

"I don't like it," Nakayla said. "There are too many elements out of our control."

"That's why we're taking it step by step to gain control. I'll have the recording of Torrence and Thrash establishing that only Thrash was given information about the lyrics' location here in the farmhouse. Since my P.I. license is good for audio-video surveillance and North Carolina is a state that allows one-party knowledge of a recording, their conversation will be admissible in court. I'll set up a video camera in the bedroom and we'll catch him red-handed."

"And how does that tie him to Cameron Reynolds?"

"His actions will provide probable cause for a search warrant. He's breaking and entering for a song we also found in Cameron Reynolds' office, a song in the very book that was stolen from my car."

"He'll say Cameron Reynolds' stole it."

"Impossible. I checked Reynolds' class schedule. He was teaching at the time. In addition to a search warrant, we might get his DNA match to the skin under Reynolds' fingernails."

"If it's not Reynolds' own skin from where he clawed at the guitar string." Nakayla eyed me skeptically. "What else are you planning?"

"I think that's enough to jump-start the investigation. I'm counting on the efficiency and expertise of the local law enforcement officers to follow-through."

"Since when?" The darkness of her complexion deepened. "Sam, are you being straight with me?"

I tried to look as innocent as I could. "If you've got a better idea, I'm all ears. You're the one who wants to bring in the authorities. I'm just creating a buffer between Arthur Thrash and Janice Wainwright."

"And that's creating a difficult situation," Nakayla said again. "My original point." She threw up her hands in surrender. "But I understand why you're doing it and I don't have a better idea."

"Good. I'll call Torrence and tell him to see Thrash tomorrow. We'll meet an hour ahead to get the body mike on him and find a parking place within range of the transmitter."

"Sam, are we going to hold Thrash if he breaks in, or let him go and turn the recorded evidence over to the sheriff?"

"It'll be stronger if we apprehend him at the scene."

"And more dangerous."

I nodded. "Only if he comes armed. We'll play it by ear. I won't do anything foolish."

"That'll be a first."

◇◇◇

"What's up?" Arthur Thrash's voice sounded distant and tinny.

Nakayla and I sat in my Honda and listened through the receiver on the console between us. The attached field recorder captured every word.

"I talked to Wendy Wainwright this morning." Torrence came through loud and clear. I'd taped the omni-directional mike to his sternum and the slight rustle of his shirt fabric was the only distortion.

A squeak punctuated his sentence. He must have sat in a chair.

"Is she back from Florida?" Thrash sounded closer. He asked the question in an offhanded manner.

"Yeah. Last night. Her aunt's coming up in a day or two."

"Is Wendy going to be able to do the show?"

"As far as I know. She said to thank you for the part."

"Well, I figured she needed something to look forward to."

Silence stretched for at least twenty seconds, an eternity while recording a conversation.

"Is that why you wanted to see me?" Thrash asked at last. He sounded annoyed.

"Yeah. You told me you wanted to know when I spoke to her."

"I want to know what she says. Was that all? Thank me for the part?"

"Yes. And she found some song lyrics in her mother's dresser."

"What?" Thrash's voice reverberated with excitement.

I looked up from the recorder and caught Nakayla's smile. "Our actor's doing all right," I whispered.

Torrence laughed. "I thought you'd be interested."

"Maybe." Thrash dropped his tone a couple of notches. "If it's something we can use in the show."

"Wendy says it's a longer version of 'I'm Troubled.' She's going to give it to one of the professors at UNC-Asheville. I said she ought to give you a copy. Maybe you'd let her sing it."

"Did you speak with Wendy in person?"

"No. On the phone."

"Did she read you the song lyrics?"

"No."

Another long silence.

"Has she already given the song to the university?" Thrash asked.

"I don't think so. She just found it this morning. You want me to call her and get you a copy?"

"No," Thrash said quickly. "It's not a big deal. And you shouldn't have suggested I'd let her sing the song. We might not be able to include it. The show's running long."

"Sorry. I was trying to help."

"I know. And I appreciate it." Wheels squealed. Thrash must have rolled back his chair and gotten up. "Say, is Wendy by herself?"

"I guess so. She didn't say otherwise."

"Why don't you take her out for dinner. Cheer her up."

"I was gonna finish the set pieces tonight," Torrence said.

My stomach tightened. He was blowing a critical opportunity for the sting. Of course, it would have helped him understand that if I'd brought him into my confidence.

"I insist," Thrash said. "My treat. You can finish set construction in the morning. Don't make it a late night and remember she's seventeen. Keep your distance."

"Okay."

"See me after you phone her. She lives near Asheville, right?"

"I think so."

"I'll make a reservation at 131 Main in Biltmore Park and give you my credit card. It's an excellent restaurant."

"And the song?"

"Tell her I'll see it some other time. She should leave it where she found it till her mother's colleague reviews it. Then I'll get a copy."

"Thanks, Artie."

"My pleasure."

A heavy thump jumped the volume level on the recorder. Thrash must have slapped Torrence on the back.

Five minutes later, Torrence crawled in the backseat of the Honda. "How'd I do?"

I turned and shook his hand. "Worthy of an Academy Award."

He beamed. "Can I hear it?"

"No. There's not time. We've got to move to phase two."

"There's more?" he asked.

"Artie expects you to take Wendy to dinner. We don't want him to know this was all an act, right?"

"But Wendy's pissed at me."

"I know. Tonight we'll playback your conversation. Wendy will hear how you and Artie were concerned only with her welfare. But you should go to dinner because Artie will be expecting a credit card receipt from 131 Main. Have you got another girl you can take? Someone who won't run into Artie between now and then?"

His eyes brightened. "There's this music major at Brevard College. She's hot."

"By all means, go for the hot one," Nakayla said.

Torrence was oblivious to the frost in her voice. "Okay. What should I tell Artie?"

"That it will be seven-thirty," I said. "Wendy has to take care of her farm animals and won't get away until seven."

"That's it?"

"Yes." I pointed to his chest. "Take off the mike and transmitter. We won't need to record any more. Just call me to confirm Artie's made the reservation."

"Cool. This was fun."

As we pulled out of the Connemara parking lot, Nakayla said, "I have to admit I had my doubts but your plan seems to be working. Thrash is coming to the farm."

"He's set things up to give himself the opportunity. And we need to make sure he finds what we want him to find."

"I should dummy up the song sheet so he thinks he's got the original. He doesn't know the song only exists as a recording."

"Good idea. Can you make the paper look aged and write the lyrics with an old-fashioned pen?"

"I have a calligraphy set. And paper soaked in light coffee should bake to a vintage brown. He won't examine it too closely, will he?"

"I doubt it. The bedroom will be dark."

"What are you going to do?" she asked.

"Get the video equipment from the office and rig the camera." I glanced at my watch. "It's one o'clock now. Be at the farm no later than five. Call Wendy and make sure she doesn't go anywhere near Flat Rock this afternoon. She can meet us at the farm at five to take care of Ida Mae. She should go back to the hotel by six-thirty. I don't think Thrash will show before seven, but I don't want to cut it too close. We'll need to hide our cars at the far end of the pasture again."

Alone back in our office, I charged the batteries in the miniature surveillance camera and loaded a fresh tape in its wireless recorder. I went to the file drawer and retrieved the thirty-two caliber pistol Wendy had fired at me. One spent and four live cartridges were still in the five-chamber cylinder. I pulled out the spent along with a live one, and spun the cylinder so that the hammer was over the last bullet with the two empty chambers next in rotation. There would be two pulls of the trigger before the firing pin hit a shell. If I couldn't kill Arthur Thrash in that time, I deserved to be shot.

Then I looked up musical instrument stores in the Yellow Pages and called them in alphabetical order. The third one had what I wanted. Elixir guitar strings.

Chapter Twenty-seven

At four o'clock I stood in the doorway to Janice Wainwright's bedroom and surveyed what I had to work with. The dresser was on the left-hand wall. Above it hung a large wood-framed mirror shaped in a horizontal ellipse. The double bed ran lengthwise under the twin windows of the exterior far wall. Lace curtains bordered half-drawn shades. The view looked out on the front yard and driveway. The bed's brass headboard stood tight against the wall opposite the dresser. A lamp and nightstand were on the right side between the bed and a closet door. The wall beside the bedroom door allowed just enough room for an armoire to fit between the space needed for the closet and hall doors to swing open into the room.

I walked in, dropped my gym bag on the bedspread, and examined the light on the nightstand. The square shade was white cloth stretched over metal rods, the base was green ceramic, and the finial, a ball of cut-crystal. There was not a good spot to mount the camera.

I opened the closet door and found it jammed with dresses, blouses, slacks, and skirts. If I positioned the camera inside, I'd have to leave the door open and eliminate my own hiding place. The top of the armoire was a possibility, but if Thrash pushed the hall door open more than thirty degrees, the video coverage of the dresser would be blocked.

I checked the walls and ceiling for a smoke detector. There wasn't one. I unzipped the gym bag and lifted out the plastic case of a gutted smoke detector. Then I unpacked the surveillance camera, remote activator, and separate recorder with a built-in three-inch viewing screen. I snapped the camera inside the smoke detector so that its lens aligned with the hole where the sensor had been.

I studied the dresser. The drawers on the right caught the light from the windows. If Thrash arrived before dark, there might be stronger illumination in that area. I couldn't count on his turning on the overhead light and I certainly didn't want him turning on the lamp on the nightstand near the closet. I loosened the bulb so he would think it was burned out.

The camera angle was important for another reason: I needed to see his face in the mirror. If the position were directly behind him, he would block his own image. And when the time came, I wanted him turning to the camera, clearly visible from his face to his hands. Placing the phony smoke detector on the wall above the closet door provided an angle on the dresser that would capture Thrash in the mirror while he searched through the drawers. Even light from a pocket flash should bounce off his face enough for identification.

I donned a pair of latex gloves from the bag and then emptied its remaining contents on the bed. Nakayla would be bringing the dummy song lyrics, but I had the library copy of the Lomax book, the loaded pistol, a box of Elixir guitar strings, and a roll of double-sided industrial tape. I took the number four guitar string from its paper envelope, looped it around my prosthesis, and pulled as tight as I could. The artificial leg wasn't the same size as a human neck, but the bend and stress of the string's metal would be close enough. I rewound the string into a loose coil and left it on the bed. I dropped the box of strings and empty envelope back in the gym bag.

The upper right-hand drawer of the dresser was small, no more than a foot wide and four-inches deep. Inside were neatly folded pairs of panties. I slipped my gloved hands under all of them and set the pile on top of the dresser. Then I opened several drawers until I found one packed loosely enough to hold them.

Into the empty drawer, I laid the Lomax book with the pistol next to it. I put the coiled guitar string on the black book cover where the faintest glow of light would snap the shiny metal out from the dark background. When Nakayla arrived, I'd slide the song sheet under the revolver.

I brought a straight-back chair across the hall from Janice Wainwright's study and placed it in front of the closet. I attached double-sided tape to the back of the smoke detector, climbed on the chair, and firmly pressed my makeshift camera mount in place. I used the remote to activate the device and flipped on the recorder's receiver. A wide-angle shot of the bedroom appeared on the viewer. I walked to the dresser and stood in front of the drawer I'd prepared. The clarity of the miniature camera's resolution was remarkable. My face was clearly visible in the mirror. I knew the quality would degrade when night fell, but there would be enough of an image that a video specialist would have no trouble boosting the luminance.

I returned the chair to the study, repacked my gym bag, and then took all of Janice Wainwright's clothes from the closet and laid them on the bed. I expected Thrash to believe that Wendy was going through her mother's things. I stepped in the closet and pulled the door until there was only a half-inch crack between the edge and jamb. Even in the daylight, I was far enough in the recess that I felt confident Thrash wouldn't notice me.

Nakayla arrived a few minutes before five. I met her on the front porch and she immediately handed me a sheet of stiff paper with two deep creases where it had been folded. The texture felt like parchment and the brown-yellow tinge appeared uneven with age. The verses of "I'm Troubled" were written in faded black ink.

"What do you think?" she asked. "I got the paper at a crafts store."

"It's great. How many tries did it take?"

"This is the third. Getting the stain and the heat balanced was the toughest part."

"I'm sure he'll just glance at it in the drawer, take it, and bolt."

We turned at the sound of gravel in the driveway and saw Wendy come up in her Subaru. She was alone.

"I'm going to run this to the bedroom," I said. "I don't want her to know what we're doing."

"Okay. She'll head straight for Ida Mae anyway."

I hurried up the stairs, put on the gloves, and lifted the pistol out of the drawer. I re-folded Nakayla's doctored song, laid it beside the Lomax book, and then replaced the gun. I didn't care about our fingerprints on the paper. In fact, their presence would prove Thrash took the sheet we'd put in the farmhouse. When he opened the drawer, he'd see everything at once. The book, the guitar string, the revolver, and the song. If he was our killer, three of the four would be a bad surprise. They'd be the signal that someone was on to him, and I figured he'd react. It was now up to him.

Do What Has To Be Done. I was giving the CID motto new meaning.

"Sam! Sam!" Nakayla called my name from the backyard.

In an instant, I understood my plan must be in trouble.

By the time I got downstairs, Nakayla was already in the kitchen. She said one word: "Mucous."

I felt the blood drain from my face. "You mean that kind of mucous?"

"Yes. Ida Mae's vaginal mucous. There are traces in the straw. Just like the ranger said. They're from earlier today so we're very close."

"Why now?"

"Because she's due. We knew it could happen any time."

"But not now. We need to get Wendy the hell away from here."

The girl ran in the kitchen from the back porch. She jumped up and down with excitement. "Her temp's dropped to ninety-nine. The kids are coming tonight! They're coming tonight!"

"You can't stay," I said. "It's not safe."

Wendy froze. A look of desperation came over her. "No. I'm not leaving." She turned to Nakayla. "You're not taking this away from me."

"You're in danger," Nakayla said. "Sam and I can't protect you and find Cammie's killer."

"You won't have to. I'll be in the shed with Ida Mae." Wendy turned and ran out of the kitchen.

"God damn it, Nakayla. She can't be on the property. We don't know what's going to happen."

"Maybe we lead Ida Mae to the woods where we hide the cars. We can load the birthing supplies in the CR-V."

"And leave Wendy by herself?"

"Yes. She'll be out of sight. Maybe everything will be over before Thrash gets here."

I headed for Ida Mae's shed. "Don't count on it."

I found Wendy outside the stall, staring at the goat. Ida Mae had turned away, facing the back wall as if she didn't want to be seen. Tremors rippled across her body. She wasn't walking to the other end of the pasture; she wasn't even walking out of the shed.

Nakayla hurried past me and put her arm around Wendy's shoulder. I stood mesmerized as three dots appeared between Ida Mae's hind legs. In only a few seconds they grew larger and became the tip of a nose and two tiny hooves. Then a wet, slippery brown and white bundle dropped to the ground head and forelegs first. Ida Mae turned and began licking the kid where it lay in the straw.

"Is it breathing?" Wendy asked. She leaned over the stall's gate.

"Yes," Nakayla said. "I can see the rib cage moving. When will it stand up?"

"Usually not for another half hour."

"What if there's another one?" I asked.

"Ida Mae's got to rest," Wendy said. "It might be an hour or two before a second one is born."

Right when Thrash would probably arrive. I knew short of knocking Wendy unconscious I'd never drag her away. "All right," I said. "Here's what we'll do. Wendy, you can stay, but we'll keep the door of the shed closed. You're not to come out under any circumstances, no matter what you hear. Use the flashlight only in an emergency. If Ida Mae and the kid are doing fine, leave it off. If a second kid comes, do what you need to, but stay in the shed. Make sure you've got everything here you need. Understand?"

Tears glistened in Wendy's eyes. "Yes. I promise."

"Good. Nakayla will be outside and she will open the door when it's safe to come out."

"Where do you want me?" Nakayla asked.

"In the tool shed where Wendy locked up the ranger. You can't see the front of the house but you've got a view of the driveway. Text me if a car comes. Then I'll turn off my phone."

"And after that?"

"Stay put. If I apprehend our suspect on the spot, I'll yell for you. If I think that's too dangerous, I'll stay hidden and we'll contact the Sheriff's Department as soon as he leaves."

I looked down at the newborn kid. The little face was framed by the downward Nubian ears. Ida Mae licked its back diligently. "Good job, Mama. Everything's going to be fine."

Nakayla and I moved the three cars into our hiding spot in the pasture. When we returned to the shed, the kid was on its feet. The three of us stood by the stall, but Ida Mae showed no sign of delivering a second kid.

"Maybe there's just the one," I said.

"The vet was pretty sure there are two. Ida Mae's got to regain some strength before she starts pushing the second one."

At six-fifteen, I decided we'd better take our places. There was the chance Thrash could come early to watch the farm from the overlook. When he didn't see Wendy's car, he might think she'd finished her chores and left. Although I expected him to wait till dark, I didn't want to take any chances he'd arrive early.

Nakayla and I stopped at the tool shed. She gave me a hug. "Don't be a hero."

"Don't worry. No one's ever confused me for a hero."

She kissed me. "No confusion here. I know you are. And that's what scares me." She looked at me for a long moment, and then turned away.

I entered the farmhouse through the kitchen door and locked it behind me. I made sure the front door was bolted. I turned on the porch light and a lamp in the living room. I figured it seemed likely that Wendy wouldn't want to return to a completely dark house.

Rather than stand in the bedroom closet, I sat in the study away from the windows. Six-thirty came and went. Then seven. The sky changed from purple to black. Seven-thirty. I wondered if Ida Mae nursed twins, and if Wendy would do as she'd been told.

At twenty to eight, my phone vibrated. The text message appeared: "car coming down the drive with lights off. love u."

Quickly I keyed back "love u 2" and then cut off my cell. I stepped across the hall to the bedroom, took the remote from my pocket, and activated the video camera. I entered the closet and pulled the door closed until the crack was only large enough to see the right side of the dresser. Then I took the Kimber from my shoulder holster and pulled back the slide. The click broke the silence. It would be the last sound I'd make until I was face to face with Cameron Reynolds' murderer.

Chapter Twenty-eight

Even though I stood in a closet in the dark, I closed my eyes and envisioned the impending action. I saw Arthur Thrash in the mirror. He would look down in the drawer. Although his body would block my view of his hands, his face would tell me all I needed to know. He would pick up the guitar string and study it a second. The presence of an identical murder weapon should unnerve him. He'd recognize the book cover but leave it alone. Then he'd lift the gun, maybe to take it or to get to the song sheet underneath it. When I calculated he held it in his hand, I would step from the closet, standing directly under the camera. I would tell him to freeze. He would spin around, startled by my voice. If he pulled the trigger, I'd hear one click. I wouldn't wait for the second. The videotape would show him pointing a gun at me after breaking and entering. Enlargement and enhancement would provide proof that he pulled the trigger first. I reacted with just cause. Still, I would be in a tricky spot. There would be questions. But my claim of self-defense backed by the legal skills of Hewitt Donaldson should prevail. The killer of Cameron Reynolds would have been revealed, and the man who confronted Janice Wainwright on Glassy Mountain would have been silenced with no one the wiser. Two separate cases closed by one death. Do What Has To Be Done.

The tinkle of breaking glass shattered my imaginings. Thrash was coming in through the kitchen. I shifted my weight to my good leg and held the Kimber close to my cheek. Through the crack in the door I saw only the murky shapes of the bedroom furniture.

Footsteps on the floor came steadily. The man had been in the house before. He knew his destination. Moving shadows danced on the wall as the motion of a flashlight played through the hall. Then the overhead light blazed to life. Reflexively, I pulled back from the door.

I heard a drawer being opened. I pressed my eye to the crack and enlarged the field of view. Arthur Thrash stood in front of the left side of the dresser. I felt relief that my suppositions had been correct. He had a black cylindrical flashlight jammed in the hip pocket of his jeans. He wore a brown leather jacket with a piece of powder-blue scarf peeking over its collar. The artistic director always dressed for the role. His hands were covered by tight-fitting driving gloves. He would leave no fingerprints.

Without pause, he scooped out the contents of the first drawer and dumped them on the floor. He moved to the one below it. Now I could see his face. His jaw was clenched in grim determination. His eyes flicked rapidly over the articles of clothing as he pulled them free.

When he snapped open the upper right drawer, his mouth dropped. For a few seconds, all he could do was stare down. Then he lifted up the looped guitar wire and examined it closely. Was he looking for blood or some other sign that the string he'd used on Reynolds had been magically transported into the farmhouse?

The moment of action approached. Thrash stuck the guitar string in his jacket pocket. Again, his hands disappeared into the drawer. He was picking up the revolver.

Suddenly the line I was prepared to cross in theory became a barricade in reality. No matter what this scene looked like to the video camera, I knew Arthur Thrash wasn't an armed man. A loaded gun that won't fire properly isn't a deadly weapon. Those first two useless pulls of the trigger might as well have been on a squirt gun. Calling him out and shooting him down was not the action of a hero, not the action of the man I used to be in the CID. And though others may have betrayed me in the course of my career, I could not betray myself. Do What Has To Be Done is always coupled with Stay True To Yourself. I not only faced Arthur Thrash in the mirror, I faced myself.

The moment came. The moment went.

Thrash stuck the revolver in his other pocket. His eyes brightened as he lifted the song sheet. His fingers trembled as he carefully unfolded the creases. There was no mistaking the smile that came when he read the added verses. Then, as quickly as he entered, he left, switching off the light as he passed through the door. The back spill of his flashlight dimly illuminated the bedroom until he disappeared down the stairs.

I waited, not daring to move until I heard his car engine start. Two minutes became five. Nothing. Had he found Nakayla or Wendy?

I left the bedroom and started down the stairs. The sound of sloshing liquid came from the rear of the house. When I reached the first floor, the pungent smell of gasoline hit me like a tidal wave. Arthur Thrash was drenching the kitchen and back porch. He was going to burn down the farmhouse, destroying any sign of his theft and leaving Wendy to believe the song sheet had been consumed by the flames. I was torn between unlocking the front door and running around the house to intercept him or going straight to the kitchen over the gasoline-soaked floor. That would be the fastest route. It would also be the fatal one if he ignited the gasoline before I could stop him.

I held my breath and ran through the kitchen and onto the back porch. Puddles of gas splashed under my feet.

A road flare threw a brilliant light in the backyard. Thrash stood at the bottom of the porch steps holding it like some mockery of the Statue of Liberty. The red glow of the spewing flame cast demonic shadows across his face.

I leveled the Kimber at his chest. "It's over, Thrash. The song's a fake."

"No. You're lying!"

"Rick Torrence was wired. The recording went to the police. And we know you killed Cameron Reynolds."

The flare wavered in his hand. He could throw it before I shot or fall forward and drop the flare into the rivulets of gasoline flowing under my feet and down the porch steps.

Tears sparkled on his cheeks. "I didn't want any of this to happen. Janice was going to turn everything over to the park service. I didn't want it all. I didn't even want half. Just enough to go to New York and get my career back on track. Have the money to be a producer."

"She told you about her theory of the silver?"

"Yes. The historical story would be part of the play. But she wouldn't tell me what she learned from the verses. I tried to reason with her on the rock. I never touched her. I swear. She suddenly clutched her back and collapsed."

"I heard her cry out 'no.'"

"Right, when her back spasmed. Then I heard someone call out. I guess that was you. I knew how it looked. There would be questions. I panicked and grabbed the backpack. She had some tree book inside. I kept it and tossed the backpack into the bushes away from where I was hiding. I would have stayed to help her, but you were there. There was nothing I could do. I swear it was an accident."

"An accident when you bludgeoned the ranger the next morning?"

"I didn't lock that woman in the shed. I didn't know she'd get out. I needed the verses. That's all I wanted."

I stared at him, momentarily stunned at the extent of his rationalization.

"And Cameron Reynolds accidentally strangled himself with a guitar string?"

Hate flashed in his eyes. "He called me a thief. Me. Arthur Thrash. He looked at me like I was a common criminal."

"You went to see him Friday night. Find out what he suspected after I saw you. He waited for you, but he tried to reach me beforehand. Reynolds was asking questions, wasn't he? He'd just learned from Wendy that you showed up late for the audition at the high school the afternoon Janice died. He figured Janice had told you about the silver."

"Don't you see? He had no proof. He couldn't touch me. But he was going to tell you about the silver. I couldn't have that happen. Then everything I'd done would have been in vain."

"So you left the book you stole from my car to throw suspicion on him and set the scene of a remorseful suicide."

"You don't understand. He threatened me. If he'd just gone along, everything would have been fine."

"But he wouldn't go along and you garroted him in cold-blood. No, you're not a common thief. You're a murderer. A monster."

"Don't say that! You have no proof!"

"You're wrong. I have you in a starring role up in the bedroom. Videotape of you caressing the looped guitar string in front of the mirror. The duplicate of the string you used on Reynolds. The jury will be captivated by your performance."

"I am not a monster!" The flare arced back slightly, the nearly imperceptible sign of his intention to throw it forward and burn me alive. The thought of the videotape in the house pushed him over the edge, even though he was right. It wasn't enough to connect him to Reynolds' death.

Before I could fire, two short pistol shots rang out behind Thrash. His eyes snapped open with surprise as he stumbled toward me. I leapt from the top step, hurling myself at him like an NFL linebacker. The flare tumbled from his hand. I batted it away as I collided with his body.

I hit the ground and rolled to my knees, desperately looking for the flare. Nakayla picked it up from the grass.

"Nice move," she said. "I didn't know you had it in you."

"Nice shooting, but you nearly cooked me in the process."

"Stop whining. You're the guy who loves barbecue." She walked over to Thrash, the flare in one hand and her gun in the other. "You want to check for vitals while I cover him?"

Thrash lay on his back, one leg and one arm curled under him. His eyes were open. One of the twenty-five-caliber bullets must have pierced his heart.

"The show's over," I said. "No curtain call."

Nakayla sighed as the tension left her body. "He gave me no choice." Her voice warbled and despite her flippant banter, I knew she was shaken. She'd just killed another human being.

"No. He didn't. And that's the tragedy. He had choices. You didn't." I wanted to hug her, but the flare in her hand and the gasoline-soaked shoes on my feet still made a deadly combination. "You did what had to be done. I'd have you in my unit any day."

"We are in the same unit. Blackman and Robertson." She walked away from Thrash's body and snuffed out the flare in a bare patch of earth.

Blackman and Robertson. We'd come damn close to having our partnership go up in flames.

"What's our story?" she asked.

I knew what she meant. We'd stopped an arsonist who would have killed me in the process. That evidence and the story were strong enough. We could destroy both the videotape and the copy of the song. The treasure would be waiting for us whenever we wanted it.

"What do you want to do about the silver?" I asked.

"What would Janice Wainwright want to do?"

"Damn. I hate it when you go all ethical on me. Then the way I see it we give the police the whole package, the conversation between Torrence and Thrash this morning, the videotape from the bedroom, and the confession when he thought he could incinerate me."

"What do you think about his version of what happened on Glassy Mountain?" she asked.

"I think there's a good chance he was telling the truth. We know Janice collapsed in her classroom. But from that point on, he disintegrated into a man obsessed with treasure." I looked at Thrash's body. "The villager with his torch come to burn down the castle with the monster inside. That's how he saw me. The monster threatening to take away what he was due. And who next? Wendy, probably."

"So, we're saying Thrash didn't meet Janice on Glassy Mountain?"

"It never happened."

Nakayla smiled. "I can live with that."

"Then call it in. Be sure they send a fire truck and chemicals to handle the gasoline spill."

"In a moment," Nakayla said. "Let's check on Wendy."

We found her in the stall, drying a second brown kid with a towel. The first stood nursing at one of Ida Mae's udders.

Wendy looked up as we entered. "Everything okay? I thought I heard shots."

"Everything's going to be fine," I said. "The police will be here shortly. I've got some tough news for you. Arthur Thrash killed Cammie. He tried to burn down your house and we had to stop him with lethal force."

She stared at us in disbelief. "Mr. Thrash?"

"Yes, he wanted the Mexican silver. He didn't kill your mother, but after she died, he saw Cammie as the only obstacle in his way."

She was too stunned to ask probing questions. We'd fill in details later, but the main goal of any fabrication was to keep Janice Wainwright's death solely a consequence of her operation and medication.

"What about the house?" Wendy asked.

"No fire, but there's gasoline spilled on the back. Nakayla's calling the police and they'll handle it."

"I guess I'd better call Aunt Cynthia and let her know. By now she ought to be getting use to the police being on the property."

The newborn kid struggled beneath the towel, trying to get to its feet.

"I see you've been busy," Nakayla said.

"Yeah. Nakayla didn't want to breathe so I poked her in the nose with a straw. Her reflex started her lungs. That's a trick the ranger taught me."

"Nakayla?" I said.

Wendy smiled. "Yeah." She pointed to the nursing kid. "And that's Sam. He hasn't stopped eating since he latched onto the udder."

"That's Sam," the two-legged Nakayla agreed.

◇◇◇

"You know Thrash lived in Kenmure," Ranger Corn said. He leaned against one of the front porch posts and watched the volunteer firemen repack their gear. The ambulance carrying Thrash's body had left twenty minutes earlier.

"Really?" I said. Nakayla and I sat together on the old glider. We'd given statements and turned over all our evidence to the Buncombe County deputies. Corn had come because we'd called him. "Did his name pop up on the guardhouse log?"

"No. I got the idea to check the names of short-term renters as well as owners. The playhouse has some arrangement with Kenmure and Thrash was using a condo."

"Interesting. So, he could have breezed right in. But he told us he wasn't there. Why admit to murder but deny an encounter on Glassy Mountain?"

"Why indeed," Corn said. "No point in pursuing it now. Better just to expunge that whole theory from the file."

"Suit yourself," I said.

Nakayla kicked my leg. The good one. "We appreciate what you're doing," she told Corn.

"Only doing my job."

"Does your job include guarding the site of buried treasure on National Park land?" I asked.

"It can. So that document Thrash came after is real?"

"No, that's a phony. And we told the deputies so. But Janice was right about the Sandburg verses. Actually they were written by C.G. Memminger. We changed a key word in case Thrash got away with them. We'll give you the real verses if you promise to give Janice credit for identifying their significance and Wendy any reward if she's due a finder's fee for her mother's research."

"I can't make any promises, but I'll look into it."

"One more thing."

He laughed. "Isn't there always?"

"When whatever Memminger buried is ready to be unearthed, we'd like to be invited. I'd like to see what we voluntarily turned over to our government. Maybe include Wendy and a few other guests."

"If you're giving us the location of millions of dollars in Confederate treasure, I'll carry you up there myself."

"No bother. I'm easy to please. An all-terrain limousine will be sufficient."

Chapter Twenty-nine

The first signs of autumn began to color the foliage before we next assembled on Glassy Mountain. The events of the previous April seemed a lifetime ago.

A search of Arthur Thrash's rented condo had uncovered some of Janice Wainwright's Sandburg books and her home calendar. None of the critical meetings with Eli Smyth, Louise Bailey, or Don Moore had been on it.

That evidence linked Thrash to the first break-in at the farmhouse. The only possible connection to Janice's injury on Glassy Mountain was a copy Thrash had of the same tree book that disappeared from Janice Wainwright's backpack. Ranger Corn concluded thousands of people own that guide and it in no way altered his opinion that Janice had tragically stumbled and fell because of her pain medication. The search of Thrash's personal bills and bank statements revealed that Thrash was nearly bankrupt and drowning in credit card debt. He indulged in Broadway tastes on a summer stock income.

Wendy was a successful freshman at Warren Wilson College. Ida Mae, and our namesakes, Nakayla and Sam, were also enjoying residency privileges on the college farm.

Corn had done his best to acquire monetary consideration for Janice Wainwright's discovery, but the U.S. Government's concern with legal precedents limited our nation's thanks to just that—"Thanks." It seemed since this potential treasure was already on federal property, there was no collection role for Janice Wainwright to play. It wasn't like she was a deep-sea diver bringing up sunken treasure off the Outer Banks of North Carolina. Even having a metal detector on park land is a crime. But a statement of thanks would be read by the local congressman into the Congressional Record and there was talk of a plaque being mounted at the site of the discovery.

The lawsuit was progressing more satisfactorily. Hewitt had made the suggestion that Wendy's attorney offer a settlement with Dr. Wyatt Montgomery for three million dollars. That was the limit of his malpractice insurance and would keep him from losing personal funds. Given the M.E.'s report, both the doctor and his insurer jumped at the offer. What was understood but never spoken or written down, was that Dr. Montgomery would also testify in the suit against the pharmaceutical company that he had developed grave misgivings about the prescribed painkiller and its addictive properties and side effects. Word of Montgomery's pending deposition leaked, and the pharmaceutical attorneys were suddenly interested in a fair-and-just, out-of-court settlement.

So, the financial road ahead for Wendy was as bright as the sunny sky of our balmy October morning. Nakayla, Wendy, her aunt Cynthia, and I were waved through the Kenmure guardhouse to drive the two and a half miles where we could park and walk the shortcut path to the Glassy Mountain overlook.

During the intervening five months, Ranger Carol Hodges at Connemara had coordinated all aspects of the proposed historical dig. Using the verses as a guide, she'd received assistance from the chief arborist of the North Carolina Arboretum in Asheville. He'd found not one but three chestnuts growing on the north side, the oldest of which was succumbing to the blight. Then funds had to be appropriated for the proper archaeological approach. The park service wouldn't haul a backhoe up the mountain and start gouging away. A sophisticated, heavy-duty metal detector was utilized to check the ground adjacent to all three chestnuts. One of them generated a hit. Then the search began in earnest. Digging proceeded in small sections and layers. No one knew for sure what would be found and how scattered the discoveries might be. Historical artifacts could be damaged or destroyed in a rush to reach larger objects. During the month of September a few coins and a button from a Confederate uniform had been unearthed. A particularly wet late summer and early fall had restricted the number of days suitable for digging.

But now the major metal source was estimated to be less than six inches below the surface. Work had been halted as Ranger Corn and Ranger Hodges honored my request to observe the final phase of the excavation.

They'd also invited Louise Bailey, Eli Smyth, and Don Moore, all of whom played a crucial role. Dr. Venable and Dr. McCaffrey represented UNC-Asheville.

As we walked in on the short trail, we passed Roger Richardson Hill's mausoleum. I wondered what he would have thought had he known he'd pitched his tent not fifty yards from a treasure of the Confederacy.

We formed a circle around the plot of open ground that was now about four feet deep. It was not unlike a graveside service except we were bringing something up rather than lowering someone down. The rangers had camp stools and folding chairs available. I sat beside Louise Bailey. She wore pants, sensible walking shoes, and a light down jacket. She was set for the duration.

"See any ants?" I asked.

She laughed and patted me on the arm. "This is quite an adventure."

When everyone was in place, the site supervisor had two of his team begin with small spades. They progressed slowly to insure they didn't damage anything. A man shot photographs of the process with a digital camera. After about thirty minutes, they had defined the perimeter of a metal box roughly a yard square. They started down on all sides.

Sandwiches were passed around at lunch. There were jugs of lemonade and ice water. Then two chains were handed down into the hole. Through a coordinated lift of blades, the rusty metal box was pried free of the dirt and a chain threaded underneath first one end and then the other. Using the chains as a hoist, men kept the box level as they raised it out of the hole and set it on a cleared spot of ground.

"It's not a keg," Louise Bailey remarked.

"No, it's not," I said. "Maybe it has instructions as to where the kegs of silver are buried."

"Maybe. You're a devious thinker, young man."

Dr. Venable took a closer look. "The clasp is rusted away. It can be opened without further damage."

The site supervisor bent down with a small crowbar. We all got to our feet. I noticed Nakayla had grabbed Wendy's hand. I took Louise Bailey gently by the arm. "Let's get a ringside view."

Metal groaned as the crowbar forced the lip of the lid upward. Dry hinges squealed. Several hands reached out to keep the lid open at a forty-five degree angle. The supervisor reached in and felt something wrapped in oilcloth. He smiled.

"The treasure of the Confederacy," he said. "I should have known." He looked to an assistant. "Charlie, help me. This whole block should lift out."

The two men struggled to raise a rectangle shrouded in the oilcloth. They carried it to a portable workbench near the hole. We followed. The men found the edges of the cloth and the supervisor said, "Drum roll, please."

He and his colleague removed the cloth and revealed an engraving plate. The dull metal relief was etched with reversed letters, numbers, and designs.

"An eight-bill plate for one side of a five dollar confederate note," Douglas McCaffrey said. "And guess whose picture is on it."

"C.G. Memminger," Louise Bailey said, and then gave a hearty laugh. "How appropriate. A buried treasure of false hopes and paper promises. As I live and breathe, life never ceases to amaze me."

"That's it?" I said.

Dr. Venable shrugged. "Apparently so. It's still a scholarly find and a good piece of detective work by Professor Wainwright."

"Good detective work," I mouthed to Nakayla.

"Let's go," she replied. "This case is closed."

We left Wendy and her aunt at their car in the Connemara parking lot. The route home had become so familiar I drove on automatic pilot.

"What a bummer," I said.

"Really?"

"Janice Wainwright dead, Cameron Reynolds dead, Arthur Thrash dead. And for what?"

"Janice died for her academic integrity and Cameron died trying to find the truth. Like us, I think he also wanted to protect any finder's fee for Wendy. That's why he held back information and offered to review Janice's research. Arthur Thrash simply died for greed. Two of the three exemplified noble causes. And then there's you and me."

"Us?"

"How would you have felt if we'd kept that location to ourselves and dug up plates for printing worthless confederate money?"

"Pretty sleazy. We'd have hijacked Janice Wainwright's scholarship."

"You made the right choice, Sam."

I said nothing, only felt her continuing to stare at me. I wondered if she somehow knew about the other choice I'd almost made in the closet of Janice Wainwright's bedroom.

"Okay. Thanks. That's comforting."

She leaned across the console and kissed my cheek. "And, there's always Danville."

"Danville?"

"Janice Wainwright didn't invent those thirty-nine kegs of Mexican silver. That's where they're probably buried. She might have been a good detective, but I know a better one."

"I know two," I said. "They're so famous even Sandburg's goats are named after them. But what's this about Danville? You and I've got a date in Paris."

"Sam, you sweet-talking devil. Where do you want to eat barbecue tonight? I'm buying."

I sped down the entrance ramp onto I-26 headed west. Headed home.

Acknowledgments

The premise of this novel, that Carl Sandburg discovered a song sheet in the foundation of Connemara, is pure invention. However, the history of Connemara from its construction to its existence as a National Historic Site is factual. I am indebted to the Connemara National Park Rangers and volunteer staff for their cooperation during the research phase of the book. Pisgah District Ranger Tim Francis was invaluable for guidance on issues of law enforcement jurisdiction. Any errors of procedure are my responsibility.

Two people who played key roles in the inspiration for the story are no longer alive. For more than forty years, Louise Bailey wrote a column for the *Hendersonville Times* entitled "Along The Ridges." Her dedication to recording and sharing the stories of the mountain people created a lasting legacy. Scenes in the novel with Louise are drawn from my personal conversations with her and from her columns. She was Carl Sandburg's part-time secretary and the incidents regarding their relationship are true. Her son Joe graciously provided assistance after her death, and I regret that she didn't live to see herself as a character in the mystery.

Donald Lee Moore was both a funeral director and published composer of sacred music. He and his brothers collected mountain songs and would visit Connemara to share their repertoire with Carl Sandburg. Donald Lee's account to me of those sessions and materials shared by his son Don Moore formed the framework for the fictional recording of "I'm Troubled," a lament that can be found in Alan Lomax's *Folk Songs of North America*. I'm grateful to Don Moore for his help and for agreeing to appear in the story.

Eli Smyth shared remembrances of his great-grandfather Captain Ellison Smyth and his family's history at Connemara; Randy Romeo assisted with details of the Kenmure community; Dr. Tom Buter provided guidance in the area of spinal surgery and its possible complications; and Henry Harkey, attorney extraordinaire, patiently listened to my questions about proximate cause and wrongful death suits. Any variances from medical or legal accuracy are my own wanderings for the sake of the story.

Mrs. Sandburg bred champion goats and ran a dairy business at Connemara. The National Park Service keeps a remnant of her herd for visitors to see. Additional information was provided by Melinda Hartley Marlette who went through the real delivery of Ida Mae's kids and veterinarian Dr. Jenny L. Milford who gave Sam and me an insight into the gestation and birthing process.

Thanks to my wife Linda, daughters Lindsay and Melissa, and son-in-law Pete for their love, support, and enduring the first draft with an open mind.

Thanks to Linda Allen, my agent, and Barbara Peters, my editor, for navigating the story through the pre-publishing procedure, and the staff of Poisoned Pen Press who keeps the whole process enjoyable.

Finally, I'm grateful to the booksellers and librarians who continue to recommend my stories to their patrons, and to you, the reader, for spending your time with Sam and Nakayla in the mountains of North Carolina.

Mark de Castrique
February 2011
Asheville, North Carolina

To receive a free catalog of Poisoned Pen Press titles, please contact us in one of the following ways:

Phone: 1-800-421-3976
Facsimile: 1-480-949-1707
Email: info@poisonedpenpress.com
Website: www.poisonedpenpress.com

Poisoned Pen Press
6962 E. First Ave. Ste. 103
Scottsdale, AZ 85251